Here to Stay

Debby Querido

About the Author

Debby Querido is a queer writer born and raised in Cape Town, South Africa. When she's not writing, she's walking her dogs, forgetting to water her plants, or getting another tattoo. *Here To Stay* is her first published work of fiction.

Here to Stay

Debby Querido

BELLA BOOKS

PUBLISHER'S NOTE

Acknowledgments

I have always found writing an extremely solitary and vulnerable process, and so first and foremost, I must thank Joy for being not only my first reader, but my first listener. Thank you for investing in the story of Abby and Chris, and for pushing me to free them from my laptop. *Here to Stay* would still be living in a Word doc had it not been for your encouragement, enthusiasm, and unfailing belief in me. Thank you.

Candice, I wouldn't be who I am today, or where I am today, without you. And that means no Candice = no *Here to Stay*. So, I suppose you could say you were instrumental to all this. Let's not make it weird, but gosh, I love you so much. Isla can read this when she's eighteen!

Thank you to the best cheerleaders a gal could ever ask for—Leah, Jeanine, and Tazzi. To trust you with my manuscript and ideas is to trust you with a piece of my heart, and I couldn't ask for a safer, more supportive space than the one you created for me. Thank you. (Anyway, you already have huge pieces of my heart, so it wasn't such a leap.) Jeanine, we're doing this! We. Are. DOING THIS!

Di, you're a constant in my life, through it all. I love you.

Savannah, you are SO talented. When you're not out fishing, please share your art with the world.

Dad, thanks for reading, even though I didn't redact the bits I wish I had (for your sake and mine!).

Mom, sorry you missed this. There's a copy just for you up in the cloud(s). I think you'd have got some nachas out of it.

Random, but Gareth…somehow when we were seventeen, you knew I'd do this. And you asked me to give you a shout-out when I did. So, here it is.

Jonathan, you nailed it! Thank you for your expert sculpting of my first, messy draft. I barely felt you shaving off those 10,000 words! You reignited my love for this book and for that I am endlessly grateful. And thank you for the memes.

Heather! With or without a snake tattoo on your biceps, you're hands-down one of the coolest people I've ever met. Thank you for the hand-holding, encouragement, anatomy lessons, and grammar insights—and for teaching me the keyboard shortcut for the interrobang (‽). The editing process has been one of my favourite parts of this process, all thanks to you.

Bella Books, thank you for believing in Abby and Chris—and in me. Gosh, I'm still pinching myself. And Jessica, for your infinite patience, thank you.

Last, and most certainly not least, thank you to you, dearest reader, for opening your heart to Abby and Chris. If you enjoyed *Here to Stay*, I'd love to hear from you! And of course, book reviews and social media shout-outs are absolute gold to writers and are more appreciated than you could ever know.

Instagram: deb_querido_author

Website: www.debbyquerido.com

Dedication

For all of you who knew I could, even when I didn't quite believe it myself.

PART ONE

CHAPTER ONE

A tiny fleck of ash floated onto Abby's keyboard, landing right between the tilde and the Z. She pressed her finger onto it and rubbed, frowning at the small grey smear it left behind.

Hmm. Weird.

Abby was doing what she always did at 7:03 a.m.: sitting in bed, checking for new bookings on FortyLinks.com.

"Mmm…" she murmured as she scrolled through her emails, her eyes still blurry from sleep. "Who will I be sharing my house with next?"

Even after all these months, short-term house-sharing was a still strange concept to her. But it served its purpose, so she tried not to overthink it. Instead, she blew on her strong black coffee to cool it and squinted at the tiny avatars of her would-be guests.

Avatars covered in tiny grey specks.

Wait a second…Ash?

ASH?

Abby jumped to her feet, laptop tumbling into her pillows, and yanked open the curtains. The sky was an ominous grey and thick with smoke. The tiny slice of bay, usually visible from her bedroom, had disappeared into the smog. When she opened a window, the acrid smell of fire hit her nostrils. Abby quickly slammed it shut.

Lurching back over the bed, she retrieved her phone from the jumble of blankets.

"Dude, I was about to call you," Evan said before Abby could utter a word. "Can you believe this fire? I mean, we always joked that The Dolphin Inn was an accident waiting to happen, but we never actually thought it would."

She gasped. "The Dolphin Inn is on fire? What happened?"

"No idea," Evan replied, slurping on something—probably a protein shake. "Saw the whole thing while I was out running—smoke, fire trucks, the works. Must've happened during the night."

"Holy crap," Abby murmured, staring back outside. "I can't believe I slept through it. Although, we did have a pub quiz night last night." She rubbed her eyes with her free hand. Her head felt thick. She took another sip of coffee.

Evan scoffed. "Oh, come on, it's a virtual quiz. How many beers did you even have? Three, max?"

"Two," Abby said sheepishly. "But I'm a lightweight, you know that. Anyway, it's Monday, okay? Give me a break."

"Nope, no breaks for you." Evan took another noisy slurp. "You're going to have to get on top of your game, Massey. With The Dolphin out of action, your spare room is going to be in huge demand."

"Good point." Abby glanced at her upturned laptop. It wasn't like there was much choice in itsy-bitsy Bay View, which boasted exactly one of everything and zero excitement.

"I gotta get ready," she said, pulling her laptop upright. "I'll see you at school."

The ping of an email notification: her FortyLinks booking for today had cancelled. So much for the fire creating a boom in business. The guest would have arrived this evening and stayed for a week. Nice bit of extra cash. Bummer.

With a shake of her head, Abby shut her laptop and headed for the bathroom—a good soak would clear the fogginess. What were they thinking, downing beers on a Sunday night?

Her email pinged again, but she didn't hear it: she'd already sunk below the steaming water.

The fire was all anyone could talk about at school. Abby caught snatches of the kids' conversations as she hurried across the front quad to the teachers' entrance.

"And then the *roof* caved in!"

"My dad said it *blew up*!"

"Yeah! A piece of it landed in our yard! *Still burning!*"

The fire was the hot topic in the staff room too.

"I heard the bartender was an alcoholic. Yeah, that young guy who helps out on the weekends. He probably got drunk and passed out smoking or something."

"Well, I heard it was that local gang of hooligans—you know, the ones who put graffiti all over the hardware store."

"Arson? No way! That place was falling to pieces. Couldn't flush a toilet without a couple bricks falling out of the wall. Was bound to happen."

Abby listened to the theories half-heartedly. While many local folks had disparaged the place, she had genuinely loved The Dolphin, with its cracked leather booths and sticky bar counter.

"Hey, hey," Evan said, sliding into the seat beside her at the long staff table. Freshly showered, his hair was still damp.

"How are you feeling?" he asked, handing her a steaming mug.

Abby mumbled her thanks as she took a sip. "Ugh. I'm sad about our Dolphin. And my FortyLinks booking for this week fell through. And…" She groaned, rolling her eyes. "I have back-to-back classes all week."

"Sounds like a case of the Mondays," Evan teased. Abby glared at him.

"Yeah, it's a rough start to the week," he conceded. "And this year's schedule is super intense. I'm going to have to invent new historical facts just to fill all the extra classes I have. How soon do you think I can include 'The Great Bay View Bar Fire of the Twenty-First Century' in the curriculum?"

Abby laughed and hoisted her bag off the floor. "Maybe you can use it to teach the kids what 'fake news' is," she said as she cocked her head in the direction of Moira Fresh, the elderly, musk-scented maths teacher who was banging on about the alleged alcoholic bartender. She'd cornered a group of teachers, most of whom were checking their watches and inching away as she spoke.

Abby and Evan said their goodbyes outside their neighbouring classrooms. As the kids filtered into her class, she sent a silent message of thanks to the gods of work husbands for sending her Evan—good-humoured, steadfast Evan. He'd been the one constant in her life since she'd moved to town eighteen months ago, and she so valued his easy friendship and thick skin. New teachers always assumed they were a couple.

The kids all inside, Abby clapped her hands together and pasted a bright smile on her face.

"Okay, class! Today we're going to watch a movie." The kids whooped, and Abby winked conspiratorially. "Just don't tell the other teachers, okay?"

It was lunchtime before Abby checked her phone and saw the email notification from FortyLinks.

Hi, my booking at Dolphin Inn cancelled and urgently need accomm for a week. Flying in tmrw AM. Do you have available. Tx—Chris A.

Abby paused. There was no avatar. Chris A had no other bookings or reviews. That would usually send alarm bells ringing, but Chris A had booked at The Dolphin…

No, you're being paranoid. And besides, you need the cash. Abby tapped Accept.

In the year she'd been renting out her spare bedroom on FortyLinks, she'd had close to fifty guests. Only two of them had turned out to be a little peculiar. One was a young woman who had stayed for a week and barely left her room. After she'd left, Abby found the room full of empty peanut butter jars, and peanut butter…everywhere. On the carpets. On the sheets. Even on the windows. She and Evan had called it the "Peanut Gallery," and it had taken them an entire weekend to deep-clean the room. Abby swore she could still detect the odd whiff of peanut on warm days.

Then there was the middle-aged engineer who left towel animals all around the house. Every day for three weeks. A towel llama peeking around a door, a towel snake uncoiling from a cupboard. The weirdest was the litter of towel puppies that must have taken an entire afternoon to create—a real labour of love.

After that, Abby took to rationing her guests' access to towels.

Her new FortyLinks booking had delayed her, and Evan had spread himself around the lunch table by the time Abby arrived. She handed him a sandwich and a bottle of water and plopped down on the chair next to him.

"You know who I was thinking about today?" she asked as she unwrapped her egg salad sandwich.

"Who?" Evan stopped midway through salting his food, looking concerned.

"Oh, no, not Dan," Abby said quickly, smiling to show that there was no risk of sudden meltdown. It had been months since she'd sobbed uncontrollably over Dan, and Evan had been there almost every time.

"I was thinking about Peanut Gallery."

"Oh, ha! That nutjob." Evan bit into his sandwich, flicking his head to move a stray piece of blond hair from his face. He was annoyingly good-looking. Almost all the women and many men in Bay View were positively googly-eyed over him.

"Wait," Evan said, a realisation dawning. "What are we cleaning up this time? I think the only thing more difficult to get rid of would be a body."

"Well, actually…" Abby grimaced. "Maybe."

Evan frowned, and Abby hurried on. "I accepted an accommodation request that came through this afternoon from some person called Chris with no picture or reviews. I was just so relieved to get a booking after this morning's cancellation. So, now I'm worried he's a murderer hunting down attractive young women."

"Well, then, whatcha worrying about?"

Abby punched Evan on the shoulder.

"Ow! Okay, okay. You want me to come over?"

"Would you mind? He arrives in the morning so you could just swing by after your run…"

Evan ran every morning at seven a.m. He ate breakfast at eight and he was in bed by ten p.m. He was always Abby's "first phone call"—the person she knew she could call in any emergency—peanut butter-related or otherwise.

Abby knew his schedule almost down to how often he took a leak. She supposed she could understand why his long-distance girlfriend seemed to feel threatened by their closeness. It didn't help that she knew about their history. Early on, long before they were best friends, there'd been that one, confusing night… But that was in the past. Abby and Evan were firmly, and only, friends.

"Sure, dude, I'll be there," Evan said, pushing the last bite of sandwich into his mouth and stretching out his long legs. "But I'm warning you— I'm gonna start charging a protection fee."

CHAPTER TWO

In her dream, she was running. Her feet went *thud-thud-thud-thud* against the ground as she sped toward a burning building in the distance.

Thud-thud-thud-thud.

She knew she shouldn't be running toward it, but she didn't feel afraid. She pushed on, even as someone called her name.

"Abby?"

Thud-thud-thud-thud.

She felt herself being sucked upward, through the thick, sticky mud of deep sleep to consciousness.

The thud-thud-thud-thud was still happening.

What the…?

Someone was knocking on her damn front door in the middle of the night.

She sat up and fumbled for her phone.

Six a.m.? What the hell!

Abby swore out loud as she swung her feet to the floor and began stumbling toward her front door. Squinting through the peephole, she made out a smartly dressed person who now seemed to be fiddling on a cell phone.

Oh, shit. Was this Chris A? So early?

Abby opened the door a crack and the person looked up.

"Abby?"

Abby nodded mutely, detecting an impatient tone.

"I'm Chris. I have a booking starting today?"

"Oh, uh, yeah…I just didn't expect you so early."

"Airlines," Chris said with a roll of the eyes. "My luggage is in the taxi. Could you help?"

Still dazed from sleep, Abby made her way down the path to the waiting cab in her pyjamas. She mumbled a "gmmrninnng" to the driver, who'd already kindly tossed the bags onto the sidewalk, where they lay like fat lazy seals.

Abby grabbed a handle in each hand and hobbled back up the path, hissing "Shitballs!" as she rolled a plastic wheel over her bare foot.

Back in the house, bags deposited in the hallway, Abby was finally able to assess her latest guest-slash-potential-killer.

Chris A was not a murderous-looking dude, but a striking, burgundy-haired woman who smelled of leather and expensive fragrance. It wasn't even breakfast time, yet she looked prepped for a power lunch in her crisp white shirt, suit jacket, and dark fitted jeans.

Even in the dim light and through a veil of sleepiness, Chris A was exquisite.

Suddenly, Abby felt horribly self-conscious in her flimsy sleep shorts and old, oversized hoodie. And her toe was throbbing. She wiggled it to get the blood flowing.

"Welcome, Chris!" she said overly brightly, extending a hand. "I'm Abby. Sorry, I wasn't expecting you so early."

Chris squeezed her hand with a cool, firm grip. "It's fine. My flight got in earlier than expected, and this town is so tiny, the drive took all of thirty seconds." Chris ran a hand through her hair. It was short and meticulously styled to look like it hadn't been styled at all. "What's a gal gotta do to get some coffee around here?"

"Oh, yes, of course!" Abby practically squeaked. "Sorry, I'm still half asleep."

Instant coffee made, and Chris's look of disdain cheerfully ignored, Abby gave her a quick "housekeeping" rundown.

"You'll find your keys in your room, next to the bed, along with an information pack—"

"No machine?" Chris cut in, lip curling as she regarded the steaming mug in her hand.

Christ, this is going to be a long week, Abby thought, taking a deep breath. It had been less than ten minutes, and the woman was already shaping up to be high maintenance.

"Oh, er, no. It broke a while back and I've been meaning to replace it." Abby worked hard to keep her voice light. "But there are some great coffee spots around here, easily within walking distance." She could think of only one, and it was average at best. "As I was saying, there's an information pack in your room with all of that—you know, shops, restaurants, activities, the whole shebang."

Well, not much shebang, really, but it was too early to shatter dreams. The most exciting thing to happen in Bay View lately was a new flavour of soft serve at the corner café.

Chris, now perched on a barstool at the kitchen counter and looking perfectly at home, gingerly lifted the mug to her lips. Too late, Abby realised it was the one emblazoned with *WORLD'S BEST WIFE*. Dan had bought it for her years ago, a tongue-in-cheek gesture after yet another unresolved conversation about marriage. Abby had grabbed it in her sleepy daze.

Chris followed Abby's gaze, turning the mug to flick her eyes over the bold text. Abby took a breath to explain it away, but a sharp rap at the door stopped her.

"Hey, Abs, you up?" Evan's voice rang out as he let himself in with his spare key.

She turned and started to call back, but with his long, quick strides, he was already in the kitchen. He started to speak, then did a double take when he saw Chris sitting at the counter.

"Oh, er, hi." He extended his hand and flexed. "I'm Evan."

"Chris," she responded, giving his hand the same brisk, businesslike shake and returning to her coffee. It didn't escape Abby that Chris, unlike most women, didn't swoon or blush furiously upon laying eyes on Evan—who was clad, typically, in too-tight running gear.

Evan turned back to Abby, clearly thrown by Chris's response—or rather, lack thereof.

"Is, uh—what's your murderer dude's name—has he arrived?" Evan stretched into an exaggerated yawn, guns popping. Chris looked at her watch.

Abby grabbed his arm and yanked him out of the kitchen. "Excuse us," she called over her shoulder as she dragged Evan to the living room. "We just have to do…a thing."

"Sorry, bit of a misunderstanding," she hissed once they were out of earshot. "That"—she jerked her thumb behind her—"is 'Chris A.'"

"Ohhhh!" he hissed back. "Why are we whispering?"

"Well, because…I feel silly."

"What for? Taking precautions against potential serial killers? Don't," he said with a shrug, and then, swivelling his hip, launched into his signature arms-above-the-head stretch to showcase his muscles. He just couldn't help himself. "You watch enough YouTube to know, better safe than sorry."

Abby rolled her eyes at him. "Thanks, Johnny Bravo."

"Sorry to interrupt," Chris announced, appearing in the room. "Could you show me to my room? I'm an absolute mess after my flight. Busy day ahead."

Abby jumped. "Yes! Of course. Let me just grab your bags…" She side-eyed Evan, who quickly snatched them up. "It's just down this little hallway…"

* * *

"So, how's it going with the new house guest?" Evan was perched on Abby's desk, spinning a pen between his fingers as she graded papers.

"I can't get a read on her just yet. Turns out, she's Mrs. Addison's daughter—you know, that reclusive old lady who lives near you? I think you helped her paint a wall once or something."

"Oh, yeah, I did. I had no idea she had kids. She never seems to have any family over. Or anyone, for that matter."

"I know, right? And I've certainly never seen Chris Addison before. She's not exactly…forgettable."

Evan inspected his nails. "Huh, I guess so, if that's what you're into." He turned his mouth down at the corners. Abby smiled to herself.

"Anyway, she says her mom is having some medical tests done and so I guess she's here to take care of her or something. How awful to be old, sick, and alone."

Abby pulled another sheet from the never-ending stack of papers and groaned.

"Remind me why I agreed to help Moira with her grading?"

"Because you're a sucker for punishment and you have no life?"

"Rude! Well, if I'm a sucker for punishment, so are you. Here." Abby shoved a stack in his direction. "Make yourself useful."

"Nope, sorry!" Evan hopped off the desk. "PE class starts in five, and then I've gotta get home. Marli's arriving this evening, so I have to follow *her* orders for a change."

"Oh, right. I nearly forgot about that."

"Aww, there, there, it'll all be okay," Evan said with a grin, roughing her hair.

"No, it won't. I'm going to be stuck here marking these damn papers until the end of time." She dropped her head on top of the stack and felt a staple pressing into her temple.

"There's my little drama llama." Evan laughed as he headed to the door. "Who said lesbians can't multitask?"

Abby lifted her head to glare at him, but Evan was already out of sight, his chuckles echoing down the hallway.

The sun was setting as Abby arrived home. Even though she'd been exhausted by the school day, she'd stopped at the grocery store on her way, popping a French press and a bag of expensive ground beans to her basket. It wasn't very often that Abby had a guest who made her feel self-conscious in her own home. And none had ever complained about the coffee.

Chris was on the phone when Abby got in, pacing up and down the small garden at the back of the house. Her outfit was different from this morning's but equally trendy. Abby decided she had to be a magazine editor or similar fashion-orientated professional. It was difficult to read her expression in the fading light, but from her body language, she seemed irritated.

Abby unpacked the coffee plunger and beans onto the kitchen counter but found it hard to shift her eyes off the woman. She watched as Chris tapped away now on her phone, staring earnestly at the screen. Then she placed the phone to her ear once again. This time when she spoke, she seemed more subdued. She'd stopped pacing and was absently running her hand through her hair.

Abby's hand drifted to the blond knot on top of her own head. She'd once cut her hair short, hoping for a cool, messy look like Chris's, but after the first wash it had flopped spectacularly. For the next several months, it stuck out every which way but up.

Hair-riffic, Dan had joked. That was before she'd lost her own hair.

Abby was picking at last night's chicken parmesan when Chris came back into the house. She seemed momentarily startled to see Abby, as if she'd forgotten where she was.

"Hi!" Abby greeted her brightly. "How was your day?"

"Oh, hello." Abby could see her visibly pull herself together. "Fine, thanks." Chris smiled stiffly and then strode into the kitchen, opening the fridge.

"Are you hungry?" Abby asked, swallowing a bite. "Want some chicken parmesan?"

"I ate earlier, with my mother, but thanks," she said into the fridge, extracting a bottle of mineral water. Abby never kept bottled water.

Chris turned and set her gaze on Abby. There was the slightest hint of dark shadow beneath her eyes. "I'm going to bed. Good night."

"Oh, er, night," Abby replied, staring long after she'd disappeared down the passage and shut her bedroom door behind her.

It was still early when Abby climbed into bed herself, so she reached for her phone and dialled the latest number she had for her mother.

"Mom? Can you hear me?"

After a beat, her mother's voice came down the line. "Darling! How are you? We're in the south of…somewhere. Middle of the ocean, as usual. Your father knows. He's at the casino now, so you've missed him. But how are *you*? Gosh, it's been *ages* since we spoke. Oh, you wouldn't *believe* this ship! Last night at dinner I was saying to Marjorie and George—you know, our friends from Sydney? I was saying to them that on our *last* cruise…"

Abby settled back and let her mother's voice wash over her. She wouldn't have to say much for the next forty-five minutes, just a couple of "mm-hmms" and "wows" until her mother ran out of steam or "had to dash" to a line-dancing class.

Abby's parents lived on cruise ships, hopping from one monthslong cruise to the next and calling it their "retirement plan." It was the perfect fit for two people who'd always sailed from one shiny thing to another, averse to any real responsibility. She was grateful that she'd inherited their sense of adventure and a fair degree of fearlessness. But she'd always felt more responsible than her parents, even as a small child, certain that she wanted a life more rooted in routine and predictability. Routine anchored her when life felt rudderless and dark.

Her parents visited her once in Bay View between cruises, but without their daily aqua aerobics and table tennis tournaments, they quickly grew bored. Abby had tried her best to entertain them, but her heart wasn't in it. After all, it was just a few months into her move, and she was still shattered over Dan. Her parents hadn't known what to say to comfort her, and she hadn't known what to do to occupy them, so after four awkward, very long days, they packed up their super-light suitcases, hailed a cab, and zipped off to Newtown Port, two hours away. The only watercraft you could launch from Bay View was a kayak. For ants. Catching up over the phone every few weeks was a better solution for everyone.

"…then bought the most *stunning* silk scarves at the port, because you know these cabins are small so it's about downsizing, no great big coats for us, but you need something for those chilly evenings…"

It was a pleasant enough conversation, and by the time it was over, nearly forty minutes later, Abby had no trouble drifting off to sleep.

CHAPTER THREE

It was already light when Abby awoke a few minutes ahead of her alarm. The air smelled pleasantly floral and spicy—nothing like the acrid smell of fire from a few days before.

The disaster had been splashed across the front page of yesterday's local rag, and her heart had sunk once more. How many nights had she and Evan propped up that bar counter? A bar counter which now lay in charred bits on the ground. It felt like losing an old friend.

She sighed and stretched, for a moment expecting to feel a pair of warm feet beside hers and then remembering. Phantom limb. Too much thinking about loss.

These days, the waves were mercifully smaller, and ebbed faster.

In a moment, Abby would begin her morning routine: strong black coffee, a scan of her FortyLinks bookings, shower, walk to school. Thank god for her routine. And for house-sharing, which made her feel like she was in a private capsule of her own but never entirely alone. Water droplets on a shower wall or a handbag slung over the back of a chair were often the only signs that another human inhabited the space, if only temporarily. But another human did inhabit the space, and that was comforting.

After a final, satisfying stretch, Abby padded to the kitchen. She loved this cottage, her little den since arriving in Bay View. Abby from three years ago would never have imagined she'd find herself here, in a small town with a handful of residents and not a name-brand store in sight. Then again, there was a lot Abby from three years ago would never have imagined. Certainly not the sucker-punch of losing Dan. Exquisite, effervescent, full-of-life Dan.

From the breakfast nook, she took in the bright sitting room, drenched in early morning light, and the garden patio beyond it, from which she watched the sky turn yellow and orange and impossible shades of red in the evenings. Dan would have liked this place. She smiled to herself as she reached for a mug.

Most mornings, there was no one in the garden. But not today.

Chris Addison was already stomping around on the dewy lawn, dressed in cashmere, her phone glued to her ear. On her feet were a pair of designer sneakers that Abby instantly coveted. They were the kind you had to properly budget for—unless, she sensed, you were Chris Addison.

The woman turned around and Abby quickly looked away, fumbling to switch on the kettle.

"Good morning," Chris said, striding into the house. She perched on a barstool, her eyes locked on her phone.

"Hi," Abby replied, smoothing her hair as she took in Chris's flawless appearance. "Did you sleep well?"

"I did," Chris said, still thumbing the screen.

"Great. Great! It can be weird, I mean, the first night sleeping in a new place and—"

Chris looked up and fixed dark, penetrating eyes on Abby. "I travel a lot for work, so I'm used to it."

"Oh! Oh, that's cool." Abby wanted to ask what kind of work Chris did, but before she could formulate the question, Chris cut in.

"So, your husband…boyfriend…?" She peered around expectantly.

Abby laughed. "Oh, Evan's just a friend. He lives around the corner from your mother, actually." She felt herself reddening. Her throwaway comment made it obvious they'd been talking about her. Chris breezed right over it.

"Ah. I just thought, because of the mug." She pointed to the cups on the counter, now just plain white ones without any hyperbolic proclamations of love.

"Oh, that." Abby worked to keep her voice light. "That was just a joke. From someone. Years ago." She didn't like getting too personal with her guests. People tended to be morbidly fascinated by tales of twenty-eight-year-olds with dead girlfriends. She quickly changed the subject. "Look what I bought yesterday."

With a flourish, Abby produced the chrome plunger and the eye-wateringly expensive pouch of coffee.

"Oh, fabulous," Chris said, reaching for the bag. "This is a great blend."

"It is?"

"Yep. Nice and strong. Here, I'll do it."

Abby watched as Chris slipped a finger under the tab of the bag to open it and set about spooning granules into the plunger. Her nails were short, perfectly manicured, and varnished in a deep oxblood shade. As she stood and leaned forward to press down the plunger, her sweater gaped ever so slightly to reveal a glimpse of smooth, tanned chest. Abby bit her cheek and looked away.

"Voilà," Chris announced, straightening and placing a mug in front of Abby. "Tell me it's not a thousand times better than that cheap crap you've been drinking."

Abby blinked, trying not to take it personally, and then tentatively took a sip.

Whether it was the crimson nails, the hint of cleavage, or the smell of Chris's perfume mingling with the aroma of coffee, it was the most delicious sip she'd ever had.

"Oh, okay, wow," Abby said, eyes widening. "You're on coffee duty for the rest of your stay."

Chris shrugged nonchalantly. "Sure. I suppose I could consider it compensation for your being my concierge."

Abby stopped midsip. Was this—gasp—self-awareness she detected?

"You're not used to this whole house-sharing thing, are you?" Abby asked with a chuckle.

"What do you mean?" Chris replied coolly, cocking her head to one side.

"Oh, I just mean…" Abby panicked. She really wanted to keep the momentum of the conversation going, but she instantly felt on thin ice. "The, uh, collaborative aspect of it. You know? It's a lot more…personal than staying in a hotel. I mean, that's what I find anyway."

Chris regarded her for a moment. "I wouldn't know," she finally said, casting her eyes around before meeting Abby's gaze again. "I only ever stay in hotels. This is the first time I've used…Forty Winks?"

"Forty*Links*."

"Mm. It was so last-minute, I didn't even have time to ask my assistant to sort it out. My son helped me do it."

"Oh, cool. How old is your son?"

"He's seventeen. Now I'm off to call him and make sure he and his siblings get their butts to school."

Chris stood and picked up her phone. It seemed semipermanently glued to her palm.

"And I must get to school, too," Abby declared, suddenly realising the time.

Chris frowned. "School? You're a student?"

"No, I'm an English teacher at Bay View Junior."

"Well then, you better get to class, too."

Abby opened her mouth to reply, but before anything could come to mind, Chris was halfway down the hallway, talking into her phone.

Curiosity got the better of Abby, and she took a slight detour on her way to school to walk past The Dolphin Inn—or at least, what was left of it.

It was a clear day out, the sky crayon-blue, the air already warm. Abby loved her daily walks to and from work. She loved hearing the birds chatting away and smelling the mix of aromas along her route: cooked breakfasts, fresh coffee, thick vines of jasmine. Most humans, no matter how much they kicked against the idea, kept to a mostly predictable schedule: they woke, worked out, and ate at roughly the same time every day. They had the same arguments with their kids in the driveway at the same time each day, and daily, they tore past her in their cars—late, again, for their city jobs, even though they swore it would be different today.

Abby had always found routines comforting. But when she'd met Dan, she'd had to relax her grip on her carefully scheduled life. For the first few years, Dan's spontaneity had taken them on unplanned road trips and hikes they could never quite retrace. There'd been impromptu all-night parties, bizarre music festivals and, once, a naked gardening convention. Abby had drawn the line at this and marched back to the car. Much later, when Dan had been really ill and really angry, she lashed out at Abby for having denied her the opportunity to liberate her body in public while it had still been healthy and fit. Even later than that, she tearfully apologised. For all of it.

When Dan got sick, Abby returned to the calming predictability of routine. She sprang into planning mode. She planned the doctors' visits and medication schedules. She planned their healthy meals and visits with loved ones. She even scheduled time for spontaneous activities, just in case Dan ever felt strong enough to do something other than fight to survive on any given day. And occasionally, she did. There was that seven-hour drive they'd taken along the coast, snapping photos of the birds and the sea and each other, and eating chocolate ice cream until they felt sick. They'd arrived home sticky and sunburnt, their cameras crammed full of memories.

Neither of them said it, but they both knew it would be one of their last outings with both of them able-bodied and carefree. That night in bed, Dan had said, "I'll be waiting for you with an ice cream on the other side," and Abby had soaked her pillow with the silent tears she'd wept.

The sound of firefighter tape flapping in the breeze brought Abby back to the present. She stopped and gasped. The front, soot-blackened facade of the hotel was mostly intact. But the entire right-hand side of the building, where the bar had been with rooms upstairs, was gutted. Rubble and burnt bricks were strewn all over. Abby was certain she could feel heat still radiating off the charred walls.

The Dolphin Inn had been an institution, the way a town's sole pub often was. It was gaudy and filthy, falling to pieces and most likely a health hazard to anyone who set foot through its doors, but it was The Dolphin. And it was adored, if ironically so.

The thing about The Dolphin was that your friends were always there, and if you didn't have friends, hanging out inside made you feel like you did. It's where Abby had met Evan. On nights when she felt particularly lonely, there was always someone at The Dolphin she could hang out with: school-teacher friends, town locals, and the pub's cheerful proprietor, a grey-haired old man named Roy Prescott. Until recently, he'd run the bar single-handedly, always in a pair of well-worn chinos and wearing a kind smile on his face. He poured strong drinks with an unsteady hand, his medical identity bracelet clinking against the glass. Lately, his nephew Chip had begun helping him out behind the bar, and the place could easily go until two or three a.m.

Carefully, Abby crept deeper inside the cavity. The windows had been blown out, and glass and bottles of booze lay glinting in a million tiny pieces all over the ground—vodka, gin, rum, tequila. The cheap stuff, Abby thought. Our favourites.

Her mouth felt dry as she took in the charred carcass of the bar, as if she'd inhaled a mouthful of ash. Quickly she retreated, gulping the fresh, clean morning air.

At the sound of voices, Abby trotted around the back of the building and spotted Roy talking to a tall man in a suit with a notebook tucked under his arm. Abby guessed he was an insurance investigator, but she was too far away to hear their conversation.

The man was frowning as Roy gestured to the building, seeming agitated, and Abby felt dreadfully sad for him. Standing beside his gaping building, he looked even more frail and stooped than usual.

Roy stopped his frantic gesturing and put his hands on his hips, his head hanging low. The man patted him awkwardly on the shoulder—two solid taps—and then climbed into his brown sedan and disappeared around the corner.

Abby didn't want Roy to know she'd been watching the exchange, but there was no way to walk past him now without him seeing her. She took a few steps in his direction, trying to do it as loudly as possible, and cleared her throat.

"Morning, Roy," she called as she got close.

He turned his head, his hands still on his hips, and squinted to see who'd called.

"Oh, Abby, hi," he mumbled as she walked up. "I'm afraid it's not looking too good…"

"Mmm, no, it isn't," Abby agreed, feeling glum. "I'm so sorry, Roy."

"An electrical fault!" he exclaimed. "It just boggles the mind. One day, without warning, something just gives out after decades of just… just…working fine! And you want to know the most unbelievable thing of all?"

Roy continued, not waiting for Abby's reply.

"It seems the fault came from the ice machine. The ice machine!" he cried, dropping his face into his hands. "Imagine that—fire, from ice!"

Abby winced at the irony. "How do you know, Roy?"

"They did their investigation. Seems it was a cable that had frayed over years and years. It was out of sight. I had no idea."

Abby didn't know what to say. She joined Roy in shaking her head sadly and then wondered how long she needed to do that before it would be polite to leave. School would be starting soon, and somehow, no matter how hard she tried to avoid it, she always seemed to skid in at the last possible minute—even though she always promised today would be different.

"I, um, I've gotta head to school…"

"Go, go." Roy waved a liver-spotted hand. "I need to fill out some paperwork for that insurance kid anyway."

Abby felt bereft for Roy as she dashed to school, hurtling through the gates just as the bell rang. Nothing made you feel as unmoored as watching your safe, predictable routine go up in smoke.

It was lunchtime before Abby felt like she'd finally caught her breath. Back-to-back classes meant she'd only managed her second cup of coffee around midmorning (Evan had made it and it had been surprisingly unsatisfying), and she was starving by the time she collapsed at the lunch table next to him.

"Mac 'n' cheeeeeeese, ladies and gentlemen!" Evan yanked the lid off his lunch box, a puff of steam escaping. The old Abby—Dan's Abby— would have berated him for microwaving anything in a plastic container. Dan absolutely abhorred it. She worried about chemicals from the plastic leaking into their food and causing… Well, now Abby didn't care.

"What, no almond-crusted salmon for Marli's arrival?" she teased, spearing a noodle with the fork Evan gave her.

"No need," Evan said, shoving a forkful into his mouth. "Trust me, this stuff is the greatest aphrodisiac."

"Ew, okay, don't tell me any more." Abby wrinkled her nose. She looked out over the playground, full of shrieking children and irritable teachers, and turned her chair so her back was to the chaos.

"I went past The Dolphin today," she said, watching a noodle droop off the end of her fork. "Roy told me it was a short circuit in the ice machine that caused the fire. That machine always looked dodgy to me, but that was more from a hygiene perspective than anything else, to be fair."

"Yeah, you always refused ice," Evan said, wiping his mouth with a napkin. "Remember that time you made me get you a whole new drink?"

"Well, yeah! I doubt it ever got cleaned."

Abby started imagining years of built-up grime in and around the machine and felt queasy. She pushed her fork aside.

"No one went to The Dolphin for its unbeaten levels of hygiene and cleanliness," Evan pointed out. "You went there because you could get shit-faced for next to nothing. And as teachers, we need to be able to get shit-faced for next to nothing. Regularly."

Abby laughed. "You can say that again. I always knew I didn't want kids, but teaching a bunch of ten-year-olds has confirmed that for me— for this life and the next few."

"Tell me about it." Evan groaned, uncoiling into his signature arms- up stretch. Behind them, two kids chased each other with mouths full of water, ready to spit. Abby knew she had to get up and stop them, and she lumbered to her feet.

Back when she lived in the city, she'd loved, absolutely loved, her job tutoring university students. The ideas, the debates, the passion, the snot-free noses. They'd challenged her in ways that had ignited her soul. Ten-year-olds challenged her in ways that crushed it.

She marched back to the table and Evan exploded in laughter. There was water dripping off her sleeve, and Abby had a face like thunder.

"So, that went well, then?"

"Ugh." She slumped back into her chair. "As you can see."

Evan was laughing harder now, and Abby couldn't help but giggle too.

"Damn, I had no idea how much babysitting would be involved in teaching children."

"Babysitting, nose-blowing, butt-wiping." Evan ticked them off on his fingers. "Marli can't understand why I freak out every time she mentions kids. I wish she'd come and spend a couple of days here to see why."

"Kids? You guys have been dating for five minutes."

"Oh, says you of the U-Haul crew."

"Oh, no, you didn't with the stereotypes. Straight couples move just as fast. The only reason you don't need a U-Haul is because all you straight dudes own is a frying pan and a crusty back-issue of *Playboy*."

"For your information, Miss Massey, I also own a large chest of drawers."

"Well, you know what they say about large chests of drawers, don't you?"

"What?"

"Small drawer compensation."

By this point they were both doubled over in laughter and Abby had all but forgotten about her soggy arm. Barely a day went by when she wasn't grateful for Evan and the joy he brought to her life—particularly now, when she'd never needed it more. If she were honest, perhaps she, too, was threatened by another woman's presence. But if they were talking kids, she'd have to start getting used to Marli. She'd have to learn to share her bestie a little better, or she'd risk losing him altogether.

"Oh shit, dude, was that the bell?" Evan said, scanning the field. Kids were running into each other like demented Minions.

"Do you think they'll notice if we don't come to class?" Abby mused. "Or will they just be satisfied to spit all over each other until the end of the day?"

"Definitely the latter," Evan replied. "But then we'll be in a huge amount of *spit* ourselves."

The cottage was empty when Abby got home, though the new, now-familiar fragrance hung in the air. She wasn't quite sure what compelled her to do it, but she walked through the sitting room, down the little hallway to the bedrooms, and—quietly, just in case—pushed open the door of the spare bedroom. Chris's room.

The bed was unmade. That didn't really surprise her. Chris probably assumed Abby would be making her bed for her. Her luggage was stowed in a corner of the room, a couple of items draped on top.

Most of Chris's clothes were hanging in the wardrobe or folded up in drawers. Feeling like an interloper in her own home, Abby ran her fingers over the different fabrics to see if they felt as expensive as they looked. They did. Abby knew she should stop. She had never encroached on a guest's privacy before, and she had always vowed she wouldn't—but for some reason, she couldn't help herself.

Next, she crept into the bathroom. All the regular things: toothbrush, whitening toothpaste, deodorant. A bottle of Tom Ford perfume which, when sniffed, proved to be the source of the smell that now clung to every corner of her house. She placed it back on the counter ever so gently, and as she looked up, she caught sight of herself in the mirror.

More often than not these days, her long blond hair was tied into a greasy ponytail or wrestled into some permutation of a bun. It had been years since she'd been called beautiful or mistaken for that popular model whose face had seemed to be everywhere for a while. She still wore makeup, but only the basics—a swipe of mascara now and then, a smudge of lip gloss. While she was being honest, her hair was, in fact, taupe these days, not Santa Monica blond like it had been when she was a city girl with her stylist on speed dial.

She was slender, still, under all those layers.

It wasn't that she no longer cared about her appearance or that she'd given up, it was that her priorities had changed. Dan was dead. The life they'd lived was gone. She was alone in a little town, teaching a bunch of sticky kids and socialising on her laptop. What was the point of contouring?

Or snooping.

Abby backed out of the room quickly and silently sent up an apology to the gods of house guests for her infraction.

Chris still wasn't back, leaving the patio free of frenetic, pacing house guests. Abby sat down at the little wrought iron table and, sipping an iced tea, looked out over the small garden with its huge bougainvillaea vine. How she loved watching the sun setting behind its lush magenta flowers in the evenings.

Abby had been lucky to find this cottage—her little pocket of peace—and as she sipped her drink and watched the sky change colour, she felt the stress of the day ebbing away. It was like this every day. It was why she could return to school every morning, full of hope for the day ahead, even though she often felt frazzled by midmorning. Her home was her retreat, a little daily reset.

Abby's reverie was interrupted by a commotion inside before Chris appeared at the sliding door in a wave of big-city energy.

"Hi," she announced. Abby sat up a bit straighter, pulling her legs off the chair she'd been resting them on.

"Oh, don't move on my account," Chris said breezily. "I need to make some calls. Inside."

Of course you do, Abby thought but held her tongue.

Half an hour later, Chris reemerged to demand a bottle opener. This time, Abby felt emboldened.

"It's really pretty out here at this time of day," she said, tossing a pillow onto the chair next to her. "You should take it in for a moment. It's one of the few beautiful things this town has to offer. Besides the sliver of muddy bay, of course."

"I still need to open this, though," Chris replied, thrusting a wine bottle in Abby's direction, but she settled on a chair while Abby hunted down a corkscrew inside.

"You're right, it really is quite beautiful," she said when Abby returned. "I hadn't noticed last night. Perhaps I was too distracted."

"When I have loads on my mind, or I'm feeling stressed, it's my little sanctuary," Abby said, handing her the gadget. "I even have a 'no phone' rule out here. Just for myself, obviously," she quickly added. "It's not a rule for guests or anything."

Chris narrowed her eyes slightly and disappeared into the house. Abby frowned. That was abrupt, even for her.

But to Abby's surprise, Chris returned a moment later brandishing another wineglass instead of her phone.

"You know what? Some phone-free time sounds like just what I need."

She planted the glass in front of Abby. "You drink wine, I presume." But she said it the same way she'd demanded help with her luggage: it was not a question.

"Uh, er, yes—thanks, that's kind of you."

"Oh, please. You're doing me a favour, doll." She pulled the cork smoothly from the bottle with a satisfying *whoosh-pop*, and Abby liked the way she called her "doll." "Otherwise, I'd drink this all alone."

She didn't know much about wine, but judging by the label—which was entirely how she judged wine—it looked fancy.

Chris handed Abby the glass and leaned back, placing a foot on the chair opposite her. Indigo jeans and ankle boots the colour of dark chocolate. They were leather, and the heel made a little metallic *clang* as it struck the chair.

Abby took a gulp of wine, self-conscious in her unbranded jeans and shapeless cable-knit sweater. City Abby would be cringing big time. She placed her glass back on the table a little too hard.

Chris raised an eyebrow. "Looks like you had a pretty stressful day yourself."

"Yeah," Abby said with a sigh. "I guess I did. I mean, every day is stressful when you're trying to get twenty kids to sit still and listen, let alone not stick pencils in each other's ears. It's a bit like trying to put a baby-gro on an octopus. Just as you get one tentacle in, another pops out and slaps you in the face or steals the other octopus's crayon. It's a goddamn nightmare."

Chris laughed, and Abby realised it felt surprisingly good to vent to a stranger. Maybe this was why people paid so much to do it with therapists.

"And the worst part is that this isn't even what I studied for. When I moved here, this position was available, and I needed it, to be honest…" Abby caught herself. "Anyway, it's not like jobs are a dime a dozen here. It was this or working as the assistant manager at the DVD shop. *Assistant* manager. Can you believe people here still rent DVDs?"

Chris was laughing now, a real hearty laugh, so Abby carried on. She told Chris about the silly things her kids had done at school: how they once stuck a giant poop emoji to her back and giggled every time she turned around, how they'd tried to prank her by putting a plastic spider in her coffee. She'd seen them do it, but she'd played along, dramatically spitting out her coffee and shrieking.

"And speaking of spitting, today I had some kids doing just that…"

When she realised she was still wearing the same sweater she'd had on at school, she looked at the offending sleeve in mock horror and then wrenched the sweater over her head, tossing it into the garden. She leapt to her feet. "Grossssssss!" she cried, pretending to scrub at her arm. It was like she was on autopilot, with Chris's laughter egging her on.

"Oh, oh! And how can I forget the time a little girl brought a 'lightsaber' to school…" It had, in fact, been an adult toy. "She whipped it out during show-and-tell, and before I knew it, it was all lit up and jerking around like a demented worm." Abby was relishing Chris's laughter. "I had to confiscate it and have a very awkward conversation with her parents after school."

Eventually, breathless, Abby took a deep bow, arm above her head, and collapsed into her chair. It must have been the wine.

"I needed that, thank you," Chris said through her giggles, dabbing her eyes. "God, I can't remember the last time I laughed like that."

Abby grinned and took another slug.

"You've got a kid, haven't you?"

"Three kids."

"*Three?* Holy smokes! I don't even want one. How old are they?"

"Seventeen."

"Seventeen? All of them?" Abby was aghast. "Triplets?"

"Yup. Two boys and a girl," Chris said, draining her glass. "That's why I need this." She picked up the bottle and refilled their glasses. "They're about to graduate from high school."

"Well, you don't look old enough to have grown-up kids."

Of course, Abby knew Chris was forty-four, having requested identity verification upon check-in as per FortyLinks protocol. But she was so cool, so trendy—it was difficult to believe she was a parent to adults.

Chris looked sceptical. "Really? These last few weeks I've felt ancient. Like I'm a hundred years old. Stress is a real bitch."

Abby frowned, then asked softly, "Your mother?"

How had no one known that old Mrs. Addison had a daughter— let alone one as sophisticated as Chris? Abby was desperate to know more about her. Guiltily, she thought back to her trespassing a few hours earlier, and she quickly pushed the memory aside.

"Oh, my mother..." Chris took a deep breath, so deep that Abby could see the skin stretching over her clavicles. "She's getting old, and she's alone. And lonely." Slowly she let out a long breath, twirling the stem of her glass between her fingers. "And full of regrets, I suspect."

Abby nodded, afraid to say anything in case Chris stopped talking.

"This is the first time I've seen her in many years. And doing it alone is hard. But that's a story for another day and another bottle of wine."

"Alone?" Abby prompted gently, really wanting their conversation to continue a little longer.

"Well, yeah," Chris said, still playing with her wineglass. "My partner needs to be home with the kids, make sure they get through their finals okay. And she's managing our business..."

She.

Abby tried to let this new detail wash over, but her heart did a curious little flip, and she frowned involuntarily.

"We're gay," Chris said sharply, having misunderstood Abby's expression. Abby felt her cheeks burning.

"Oh, uh, yes! No, I got that. It's cool, obviously."

Tell her you're gay, too!

"I was just wondering what kind of business you and your partner own."

Ugh, Abby!

"A clothing boutique."

"Oh, well, of course! That makes total sense," Abby babbled on, still flustered. "I mean because you dress superbly."

That seemed to warm Chris back up, and she smiled. "Thank you," she said. "We do consider ourselves walking, breathing advertisements for our brand, so I'm glad to hear it's working."

"Definitely!" Abby breathed a sigh of relief. "What's your boutique called?"

"Saint Jamie."

"Saint Jamie?" Abby sat up straight, her eyes wide. "*The* Saint Jamie?"

"One and the same," Chris said, a look of deep pride blooming across her face.

"No way." Abby slapped her hand against the table. "We—I—used to go into your boutique all the time when I still lived in the city. The jackets!" Abby collapsed back into her chair, remembering the exquisite woollen coat she'd bought for Dan on their first anniversary. Dan would pop the collar up to her cheekbones so that only her large sunglasses and spiky platinum hair stuck out at the top. On Abby, the coat had hung like damp laundry. But on Dan, it had *lived*.

"Oh yes, our coats and jackets are some of our favourite children," Chris said with a smile. "And, speaking of children, I need to check on mine."

"Oh. Okay." Abby felt disappointed as Chris scraped back her chair and got to her feet. "I should probably make some dinner anyway. Have you eaten?"

"Earlier, yeah, with my mother," she replied. As if on cue, her phone began to ring inside, the sound muffled by sofa cushions.

"Speak of the actual devil," Chris said wryly as she strode into the house and retrieved her phone. She closed her eyes for a moment as if steeling herself, then answered, "Hi, Mom. All okay?"

Chris turned back and gave Abby a quick wave before disappearing down the hallway to her room. The door shut with a soft click behind her.

Abby could have sat up all night talking to Chris, and she felt a little stung that Chris had cut it short.

She settled on a bath. It always calmed her mind.

* * *

Dan was standing behind the bar at The Dolphin Inn, fixing Abby a drink. She filled a giant glass with ice—more and more and more ice, until it was tumbling out over the top and onto the dirty wooden counter. Then she poured a shot of wine over the ice, and with a flourish, set the drink alight. Blue flames leapt over the ice blocks as Dan slid the drink over to Abby. "Cheers, doll." She grinned, the zippers on her leather jacket jingling as she raised her glass to Abby's.

Abby jolted awake and scrambled to turn off her alarm. She desperately tried to cling to the dream, but it was futile, like trying to hold on to steam.

When she reached the kitchen, a fresh plunger of coffee awaited, but there was no sign of Chris. Gingerly, she touched the back of her hand to the glass beaker. Lukewarm. Abby pushed aside the vague feeling of disappointment that rose in her chest and filled a cup, banging it into the microwave to heat it up. She leaned her back against the kitchen counter with a sigh, scowling as she jammed her fingers into her eyes.

The one thing Abby had had plenty of experience with over the last few years was feelings. And these long-dead feelings that were stirring in her now… They were the kind best left buried—or they buried you.

As she returned to her room with the second-most delicious cup of coffee of her life, she wondered grumpily what it was about Chris Addison that had her feeling this ruffled.

As if on cue, her email pinged to signal a new message: a FortyLinks booking for the day after Chris would be leaving. Abby quickly clicked Accept, barely scanning the applicant's information and social media pages. She took a sip of coffee and stared out of her window.

* * *

Once again, Abby found herself taking a detour past The Dolphin Inn on her way to work. A little annoyed by the unconscious error—this was a longer route and she was again running late—she quickened her steps.

The firefighter tape was even more tattered than it had been yesterday, torn bits of it now hugging the base of a nearby lamp-post. But the juxtaposition of burnt-out building and storybook sky was an arresting sight, and Abby couldn't help but slow down. Which was when she heard it: a faint, unmistakable mewling sound.

She held her breath and listened.

Nothing.

Abby crept closer to the building.

Mew. Meuuuuuwww. Mewwww.

The sound seemed to be coming from the rubble. "Shit. Shit, shit, shit," she cursed as she picked her way over the debris. She was definitely going to be late now.

She stopped and listened again.

Nothing.

She called. She carefully moved bricks and bits of wood aside. Still nothing.

"Oh, come on," she groaned, turning on her heel—and missing the kitten by a whisker. Catching sight of the tiny grey puff of fur, she instantly changed the trajectory of her airborne foot and landed with a painful crash on the ground.

Her school bag tumbled beside her, spewing its contents all around. The kitten darted behind a burnt brick.

She swore again and rubbed at a spot on her ankle where the bone had connected with a piece of brick.

"Come here, kitten," she cooed from her spot in the dirt, rubbing her fingers together. "Pss-pss-pss…Come on, I won't hurt you."

She knew that when you found a kitten, you were supposed to leave it where it was, because its mom was probably nearby, transporting the rest of her litter and coming back for it. But, shit.

"Come on, please? I've gotta get to work and I'm not leaving you behind. Please! Pss-pss-pss…"

Abby reached over and grabbed her lunch bag, unzipped it and, as noisily as possible to keep the kitten's attention, unwrapped her chicken sandwich. It was store-bought so probably loaded with all kinds of unhealthy stuff, but she figured if the cat had survived this far, it could handle a bite of artificial additives. She pulled apart the bread and took a chunk of chicken in her fingers, rolling it around to release its aromas.

"Come, kitty, come have some yummy chicken. Mmm…Pss-pss-pss…come on…" Abby threw the meat on the ground.

The animal finally emerged. Ten minutes later, Abby was back on track to school, down one sandwich and up one little kitten with a belly full of chicken.

The kids were surprisingly gentle with the kitten, helping Abby to make a comfy bed for it and stroking it lovingly with their stubby little fingers. The more they stroked it, the clearer it became that the kitten wasn't grey at all, but actually snow-white and just filthy with soot.

It was sweet to see them clustered around the box, heads pressed together as they peered at their newest classmate. The kitten was still shell-shocked, so Abby shooed the kids back to their spots on the mat, where they spent the remainder of drama class mimicking playful kittens.

"What are you going to call it, Miss Massey?" Jordan asked from her position on all fours, pretending to lap up milk.

"Hmm, good question, Jordy," Abby replied. "Do you have any ideas?"

"Well," she said matter-of-factly, "it depends on whether it's a boy or a girl."

"Does it really?" Abby asked seriously.

Jordan flopped onto her bum and rolled her eyes in exasperation. "*Duh*, Miss Massey. Of *course* it matters! Girl names are for *girls* and boy names are for *boys*."

"Well, what about something gender neutral?"

"What's 'gender neutral,' Miss Massey?" Enzo piped up. He'd been cleaning his whiskers and paused with his hand cupped against his cheek.

"It means that it's not just for one gender—it's for any gender. Boy or girl, or those who identify as neither, or something else."

The kids thought about this for a moment, then Jordan piped up. "Hey, my name is gender neutral! I once had a boy friend—" She scowled as the other kids started to titter. "No, no! Not a *boyfriend*, a friend who was a *boy*, and his name was Jordan."

"Yes, exactly." Abby nodded. "Your name is gender neutral."

"Then let's name the kitten 'Jordan'!" she said triumphantly.

Abby laughed as this sparked a spirited debate—everyone wanted the kitten named after them. Eventually, a serious ginger-haired girl called Poppy spoke up. She was a smart, perceptive child who always seemed bored with her rambunctious classmates. Pushing her glasses up on her nose with one finger, she announced, "I think you should call her Snowy, because she's white and really fluffy. And even if she turns out to be a boy, it's fine because Snowy is a *gender-neutral* name." She put particular emphasis on "gender-neutral" and finished with a little pout.

Nobody—not even Jordan—could argue with this logic. So it came to pass that by ten thirty that morning, Abby was the reluctant owner of a kitten called Snowy. None of the other teachers were interested in adopting it, not even Moira Fresh, who Abby thought would be a sure bet. She'd bundled the tiny animal to bosom, her gold bangles jingling wildly as she stroked it to within an inch of its life.

"Oh no, no, no," she said gravely, her eyes wide. "Mr. Toby would never allow it. Never allow it! Not even for a cute little thing like you." She emphasised the last few words with little bops to Snowy's nose. "He's a grumpy old kitty. But you'll find a lovely home," she cooed as she pressed the animal into her crinkled cleavage.

"I think you're going to have to keep it," Evan said later as they watched Snowy prepping one of the school's flowerbeds for a pee. She pawed at the earth with tiny, stilted movements.

"Although I know Marli would love her. She's been saying we should get a pet..."

"No, no, it's fine," Abby said quickly, feeling possessive at the thought of Marli getting her hands on Snowy. "Anyway, shouldn't you wait until you're actually living in the same town before you start adopting animals together?"

Evan ignored her comment and continued to stare at the kitten with his hands on his hips. "He's fucking cute, though, gotta say. Why wouldn't you want to keep him?"

"Her. I think," Abby said.

"No offence, Abby, but you haven't got much else going on in your life."

Abby scowled at him as she scooped up the cat and put it back in its box.

Evan laughed. "What? You're denying it? How's your week looking? What are you doing tonight?"

Abby raised her chin defiantly. "Tonight I have a virtual pub quiz. With at least two beers."

Evan guffawed. "Honestly, I couldn't have asked for a better answer. Just keep the cat."

"I don't have a good track record with them," Abby grumbled. "The last one I had hated me. The one and only time she let me hold her was when we drove her home from the shelter. After that, I was persona non grata."

"Shit, what did you do to make a cat dislike you that much?"

Abby sighed. "I just wasn't Dan," she said sadly.

Evan softened as they sat down at their regular lunch table. "Abs, you need more than single-serving housemates in your life," he said gently. "A little bit of company is not the worst idea. And I'll tell you what. If it doesn't work out, we'll adopt him. Her. Them! Whatever."

Abby knew he had a point. It was ridiculous to swear off cats for the rest of her life because of how things had turned out with Alice.

It was not, however, ridiculous to swear off relationships forever because of how things had turned out with Dan.

* * *

"Where are we going?" Abby asked as they headed out on an unfamiliar route, but Dan just wiggled her sparse eyebrows. Their destination was a secret, she said, as they drove with the windows down and their favourite music blaring, scream-singing off key at the top of their lungs. Maybe they'd been wrong, thought Abby. Maybe Dan really had turned a corner. Maybe the drugs really were working. Maybe it was all the love, light, positive vibes; the candles, the crystals, the endless supply of cannabis.

Abby had been on cloud nine until, forty-five minutes later, they pulled up at an animal shelter outside of the city. She turned to Dan, confused.

"I think we should get a cat," Dan declared.

"But...you hate cats," Abby stammered, a cold, sick feeling filling her stomach.

Dan shifted in her seat, tugging on the seat belt. "I never *loved* cats, but I think I've mellowed in my old age." Dan had turned thirty-eight the previous week and joked that at least she'd never have to see forty. Abby had yelled at her for her insensitivity and had then taken a drive to avoid crying in front of her. The problem with having a terminally ill girlfriend at home was that you no longer had the luxury of taking long drives. It felt like each minute away from them propelled you closer to a finish line you never wanted to reach. The sound of the indicator tick-tick-ticking was a brutal reminder of the seconds burning away. So, after a six-minute sob around the block, Abby had returned so they could finish opening presents and tuck into the cake Abby had baked.

Back in the car outside the shelter, Abby felt her lip begin to wobble. *She wants me to have a distraction for when she dies.*

"Oh, my baby!" Dan threw her arms around her. "What's wrong?"

"I don't want a cat anymore," Abby choked out, burying her face in Dan's neck. "Let's just go home."

"What? Why?" Dan pulled back, her face creased with concern. "We've literally fought about this every three months since we met."

"Because, if we get a cat—" But her voice cracked before she could finish the sentence. She hated herself for ruining this beautiful day, this moment, this happy time with her detestable tears. She hated that a cat couldn't just be a cat, that a car ride couldn't just be a car ride, that her girlfriend's allotted time on Earth was running out and she only had one life, not nine.

Dan put her arms back around Abby and pulled her close. She smelled warm and familiar, and Abby felt herself giving in.

"It's just a cat, okay? I swear. I'm not going anywhere. In fact, I'm feeling better than ever. See?" She pulled back and opened her eyes wide, giving a broad, lopsided grin.

Abby laughed softly, but she wasn't convinced.

"I mean it, babe. Let's do the whole lesbian adoption thing and get a cat. Besides," she said with a wink. "It'll give me a reason to see forty."

Abby punched her gently on the shoulder and sniffed snottily. "Okay, on one condition. You have to promise me you aren't going to die."

"But I *am* going to die. And so are you. And so will this cat! So will everyone, in fact. Let's call the whole thing off."

That was Dan. Even in the most serious moments, she deflected with light-heartedness. Sometimes it drove Abby nuts, other times she was grateful for it. But in that moment in the car, it really didn't matter what Dan said or how she said it. She was going to die.

Abby sighed. Her whole body was shaking. She added her tears to Future Abby's clean-up duty, and then wrenched open the car door. "Come." She summoned Dan with much more determination than she felt. "Let's go get a baby."

In the end, it had been an easy choice: a slightly older, cream-coloured kitten whose fur was the same colour as Dan's hair had been.

"She reminds me of you," Abby said as the kitten purred contentedly on her lap on the drive home. She could see Dan was exhausted, but she'd insisted on driving and Abby hadn't had the heart to argue. *How many more times…* hung in the air.

"A cute pussy reminds you of me?" Dan said, winking.

Abby rolled her eyes. "Well, besides that, you dirty ol' dyke. You guys have the same colour hair. And she looked so serious, just sitting there in her little cage."

"But now that she has her face buried in your lap, she's in her happy place?" Dan finished.

Abby laughed this time. "Exactly! And, of course, she was older than all the rest."

Dan frowned and stuck out her tongue at Abby.

"What, you're the only one allowed to joke about age now?" Abby teased. "I'm the one dating a geriatric!"

"Dating!" Dan snorted. She hated that word.

"That's the word that bugs you in that sentence. Not 'geriatric'?" Their banter felt so much like old times.

"So, what are you going to call her?" Dan asked, flicking her eyes over to Abby as they waited at a traffic light.

"Oh no, you don't," Abby said sternly, looking up from the cat. "You're not getting off the hook that easily. You're going to name her."

"Moi?" Dan sounded surprised as the light turned green. She flicked her eyes back to the road.

"Yes, you!" Abby laughed. "This was your idea after all."

"Hmm…Well, in that case, it's an easy decision. Alice."

"I knew it!"

At that, the kitten's eyes popped open, and Abby rubbed her furry little head with one finger. "You're too blond to be a 'Shane,' aren't you?"

"So, you approve?" Dan asked.

"Yip, I think it's perfect." Abby smiled, reaching out to squeeze Dan's thigh.

Later, when all three of them were settled in bed, Abby brought her face close to the kitten's and cooed, "Hello, Alice. Welcome to our lives. I hope you like *The L-Word*."

It turned out that Alice *had* enjoyed *The L-Word*. And *The Big Bang Theory*. And pretty much anything they watched squashed into bed together, Alice purring and long-catting between them.

Poor Alice. She'd become Dan's shadow, her constant companion. Dan used to joke that her side of the mattress must have had two indentations: Dan's shape, and Alice's, right next to each other.

Except for the day Dan died.

Early that morning, Alice had gone to lie under a tree outside, her paws tucked under her, her head resting on the ground. She refused to budge, to eat, to drink, to respond to their calls. She'd never left Dan's side before, and Abby had instinctively known what it meant.

All day Alice had grieved, and Abby had waited, sick to her stomach, trapped in a horror movie.

It was no wonder Alice had cracked in the end. At first, her mournful yowls had been almost too much to bear, but it was even worse when they stopped. She slept all day and all night on Dan's side of the bed.

She wouldn't go near Abby or let her touch her. And when she wouldn't eat and Abby had had to force-feed her twice a day, she began to despise Abby even more. Alice blamed Abby for taking Dan away from her. And Abby welcomed it. She deserved it. After all, she hadn't been able to make Dan stay.

Mercifully, Dan's parents—her wonderful, bereft parents—had scooped up this yowling, raging sack of fur and bones, and revived her. They restored her with a diet of home-cooked meals, boundless patience, and piles of Dan's clothing. They still sent the occasional photo of Alice reclining on a chair or on a warm lap. Alice, like Dan, had finally found peace, albeit in a different place.

Back at the lunch table, Abby sighed as she looked at the grubby kitten pressed into the corner of an office paper box. With her huge grey-blue eyes and fighting spirit, she seemed set on burrowing her way into Abby's life.

* * *

Abby was setting up for her virtual quiz when Chris arrived home laden with groceries. She was slightly out of breath, her hair tousled from the breeze outside.

"Hey," Chris greeted her, running a free hand through her hair. The sleeve of her jacket slipped to reveal a tanned forearm.

"Hi," Abby replied too brightly, ignoring the strange twinge in her stomach.

"I'm making sushi," Chris called as she strode into the kitchen. "I've had to improvise on some of the ingredients, so it's going to be something of an experiment."

"Sushi?" Abby repeated dumbly. When last had she'd had sushi? Certainly never in Bay View.

"The most exotic food I've seen in this town is eggs Benedict," Chris was saying as she tossed ingredients onto the counter. "And I'm pretty sure they used *may*onnaise instead of *holland*aise."

She plucked a fillet of salmon from the bag, vacuum-sealed in plastic, and waggled it at Abby. "Amazed to find this here."

"Huh," Abby said, pulling her lips down. "That is pretty so-*fish*-ticated for our town."

"Really?" Chris rolled her eyes at her. "Those ten-year-olds are clearly rubbing off on you."

Abby watched as Chris rifled around in a drawer. She had a feeling she probably wasn't a cat person—or a dog person, or any kind of pet person for that matter—but she knew she had to break the news about the kitten. She just hoped she wasn't an allergic person.

"Speaking of unexpected discoveries…" Abby segued. "Look what I found today."

Chris was pressing her fingertip to the blade of a long, sharp chef's knife, her lips pursed in concentration. "What?" she said distractedly.

Abby held up Snowy, her tiny head poking out from a fluffy blanket. "Maybe you should put the knife down first."

Chris looked up, her finger still nudging the blade. When her eyes finally locked on the tiny, furry head, she squinted and said, "Hmm. I think it's a bit *too* raw for sushi."

Abby chuckled as Chris came over to the sofa, bending to peer at the cat, who Abby now clutched to her chest.

"Was this planned or an accident?" Chris asked, arching a sculpted brow.

"Accident," Abby confirmed. "I found her in the rubble at The Dolphin Inn this morning."

"Poor baby," Chris cooed, leaning in close and stroking Snowy's head with the tip of her finger.

"You like cats?"

Chris looked up, surprised. "Who doesn't like baby animals?"

"Oh, I just mean…I just thought you might be allergic."

"No. But I detest having animal fur on my clothing." Chris straightened up and brushed imaginary cat fur from her jeans. Ah, Abby had nailed that one.

"So, now you're a single spinster with a kitten," she said, sauntering back to the kitchen. "It's not really helping your chances, is it?"

Abby reddened. "Who said I was single?"

"Sorry. Aren't you?"

"Well, yes, I am, but…" She tried to come up with a clever reply, but her brain stalled.

"What are you into, anyway?" Chris asked, lopping off the end a cucumber. "Boys? Girls? Neither? Both?"

Abby stared at her. "You can't just ask a person that!"

"Why not?"

"Because it's invasive. And politically insensitive."

"Really?" She looked up, her brows knitted. "But I'm gay. Doesn't that make it okay to ask?"

"Maybe, I don't know…and there are more than two genders!"

"Okay, okay, shoot me," Chris said, dropping the knife and holding up her hands in surrender. "Why are you so defensive about it, anyway?"

Abby took a breath to reply but paused. It was a good question. Why had Chris's questions got under her skin? Was it because she'd hoped that Chris would have intuited that she, too, was gay?

"If you must know," Abby replied at last with a little huff, ignoring the second question, "I, too, am a *Homo* sapien." She looked back at Chris to gauge her response. Surprise? Excitement? Recognition? Nothing—not even a snigger at her joke.

"Well, I guess it's fine that you have a cat, then," was all she said in acknowledgment. "A plus, even."

Abby forced a laugh. "Something like that, yes."

She sighed and turned back to her laptop. She watched as the faces of her friends popped up on the screen in a burst of raucous conversation.

"What's all that?" Chris asked, gesturing toward the laptop with her chin.

"Virtual pub quiz night with my friends back home," Abby said, glancing over to check on Snowy, who was purring contentedly in her bundle of blankets. She couldn't wait to introduce the kitten to her friends. They'd all walked the long, painful Alice Road with her.

"Is this really your life, doll?" Chris asked as she peeled cucumber into long ribbons. "School, home, virtual get-togethers? I'm starting to change my mind about that cat. Maybe it's an awful idea after all."

Abby drew a breath for her favourite retort—"I have a dead girlfriend, I'm allowed to"—but when Chris looked up and winked at her, the air stuck in her throat.

Abby had set up these online meet-ups as soon as she'd moved to town, and sometimes they'd been the only bright spot in her week. She missed her friends terribly, but she never regretted leaving: Missing was better than pity. Life back home AD—After Dan—had been entirely intolerable. Dan's early exit from this world had grated against engagements and graduations and weddings and births. Abby had needed to put distance between herself and the friends she'd collected throughout her life. Pity was harder to detect in 2D. But now, seeing herself through Chris's eyes, it struck her that perhaps her life had become almost one-dimensional.

"Well," Abby said at last, her cheeks hot as she turned back to her laptop. "I guess I'm destined to be a boring old cat lady."

"Is that a tiny baby kitten?" Lulu squealed moments later as Abby held the bundle to the screen, *Lion King*-style. Several pixelated faces cooed and gushed before Abby tucked Snowy back into her cosy spot on the sofa.

But as the game got underway, she struggled to focus. Her eyes kept drifting to the kitchen: to Chris chopping things, arranging things on platters, chatting on the phone with white earbuds plugged into her ears.

"Dude." Nathan snapped his fingers in front of the camera several times. "You here? What's going on?"

"Sorry, sorry!" Abby blinked, refocusing on the screen. "It's my turn to ask the next question, right?"

"Yup," Lulu replied, looking bored.

"Okay, um. Okay! What year was the first iPhone released?"

Phew. What was going on with her? She doubled down on her efforts to focus on the quiz, turning her back squarely to the kitchen. It worked so well that she didn't notice Chris coming into the living room until she was just a few steps away.

"Sushi?" she offered, setting the platter down beside Abby's laptop. She didn't seem fussed about the game underway.

Abby looked up and nodded wordlessly.

Turning back to the screen, she said, "Carry on without me for the next round, guys" and then quickly killed the volume to mute her friends' protestations.

"Whoa, this looks like something out of a magazine shoot," Abby said, ogling the colourful selection before her. Back home, sushi had been a weekly treat. It felt like a different lifetime.

"I couldn't find nori or wasabi, so we'll have to make do with cucumber ribbons and chilli paste," Chris said as she sat down beside Abby. Snowy stirred, and Chris pinched off a piece of salmon and held it out to her. She gobbled it down, her eyes still half-closed in sleep, then tucked her little head under a paw and went back to sleep.

Abby was still staring at the plate as Chris deftly picked up a piece of sashimi with chopsticks and popped it into her mouth. "Come on, doll," she said, nudging the platter closer to Abby. "This is just gorgeous."

Abby lifted a piece of salmon sashimi to her mouth. It was delightfully buttery and smooth, even better than she remembered. She closed her eyes as the fish melted on her tongue.

"This is incredible," she murmured around a mouthful of nigiri a moment later. "I think this might be the best sushi I've ever tasted."

"I took a couple of classes in Japan, a few times I was there on business," Chris replied breezily, as if taking a sushi-making class in Japan wasn't any different to grabbing a coffee at the corner café. "Are you still busy with this…" She motioned vaguely to the laptop screen. "Online game?"

"The quiz? Yeah. We're only on round two."

"Can I play too?"

Abby jerked her head in surprise. "You…want to join our quiz?"

"Yup," Chris said, licking a fleck of food from the corner of her lip. "I'll admit that it sounds like fun."

"Oh, really?" Abby tried not to smile as she turned the sound back up. "How odd that a virtual get-together should be fun."

"Oh, just show me how it works," Chris grumbled, but the corners of her mouth were curling up as Abby adjusted the screen.

"Guys." She raised her voice to get their attention over the ruckus. They were debating modern architectural styles. "This is Chris. She's staying here for the week."

There were friendly greetings all round. They were used to her house guests dropping in on their games.

"Brutalist," Chris said by way of greeting. "And hello."

JD nodded as he double-checked the answer. "Yup, Brutalist."

"Knew it!" Nathan punched the air.

Chris winked at Abby and turned back to the screen. "So, I can stay?"

"Absolutely," Nathan said with a laugh. "I just wish you could be on my team. It looks like Abby has a secret weapon tonight."

Abby's pub quiz performance generally vacillated between mediocre and not-too-terrible, but not tonight. Chris was smart and engaging and very, very quick. Abby found herself mesmerised.

"I used to have so much fun playing general knowledge games with my kids when they were younger," she said to Abby between rounds, eyes sparkling. "I'd forgotten how much fun this is."

She reached for her beer, her thigh pressing gently against Abby's. For a moment, she was close enough for Abby to smell the sweet, fruity fragrance of her shampoo.

"God!" Chris winced, sitting back. Their thighs were no longer touching, and Abby felt strangely disappointed. "I never thought I'd live to see the day I paired sashimi with a pale ale, but here we are."

"Mmm," Abby replied vaguely.

On screen, some excitement was brewing. "You guys are on fire!" Nathan exclaimed as he added up the latest scores. "That puts you in the lead by fifteen points, Team…Wait, what is your team name?"

Chris and Abby turned to each other and shrugged. Then Chris's eyes lit up.

"Well, we're eating sushi, and we're Chris and Abby…so it's gotta be 'Team Crabby.'"

The others burst into laughter. It was witty and cute, and Abby grinned as she repeated it to herself.

Team Crabby. Chris and Abby.

By the end of the evening, newly minted Team Crabby was declared winner of the invisible floating trophy and a week's worth of quiz kudos, despite Chris's tendency to flout the rules. "You can't just shout out the answers," Abby had admonished more than once through fits of giggles.

The game over and the farewells bade, Chris turned to Abby and held her hand in the air for a high five.

"We make a pretty great team," Abby said, concentrating on Chris's elbow to land the perfect high five—an old trick she'd learnt from Dan. "That's the first time I've ever won."

"Well, best you stick with me, doll. I've been around the block a few more times than you. It comes with the territory." She smiled lazily at Abby, and it made her look cheeky and wise all at once.

Abby looked away quickly. She felt a peculiar, long-forgotten flicker inside her, and she busied herself with gathering up Snowy.

"I'm heading to bed," she said, clutching the cat and her laptop to her chest.

"Already?" Chris sat up straighter, her perfect brows knitting together ever so slightly.

"Yeah," Abby said with a sigh as she backed out of the sitting room. "It's late. Those kids will eat me for breakfast if I don't get enough rest."

"Okay," Chris said, flopping back against the sofa. Abby suddenly yearned to stay a little longer, but instead she said, "Good night. Sleep well," and dashed to her room.

It was hours before she was finally able to fall asleep.

CHAPTER FOUR

There were a couple of absentees in Abby's class on Friday. And then there was reading time, when Abby noticed that Poppy, engrossed in her ballerina book, was scratching her head absent-mindedly. She hadn't paid particular attention at the time, but now that they were all sequestered in the principal's office, she was quickly realising she should have.

"Lice?" The newest member of staff was aghast. He was young, perhaps twenty-two, and his face was turning an interesting shade of chartreuse.

Abby looked at Evan and grimaced. "Gross," she mouthed.

He grinned and pretended to stick his finger down his throat in a mock puking action, his biceps bulging. They both giggled until Moira Fresh turned around and shushed them sharply, her bangles jangling like a rebuke as she jammed a finger to her lips.

The instruction, as usual, was for everyone to leave school immediately and check their hair. Shaving hair off only really happened in the movies. In reality, it was all about patient combing and that awful, medicated shampoo if nits or lice were detected. It wasn't Abby's first rodeo—she even had a dedicated kit at home.

"So, your place or mine?" Abby joked as she and Evan headed out at noon. Like shared lunches and coffee breaks, it had become part of their routine: If there was a lice infestation, they'd check each other's hair like a couple of chimps.

Evan looked sheepish. "Sorry, dude…Marli's here, remember? So, I guess she'll do it for me…"

"Oh, of course—duh." Abby's cheeriness was more forced now. "Well, it sounds like a fun date night for you two."

They said their goodbyes at the intersection on Main Street, where Evan carried on straight and Abby turned left. Her head was starting to itch, but that could also have just been…well, *in* her head. She gave a good scratch and peered under her longer-than-usual fingernails. Nothing obviously suspicious.

It was a beautiful day out—sunny with clear skies and the promise of a mild evening ahead. As soon as she finished with her hair, she planned to sit outside with her book and an icy drink, and let the sun bake her hair dry. She'd even make a comfy little spot for Snowy. She was surprised by how much she already loved the kitten and how excited she felt to see her.

As Abby entered the cottage, she noticed with an annoying jolt of happiness that Chris was already home. This morning, as usual, she had awoken to an empty house and a half-full pot of coffee. She hadn't expected to see Chris home before nightfall.

She was sitting at the little wrought iron table on the patio, her back to the house, and Abby was about to call out in greeting when she noticed that she was, somewhat predictably, on a call. Besides, she'd drawn the door shut behind her—they had to be extra careful not to let Snowy escape—so Abby changed direction and headed to her bedroom instead.

Snowy was curled up in a tiny white ball on the bed, enshrouded in her favourite fluffy blanket. She slowly opened her eyes as Abby stroked her head, then she stretched out her legs and gave a great big yawn. Abby giggled and picked her up, covering her in kisses before setting her back down on her blanket. She sat and stroked the little animal until a tickle on her scalp brought her back to the task at hand.

In the bathroom, Abby turned on the shower and waited for the water to heat up. It was her favourite room in the house. Unlike the rest of the cottage, which was airy and bright, the bathroom felt like a separate, mysterious little universe all of its own.

Dark wood shelves adorned a charcoal feature wall behind the bathtub, which was a spectacular white ball-and-claw number with bronze feet. Mismatched pots of pothos and philodendrons lined the shelves, their leaves tumbling all the way down to the floor. Abby had whiled away more hours than she cared to count in that tub, bubbles up to her chin, steam making dragon's-breath patterns in the air. She'd light every candle she owned—ylang-ylang, vanilla, jasmine, sandalwood. It was her sanctuary, her little private paradise. She always felt restored when she walked out of it.

But today was about efficiency, not indulgence. She showered quickly to wet her hair and then dressed and combed conditioner through the strands.

She was rifling through the bathroom cabinet for her lice kit when Chris walked past the open door.

"Hey," Abby greeted her, leaning around the doorframe. "How are…" She stopped when she saw Chris's expression.

"Oh, uh, hi," she said distractedly. "Aren't you…Don't you have school today? I wasn't expecting you home so early." She had clearly been crying.

Abby pointed to her scalp. "Lice scare," she said with a shrug. "Are you…Are you okay?"

"Yes," Chris said abruptly. "Totally fine."

"O-*kay*," Abby replied quietly, turning back to the cabinet to retrieve the kit. She recognised a boundary when she heard one.

"So, are you clear?" Chris asked, lingering.

"Clear? Oh, the lice. I don't know yet." She scrunched a hand around her damp mop of hair. "I really hope so. I'd hate to have given these little parasitic scalp dwellers to you."

Chris shrugged as if little parasitic scalp dwellers were the least of her concerns and regarded Abby with puffy eyes.

"You're doing it yourself?"

"Yep." She spoke with far more confidence than she felt.

"Have you done it before?"

"Well…no. But I've checked Evan's hair. And anyway," she said, picking up her phone from the edge of the basin and waggling it at Chris. "That's what YouTube is for."

"Give me that," Chris said with a *tsk*, yanking the device from Abby's hand. "I've raised three kids. Amid plenty of lice outbreaks. I'll do it for you."

"Um…"

But Chris had made up her mind. "Come. Outside, now. We'll do it in the sunlight. Where's the comb?"

Abby fumbled around uselessly, thinking only about how Chris would be running her fingers through her hair over and over again, and how that would be strange and awkward but also…

"Are you sure you don't mind doing this?" Abby said, twisting her hair tightly in her hands.

"Oh, for fuck's sake." Chris grabbed the kit and wedged it under her arm. "I wouldn't have offered to if I didn't want to." Then she marched out to the patio, calling over her shoulder, "Besides, I need the distraction. Come!"

Abby took a deep, steadying breath and scampered out after Chris, who was already seated on one of the wrought iron chairs, a cushion tossed onto the grass at her feet. A towel hung over her denim-clad thigh.

"Sit," she barked, and Abby did.

For a few minutes, they sat in silence, Chris working methodically through tiny sections of hair: comb, wipe, comb, wipe.

Abby tried to focus on the magentas of the bougainvillaea and the sounds of the passing cars rather than the feeling of Chris's calves gently nudging the sides of her body. She'd had close encounters with guests many times before, applying sunblock to shoulders and releasing zippers on the backs of dresses. It came with the territory. Why did this feel different?

"I have to point out the irony of all this, after calling ourselves Team Crabby last night." Chris chuckled, cutting into Abby's freight-train thoughts. "Actual bugs in your hair."

"Hey! We don't know that for sure just yet, thank you very much."

Abby was beginning to relax into the not-unpleasant feeling of having her hair tugged when Chris's phone rang in her pocket, and she jumped.

"Sorry…" she muttered, a hand still holding a comb to Abby's head as she squirmed to reach the bleeping device.

The ringing cut abruptly, but there was a beat before Chris sighed "Hi, Karys" into the phone.

A tinny voice came through the speaker, loud enough for Abby to hear. "Hey" it sighed back.

Abby held her breath and picked at a weed in the ground.

"How are you feeling?" said the voice stiffly.

"I'm fine. Thanks." Equally stiff. Abby yanked at the weed, pretending not to be straining her ears.

"I still think you're making a big mistake."

"I know you do."

"You're wasting your time, Chris."

"You've said that. Many times. But I disagree." Chris's voice had turned from cool to icy, and as she spoke, the teeth of the comb pressed painfully into Abby's scalp.

"You need to come home, Chris. The kids need you. The business needs you."

"And you?" Chris snapped. The comb bit into Abby's head. "Do you need me?"

Abby jerked away, rubbing the sore spot on her head. But when she turned back to Chris, she saw the woman hadn't noticed. She sat frozen on the chair, her cheeks flushed, eyes flashing.

"I called to ask if you're okay," the voice said at last, so softly Abby almost couldn't hear it this time. "Isn't that something?"

"Sure," Chris said dismissively. "I guess it's *something*. I've gotta go. Tell the kids I lov—Hello? Karys?" She pulled the phone away from her ear and stared at the black screen. "Fuck!" she snapped, hurling the phone onto the table, where it landed with a dull clang. "And that's why I have an indestructible phone cover."

She took a deep breath before reaching for Abby's shoulders to guide her back into lice-check position.

"So…" Abby said after a long moment, flicking the now-crushed weed from her fingers. "That was your wife?"

"Karys. My partner."

"Sorry, I thought because of the ring you wear…"

"I just wear it."

Abby started to nod, then remembered about the combing and stopped. "She must miss you."

"No." Chris tugged at a knot and Abby's head jerked backward. "She's just really angry that I'm in Bay View."

Abby yanked at another weed. "Is that what you were upset about earlier?" she asked carefully as the comb skimmed the nape of her neck.

Chris's hand paused. "The short answer? Yes." She resumed combing.

"And the long answer?"

Chris sighed again, gathering Abby's hair in her hands. "The long answer is much too long for today. We're done."

"Done?" Abby wheeled around. "So my hair's fine?"

"Well, you have no lice. But your hair is most definitely not fine. When was the last time you saw the inside of a hair salon?"

Abby scowled, getting to her feet. "No idea," she grumbled. "But it's not that bad…"

"Oh, it's bad. Different lengths, different colours. You need to sort it out."

Abby tried to feel hurt at Chris's directness, but she knew she was right.

"My hair's fine," Abby repeated, giving it a stubborn shake. It was almost dry, and she had to fight the urge to wrestle it into a knot using the hairband around her wrist. Instead, she pulled out the chair next to Chris's and sat down.

"It's not, and I'm booking you an appointment at the hair salon," Chris said in that voice that meant she'd made up her mind and there was no changing it.

"Oh no-no-no, please no, you can't!" Abby grabbed her arm in a panic. "Sorry," she added, releasing her clutch. She'd rather pluck it all out, strand by strand, than walk into the Shave Shack.

"God," Chris said, rubbing her arm. "Why ever not?"

"Long story," Abby muttered.

"Ha!" Chris scoffed. "You think I'm going to let you off that easily after I just spent the last hour inspecting your crazy mop for parasites?" The annoyance of a few minutes ago had faded, replaced by a naughty twinkle in her eye.

"Fine. It's a short story but I still don't want to tell you."

Chris stared at Abby, one eyebrow arched. She was refusing to back down, and by now, Abby knew better than to try.

"Ugh!" Abby grunted in defeat, flopping back against the chair. "Cody is the only stylist in town I'd ever allow to touch my hair, and I can't go to her anymore."

"Why? Because you dated her?"

"Not quite."

"You fucked her?"

Abby shifted in her seat. "Yeah."

"Oh, for god's sake." Chris scoffed again. "That's the most ridiculous reason to avoid someone. Especially when you live in a town the size of a lentil."

"Well, it's extremely awkward."

"So? Get over it."

"Easy for you to say. You've had decades and decades to learn how to just get over things," Abby retorted, and Chris laughed before standing up and stretching.

"I'm parched from all that hard work. Drink?"

"Great idea. I'll get us some snacks."

Inside, Chris set about organising drinks while Abby foraged for food. She hurried to dump something edible on a platter. The sun would be setting soon, and it would be beautiful to watch it from the patio. Was that the only reason she was rushing to get back outside?

The sky was changing from kitten-heel pink to tangerine as Abby set the platter down. A moment later, Chris emerged with a couple of beers in one hand and her phone in the other.

"Done," she said triumphantly, waving her phone in the air.

"What is done?" Abby asked, narrowing her eyes.

"Your appointment with Cody, tomorrow morning. To fix your hair."

"Oh my god, you didn't," Abby wailed. "I can't face her."

"Well, you won't have to." Chris shrugged and slipped into a chair. "You'll have your back to her the whole time."

"Ohhhh, you!"

She was dying inside at the thought of seeing Cody again. The last time had been the night they'd hooked up. Turned out, chemistry in the stylist's chair didn't translate into chemistry in the bedroom. Abby had snuck out as soon as Cody had fallen asleep.

Walking home alone in the early hours of the morning, Abby had felt lonelier than ever. She'd burrowed deeper into her hoodie and sworn to herself that she was done.

Dan had been a unicorn. Everyone else was a barnyard pony.

"Oh, you'll thank me for this," Chris was saying as she popped open the beers, and Abby blinked herself back into the moment. "It'll be weird for a couple of minutes, and then it'll be behind you and you'll have great hair again. Besides, she's probably forgotten all about it."

"Unlikely," Abby grumbled, feeling herself flushing at the thought of her ghosting move.

"Oh!" Chris said suddenly, jumping up and grabbing her phone. "I almost broke your golden rule." She dumped her phone onto the sofa and, back outside, plopped into her chair. Abby smiled, and a strange tingling feeling warmed her belly.

"Here, have a nacho," she said, pushing the plate toward Chris. "Sorry, it's not exactly salmon roses."

For a while they chewed in silence, watching the sky turn a deeper shade of orange, then red, and then Chris turned to Abby with an expression she couldn't read.

"Tell me about the woman you loved and lost," she said, not breaking eye contact. Abby felt her body stiffen.

"How—" She cleared her throat and tried again. "How do you know about that?"

"Well, you're what? Twenty-six? Twenty-seven? You've moved to a shitty little town—"

"It's not shitty, it's just little. And I'm twenty-eight."

"Fine. You're young, you've moved to this shi—*little* town, you've clearly gone through some sort of drama because I've seen the photos around the house of you and your friends, and you used to take a fuck-load better care of yourself when you lived in the city. And, c'mon, what twenty-eight-year-old moves to a…a…retirement village? So, I suspect you're running away from something—or someone, and I suspect that someone is a woman." Chris crunched down on a nacho to make her point. "Or maybe you had a menty-B."

"A 'menty-B'?"

"Mental breakdown." Another crunch.

"That's rude." Abby scowled. Had it been, though? She'd certainly skirted close to breakdown many times.

"Oh, well, sue me. So, which was it?"

Abby looked away, taking in the darkening sky and the tiny pinpricks of stars emerging. "Why do you want to know so badly?"

"Because you used to shop at my shop and you don't anymore because you moved here, so I'd quite like to know why I lost a customer."

"Oh, please."

"What?" Chris held up her hands in mock defence. "I'm invested in customer retention."

"Well, then you really should deliver to Bay View."

"Tell me a good enough story, and maybe I will."

CHAPTER FIVE

Excitement fizzed in her belly as they walked up the palm-lined path to the double-volume glass-and-stone house. Abby smoothed her cocktail dress, glad she'd taken extra care with her outfit tonight. Already her feet ached in the patent-black stilettos, but she knew they completed her outfit perfectly. And they were Matt's favourites.

"You look gorgeous," Matt murmured into her ear as the sounds of the party floated through the air. He slid an arm around her waist, letting his hand come to a rest on her butt and giving it a squeeze. "God, I love this dress on you."

Abby smiled and took his hand in hers. She wanted to seem mature and self-possessed. Being groped by her boyfriend outside her lecturer's house wasn't going to cut it.

"Let's go," she said, using her other hand to pull the short, tight black dress back into position. Music and laughter filtered down from the crowded second-floor balcony. Abby couldn't wait to get inside.

Carol opened the door on the second ring, looking every bit as relaxed as she did at the front of the lecture hall. She may have had a doctorate in ancient languages and a string of other academic accolades to her name, but she had no airs and graces, and insisted her students call her by her first name. With her colourful, loose-fitting clothes and spring-coil grey hair that hung to her shoulders, Carol had always felt more like a camp counsellor than a stuffy old varsity professor.

"Abigail." She opened her arms, folding Abby into a warm, fragrant embrace. "I'm so glad you made it. Welcome." She opened the heavy wooden door wide and ushered them in. Abby introduced her to Matt, and Carol led them upstairs to the party.

Abby could feel the excitement in the air: students celebrating the culmination of four years of hard work and countless hours in libraries, exam halls, and study groups. She was proud of her achievement, proud to have been invited to a graduation party hosted by her favourite professor. There were dozens of people dancing and mingling upstairs and spilling out onto the wide balcony. Multicoloured lights were strung from the ceiling, and a pink-haired DJ stood behind a mixing deck, one hand held up to her earphones. In the far corner of the room, waistcoated bartenders spun cocktail shakers in the air, and Abby gratefully accepted the glass of wine that Matt pressed into her hand. Her feet were seriously hurting. Perhaps the wine would help. She wanted to dance.

Abby scanned the room as her eyes adjusted to the dim lighting. "Over there," she said into Matt's ear, raising her voice above the din. She tugged his hand as she tottered over to her friends—Lulu, Cassie, Seb, and some of Matt's friends, too. They'd been dating a year now, and slowly their friendship groups were merging.

"Lu!" Abby cried as she threw her arms around her friend. "How incredible is this party?"

"I know, right?" Lulu beamed. "This place!" She gestured with her wineglass, eyes wide. "Carol. Who knew?"

Seb and Matt were bro-hugging, and Cassie winked from her spot on the sofa. Abby squeezed Lulu to her again and then grabbed her shoulders. "Can you believe it's finally here?" she squealed. "No more essays, no more exams…No more theses!"

Lulu grinned back, then gave Abby's hand a yank. "Come, let's dance. We have so much to celebrate. We're graduates!"

As Abby followed her friend to the makeshift dance floor in the centre of the room, she couldn't recall the last time she'd been this happy. She'd successfully completed her studies, she had a smart, good-looking boyfriend, and she had the best friends in the world.

And Carol invited me! That part was key. Tonight may have signalled the end of the varsity days she'd loved so much, but if things swung her way, she wouldn't have to say goodbye to the university just yet.

She hadn't told anyone, but she'd applied for a junior lecturer position starting at the beginning of the new school year, and Carol had agreed to be her referee. That Carol had invited her to this party spoke volumes.

Abby held Lulu's hands and threw her head back as they laughed and twirled each other in circles. Her heart was *so* full.

At some point, the rest of their friends joined them on the dance floor, and Matt wrapped himself around her. Cassie handed them shots of tequila, and as usual, Matt drank Abby's because he knew she couldn't stomach the stuff. They plucked sushi off platters and drank more wine, and Abby felt very grown-up, and very, very glamorous. If only her feet weren't so fucking sore.

"I'm just going to the bathroom," Abby yelled into Matt's ear, teetering on her tiptoes. It helped her to reach his ear, but it also gave her heels a moment's respite.

Matt nodded and grabbed her butt, pulling her toward him to kiss her. He tasted like tequila and cigars. They were all playing at being grown-ups tonight.

Abby made her way downstairs to find a bathroom. The party was different down here, the music from upstairs muted, the vibe more laid-back. Carol was seated near a fireplace, with several now-former students in a semicircle around her. Another cluster of guests milled around in the kitchen, discussing their future plans. Eventually, Abby found the restroom and slipped inside. She was grateful there'd been no line outside—she didn't think she could stand for a moment longer.

She kicked off her shoes the second she closed the door, letting out a sigh of relief. Heaven was stepping out of high heels.

Barefoot, she walked over to the basin and looked into the mirror. Her cheeks were glowing from the dancing (and the eye-wateringly expensive highlighter she'd applied before leaving the house), and her eyes sparkled back at her. Remarkably, her hair was still in perfect shape, the fresh, golden-blond streaks almost luminous after hours at the salon earlier that day. Her mascara had smudged a little, but a quick swipe under each eye sorted that right out. She smiled at her reflection, capturing the moment she went from student to graduate and soon, if things went according to plan, from graduate to tutor.

An abrupt rap at the door.

"Hey! What's taking so long?" a voice demanded, startling Abby out of her daydream.

"Oh, uh, sorry," she called back, hurrying to the door. She shoved her feet back into her heels, but it felt like they'd swelled to double their size in the few minutes they'd been free and pressed against the cool tiles. Pain shot through her body as she stood up and pulled open the door.

"Sorry," she muttered again as a guy she didn't recognise pushed past her into the bathroom. She sighed and looked around for somewhere quiet to sit for a few minutes while she waited for the pain to subside. She supposed she could just leave her shoes off, but that felt…tacky, somehow. Appropriate for a drunken twenty-first party, maybe, but not a fancy graduation celebration.

Glancing up and down the hallway, she spotted another, quieter staircase wedged into the back corner of the house. She hobbled over and collapsed onto a carpeted step, breathing out heavily as she rubbed her aching feet.

Just two minutes, she told herself as she sat on the step, savouring every second of unshod ecstasy. *Then I'll put these damn things back on and just put the pain out of my head. Mind over matter! I'll be home in a few hours. I can suck it up until then.*

"I've never understood how people can wear those things," said a voice behind her. Abby spun around. Walking toward her, down the dimly lit staircase, was a tall and striking blond human—elfin, perhaps, if elves were almost six feet tall with popped collars and messy undercuts.

The woman paused when she got to the bottom of the staircase, turning to face Abby. Wisps of blond hair fell over her eyes, and a vague smile played at the corners of her lips.

With one burgundy Doc Martens boot, she nudged Abby's discarded stilettos. "These look like torture devices."

"They feel like it too," Abby replied wryly. "It's like I've put my feet through a meat grinder."

The woman grinned, revealing a dimple in her left cheek. There was something familiar about that grin, about the dimple and the particular sparkle in her eye, which caught Abby's attention even in the dim light of the staircase.

Abby raised her eyebrows. "Care to trade?" she asked, gesturing with a nod at the woman's boots. "Those flat soles look an absolute dream."

The woman laughed, wiggling a foot. "They are, babe, and there's no chance of a trade. I'd rather wear clogs than those spikes."

"I'll take clogs if you're offering," Abby retorted. "Hell, I'll take *Crocs* if you're offering."

"Crocs? You must really be in a bad way if you're willing to commit social suicide."

"I know, right?" Abby sighed. "And it's not like you're being much help." She was enjoying the banter, but there was something more to it—something she couldn't quite put her finger on.

The woman grinned again. "I'm Dan," she said, sticking out a hand, and Abby took it. It was warm and firm, and she was surprised by the jolt that ran through her as they touched.

"I'm Abby," she said, and Dan's lips curled into a smile.

"So, you're Abby," the woman drawled, still holding her hand.

"Have we met?" Abby asked, taken aback, knowing full well they hadn't. As she spoke, she pulled Dan's hand ever so slightly closer to her.

"I don't think so." Dan took back her hand, much to Abby's disappointment. "But I've heard Carol talk about you. She tends to talk about her best students. And her worst, of course. But I believe you were one of the former? Although it's hard to tell right now, given your extremely silly taste in footwear."

"Hilarious," Abby said drily, pretending to be insulted. Her hand felt hot where Dan had held it. "Anyway, I'll have you know I've always been more book-smart than shoe-smart."

"Don't you mean 'feet-smart'?" Dan quipped, leaning against the wall. She slid her hands into the pockets of her long, sleeveless olive-green jacket.

Abby found that she could not take her eyes off the woman, and not only because she couldn't place her.

"You're not one of Carol's students, are you?"

"Indeed, I'm not. I live here." Dan flicked her head in the direction of upstairs, and a small silver piercing glinted in her septum.

"Oh!" Abby had a flash of recognition. "That's where I've seen you. Photos in Carol's office. Are you her…daughter?"

Dan threw back her head and laughed, and Abby felt herself flush.

"No," Dan finally replied. "I'm not her daughter. I'm her ex."

Abby opened her mouth to respond then closed it again like a hungry hippo. Why hadn't Abby made the connection? Carol had always been open about her sexuality. Abby felt embarrassed for her faux pas.

"I, I'm so sor—" she stammered, but Dan cut her off with a wave of the hand.

"Oh, babe, please don't. Loads of people think that. Well, straight people, anyway. It's the age gap."

Abby nodded slowly, the pieces coming together. "And you live here?" she asked. It seemed odd. She couldn't imagine breaking up with a boyfriend and continuing to live with them.

"Yeahhhh." Dan chuckled in a way that made it seem like a joke Abby wasn't in on, and then she fixed her gaze on her. Abby shifted on the step, suddenly feeling very self-conscious and small. Her earlier bravado dried up, and she was aware of her heart hammering wildly in her chest. She was distantly aware of the sounds of the party, but it felt very far away.

"Anyway, now I think your boots are slightly less cool, since you won't lend them to me," Abby said, returning to safe ground. She'd talk to this woman about the texture of rain if it would keep them here, together, a moment longer.

"Well, come over to the other side of the rainbow and you can wear boots every day of your life." Dan winked, and Abby wasn't quite sure what she meant. "We'll even find you a pair that works with that dress."

At the mention of her dress, Abby was transported back to the present, remembering that she'd abandoned her friends, and Matt, upstairs. And for reasons she couldn't explain, the last thing she wanted right now was Matt coming to find her. There was something about this moment with Dan that she wanted to keep just for herself.

I don't want this conversation to end, is what Abby wanted to say, but she had the sense to go with the more measured, "I've gotta get back to the party. My, uh, friends are probably wondering where I am."

"Friends, huh?" Dan raised an eyebrow, her eyes still locked on Abby. Abby felt her cheeks redden again, and suddenly she wished they were alone in the house—just the two of them and this new, exciting, terrifying feeling inside her. She had to break the spell.

"Want to help me get these spikes back on my poor feet?" she asked, reaching for her shoes. Just the thought of putting them back on made her wince.

"Oh, babe." Dan sighed. "I can see from up here that you're never going to get back into those hell-traps. It'll be like trying to stuff a sausage back in its casing."

"Hey, are you calling my feet 'sausages'?"

"Well, you're the one who said you feel like you've put them through a meat grinder." Dan pushed her lips to the side. "I'm going to lend you a pair of my shoes."

Abby paused midway through jamming three of her toes into the front of a stiletto.

"Umm…that's really kind of you, but I couldn't…I mean, you don't even know me."

"Oh please, it's no big deal." Dan shrugged, moving back up the stairs. Abby tried to protest again but it seemed Dan had made up her mind. She disappeared into a darkened room at the top of the staircase, and moments later a light went on. Abby heard a cupboard door opening, a whole lot of rifling around, something falling, and then a cupboard door slamming shut. The light went off again.

"Here," Dan said, reemerging from the darkness. A pair of white sneakers dangled from her fingers. "These are super comfy. You'll be able to dance until six in the morning if you like."

Abby reached for them gratefully, her fingers brushing Dan's as she took them.

"I'm on my way out, but you can just give them back to me another time," Dan said, like it was nothing. Like she regularly handed out pairs of expensive sneakers to random girls and hoped she got them back.

"Thank you so much. I—"

"There you are!" called a voice, and Abby spun around to see Matt lumbering toward her. He was the very last person she wanted to see in that moment, and the force of her resentment surprised her. She wished she could spin Dan around and rush her upstairs so she wouldn't catch sight of Matt, like in a cartoon.

"Hi! I'm Matt," he said, closing the gap and sticking out a meaty hand.

Dan smiled, but it didn't seem to reach her eyes. "Dan."

Matt looked from Dan to Abby, then back again. Abby could tell he was trying to get a read on the situation, and she shifted on her feet. The movement brought his attention to the shoes in her hand, and his face lit up. "Oh! You girls doing the whole 'girl thing,' swapping clothes and stuff?"

Abby looked over at Dan, thrilled to discover that Dan was already looking at her. She winked conspiratorially, and Abby felt buoyed. So buoyed, she feared she may float away.

"Yep, exactly." Abby turned to Matt. "Dan's lent me some shoes so I can keep dancing. My feet are killing me!" Her voice sounded strangled and she kept waiting for him to realise he'd walked in on something more than a straightforward shoe exchange. But what, exactly? Even Abby didn't know.

"Sweet, thanks, dude," he said to Dan, bending down a little unsteadily to grab Abby's discarded heels. "Baby, you need to get back upstairs. They're doing the most insane shots, and Seb is hooking up with that chick—you know, the one he's been into since first year? It's crazy!"

Abby watched him, irritated.

Holding on to the banister for balance, she slipped her feet into the sneakers—like encasing her feet in fluffy clouds—and turned to Dan.

"I'll return them, promise," she said. Then, because it was graduation night and she'd never felt better, maybe ever in her life, and especially in the moment she'd shared with this woman who looked like a summer's day and an ice storm all at once, who was cheeky and funny and kind, who wore army green like god herself had created the colour just for her, who seemed to hold the secrets of the universe in the dimple of her left cheek, Abby leaned in and embraced her. As she circled her arms around Dan, she breathed in her scent. She felt the wool of her jacket brush her face as the woman hugged her back, and then shifted ever so slightly so their cheeks grazed.

And then, Matt had her hand and they were weaving their way back through the crowded rooms, back to the party and their friends and the DJ with the pink hair and the lights and the drinks, and as she turned back, the last glimpse she had of Dan was as she slipped out the back door, her platinum hair disappearing into the darkness, leaving Abby feeling bereft and elated all at once.

It wasn't quite five a.m. when they left the party. Abby had danced more, drunk more wine—a lot more wine—and she'd squeezed her friends and asked the DJ to play their favourite songs. In a few weeks, Lulu would be starting an internship three hours away, and Cassie would be moving to Botswana to work at a wildlife reserve. It was the last time they'd all be together for a long time, and Abby had wanted to relish every minute.

Yet her mind had kept drifting back to Dan. In between shots and guffaws and increasingly silly dance moves, she thought of Dan's tousled hair and the way one strand had dipped down almost to her eyes, like a lazy palm frond on a tropical beach.

A few times, her friends had snapped their fingers in front of her face and asked her where she'd disappeared to. She blamed the booze and was penalised with more.

By the time they got back to the house Matt shared with a couple of friends, Abby felt like a different person.

Matt had stripped and climbed straight into bed. He was asleep in moments, his mouth hanging open as he snored. But Abby, slowly sobering up, was wide awake. She removed the sneakers and placed them neatly on the floor, feeling guilty that she'd forgotten to leave them behind. It was nearly inconceivable since she hadn't stopped thinking about Dan all night, and she wondered what kind of trick her brain had played on her to ensure she'd have a reason to see her again.

Next, she peeled off her black cocktail dress and stared at herself in the full-length mirror. Hours earlier, she'd carefully chosen a red lingerie set for Matt's benefit. He loved her in anything lacy and barely there. But now, the thought of him ogling her in sexy underwear just irritated her.

She climbed into bed and switched off the light, careful not to rouse him. Her mind flooded with thoughts of Dan: her eyes, her hair, how she was so effortlessly cool, and what it must be like to be her friend…

Abby smiled to herself in the dark and soon, she was asleep.

Abby woke to Matt pawing at her like a bear. Her head felt thick and confused as she disentangled herself from his arms.

She'd dreamt about Dan. She'd woken up thinking about her. And this morning she couldn't stomach the idea of having sex with Matt. It felt like she'd had a software update in the night and now she was simply incompatible with Matt 1.0. It made no sense. Nothing made sense, and as she stumbled to the bathroom to vomit, Matt calling out helplessly after her, she felt guilty and confused—and desperate to leave.

Minutes later, she hurried out of his house, still in her clothes from the night before, and on her feet, a pair of sneakers that felt like they'd been made from a little piece of heaven.

* * *

It took Abby several days to work up the courage to return to Carol's house with the shoes. Days that had been spent planning her outfit and rehearsing what she'd say.

She'd really thought that Dan would disappear from her mind, but she couldn't have been more wrong.

She hadn't been able to get her out of her head. Not for a moment.

Abby had replayed their conversation over and over, trying to figure out how their brief interaction had completely upended her world. Since that night, she'd been unable to focus on Matt, on her friends, on anything really. Friendship was almost certainly what she wanted, wasn't it? But then why had Dan almost entirely taken over her thoughts?

The more she tried to untangle her feelings, the more knotted up they became.

It was storming as Abby drove to Carol's house, the sky the colour of wet cement. Rain pelted her windscreen, and the wind was whipping trees into strange shapes and angles. Next to her on the passenger seat were the sneakers. She'd tested putting them in a variety of different bags for the grand handover: *Which brand best represents my personality? Which brand would make Dan want to be my friend?* She'd tried, then discarded, cosmetic brands, clothing brands, even a branded coffee bag. She decided that a bag made the whole thing seem over-thought, which it obviously wasn't, and that handing them back in the same way Dan had given them to her would a) seem cool, as if the entire shoe-exchange was a near nonevent in Abby's life, and b) increase the chances of their fingers touching again.

Abby did, however, spray the shoes liberally with her favourite perfume. She'd considered writing her phone number on a piece of paper and slipping it into one of the shoes, but that didn't seem like something a potential friend would do. Then she considered writing it on the underside of the tongue of one of the shoes—that was cute, right? Quirky? But fortunately, a long, hot bath had given her the pause she'd needed to rethink that.

Her heart was pounding in her chest as she navigated the waterlogged streets to Carol's house. Her plan was: say a quick hello to Carol, engage in a little small talk. She was keenly aware of the fact that she was there to see *her favourite lecturer's ex-girlfriend*, the same lecturer who may have the power to make or break Abby's fledgling career. She'd have to feel out the situation carefully and not seem overly eager to see Dan, lest it seem like more than it actually was. Which it wasn't.

Abby had run through all the reasons that Dan could still be living with Carol, but the only thing that made sense was that there was still something going on between them. Surely?

She'd also practised some opening lines—even though the idea was, of course, not to sound rehearsed but rather cool—even coolly detached.

She pulled up at the house and realised with dismay that her decision to forgo the bag meant that the rain would wash the perfume off the shoes.

"Fuck," Abby groaned, groping around the car for another bag. All she could find was a discount grocery store one. "Shit-fuck!" The choice was: let the rain wash off the perfume, Abby's signature smell that she hoped would subtly invade Dan's space and therefore all her thoughts, or preserve the fragrance but hand over the shoes in a cheap plastic packet. A conundrum indeed.

At last, she jammed the shoes into the packet—she'd blame the rain—and hurried from the car up the path. With her head down to protect her makeup from the deluge, she jabbed her index finger against the doorbell, remembering that last time she was here, Carol had only opened up on the second ring.

The door flew open just a second later, and Abby was so surprised that she pitched backward, almost losing her balance on the slippery ground.

"Whoa!" Dan exclaimed, grabbing Abby's arm to steady her. The plastic bag swung wildly, the shoes smacking the front door with a heavy thud.

"You okay?" Dan gasped, eyes like saucers.

Oh. Jesus.

In the doorway was Dan. Dan with her icy-platinum quiff and her cheeky smile and that dimple. That goddamned dimple. This was not the entrance she'd been planning to make. Not even close.

"Come, come inside—it's pouring," Dan was saying, still holding Abby's arm. She drew her into the house and closed the heavy wood door behind her. Abby still hadn't said a word, but when she tried to cycle through the lines she'd rehearsed, her mind was totally blank.

For a moment, she panicked that she may wordlessly hand over the shoes and leave without ever having made another utterance to the woman she'd been dreaming about for the last several nights. But then her neurons suddenly fired, the machine jerked back into action, and what it spat out was worse than she could ever have imagined.

"Well, clearly, I have fallen for you" was what Abby said.

Dan laughed—a sweet, husky melody—and Abby, dazed but relieved, laughed too. Dan had taken her unplanned confession as a joke.

"Oh, you're funny, Abby," she said, her grey eyes sparkling. "No wonder you're one of Carol's favourite students."

"Favourites? Really?" Abby awkwardly held out the bag of shoes to Dan. "So, not just a pretty pair of sausage feet then?"

"Apparently not." Dan reached out and took the bag, absently wrapping the plastic tightly around the shoes. "These," she said, motioning behind her, "are going straight into a box."

For the first time, Abby noticed the row of mismatched, overflowing boxes lining the hallway, clothes and electrical cables spilling over their sides.

"Oh…You're moving?" Abby asked. "Both of you?"

"Oh, gosh no," Dan said with another laugh, pushing the shoes into the corner of a box. "I'm moving into my own apartment, finally."

Dan huffed as she shoved the box into the corner of the room. "There were construction delays, and then some sort of structural issue, and *then* a weatherproofing problem." She rolled her eyes as she ticked each item off on her fingers. "Carol's been great, though. She's let me crash in her spare room the entire time. Almost a year."

Abby frowned. "Isn't it weird, though, living with your ex?" She was careful to keep her voice low in case Carol was within earshot.

"Nope," Dan said with a shrug. "We realised ages ago that we're far better as friends than partners. And we're pretty great at being housemates." She pushed up the sleeves of her light-grey hoodie as she watched Abby's expression. "We're alone, by the way. She's not here."

Something about the way Dan said "We're alone" ignited a strange sensation in Abby's belly—a swirl of excitement, nervousness and… something else she couldn't quite put her trembling finger on.

"So, what were you doing in your car for so long before you came in?" Dan asked, cutting into her reverie, and Abby felt sheepish all over again. That mischievous smile spread across her face, and Abby suspected she was being teased.

"You saw that?" Her cheeks burned.

"Yup. In case you hadn't noticed"—she made a sweeping gesture with her arm—"this place is roughly ninety percent glass."

"I, um…" Never had she wanted so much to disappear and remain in exactly the same place, all at once. "I was hoping for the rain to subside."

"Hmmm…" Dan glanced outside. "Yeah, that's not going to happen."

"I guess not," Abby murmured, her eyes following Dan's as her heart thundered in her chest.

"Well, I need a break from all this packing and I'm sure you don't want to risk, you know, another fall." Dan shot her a teasing look. "How about a hot chocolate? I make it with almond milk. Or soy."

"Hot chocolate sounds great!" Abby's reply was too quick. She flushed, but Dan was already making her way to the kitchen and Abby trotted quickly behind her.

Minutes later, their hands wrapped around steaming mugs, Dan led them upstairs to the enclosed balcony. They sank into soft, side-by-side armchairs facing the rain-lashed windows, Dan drawing up her long legs like a gazelle.

"Mmm," she sighed, looking over at Abby. "How's yours?"

Abby took a gulp and nodded enthusiastically. "Oh, delicious, thank you." She hadn't tasted the drink at all.

She hoped Dan hadn't noticed her trembling hands. Her palms were so clammy, she'd worried she'd fumble with her mug. But Dan was oblivious, chatting away about the rain, her apartment, the unpacking she was dreading. She spoke about her work as a freelance wedding website designer. "The irony," she had scoffed, "being anti-marriage and all."

Abby focused on Dan's lips, on the way her long fingers curled around her mug, on the tiny studs and rings dotting her earlobes. Abby noticed how one shoulder of her hoodie had slipped down, revealing a thin white bra strap against smooth, glossy skin.

"Once it's all set up, you'll have to come around and see the place," Dan was saying. "But it's up a flight of stairs, so I don't recommend you wear your death-trap stilettos."

Abby snapped back into the conversation. "Oh, don't worry," she replied quickly. "I plan to trash those." She didn't, of course, but she thought it sounded like a cool and edgy thing to say.

"I must warn you, though," Dan said, absent-mindedly pulling her top up onto her shoulder. It slipped back down immediately. "My apartment is all the way on the other side of town. So, I may need to bribe you to get you there."

"Bribe me?" Abby laughed. As if. "With what, exactly?"

"Hmm, oh, I don't know. A pair of sneakers?" She gave Abby a sidelong glance. "It seems to have worked before."

Abby flushed. Could Dan be…flirting with her? The woman's marble-grey eyes were sparkling again, like sunlight hitting a stream, but Abby wasn't sure how to read them. That dimple, though… Abby was starting to recognise it.

After a long moment, Dan looked away. "So, your boyfriend seemed…boyfriendy," she said, leaning down to place her empty mug on the floor. Her sweatshirt gaped, and Abby, beside her, tried not to stare. She averted her gaze before Dan could catch her.

"Boyfriendy…that's a good description. I guess he is very boyfriendy." She really didn't want to talk about Matt, especially when she'd barely spoken to him over the last several days.

"So, you guys are serious?"

Abby took a deep breath. "I don't really know how to answer that."

Just then, sound and movement downstairs: a door opening, the shuffling sounds of someone arriving home with shopping bags, a bellowed, "Hi!"

Oh, no!

"Hi!" Dan called back, then reached out and touched Abby's arm when she saw her stricken face. "Don't worry, Carol won't come up here. She'll probably just go and potter around her side of the house."

Sure enough, after a few more moments of shuffling, they heard Carol retreating, and eventually, the sound of a door softly closing.

Abby breathed out. "I really don't want to piss her off," she said, her heart thumping now for completely different reasons.

"Why on earth would you piss her off?" Dan asked, genuinely confused, and Abby wondered if she'd completely misread the situation.

"Oh, um, you know…nothing. I'm just waiting to hear about a job application."

"At the university?" Dan sat up straighter, her eyes wide. "How exciting!"

"Yeah. I've asked Carol for an academic reference. So I don't want it to seem like…well, I don't want her to think I'm stalking her. Or like I'm trying to influence her decision." *Or trying to get close to her live-in ex-girlfriend.*

"Oh, babe, no, I wouldn't worry about that." Dan waved a hand. "Carol's super chilled."

But suddenly, Abby felt very much like an interloper.

"I think I should let you get back to your packing," she said, looking in the direction of the boxes downstairs.

Dan was watching her, a smile tugging at the corner of her lips, and Abby felt annoyed. She was growing quite tired of this knowing look, plus she was irritated that Carol's arrival had interrupted their quiet moment. And was Dan really going to just let her leave with no protest, and no clarity on her leading comment about the sneakers? Fine, then!

But the second she stood up, Dan grabbed her hand. Abby swung around.

"But finish what you were saying first."

Abby's hand throbbed where Dan held it, and she worried that she would feel it through her fingertips. "Oh," she said, trying her best to sound bored. "What was I saying…?"

Dan tugged her lightly, coaxing her back down into the chair. But she didn't let go of Abby's hand. Instead, she pulled it closer to her, tracing the lines of her palm with her fingers.

Abby froze. Her heart was hammering so wildly, she was sure it must be audible. Slowly, Dan turned Abby's hand over and ran her fingertips over the long, polished fingernails and smiled.

"You were about to tell me whether you and your very boyfriendy boyfriend were serious…remember?"

Of course I remember.

"Oh, yes, that…"

If Abby sounded vague, it was because she was trying to steady the rhythm of her breathing. Her hand, still caught in Dan's, was clammy and trembling. She drew her lips into her mouth and tried to catch her breath.

"What I mean is," Abby started, then cleared her throat. "I thought it was serious. I thought I loved him. I mean, I love him. I think I love him."

She shook her head and squeezed her eyes shut for a moment. When she opened them, her vision was blurry, but her thoughts, at least, were clearer.

Dan was still watching her, saying nothing, still holding her hand between her smooth, cool fingers.

Abby searched Dan's face, taking in her eyes, her mouth, her persistent, teasing smile. She felt her own heart beating in her chest, her throat, her belly, and lower, too—much lower—as Dan slowly laced her fingers through Abby's.

And then she leapt.

"When I said, earlier—when I made that joke, about falling for you?"

"Mmm…"

"I think…maybe…I wasn't joking."

Abby hurried on. "I mean obviously, I've just met you. I haven't, like, *fallen* fallen for you. But there was something…last Friday night. I haven't been able to put it out of my mind." Abby cleared her throat again. "Put you out of my mind."

She took another deep breath, and then she let the last of her confession tumble out. "I can't stop thinking about you. All the time. And I don't want to. I don't understand it and I don't know what it is but I'm here and that makes me really, really happy."

Dan smiled—a wide, deep, dimpled smile that lit up her whole face—and said, "Good."

Then she leaned forward and placed her fingertips under Abby's chin. As the rain poured outside and Carol shuffled around below, Dan tipped Abby's face up to hers and kissed her.

Everything inside Abby blew up. And in that moment she was home, and she knew there'd be no going back.

Whether the kiss lasted minutes or hours, Abby couldn't tell. She felt the tips of Dan's hair tickling her eyelids, she tasted chocolate and caught glimpses of her bare shoulder and delicate bra strap. She was aware of the arms of chairs between them, hers pressing uncomfortably into her ribs, but she dared not move for fear of breaking the spell.

It was their first of oh-so-many kisses. Abby couldn't have known that then—nor that one day, far too soon, they'd have their last.

"I've been wanting to do that since the moment you told me about your sausage feet." Dan laughed hoarsely as she finally pulled away. "It was probably the sexiest thing a woman has ever said to me."

Abby laughed too. The sound caught in the place under her ribs. She gulped. "Well, then, just wait until I tell you about my juicy rump," she whispered back, and they kissed again, partly because talking was awkward now, but also because kissing Dan felt like her newly discovered purpose in life. It felt the way people said kissing felt, even though she'd never experienced it like that before.

And kiss, they did: in Dan's new apartment, in Abby's car, in coffee shops and libraries and Abby's tiny bedroom in the apartment she shared with three housemates. Matt was gone—he'd been hurt and angry and confused, but he let her go graciously. For that she was grateful. He wasn't a bad guy, he just wasn't her guy. Neither of them could've seen this plot twist coming.

She cut her nails right down. She tossed the stilettos to the back of her wardrobe, and later, away altogether. She contemplated a piercing, a tattoo, a new hairstyle. She settled on a few flannel shirts and several pairs of white sneakers.

Late one afternoon, as the day seeped lazily into evening, Abby pulled Dan's loose white shirt over her head and buried her face in the soft, perfect breasts beneath. She pressed them together and let her lips graze the delicate pink nipples. It had only been a few weeks. Perhaps Dan had been taking things slowly for Abby's sake. But Abby couldn't stand it anymore. She wanted more of Dan, needed more of her, and as her teeth teased the steel bar through Dan's nipple, the throbbing grew deliciously, exquisitely unbearable.

Abby had worried that she wouldn't know what to do when the moment finally came, but she needn't have: her body just did. Their bodies just did. There, on Dan's eco-friendly mattress on the hardwood floor—her bed frame hadn't yet been delivered—their bodies wet with sweat and wanting, they came together in ways that Abby couldn't ever have imagined, even in her most vivid fantasies, and there'd been plenty of those. Maybe it was hours that they lay together, or days, surrounded by scented candles and bottles of water and lanterns strung from window frames.

The bed frame arrived, then the bedside tables (obviously one was immediately allotted to Abby) and then, the question of Abby moving in became more of a technicality than anything else ("I *hate* it when you leave, baby." "Well, I hate *to* leave, baby!")

Moving-in Day was the happiest of Abby's life, and a very close second was the day she was awarded the tutoring job at the university. They celebrated the latter with champagne and friends and a special toast from Carol. They'd celebrated the former in their apartment, with far fewer attendees, and on a brand-new bed frame.

The way Abby saw it, things simply couldn't get better. She had a job she loved, a partner she adored, and a supportive circle of old and new friends that was slowly, beautifully, knitting together.

Then there was that other, lesser spoken-of benefit of being a lesbian: double the wardrobe, double the makeup, half the risk of running out of tampons. Having full access to Dan's collection of designer clothes forced her to up her own fashion game and gave her an appreciation for gorgeous fabrics and cuts. They were a striking couple—everyone told them so—but more than that, their relationship was solid. They were best friends, soulmates, each other's favourite people. Things felt almost too good to be true.

It was Abby who found the lump. From the moment she'd first traced the shape of them with her fingertips, Abby hadn't been able to get enough of Dan's breasts. And so, while it was a shock to find the small, hard mass, it wasn't a surprise, really, that it had been Abby who made the grim discovery.

They'd been together three years. Dan was thirty-seven—young, but not too young for a lump. But surely not old enough for it to be… that bad of a lump. Surely young enough for it to be…just a blip on the radar. Surely.

Dan drank freshly pressed juices and ate berries and cauliflower and nuts. Cups and jars were filled with strong-smelling tinctures. They littered the countertops and bedside tables. At night, drops of CBD oil; in the morning, mug after mug of bitter green tea.

But none of it fixed her, and slowly the fruit and herbs were replaced with drips and pills. Always more drips and pills. The bitter tea gave way to bitter words and thoughts.

Cancer changed Dan. Correction: terminal cancer changed Dan. She'd always been positive, fuelled by a particular lightness of heart and soul. Now, she was… Well, she called it "realistic," but to Abby, it leaned uncomfortably close to "fatalistic."

They fought about it, often. Just as Dan put only healthy foods into her body, so Abby felt she should put only healthy thoughts into her mind. But that required stamina Dan was swiftly running out of.

As the illness progressed, it seemed to sap Dan of her very essence— the bright, happy energy that made her who she was. While they both felt increasingly powerless in the face of the disease, their vulnerability manifested very differently.

"You're twenty-six!" Dan would rant from her prison of damp sheets. She had to work hard to muster the energy. "You should be out fucking hot, healthy people, not providing palliative care to an *invalid*."

Abby, meanwhile, vowed to stay positive, doubly so to combat Dan's singular dose of "realism." She took the tiniest sign as an indication that it was working, like Dan having a craving for a food she hadn't touched in months or experiencing a half hour without debilitating nausea or pain.

She never thought further than *today*, and sometimes, *this hour*.

Their apartment became a train station of well-intentioned visitors, there to entertain, relieve, soothe, feed, clean, and everything in between. Carol was as reliable as the tides.

Abby was encouraged to take breaks, to "go out and have fun for a few hours," but she resented the implication that she needed to escape or that she could somehow, even for the briefest moment, have fun without the person who was her entire world. Fun was fun because of Dan. Was she supposed to go to a movie, a party, a music festival alone? Who should she mock-gag over beetroot juice with? Who would understand what she meant when she uttered only the first three words of a sentence before dissolving into laughter?

Everything was pointless.

Instead, she'd go to the kitchen and cut up fruit she'd later bin.

She'd almost convinced herself that one day—one day—they'd take road trips like they used to and throw dinner parties for their friends and celebrate birthdays without the spectre of death sucking the life from the room.

Blowing out candles meant something different now.

There were good days—like the ice cream day, like the day of Alice's homecoming—and plenty of shitty days. Extreme highs, and then hopes dashed to dust. There was moisturising lotion and an endless stream of medication. There was food going mouldy in the fridge and on the counters because Dan didn't have an appetite and neither did Abby. There was the laundry pile that sometimes seemed unending, laden with sodden bedsheets and pyjamas, never designer clothes or pretty underwear. Eventually, there was the hospital bed, the hospital smell, but never those first shaky steps down a grey corridor, toward recovery, toward the light of the world once more.

Once, during one of their many debates about marriage—which Dan had never understood, because she'd told Abby right up front, before their first kiss even, that she was decidedly, vehemently, anti-marriage—Dan had said it was too late anyway. Getting married when one partner was terminally ill was macabre and fake. "Do you really want to be a twenty-six-year-old widow?" she'd spat, but she was crying, and Abby had put her arms around her and enclosed her battered, battling body in her arms. She placed her head on Dan's chest and listened to her heartbeat. She wanted to memorise the sound. She listened and let it drown out the sound of Dan's humiliation, which had turned her cruel and mean.

They'd actually had a really good few days until Alice took up her vigil in the garden downstairs. Happy, light, hopeful even. It was a bit like the darkest hours being before dawn, but whatever the opposite of that was.

And then, she was gone.

Abby, by default more than design, inherited Dan's clothing collection—coats, jackets, denims, shirts, shoes probably worth a fortune, probably worthy of display in some sort of museum of fashion. But Abby was barely out of babyhood. She didn't want to inherit anything from her dead life partner. She didn't want to be the default owner of a couture collection because the person who'd painstakingly curated it over two decades had died a dreadful death, died slowly, had had the life leeched from her body, stolen drop by drop, starting in the bed they'd shared.

Abby felt like she had the flu all the time. Every inch of her body ached, every time she moved, every time someone touched her. Each night, she closed her swollen eyes hoping to die, and every morning, she woke up exhausted and in agony, always on the sofa, always still alive.

She gave the bed away.

She gave away the furniture, the art, the expensive equipment she'd bought to liquidise, pulverise, obliterate food.

Little by little, people picked away the pieces of their life.

And when they all looked at Abby with pity in their eyes, she tucked her boxes under her arms and left to where no one would ever follow. And even though Alice had hated her by the end of it all, and her pain had set Abby's teeth on edge, she missed that cat dreadfully. Alice was the only one who had understood it all.

* * *

It was almost dark by the time Abby stopped talking. She could still hear Alice's anguished yowls echoing in her memory.

Usually, by the time she reached the end of her story, her listener's face would be slack-jawed with shock—a ragged patchwork of pity and discomfort. Then their mouths would crack open and some platitudes would dribble out.

People tried so hard, but they never really knew what to say. So, Abby would rearrange her own expression and reassure them that she was Okay Now. Doing Fine These Days. It Really Was *Okay*.

She braced for pity, but when she looked into Chris's face now, she found none. To her relief, there were no repairs to be made. There was no awkwardness, even in the silence that Chris allowed to linger between them.

"Abby, I'm so sorry," she said at last, her voice soft, her gaze not wavering. "Life dealt you a real shit blow. You didn't deserve any of that, and neither did Dan. No wonder you've retreated to the sticks."

"Right?" Abby laughed, but the sound was jarring and caught in her throat.

"No reminders of Dan out here."

"Nope." Abby dropped her gaze. "None at all." She noticed that Chris's hand was resting gently on top of her own, but she had no idea when it had happened.

She looked up again and forced herself to look Chris in the eye. What was it about her that made Abby want to crack open her chest, show Chris the scars and bruised mess inside?

"Thanks for listening," Abby said after a moment, taking back her hand and wrapping her arms tightly around herself. "And for not pitying me. That part means the most."

"I know it does."

"Do you?"

Now it was Chris's turn to look away. In the dim light, Abby thought she caught a flicker of something cross her face, but in a second, it was gone.

"Abby, this might be a strange question, but…do you still have all of Dan's clothes?"

"Of course I do."

Chris took a breath. "I would love to see her collection. I mean, if you're comfortable with that. If it's not insensitive. It sounds like she had an incredible eye."

Abby blinked in surprise. She was aware of her palms moistening, of her heart rapping against her ribs. But, yes. Yes, she wanted to.

"No one's ever asked me before. I'd love to show you."

Dan's clothing used to be stored in the FortyLinks bedroom until Abby had caught a guest trying to exit the house in one of Dan's winter coats. Upon questioning, she claimed to believe it was part of the service offering. A bit like bed and breakfast—but in this case, bed and double-breasted coat. Now, the boxes were safely in her own room, taking up ninety percent of her closet space. Fortunately, there wasn't much temptation to shop in Bay View, unless you were particularly partial to Lycra and tie-dye, so Abby didn't miss the cupboard space.

They hauled the boxes one by one into the living room. They were grubby and torn, but Abby knew exactly what each one contained based on its scuff marks and tears. Chris fetched them drinks and perched expectantly on the sofa, poised for the big reveal.

She fiddled with her phone—Abby assumed she was messaging someone—but a moment later, music began playing from Abby's laptop. Snowy started at the sound from her spot on a cushion, but after a moment, she stretched her little legs and curled back into an even tighter ball.

"This," Abby said, kneeling on the floor and loosening the criss-cross folds of a box lid, "is a *jacket*-in-the-box." True enough, as she opened the lid, clothes almost sprang out of it. Maroons and greys and denims and velvet. Abby plucked a black leather jacket from the box, the same one that had featured in her dream the other night.

"This was one of my absolute favourites on Dan," she said, pressing it to her chest. It smelled the way well-worn leather always did—earthy and sweet. When Abby squeezed the fabric between her fingers, she felt a tube of lip gloss in the pocket. Blinking fast, she pulled it out and tucked it into her jeans pocket, and then turned back to the box.

"Oh! Here's one from Saint Jamie." She handed a pristine cream trench coat to Chris, who had now moved off the sofa and joined Abby on the floor.

"I remember this line well," she said, carefully taking the garment from Abby. "Four or five seasons back. We sourced it in Milan."

"Uh-huh," Abby replied, reaching out to finger the fabric. "I wasn't kidding when I said we were regulars in your store. Dan spent all her money on good jackets and organic fruit."

"Oh, this! My god." Chris's eyes widened as she lifted a black blazer, handling it as if it were a baby.

"That," Abby said, "was a birthday gift from a bunch of Dan's friends. Cost a month's rent at least. Exquisite, isn't it?"

"Absolutely gorgeous," Chris agreed.

"I used to wear some of these," Abby said, appraising an emerald-coloured jacket, "even though they always looked so much better on Dan. I just liked how it felt to wear her clothes."

"I get that," Chris said, her smile slightly tinged with sadness. "And now? Do you still?"

"Oh god, no…no. Now I could never. It would feel too strange. And anyway—it's not like I need a fancy wardrobe here."

When they had gone through every item in the box, they moved on to the next, and the next. They picked over shoes and shirts and twenty different styles of plain white T-shirts. Chris had given Abby the backstory of each Saint Jamie piece, most of which she'd hand-picked during her travels. Abby had shown Chris the army-green jacket Dan had worn the night they'd first met, and bemoaned the fact that sleeveless coats even existed. "What's the point of them?" Abby had cried, to which Chris had exclaimed, "Fashion, doll! Fashion is the point!"

Abby had fished out her least favourite of all Dan's jackets, an oversized faux fur disaster that reminded her of a grubby polar bear. "She wore this one to festivals, which is why it's all matted. I hated it! I begged her to get rid of it. And now, I can't…*bear* to."

They both howled with laughter, and eventually Chris spluttered, "Why not repurpose it as a bathroom rug?" and they howled some more.

She usually found it so hard to look at Dan's things, but this evening, poring over them with Chris was…fun, she thought guiltily. She watched Chris hold up a cape—a cape!—and they both dissolved into fits of laughter once more. It had proven too dramatic even for Dan, who had worn it once and never again.

Abby hadn't ever laughed about the cape after Dan died. She'd taken the cape Very Seriously Indeed. Until tonight, in this precious and unexpected space—a space in which she could appreciate Dan for all she'd been: a real, fallible person with a wonderful and sometimes totally weird sense of fashion.

Afterward, they sat side by side on the sofa, legs drawn up and sipping their drinks, and Abby felt lighter than she had in months.

"What are you going to do with all of it?" Chris asked, nodding in the direction of the clothes draped over sofa arms and upturned boxes.

Abby pursed her lips. "I dunno. But I'm not ready to start thinking about getting rid of it all. I do know I'll have to, eventually. I mean, it's literal baggage. But I'll give you first dibs, okay?"

"Hey, no, that's not what I meant." Chris looked stung, and Abby hurried to fix what she'd said without thinking.

"No, I know, I just mean that you see the beauty in all of it—even in the crazy. And I'd want all these pieces to go to a loving home, you know?"

Chris nodded. "I understand," she said, and then gestured expansively with one arm, her wineglass poised between her fingers. "So, is this really going to be your life now?"

Abby laughed, relieved to be back on safe ground.

"I like it here," she replied with a shrug. "But I also don't know how I'd ever go back home." Truthfully, she knew she'd never move back to the city, but she worried that Chris would judge her for wanting to stay in a town she clearly thought so little of.

Chris cocked her head and narrowed her eyes at Abby. Abby shifted uncomfortably beneath her gaze, slopping a bit of her wine on her arm. She dabbed it dry with her other arm, and now that both arms were indisposed, she tossed her head to move her unruly hair from her eyes.

"Firstly," Chris said, pausing to purse her lips in a thoughtful expression. "Thank god we're getting your hair done tomorrow, and secondly, your not wanting to go home…It's not really about the memories, is it? Because you've filled this house with so much of your life with Dan."

Abby scowled at Chris and reached for the bottle of wine.

"This bird's nest has kept the lice away, as you well know," she said, filling their glasses. "So how do you know that wasn't actually strategic?" She purposefully ignored the second question as she took a sip of wine. Chris didn't push.

"I know it wasn't strategic because you literally told me a couple of hours ago that you're trying to avoid the only decent hair stylist in town because you boned her once and regretted it."

"Oh my god!" Abby spluttered, jamming her free hand to her ear melodramatically. "Boned? Really? Ugh!"

Chris grinned. "Who knows? Perhaps that *boning* might end up being the start of a beeeautiful romance."

"Nope, no way, not with her, not with anyone, thank you very much."

Just as Chris took a breath to respond, her phone trilled and the sharp sound shattered the moment. Abby's heart sank as Chris reached toward the coffee table to grab it. But, instead of answering, she glanced at the screen and pressed a button to mute the call. Then, tossing her head back, she sent a long, loud "Gah!" up to the ceiling.

It was silent for a few moments after that.

"Sometimes you just need to roar at the sky, right?" Abby said.

Chris smiled at her. "You get it, Abby," she said, and then held her glass out. "Cheers to strangers and group therapy."

"Hey," Abby said, narrowing her eyes. "You still haven't told me what upset *you* today. It's your turn to share."

Chris sighed. "Mom stuff, life stuff…It's really not worth getting into. Now, don't leave me hanging," she added, motioning to her raised glass.

Reluctantly, Abby clinked her glass against Chris's. She had shared so much, and she'd hoped by now, Chris would feel comfortable sharing, too.

"Hey!" She frowned. "You need to look me in the eye when we toast. Otherwise, it's seven years of bad sex."

Abby made her eyes very wide. "Well then, here's to seven years of great sex," she said as they clinked glasses again.

CHAPTER SIX

As she stared at her reflection in the salon mirror, two things became clear: she needn't have worried about putting on makeup, and she needn't have worried about Cody.

Cody was flitting around Abby's head, chopping, clipping, and highlighting with a vulgar amount of energy for a Saturday morning. She was the same as always—a jovial, softly butch teddy bear with colourful streaks shot through her cropped dark hair.

"You're sure you just want me to trim it?" she'd asked as she'd raked her fingers through Abby's hair. She'd sounded disappointed, as if this were the world's greatest missed opportunity.

"Yeah, I think so…" Abby replied, staring at her caped reflection in the mirror. Neckless, with wet hair, she looked like a toe. "Actually, Cody—you know what?" Cody's head shot up, her bangs dipping into her eye. "Zhoosh it up a bit. It could do with a fresh style, maybe some colour…" Her eyes drifted to the woman's shaved side cut. "Just no clippers."

Cody laughed a deep, easy laugh that Abby recalled from their single date. "Yeah, dude! You got it," she said enthusiastically, and set about with renewed gusto as she gathered clips and brushes and mixing bowls. "I think this butter blond could work great in your hair," she said, rifling through a stack of colour swatches. "Or actually—nah, I think you're more a Scandinavian blond kinda gal." She blushed, and with a toss of her head, flicked her hair out of her eyes.

Abby smiled. "I trust your expert judgment. Go wild…ish."

"Excellent," Cody replied, rubbing her hands together. She had thick rings on most of her fingers, and Abby had always wished she could pull off the look. It was cool on Cody. On Abby, it just looked like she couldn't decide which of her seven awkwardly clashing rings to wear that day.

Cody dove in, mentioning her girlfriend within a couple of minutes of getting started. She continued to punctuate her sentences with the word as she chatted away. Her energy was just as Abby had remembered it: light, friendly, warm. She didn't seem to hold any kind of grudge.

"Oh, that," she'd said airily as Abby had begun to reference their last encounter. Better to get it out of the way, she'd figured. "That was ages ago, dude." She fiddled with the cape, tightening the Velcro. Abby's transformation into a pasty, blobby frog was complete. No neck, but inexplicably, seven chins.

"I was actually chatting to my girlfriend the other day about…" and she was off. Abby breathed a sigh of relief as she rubbed at the mascara smudges under her eyes. She'd been wearing more makeup than usual lately—"more" as in "any," and "lately" as in the last several days.

As Cody prattled on, it occurred to her that in a town as small as this, there really wasn't any space for grudges. Among a mere eight thousand or so people, perhaps a bad memory was considered a good character trait.

Abby let her mind drift back to last night. Chris's question about whether this would be Abby's life indefinitely had stuck with her. Abby may have committed to this town from a practical point of view—she had a job, a couple of friends, even a second income stream and now a pet—but if she intended to stay, she needed to commit to it emotionally, too. She couldn't avoid Cody forever because of an awkward encounter in the past; the place was just too small for that. She needed to turn her temporary state of mind into one of permanence, which meant integration and reembracing all the things that made her *her*. Getting her hair done. Wearing makeup and nice clothes. She didn't want to be anonymous anymore, floating through this town invisibly, suspended in time. She needed to start carving out a place for herself, and that meant taking up space as Abby Massey.

"…And she's staying with you, right?" Cody was saying, but in that slightly pointed tone that people used when they were repeating themselves. She was mixing hair dye with a rubber brush, and the ammonia was making Abby's eyes sting.

"Sorry, who?" Abby asked, blinking.

"Mrs. Addison's daughter. I hear she's in town. Weird, my girlfriend and I didn't even know she had a daughter."

Abby felt strangely defensive of Chris's privacy, especially after seeing her clearly shaken and upset yesterday. "Remind me the name of that hair colour?" Abby said, changing the subject. Each time Cody tried to steer the conversation back to the Addisons' affairs, Abby would redirect her, and eventually she gave up.

Abby hadn't been surprised to wake up to the smell of fresh coffee and fragranced air this morning—it was, after all, the aroma that indicated the very existence of Chris. She *had* been surprised to discover that Chris had already left the house.

She wasn't sure what time she'd fallen asleep. They'd stayed up late chatting, drinking wine, and when they finally went to their respective rooms, Abby had lain awake for hours, her mind whirring. It felt like she'd only slept a wink when Snowy woke her by attacking her hair with razor-sharp baby teeth and claws.

"I know, baby, I know. I'm getting it done today," she'd croaked as she'd extracted the kitten from her matted locks. It was early, and there were the now-familiar aromas floating through the air, but as usual, the house was silent. She felt her stomach drop at a thought: *Just a couple more days.*

Abby heated the coffee that awaited her, poured some food into Snowy's bowl, and shuffled back to her bedroom to check her emails. With the tiny beast fed and tucked into her lap, she scrolled through potential bookings. A few enquiries had come through, but when Abby thought of someone else staying in Chris's room—*Chris's room!*—her stomach dropped again.

"Aww, little cat," she cooed, scratching Snowy's head. "Why can't my life be as simple as yours?"

Snowy yawned in response and stretched all her little legs downward. Then she promptly fell asleep. She really was of very little help.

By the time Abby had arrived at the hair salon several hours later, she'd managed to put the booking enquiries out of her mind and talk herself in circles about what she wanted to do with her hair. Now, several more hours later, Cody was whipping off the cape with a flourish.

"Whatcha think, dude?" she asked, proudly holding up a mirror behind Abby to give her a three-sixty-degree view.

"Oh my god, I love it," Abby whispered, touching the delicate waves. Her new colour was a warm honey shade that felt trendy and more sophisticated than the lemon-yellow of her early twenties. Cody had styled it to hang just below her shoulders in subtle waves. "You've worked magic here, Codes, you really have."

"Yeah, I'm super happy with how it's turned out," she said, looking at her boots, suddenly shy. "And you can easily re-create this style at home with a flatiron. I mean, if you have one…?"

Abby laughed. "Yeah, somewhere. Believe it or not."

Abby paid and then, gingerly, reached out to hug Cody. Cody squeezed her right back. "Oh, and hey! I hope you have plans to show off your new look tonight," she called as Abby left the salon. "We'll be at The Planetarium. You should come dancing!"

Now, as she walked home, her hair bouncing around her face, she mulled that over. Old Abby, City Abby, would've hit the trendiest clubs, and she and Dan would've danced until the wheels came off or the lights came on. But for Anonymous Abby, small-town, muted Abby, what did the night have in store? Netflix? Frozen pizza? Maybe, if she were lucky, a virtual pub quiz with her paired-off friends?

No, that really wouldn't do.

She was still pondering her evening plans—or lack thereof—when she passed The Dolphin. The firefighter tape was all but stripped away, and the afternoon sun was baking whatever wasn't yet burnt to a crumbly brown crisp. Before the fire, she might have spent this evening hanging out at the bar with Evan, eating stale peanuts as Roy poured them round after round of cheap vodka.

Next, she walked past the road that would take her to Evan's house. Often on a Saturday, she'd swing past and spend the afternoon just hanging out, but not now, with Marli here.

Suddenly, she found herself wanting to take a detour past Mrs. Addison's house, in the hopes of catching a glimpse of Chris and, more importantly, Chris catching a glimpse of her, new hair and all, but she managed to fight the urge and head home instead with a sigh and a slightly heavier tread than before.

The house felt stuffy when she opened the front door, all the windows and doors closed on account of the kitten. But it was worth it. Abby smiled as she cuddled the purring ball of fur to her face. She was falling more in love with the kitten by the hour, with her earthy scent and pink pads, and Abby thought how ironic it was that something so full of life could have crept out of the charred cremains of The Dolphin.

Abby headed outside onto the patio, keeping Snowy close. She wondered when Chris would be home, hoped it wouldn't be as late as usual, hoped the waves in her hair wouldn't have collapsed by then. She video-called Lulu, ate some lunch. She considered taking a nap—her head was feeling a little thick from the effect of last night's charged conversations, and no doubt, the wine too—and she jumped at every sound, anxiously anticipating Chris's return. Perhaps if she killed a few hours by napping, Chris would be home when she woke?

Just as she lay down on her bed, her hair carefully spread out to ensure minimal wave disruption, she heard the front door spring open.

"Hel-lo?" Chris called, and it was all Abby could do not to race to her like a Labrador puppy. She forced herself to wait a beat or two before getting up and frantically rearranging her hair in front of the mirror.

"Hi," Abby said as she attempted a casual amble into the kitchen. Chris was dumping her things on the counter. Then she had to repeat herself because her voice had caught in her throat. Chris was wearing a white V-neck T-shirt and a pair of black, washed-out boyfriend jeans. Between her teeth, she clasped the arm of her aviator sunglasses. Abby tried to hold on to the moment before they spoke, Chris standing in her kitchen like a life-size cut-out, brighter and glossier than everything around her. To Abby, she seemed impossibly perfect.

It's just a little crush, she told herself in the eternal words of… whoever that singer had been.

"Hi," she said again, and Chris heard this time and looked up.

"Oh…oh my god, it's totally fabulous!" she gushed, the sunglasses falling from her mouth and clattering to the floor. She bent to pick them up and Abby averted her gaze—with difficulty. She really had to stop with the down-shirt cleavage gazing.

"I love it. Love it! And to think, I'd worried about sending you out there today without strict written instructions on what to do with your hair. I thought maybe you'd end up with some sort of half-shaven, half-peroxided nightmare."

"My god, you are old-fashioned." Abby scoffed, but she twirled anyway to let Chris take in the full style. "There's an undercut underneath."

"Really?" Chris gasped, looking truly horrified.

"No, not really." Abby laughed and shook her head. "We ran out of time. I have to go back for that."

"Oh, shut up." Chris tutted. "Actually, wait—lift your hair. I need to check that your former lover didn't shave the devil's sign into the back of your head."

"Oh, that's a good point." With her back still turned to Chris, she coyly lifted her waves and let them fall slowly back down. "Any revenge snips?"

If Chris noticed her flirting, she chose to ignore it. "Nope, and no sneaky dye job either. Your girlfriend's obviously forgiven you."

"Well, she has an actual girlfriend now, so I think we're good," Abby said, her heart dropping as she watched Chris reach for her phone. Abby grasped for a new subject. "Uh, er, how are you feeling today? Did you see your mom?"

"I didn't actually," Chris replied, gesturing with her phone in her hand. "I'm going to call her now and check in."

Abby stared at her oxblood nails and the thick rings on her fingers as Chris unlocked her phone. Her tanned fingers always seemed to Abby to be strong and decisive. Fleetingly, she found herself wondering how they'd feel entwined in her own.

Abby could hear a muffled ringing tone through the phone just before Chris lifted it to her ear. She rolled her eyes at Abby as if the call were the last thing she felt like doing, and it made Abby feel like they shared a secret in-joke. Just between them. Last night, Chris had been kind to Abby, but Abby needed to remind herself that that's all it was.

She'd have to distract herself. Evan would be indisposed for the rest of the weekend, and her other friends were on a laptop screen. Tonight, she'd have to take the first step toward the Non-Anonymous Abby she wanted to be.

The jeans were so tight, Abby had to lie down to button them up. Ah yes, she remembered this feeling well—and it would mean that her ass looked great, and soon she'd be numb so it would be fine. A few years back, this was the first pair of designer denims she'd bought online and, beginner's luck, they'd fitted perfectly. Well, if you considered "tight enough to restrict breathing" to be a perfect fit, which Abby had back then.

She took tiny steps around her bedroom to crease the fabric into submission, then bent down to lace up her high-tops and nearly severed herself at the torso. Yep, perfect.

Tonight, Abby was Going Out.

She shrugged on a vintage T-shirt and briefly considered wearing one of Dan's jackets but quickly dismissed the thought. Instead, she slipped into her own leather jacket and felt around in the pockets. Damn, no forgotten cash or treasure, just tissues matted with old chewing gum.

Snowy was playing on the new kitty jungle gym Abby had procured that afternoon. With her tiny claws, she tore at the twine wrapped around the poles and rungs, then lay on her back and swatted a feathered toy. Alice had never liked toys. She'd never known quite what to make of them. Strangely, the only thing she'd been passionate about—besides Dan—was chewing up blankets, leaving gaping holes and bits of fluff all over the house.

Around her bedroom, the aftermath of her getting-ready process: discarded clothes, scattered shoes, the flatiron she'd managed to dig out from the back of her wardrobe, its cord lying frazzled and frayed on the floor. Makeup, hair products, even a handbag—which Abby might be forced to use tonight, since the pockets on her jeans would be purely decorative.

It had taken hours, literal hours, to get ready to go to the only club in town, The Planetarium. What was with these townsfolk and their ironic names for things? There was no sea life anywhere near The Dolphin Inn, and The Planetarium catered to the world's tiniest solar system. She'd been to the club once before, but since tonight was the first night of the rest of her life, she wanted to make the right impression.

When Abby emerged from her bedroom at last, Chris was sitting in the living room, drinking a glass of wine and reading a book. When she heard Abby behind her and glanced up, she looked momentarily stunned.

"Hey." Abby smiled, trying to act casual by slipping her hands into her pockets and realising too late that she couldn't. Her fingers hovered awkwardly over the fabric as she leaned against the wall.

"Wow, hi!" Chris laughed, virtually doing a double take. "I know I've been joking, but do you have an actual date tonight?"

Abby flushed on the outside and died a little on the inside. To cover up her pocket faux pas, she folded her arms across her chest, which just so happened to accentuate her cleavage.

"I'm going to go out dancing. I didn't want to waste my new hairdo just sitting at home—although to be fair, Snowy has launched at it a few times in appreciation."

Chris placed her book face down on the coffee table and then swivelled around to fully face Abby. "Well, good for you for getting out there," she said.

"Yeah, it's been a while."

"I know. I mean, after what you said last night."

They blinked at each other for a moment, then both spoke at once.

"Do you—"

"How about I—"

"Oh, sorry. What were you going to say?"

"No, no—you go."

"No, really—what were you going to say?"

A smile spread slowly across Chris's lips. She was leaning back against the sofa, resting her chin on her hand. "Well, I was just thinking—do you want some company? I wouldn't mind…if it wouldn't be intruding?"

"Yes!" Abby replied too quickly. "I mean no, it's not intruding. At all."

"Great. I can't remember the last time I went dancing. Oh, I think Karys and I went to a club in Barcelona about three years ago…or was that Lisbon…anyway, doesn't matter. Give me a few minutes to scrub up?"

Abby nodded as Chris got up and headed toward her bedroom. Then she stopped, turned around, and looked at Abby with a mischievous expression on her face.

"So, it's not that you thought I was too old for a night out on the town?" she asked, an eyebrow cocked.

"No, god no," Abby replied, feeling her cheeks warm. "I didn't think you'd be interested in going to some silly little club here." *With me.*

Chris grimaced. "I'm sorry, I guess I have been a bit of an asshole about this place."

"Go! Get ready." Abby shooed her away. "And by the way," she called down the hallway, "just because it's called 'The Planetarium' doesn't mean it's going to be a stellar night out, so just manage your expectations."

"What are you talking about?" Chris called back from the depths of her room. "We're Team Crabby—you bet Uranus we're gonna have a great time!"

Abby was glad she'd undersold The Planetarium to Chris, because it meant that once they tumbled inside, cackling at their umpteenth Uranus joke, they could be pleasantly surprised by how not-shit it was. Chris had elected to leave her phone at home, and she seemed a whole different person when she wasn't fielding calls from family members or dealing with the admin that came with caring for her mother.

"Actually, this place isn't such a *black hole*," Chris quipped as they leaned on the bar counter, waiting to catch the bartender's eye.

"Runs rings around The Dolphin Inn," Abby replied, and they were off again, giggling like kids.

Unlike city clubs and bars that each seemed to attract a niche market—the queers or the celebrity set, the models or the hipsters—The Planetarium pulled everyone into its orbit. It was, after all, the only club in town, and indeed, the only one for miles in any direction. On a Saturday night, the only night it was open, it was a tiny, pumping, pulsating epicentre, packed to the hilt with locals and visitors from towns north, west, east, and south of Bay View. It was The Planetarium or Netflix. Those were your options. And the Internet couldn't always be relied upon in Bay View.

Inside the club were several different pockets that the owners referred to as "solar systems." There was the large bar area taking centre stage—a space for shooting the breeze with friends or the bartender if you happened to arrive too early or stay too late. It was a dim, square space with dark, highly polished marble counters running around all four sides. In a far back corner was a plush lounge area, protected from the deepest of the bass, where newly minted couples made out in dark corners.

It was also the ideal place to park your ass if you couldn't bear to miss your weekly fix but didn't have the energy for crowds, dance floors, or inane bar banter. Abby had spent much of her first visit to The Planetarium in the lounge, still new to town, still reeling, and totally anonymous. It had felt like the safest space from which to observe her new ecosystem.

Tonight, however, she intended to venture to the other side of the club: the dance floor, with the DJ decks, the bass, the sweaty bodies, the starry ceiling. She wondered whether Chris liked to dance, whether she was a lounge girl or a bar girl. Or whether she'd want to rush back to her phone after a single drink.

"Wow, doll, I'm really impressed with this place," Chris said as they settled onto their stools. "I really was expecting a hole in the wall."

"Yeah, you don't really expect it—here of all places. It's like a desert oasis."

"Or the bright spot of life in an entire solar system." Chris smiled. She took a sip of her drink and placed it on a coaster. "Hey, I think someone's trying to get your attention."

Abby looked up and spotted Cody with a group of friends. She was holding her beer up in an air toast, so Abby waved, then made an elaborate display of showing off her hair. Cody grinned and gave an enthusiastic thumbs-up.

"Your hairdresser ex?"

"Oh, would you let that crap go!" Abby sighed. "She really isn't an ex. We went on one date. Relationships are not a thing for me anymore."

"How can you say relationships aren't 'a thing' for you anymore? You're so young." Chris gestured around the club with her drink. "Just look at all the potential here," she teased—at least, Abby hoped she was teasing. "Okay sure, I can see perhaps Cody isn't your type."

"Oh, really, you can?" Abby said with a smirk. "So, what's my type?"

"Well, based on what I've learned about you so far, I'd say your type is…blond, masc and…nope, that's about it. Blond and masc. Or, masc-ish."

Abby pulled her lips into her mouth and contemplated Chris through narrowed eyes. Chris was basing her assumption on one relationship and one single, failed date. But to be fair, there wasn't a whole lot of data to go on.

You're my type.

The words popped into Abby's head so unexpectedly, she felt herself flushing. Quickly, she pushed them away.

"I don't have a 'type,' because having a type would imply that I'm looking for someone, and I'm not," she replied at last, as emphatically as she could muster.

Chris started to laugh it off, then stopped. She could tell Abby wasn't kidding.

"I don't want another relationship. Ever," Abby said, more forcefully this time. Who was she really trying to convince? "My relationship with Dan was good—no, it was great—but it was hard, like all relationships are. And I'm not just talking about the cancer part. I'm talking about all of it. You know that good relationships are hard work. It's worth it if you love the person enough, but that doesn't necessarily make it easier. Sometimes it makes it even harder."

The club was starting to fill up, getting hotter now and noisier. Abby shifted closer to Chris so she could hear her better—or at least, that's what she told herself.

"The thing is," she continued, close enough to feel warmth radiating off Chris's skin. "Everyone back home felt so sorry for me when Dan died. But I'd done my mourning by then. By the time she died, I was…"

She felt her throat close. She pulled away and sucked deeply on her drink. Chris said nothing, just waited.

"Relieved." Abby eventually choked the word out. She felt sick saying it. She'd never admitted this to anyone. What was it about Chris that Abby wanted her to see every dark crevice of her soul?

"I couldn't tell anyone that, obviously," she hurried on, stopping herself from leaning in again. She cleared her throat and wrapped both hands around her drink, focusing on the half-melted ice blocks inside it. "Nobody would've understood, and so I felt lonely, and guilty, and disgusted at myself. I used to wake up during the night and vomit. But during the daytime, I had to pretend I wasn't relieved—just like I'd had to pretend I was okay when Dan was still alive. I was so tired of pretending. So, so tired of it, that I *had* to get away. It's how I ended up here. And it's how I eventually came to the conclusion that there really is no point in going through any of that relationship stuff ever again. Everyone leaves or dies, that's life. What's the point of all the hard work if the person is just going to exit your life eventually? I used it all up on Dan, and I'm okay with that. So, no, I don't have a 'type,' because there's no way I'll get into another relationship."

Abby looked up from her drink to see Chris nodding slowly, taking it all in. But for the first time, she didn't believe her own words. It felt like her heart was straining to break free of the chains she'd wrapped around it, and she wondered who she was really trying to convince here.

"Relationships are hard," Chris was saying now, fiddling with her paper straw. "I guess for you, after everything you've been through, the good would have to be phenomenally good to outweigh the bad—and the potential bad."

"Yeah, exactly," Abby said, shifting back in her seat. And then, without thinking, "Chris…is your relationship phenomenally good?" As soon as the words were out, she realised she probably already knew the answer.

Chris took a breath to reply when they were interrupted by a high-pitched squeal of excitement behind them.

"Abbyyyy!" *Jab, jab, jab.* "We thought it was you!"

Abby swivelled on her barstool to discover that the person prodding her shoulder was one of her colleagues from school, a woman with a gummy smile who kept her pens colour-coded and her books alphabetically stacked. She and some friends, a few of whom were also teachers, were drinking pink drinks out of glass bottles and by the looks of things, had been for some time.

"Oh, hey, guys." Abby smiled, then made some quick introductions. "Those look like fun," she said, motioning to the drinks.

"Yeah!" Gummy Smile smiled even more gummily. "It's cosmic-politan night—two for one. You guys should get some! Anyway, it's so great to see you out, Abby. You look amazing! Have you changed your hair?"

Abby smiled and swung her head from side to side, giving a little lift to her waves. "I have—Cody did it for me earlier."

"Well, it looks stunning!" Gummy gushed. "Anyway, I didn't know you came here? I've never seen you here. Are you guys going to come dance?" She gave a wiggle of her shoulders and did the same with her brows as she eyed Abby and Chris. "You girls have to come and join us. I loooove this DJ. He's just so amazing!"

"You come here a lot?" Abby asked, immediately cringing when the words came out sounding like a pickup line. The Tipsies didn't seem to notice.

"Basically, like, every weekend—right, girls?"

"Yeah, pretty much," said a tall woman Abby recognised by sight. "It's either this or making tally marks on our walls." She winked, and Abby laughed. She liked them, and had she been alone, they'd have been perfect company on a night like tonight, but their timing couldn't have been worse.

"We'll definitely come and join you a bit later," Abby said, hoping they'd take the hint. She side-eyed the dance floor; she couldn't wait to try it out. The ceiling was painted onyx black. Special star projectors cast lights all over it to make it look just like a night sky, complete with the Milky Way and swirling galaxies. It wasn't yet ten p.m., but already the floor was thick with swaying bodies, drinks held in the air, sequined clothing catching the strobe lights.

"Aww, okay, Abs. But come join us soon, okay?" It was rhetorical, and the group trotted off to be gulped up by the dance floor.

"I love to dance," Abby said, turning back to Chris. It felt like she needed to catch her breath after the interaction. "I haven't done it in… years, come to think of it. How about you?"

Chris shook her head. "Nope, I absolutely hate it." As if to emphasise her point, perhaps subconsciously, she crossed her arms and legs. "But you should go and join them."

"No, no…I wouldn't…"

"Oh, come on." Chris rolled her eyes. "Earth to Abby! Go and have fun. Do you remember how to do that?" She nudged Abby's arm with her elbow. "Here's a clue—you start by getting *Uranus* onto the dance floor."

"Oh, my god! That joke is getting as old as you are."

Chris grinned. "Well, leave me here to work on some new material. Go. Go, go, go! I'll be fine."

She shooed Abby off, virtually pushing her from the barstool. "Okay, okay, hold your horses, I'm going." Abby giggled. "But you better still be *Saturn* here when I get back."

Chris wasn't sitting there when Abby finally spun out to the edge of the dance floor to check on her. Abby had been swallowed up by the swaying crowd and had no idea how much time had passed since she'd left Chris at the bar. It had been so long since she'd let loose, she'd almost forgotten how she'd get swept up in the music, and how sometimes it would be hours before she'd reemerge, sweaty and dehydrated, her muscles burning from exertion.

Now, as she unstuck her hair from her neck, she scanned the crowd for Chris. The club was heaving with people, but Abby could see the barstool Chris had inhabited was empty.

Slowly, she wound her way through the club. At some point, most of the friends she'd been dancing with had done the same. As usually happened, she'd been the last woman standing. She checked her phone—it had been well over an hour since she'd left Chris—and her mouth felt sticky and dry.

As she pressed through the crowd, she saw familiar faces: some from school, some who used to prop up the bar at The Dolphin Inn. It was only her second-ever visit to The Planetarium, but she didn't feel like a complete outsider. How much had this town already begun to absorb her without her even realising it?

Finally, Abby spotted her in a dim corner.

As she got closer, she saw Chris was talking with a group of women. Among them was Cody, a tattooed arm slung lazily around a woman's shoulders—presumably The Girlfriend—and one heavily booted foot crossed over the other, toe to the ground. The two other women with them gazed hungrily at Chris, who stood with one arm across her waist and in her other hand, a blue concoction that swayed in her glass as she laughed.

"Hey!" Cody turned to Abby as she walked up, giving her a high five. "You made it. This is my girlfriend, Jade." She gestured to the woman at her side. "Jade, Abby."

Abby began to acknowledge her with a smile, but Jade pulled her into a hug. "Hey, Abby! So great to meet you." She struck Abby as one of those perennially upbeat types. "We've been keeping Chris company while you were away. Do you wanna drink? We have a whole tray of Mars-tinis." She jerked a thumb, and sure enough, there were several radioactive-looking drinks sweating on the bar behind her. Abby politely declined. The city girl in her balked at the idea of drinking something she hadn't watched being poured herself.

Chris still had an arm across her body, but she seemed to be enjoying the attention of the other women, who were huddled in close, intense looks on their faces as they spoke. One of them was talking earnestly into Chris's ear, a hand lingering on Chris's arm. Abby felt a tinge of jealousy flare inside her. Couldn't they see the thick band on Chris's ring finger? She could sense her irritation rising, and it didn't help that her denims were biting into the flesh of her hips, something she hadn't been aware of while she'd been dancing just minutes ago.

Forcing herself to act normally, she moved into Chris's line of sight and gently touched her elbow. The fabric of her aubergine-coloured bomber jacket felt slick under Abby's fingertips.

"Oh, hi." Chris beamed, throwing an arm around her and pulling her closer. "These lovely ladies have been entertaining me."

Abby arranged the lower half of her face into a smile. "Yes, so I see," she muttered. "Are you friends of Cody's?" But she instantly zoned out as they explained how they fitted into the lesbian organogram of the town, which apparently required repeated touching of Chris—who, Abby had to keep reminding herself, she had no claim on, and who, besides, was in a long-term, committed relationship.

And you don't even want a relationship!

Her head spun.

A tray of tequila shots floated under Abby's nose and everyone dove in. As the others knocked them back, Abby grimaced, searching for a way to subtly dispose of hers. Before she could figure it out, Chris had plucked it from her fingers, downed it, downed her own, and handed Abby back an empty glass, all within seconds.

She remembered, Abby thought, and something inside her surged.

"Ladies, you've been fabulous company, but I'm going to see what the big deal is about this dance floor," Chris said, jerking her head in that direction. "I hear it's got something to do with a star projector?" She turned to Abby and winked. "Care to show me?"

Abby, only briefly starstruck, quickly recovered. "You're on." She grinned and impulsively grabbed Chris's hand. "See you guys later." She waved as she pulled Chris after her, not wasting a second, not giving the others a chance to argue.

Then they were pushing through the crowd, Chris's palm between Abby's fingers as they weaved between tightly packed revellers. She didn't know if she should let go, but she didn't want to, so she didn't.

The strobe lights flashed, and bass throbbed all through Abby's body as they squeezed their way to the dance floor.

"Is this good?" Abby yelled as she guided them to a quieter pocket of the dance floor.

"Nope." Chris shook her head, and Abby frowned. "Come." She grabbed Abby's arm and dragged them closer to the DJ booth. Abby hadn't been expecting this at all.

"Here? Really?" Abby yelled into Chris's ear, the bass pounding in her throat.

"Yes!" Chris yelled back. "If we're gonna do this, let's do it properly." She motioned upward. "This light show is really impressive."

Abby nodded enthusiastically, following Chris's eyes to the ceiling. Earlier, she hadn't really taken it in—she'd been so caught up in the music and the energy of the people around her. And, if she were being honest, she'd have felt a bit silly staring up at the ceiling that everyone else coolly ignored. They were obviously used to it, and Abby hadn't wanted to seem like a gawking tourist. But now, with Chris watching the lights beside her without a hint of self-consciousness, Abby felt emboldened too. And for a little while it felt like they were in a tiny pulsating galaxy all their own.

And then they were moving under the fake starry sky, their drinks long forgotten. Chris was a great dancer, and Abby was mesmerised by the way her body moved, by the curve of her neck as she swayed to the music.

"I thought you hated to dance," Abby teased, coming in close, lightly grazing Chris's hip with a fingertip.

Chris grinned at her. "I do," she replied, peeling off her jacket and tying it around her waist. Freer now, she swayed more, lifting her arms into the air. Abby pulled her eyes away.

The dance floor seemed to get fuller and fuller, pushing them closer together, so close that occasionally their flesh touched, and Abby could feel slick sweat on Chris's arm. At some point, Cody and her crew joined them, but Abby barely noticed.

And then, as if only minutes had passed, last rounds were called and the lights came on, and Abby and Chris turned to each other, blinking, disorientated and laughing. A guy near them groaned, "Someone turned on the sun!"

"Oh, my god, it's two in the morning," Abby croaked, glancing at her phone.

"There's life in us yet." Chris panted as the groups around them began to disperse. Her eyes were sparkling. "My god, that was great."

With the lights switched on, The Planetarium felt much smaller than it had in the dark, a comet rather than an entire universe, its magic evaporating like stardust under the stark fluorescent lights.

Slowly, they made their way back out to the street. Chris untied her bomber jacket from her waist and put it on, zipping it up to the neck.

"Well," she said, puffing out her flushed cheeks. "I would never have imagined that the girl who was rescuing kittens and hosting online pub quizzes a few nights ago would be out partying into the morning."

The night was dark and breezy, and Abby was still slick with dance-floor sweat. The chill bit into her as she hurried to pull her leather jacket on.

"You know those things aren't mutually exclusive, right?" she said, shoving her arms through the sleeves.

"Sure, not for everyone. But remind me of your social calendar…?"

Abby rolled her eyes. "You know, just when I think I'm starting to like you."

They were walking briskly in the direction of home, the crisp air nipping at Abby's wrists and ears.

Chris laughed, swatting her playfully. "Well, if it weren't for me, you wouldn't even have had a reason to come out tonight. Aren't you glad you listened to your fairy gay-mother?"

"Fairy grandmother, more like." Abby scoffed, her teeth chattering now. Leather jackets were so impractical for clubbing, how could she have forgotten? Too hot for dancing, too thin for late-night walks home.

Chris stopped and, without a word, pulled off her bomber jacket. Underneath, she wore a sleeveless black polo-neck top. "Here." She held the jacket out to Abby. "You're freezing."

Abby blinked at her. "But what about you?"

She shrugged. "I'm not cold at all, actually."

Abby hesitated. "I would feel bad taking your jacket."

Chris sighed, a hand on her hip. "Oh, for god's sake. Fine—give me your jacket. We'll switch."

That seemed like something of a more equitable solution, so Abby shrugged out of hers and they switched. Chris's jacket was still warm with the heat of her body, and Abby's pulse quickened as she pulled it over her arms, then zipped it up to her neck. As she did, Chris's familiar scent puffed out of the top in a thick, warm cloud. Without thinking, Abby inhaled deeply through her nose.

"Oh, it may smell a bit sweaty after tonight. Sorry," Chris said.

Abby was grateful for the darkness of the night, because she could feel the blush bloom across her whole face. "Actually," she said, trying to deflect as quickly as possible. "I thought you said you hated dancing? You sure seemed to be loving it tonight."

Chris took a deep breath as they started walking again. "When I first started travelling abroad for work, I'd party every chance I got. I loved dancing. I was young, and I'd find myself in these incredible fashion capitals of the world, with beautiful clubs and beautiful people..." She trailed off, and Abby wondered what—or perhaps who—she was thinking about.

"So, what changed?"

"There's a lot of temptation in places like that, and a lot of people very willing to lead you into it. And that can be really appealing when you've got a bunch of babies at home, and a bunch of responsibilities you'd rather not think about. It's incredibly freeing to feel anonymous. Too freeing, sometimes."

"Yeah, I get that," Abby said. "So, did you feel free tonight?"

"Yeah," Chris said thoughtfully. "Yeah, I did, in a safe way."

Abby couldn't help smiling to herself as she felt her tummy flip. "There's something special about new-town anonymity, isn't there?"

"There certainly is," Chris agreed.

They walked on in silence for a few moments, the zips of the bomber jacket jingling in time with Abby's steps.

"Feeling warmer?" Chris asked, raising an eyebrow in Abby's direction.

"Much," Abby replied, feeling very warm indeed. She wondered how she'd ever extricate herself from the jacket.

She was stuck in her head, a million thoughts like swirling galaxies in her brain. She didn't want the fact of wearing Chris's clothes to confuse her, or to trick her brain into thinking it meant something different to what it did. She knew that the feeling of the fabric, its smell, the weight of it on her skin were already creating an indelible impression on her subconscious. Of course she'd swapped clothes with friends before, but this... This was different.

"You never answered my question, before," Abby said after a moment.

"Question?" Chris frowned. "How many Mars-tinis ago was that?"

Abby chuckled. "I asked if your relationship was phenomenally good." She knew the question was cruel. The answer had become increasingly clear over the past few days, but she was desperate to know more.

Chris sighed. "Okay, I guess it's only fair to answer. But first," she declared. "Food! I'm starving."

Abby giggled and elbowed her, motioning to her to be quiet. The only sound in the street was the chirp of crickets and the odd ribbiting frog.

"Shall we make something delicious?" she whispered as Abby's house came into view.

"Sure," she replied as she opened the front door. To her surprise, Snowy was waiting just behind it, cautious but curious about what lay beyond. Quickly, Abby scooped her up and pressed her lips into the fur of her head. "Hello, baby. Did you miss Mommy? Is that why you're trying to escape?" she cooed. "You're far too little to go out there. Come, let's get you a snack."

"And me, too." Chris followed Abby and Snowy into the kitchen. "I'll take anything but kitten food right now. Actually," she said, picking up the cat food bag and examining it closely. "Maybe I'll even take some of this. I'd forgotten how dancing works up an appetite."

"Oh no, you won't," Abby said, plucking the bag out of her hands and pouring some into Snowy's bowl. "Us humans don't get such fancy treats."

"Okay, so what's on offer then, chef?"

Abby put on a genuine display of rifling through cupboards and fridge shelves, but she knew all she had in the house was cat food, coffee, and frozen chicken nuggets. How to break the news to a snob like Chris?

"Sooo…" she began. "Do you want the good news first or the bad news?"

"Bad, obviously. Always," Chris replied. She was perched now on a kitchen barstool, leaning forward onto the counter, jacket zips ting-tinging on the marble counter.

"Well, the bad news is that I've just run out of wagyu steak and caviar. Mere moments ago. Bummer, I know."

"Oh, I can't bear it." Chris collapsed dramatically onto the counter. "The service here is just awful. Think of your ratings, Abigail. This is doing you no favours."

"Oh, please, ma'am, I beg you, before you doom me to a single-star review, allow me to surprise, delight, and amaze you with…" Abby yanked open the freezer door and with a flourish pulled out a frost-covered box. Some of its contents plopped onto the floor. "Chicken nuggets!"

Now, Chris recoiled in real horror. "Frozen, reconstituted *chicken puree*? No. Absolutely not. Disgusting."

"Oh, come on." Abby laughed, shaking the box in Chris's direction. Bits of the frost fell to the floor. "You can't be that fussy at three a.m. after…how many Marsopolitans?"

"They were *cosmic*-politans and *Mars*-tinis, and alcohol works differently in outer space, so I'm *sotally tober*," Chris joked, reaching for the box. "We didn't even feed this crap to our kids. We called them McNopes."

"I also call kids McNopes."

Chris was indignant. "You know what I mean."

Abby cackled as she tipped the contents into a metal tray and slammed it into the oven, causing the whole thing to shudder. She cranked up the heat to high.

"Well, I certainly won't tell anyone your dirty little chicken nugget secret," Abby said, grabbing mustard and a stack of napkins. This was going to be messy eating.

"I can't believe I'm doing this." Chris groaned. "This has been the weirdest week of my life."

"Really?" Abby asked, planting her hands on her hips. "You're in the middle of a family crisis and processed meat is your biggest worry right now?"

"I don't even think they're made of real chicken," Chris wailed.

"Even better—we can pretend that no innocent chickens were harmed in the making of these gloopy blobs."

"Do you always have an answer for everything?"

"Do you?"

"Oh, you are exhausting, Abigail Massey."

"See what I mean?"

"See what *I* mean!" Chris shot back, but they were laughing. Abby thought about how strange and lovely it sounded when Chris said her full name.

It was warm in the small kitchen, like a cocoon, as they bustled around fetching plates and drinks. When the oven timer went off, it startled them both, which set off a fresh round of giggles. They both peered through the oven door.

"Careful." Abby hustled Chris out of the way of the hot air escaping the oven. "Oooh, these smell amazing," she said as she placed the tray on the stovetop.

Chris looked dubious. "Do you think they're properly cooked?"

"Only one way to find out," Abby said, reaching for a piece of crumbed chicken. She'd grabbed nuggets out of hot pans more times than she could count, but tonight, she was off her game. Whether it was the liquor, the lateness of the evening, or the hormones crashing around inside her, she wasn't sure. But as she tried to pluck a pat of meat from the pan, she brushed her fingers against the searing metal bottom, and she winced in anticipation of the pain that would register in her brain in three…two…one…

"Gah! Fuck!" She hissed in pain, flapping her hand up and down. "That's really hot."

Later, she'd wonder whether Chris had been as surprised by her own reaction to Abby's burnt fingers as Abby had been, or whether she even thought about it at all afterward.

She'd wonder whether Chris would've caught Karys's seared fingers the same way—between her own soft, strong fingers—and whether she'd have pressed them to her lips to dull the pain, as she had Abby's. She'd wonder whether they'd have held each other's gaze for the two longest seconds that had ever passed on Earth. She'd wonder whether Chris, too, lay in bed at night thinking of that one time, in a little town, when she'd held a girl's burnt fingers to her lips and how the tips had left crummy, oily traces behind.

She'd wonder whether some instinct in Chris, something motherly perhaps, compelled her to hold stinging fingers to her lips, like you might press cool palms to grazed knees. Or whether she'd been compelled that night by an entirely different instinct altogether.

But mostly she'd wonder, as she played the moment over and over until fact bled like watercolour into fiction, whether Chris's lips really had moved ever so lightly against her fingertips, or whether she'd simply dreamed up this detail, this briefest shadow of a kiss. Or perhaps, altogether, dreamt it all.

"I, I'm sorry, I don't know why I…" Chris stammered, dropping Abby's hand.

Abby blinked at her. "It's okay." But it wasn't, really.

"Here, let's just do this…" Abby muttered, scraping through the awkward moment with a metal spatula, lifting nuggets out of the pan and dumping them onto plates. Separate plates. Her fingers were burning, but she couldn't tell if it was from the pan or the memory of Chris's lips against her skin. She knocked over the mustard, elbowed a wall she'd never elbowed before.

Chris bustled around. She'd already recovered and was deftly carrying their plates and condiments to the sitting room. Then she was dipping the nuggets into mustard and not really putting up too much of a fuss, certainly acting as if the moment in the kitchen had never happened at all.

"Good?" Abby asked tentatively, watching Chris munch down on her third piece of chicken.

"No comment," she said, but it was muffled because of the food in her mouth. She winked at Abby. It wasn't a coy wink, but a conspiratorial one. It didn't say "Don't tell anyone I just did a weird thing with you in the kitchen that could be misconstrued as flirtation." No. It said "Don't ever remind me about that one time I ate chicken nuggets at three a.m. when I was starving and tipsy, because I'll deny it."

Abby swallowed the piece of rubber in her mouth and took a big sip of the water that Chris had poured for each of them. Chris was right—this really was a weird week.

"First dancing, now chicken nuggets," Abby said, motioning to Chris's plate. "Is your wife even going to recognise you when you get back home?"

Chris shook her head. "Not my wife. My partner. We're not married. And who knows?"

Abby looked pointedly at Chris's hand, where the thick metal band cuffed her ring finger. Nothing reflected in it. Whether by design or wear, it was very dull.

The moment in the kitchen was playing on an endless loop, and Abby had to shake her head. The phrase *phenomenally good* kept knocking around in her brain.

As if reading her thoughts, Chris pushed her plate away and leaned back against the sofa cushions.

"To answer your earlier question," she said, flicking a crumb from her fingers. "My relationship has had its phenomenally good times."

Abby snapped back to attention, but she stayed silent, letting Chris continue at her own pace. "But…" She paused, fiddling with the ring on her wedding finger. "If I'm entirely honest, I'm not sure that it has been a phenomenally good relationship for me."

* * *

Chris was seventeen when she and her high school best friend, Karys, fell in love. Buoyed by teenage infatuation and the indomitable invincibility of youth, the girls made a pact to tell their parents. And that's when life as Chris knew it changed forever.

While Karys's parents took the news in their stride, barely batting an eyelid, Chris's parents had outrightly rejected the idea that their child could be gay. Furious and unmoved by Chris's pleas to be understood, they'd threatened to disown her if she didn't break up with Karys immediately. But Chris refused to yield to their demands. It wasn't just typical teenage wilfulness. Even then, she understood on a cellular level that this was a battle worth waging.

When her parents made good on their threat, tossing her out with a suitcase and a scribbled note that ordered her not to return home until she was "no longer a homosexual and an embarrassment to the family," it had seemed like it would blow over. She hadn't even had a chance to say goodbye to her little sister. They were only a third of the way through that thousand-piece puzzle, their favourite one, and it was getting to the hard part now, the part where the blue of the sky melted into the blue of the sea, where Jamie always needed Chris to help her discern the difference, even though they'd done the puzzle so many times before. Jamie was so good with the border, maybe she could just take it apart and do it again until Chris got home. It wouldn't be long.

Karys's family accepted her as one of their own. Days turned into weeks, and eventually, Chris was no longer living out of a suitcase. She wasn't even sure where Karys's parents had stored it. They treated her like another daughter, feeding her, giving her shelter, tutting when she watched TV instead of studying for her finals. They'd taken her in without hesitation or second thought, and as she fell more in love with Karys, she fell more in love with them, too.

Chris hadn't seen her sister in almost a year—324 days, in fact. She calculated it when she tried to call her on her eleventh birthday. Her parents hadn't permitted them to speak.

Chris regularly called her parents. They were cordial, but unmoved. Sometimes Chris would cry, other times she would plead, and sometimes she'd simply talk to them, hoping that through the steady sound of her voice, they'd remember the daughter they'd rejected—the same daughter they'd loved until she fell in love with a woman. She knew there was nothing wrong with her. She knew the fault lay solely with her parents, but it didn't stop her from missing them with an ache that tore through her nightmares and clawed into every waking hour.

For years, she had pillowcases stained with mascara.

But her parents were resolute. Sometimes she felt that the more she called them, the more she begged for their understanding, the higher they built their walls.

Astonishingly, Chris passed her high school finals. They both did. Karys went off to college to study business management and Chris started working in a clothing boutique. At some point, they moved out of Karys's parents' house into their own apartment. Karys got her degree. Chris became a junior clothing buyer. They were earning good salaries for their age, they lived in a trendy apartment, and they spent their weekends throwing dinner parties for their large group of friends and feeling very grown up. They were the glowing centre around which their friends gravitated, and the one constant when everything else in life was uncertain—friendships, relationships, jobs, earnings—as it is in your twenties, when life is lived on a whim. They had a sofa for friends to crash on when leases expired or relationships ended. What Chris had lost in her own family, she'd built with Karys.

One night, when Chris sensed that Karys was uncharacteristically restless—had been for several nights, in fact—she asked her what the matter was. But even before Karys replied, Chris knew she'd shattered something in asking the question, and she wished she could ram the words back into her mouth, even if they ripped her tongue like broken glass.

"I need to experience more of the world," Karys had said softly. "We're only twenty-five. I need to know what it's like to…"

"To?" Chris had asked her hoarsely. "To?" she'd repeated more urgently. "To what, Karys? Tell me!" She shook her shoulder in the dark, begging her to say the words out loud. Karys stared straight ahead, but Chris wouldn't let her off the hook. If she was going to commit the ultimate lesbian betrayal, after everything they'd sacrificed to be together—to get here!—Chris was going to make sure she said the words.

"To be with a guy." It was barely a whisper, no louder than fingertips brushing a bedsheet.

Just like that, Karys blew up Chris's universe—her safety, her family, her sense of belonging in the world.

Karys moved out. Chris went into autopilot. She worked, she cried, she slept.

She'd lost her family. Her whole world. Again.

There was a constant stream of friends in and out of their—her—apartment, offering hugs, platitudes, ice cream—good ice cream, not the cheap stuff. Chris never remembered what they spoke about. In times of grief, it's not what people say to you, but simply that they're there. It taught her that it's okay not to know what to say when someone is aching to their bones. It is enough just to distract them for one more minute of their agony.

Inevitably, Chris reached her grief peak. There wasn't a tear left to cry, and her heartbreak plateaued. That was around the time she decided to test the theory that the best way to get over someone was to get under someone else. She'd had enough of rawness and pain.

She put on one of her coolest outfits (waistcoat, super-low jeans, G-string most definitely sticking out of the top)—she was already amassing quite the selection of trendy clothes, thanks to her work travels—and hit the city's gay strip.

Turned out, women loved her. They clamoured for her attention, lavishing her with drinks and compliments. Once, she managed to go out five nights in a row without taking her wallet out once. She went home with girls, she brought girls home. Secretly, she got a kick out of the fact that neighbours saw one girl leaving in the morning and another arriving that same night. She'd only been with one person her entire life, and suddenly a world of opportunity had opened up to her. It was as if she'd spent her entire life thinking chocolate was the only flavour of ice cream, but now she was discovering pistachio and strawberry and rocky road—sometimes even having more than one flavour at once.

Chris learnt that some girls fell hard and fast. Perhaps she would've, too, if she hadn't been so badly burnt. She learnt that some were crazy, crazy to the point of howling beneath her window. Those ones were always the hardest to get rid of, and not only because they had the tenacity of mountain goats. They were just so damn great in bed. She learnt that the theory was right: that, at least on a surface level, she could forget about Karys if she just distracted herself with a merry-go-round of willing bedmates. Attention, flirtation, sex, banter—drugs that numbed a deep, excruciatingly familiar pain.

Karys and Chris—who now jokingly referred to themselves as "Car Krash"—spoke occasionally. Karys was staying with a friend, and together they were living out all their straight-girl fantasies, hitting the coolest clubs weekend after weekend. Chris never asked for details and Karys never offered them, but Chris just knew. After a couple of months, they stopped speaking. It was too hard for Chris, who had now lost the only family she had, and too hard for Karys, who knew she'd rejected Chris just like her parents had all those years ago—and not for entirely dissimilar reasons.

Just as one girl in particular was about to stick—a girl who filled Chris's apartment with cute, hand-picked posies and baked goods—Karys called. She was sobbing, sick with stomach flu. And she could think only about Chris.

It had felt strange to hear Karys knocking, rather than the familiar jingle of her keys in the lock. Karys had looked good—rosy-cheeked, Chris noted, though she supposed that could've been the fever. Chris had tucked her into her own bed—the bed they'd once shared—and fed her tea and heart-shaped cookies. She didn't tell her the cookies had been baked by Potential New Girlfriend.

But Potential New Girlfriend would never materialise. Karys never left. Through the evening, into the night, and until the next morning, they spoke about their feelings, their time apart, and how deeply they still—and always would—love each other. They paused only when Karys had to race to the bathroom to puke. They didn't have to discuss whether they were back together. From that moment, they just were. Chris cleared away the cute posies and the rest of the heart-shaped biscuits. She had her family back.

Chris had suspected, from the moment Karys arrived on her doorstep, that she was pregnant. She knew her body so well. The shape of her. She knew how she changed from time to time.

But this was different.

Karys, however, had been stunned to tears when the two lines appeared almost immediately on the stick. Later she said that perhaps she'd refused to believe that pregnancy could be a possibility because she was afraid Chris would never take her back. But Chris would never have rejected her. She clasped Karys's hand tightly, drew it to her heart, kissed it. "You and me forever, babe," she'd said. "No matter what."

The shock of the positive pregnancy test was nothing compared to what went down at the first baby scan and the doctor discovered not one, not two, but three heartbeats. The father was an English rugby player who'd been playing for the local club for a few months. He'd been "dead keen" on Karys, and she'd liked him well enough, but deep down, her heart had always been with Chris.

"Three rugby babies," Karys wailed over and over again. "I have to push out three rugby babies."

In the end, of course, she didn't push them out—they were extracted one by one, boy then girl then boy. Each was perfectly healthy with a strong set of lungs. Chris had held Karys's hand through every second of the birth, while her family and Rugby Dad waited anxiously outside, erupting into whoops and cheers when the doctors announced the safe delivery of three little babies. Karys was exhausted, and Chris had never been more in awe of her. She didn't think she could love the babies more if they'd come from her own womb.

Rugby Dad went back to England, where he was a committed long-distance father who waited at airport terminals with wide-open arms every holiday. He was interested and generous and as involved as he could be from several thousand miles away, and at the height of his professional career, regularly flew the kids around the world to watch his games. He got married, got injured, retired, started a successful coaching academy. The kids, now teenagers, planned to study in England once they finished high school this year.

Chris's parents never met the triplets. They weren't interested in knowing the offspring they refused to think of as their grandchildren. They spoke less and less, Chris and her parents. When the kids were around five, Chris received the first phone call in years from her mother—her father didn't speak to her at all anymore. She'd called to tell her that her sister had been killed in a motorbike accident: she'd been a passenger on her boyfriend's bike, he'd been drunk and driven into a wall, and if Chris wanted to come to the funeral, that would be "okay."

Chris felt like she'd been hit in the chest with a thousand-pound wrecking ball. She remembered that she'd never said goodbye to Jamie, that they'd never finished their puzzle, that she never got to give her the gift she'd bought her for her eleventh birthday—a pair of pink sneakers with thick, glittered soles, the shoes that Chris still had tucked away at the back of her wardrobe. As if in a trance, she went to the cupboard and yanked everything out—sweaters, bags, scarves all flying to the floor. She found the shoes, still in their box, the price tag still attached, and held them in her hands. She wondered what size shoe her sister had been. She was devastated for the tragic loss of a young life—a death that had been so preventable—and for the loss of a sister she'd been robbed of knowing. But most of all, she knew that if she'd been in her sister's life, she could have—would have—been able to prevent this tragedy. Jamie wouldn't have been on the back of a drunk boy's bike. Chris would have made sure of it.

For days, Chris howled like an animal. Karys held her and told her that whatever she decided, she would support her. Karys kept her composure, but Chris knew she could tear down the house with the rage inside her. She hated Chris's parents, and them "allowing" Chris to attend the funeral of a sister they'd forbidden her from knowing was almost too much for her to take. She ground her teeth in her sleep, she chipped the crockery as she stacked it. But she was infinitely gentle with Chris, and patient, night after night.

In the end, they hadn't gone to the funeral. They'd spent the day in their garden, as a family, planting flowers and roasting marshmallows and horsing around until their hair was matted with grass and sticky, melted mallows. They all slept together in Chris and Karys's giant bed that night, and the next day, life returned to theirs again. Chris packed

Jamie away and promised to return to her memory one day. But right now, she couldn't afford to break. Her family needed her.

Their life was a good one, built on the kind of stability and routine that gives people the confidence to take calculated risks. When the clothing boutique was threatened with closure, they bought it, knowing that between them, they could make it a success. They gutted it, rechristened it, and gave it new life in the form of Saint Jamie. Today, it was one of the country's most successful fashion emporiums, its multiple stores filled with jackets, beautiful blouses, tailored trousers that Chris hand-selected from across the world. Now, with the kids soon moving abroad to study, it was Karys's dream that they take Saint Jamie international, too.

Chris correctly predicted that the next time she'd hear from her parents was when one of them died, and she was right. She felt little when her mother called her, after another period of several years, to tell her her father had passed. Chris had long since mourned her parents, and the call felt perfunctory, like the post office ringing to let you know a parcel had arrived with your name on it, blurry and warped under the weight of countless stamps.

In Abby's living room, Chris shifted on the sofa, drawing her legs up under her. With a start, Abby realised she herself had been crying. Tears had slipped from the corners of her eyes, down her cheeks, onto her chest, into the dips above her clavicles. She pulled her legs up to her chest, wrapping her arms around them. "And then your mom…" she said quietly, knowing what was coming next.

"Yep. Out of the blue, a couple of months back, she starts calling me."

There was no one left to die but her mother. The first time she called, Chris knew it couldn't be that. Her mother spoke much in the way Chris used to all those years back—talking about everything and nothing, building up to no great reveal, heading in no discernible direction. The call ended and Chris was confused—furious at herself for not screaming at her mother "You never loved me!" or "I despise you!" or "Why couldn't you just have accepted me?" Things that would be wholly justified as a forty-four-year-old abandoned child, still a humiliating secret, still an infected branch of the family tree hacked off to save the whole, to prevent further poisoning.

But she didn't say any of those things. She said, "mmm" and "yes" and "oh?" and she dreaded telling Karys about the call, because Karys's rage would be worse than any disappointment Chris could level at herself.

She did tell Karys—and she told her every time her mother called after that, soon weekly, even though she saw how hard it was for Karys to bite her tongue, how her shoulders rose up around her neck, where tendons bulged like ropes. Her mother would ramble, and Chris would listen, saying little, never speaking about her own life—and her mother never asked.

That her mother was lonely was obvious, said Chris. But why Chris cared, and why she kept answering her calls, she didn't know. And why, oh why, she made the decision to fly two hours across the country to be by her side while she underwent tests and awaited results, when Chris's children needed her as they completed their final high school exams, and her partner needed her, and the business needed her, she didn't know.

She squeezed her eyes shut, shook her head.

Of course, she knew why she was here, reading tattered magazines in waiting rooms, cooking healthy meals for a woman she no longer knew.

Slowly, she opened her eyes.

"Despite it all, I've still hoped for acceptance, after all these years," she said quietly, almost to herself. "It was all such a tragedy, and perhaps I don't want to believe it was all for nothing."

Abby was totally sober now, and she could see Chris was, too.

"The other day," Chris continued, then her voice cracked.

She swallowed hard and tried again. "When you came home, and I was upset? That day was the same as the day before, and the day before it—every day that I've spent with my mother this week. Doctors, tests, back home. Superficial conversation, dinner. Except that day—that day, when I handed her a cup of coffee, she looked me straight in the eye and she said, 'How is Karys? I always liked her.'"

Tears rolled down Chris's cheeks now, and instinctively Abby reached across the sofa for her hand. Chris gripped it.

"I thought that was what I wanted, you know? Acceptance. Or just some form of acknowledgment. But it all feels like such a waste, Abby. She *liked* Karys? Then what were all these years of trauma and rejection for?" Her nose was running too now. "Why couldn't we have had this conversation years ago? Why did I have to lose a sister? Lose my whole family? And she tells me she 'always liked Karys'?" Chris was angry now, her shaky voice rising. She was still clasping Abby's hand, her body vibrating with injustice.

"Have you told Karys?" Abby asked softly, treading carefully.

"No, I haven't," Chris said, letting go of Abby and giving a loud sniff. "I could never tell her. She would be…furious isn't even the word. I think it would be the final straw."

"Final straw?"

"This whole situation. With my mother. She wasn't exactly on board with it. She feels that I'm sacrificing the needs of our family for someone who tossed me out onto the street. Perhaps she isn't wrong. But I can't explain it. I need this. I need to be here. It isn't just for my mother. Perhaps I need to feel like the better person. The bigger person. Maybe I need answers, or closure. Fuck knows. But whether that's right or wrong, it's what *I* need. And for the past seventeen years, I've put the needs of four other people ahead of my own…I just can't do it this time."

Abby nodded at Chris in silence. She didn't know what to say, but she suspected that Chris didn't need her to say anything at all. Just listen. She put out her hand again, and Chris took it with a weak smile.

"So, that's the answer to your question. I'm sorry for dumping it all on you."

"Thank you for telling me," Abby replied, squeezing Chris's hand until she met her eye. "It's safe with me, I promise."

Chris nodded. "I know. I'm not sure how but, I do. Weirdly, you're my closest confidant right now."

Abby felt a little spark inside her and flushed.

"So, if we're talking about 'phenomenally good,'" Chris said, straightening up and clearing her throat. "Perhaps that was something of an overstatement on my part. We both know it's not a realistic bar to set for any relationship, but I think it's how you've managed to convince yourself not to get back in the game."

"Wow, nice diversion, Addison!" Abby teased, and Chris's shoulders relaxed for the first time in half an hour.

"And here's another: those weren't bad McNopes, actually, but I will kill you if you ever tell anyone I said that."

Abby smiled and stifled a yawn. She glanced out of the window and noticed the sky was changing colour.

"It's so late," she said, still peering at the inky sky. "The sun's about to come up."

Even though the sky was still punctured with stars, birds were beginning to chirp. Morning would come rapidly, and then it would be too late to go to bed, but Abby didn't want the night to end. Earlier, Abby had changed into comfy clothes. Chris hadn't. Not for the first time, Abby wondered if she owned a single piece of nonstructured clothing.

Chris frowned at Abby. "Does that mean we have to go to bed? And wake up, and be adults all over again, and stop making Uranus jokes?"

"No." Abby shook her head vehemently. "Team Crabby must never stop making Uranus jokes. It's the antidote to adulthood."

"Ha, ha, deal," Chris agreed, sniffing a little. She stood, then offered her hand to Abby, pulling her to her feet. "I can't begin to tell you how much I needed tonight, doll," she said earnestly, her hands on Abby's shoulders. "And now, I must ask you a serious question."

Abby frowned. After everything that had happened, after everything they'd spoken about, what could Chris possibly need to know?

"Yes?"

"Do you have a ladder?"

"A ladder?"

"I want to climb up on the roof and watch the sun rise. I'd actually like to see the famous bay for once."

"Wha—wait, you're serious?"

"Dead serious. Well, I mean, not *dead* serious. But we haven't stayed up until almost dawn to miss the best part. Let's push out the boat on this adulting thing one more time. I'll make the coffee."

Getting said coffee up onto the roof was probably the least successful part of their mission, but the rest went smoothly. The roof tiles were damp under their butts, but they sat anyway, the wetness spreading underneath them as the sun rose. If they looked carefully, they could see the bay in the far distance, across the roofs of the houses, and beyond it, streaks of dawn colouring the sky.

They drank the dregs of coffee that had survived the trip up and compared notes on the crazy, ridiculous, beautiful people they'd seen at The Planetarium. Then they leaned back against the tiles as the sky turned from black to blue to pale yellow, like a healing bruise, and it was not hard to imagine they were floating on a cloud, high above Bay View, untethered to the Earth and everyone on it.

"We're going to fall asleep up here," Abby murmured as the sun warmed her cheeks. She sat up and made her way to the ladder. "We better get down."

Chris stretched and yawned. "You're right. My old back would never recover from that. You'd have to leave me here like a body on Everest."

"Don't make me laugh like that while I'm trying to get down the ladder!"

"Oh, my god, you really are leaving me up here?"

"Shh, it's still early, we're going to wake the neighbourhood."

"Again."

It was almost eight by the time Abby was in bed, showered, her head swimming from the events of the past twelve hours. On her bedroom floor was her discarded pile of clothes, Chris's silky purple jacket resting on top.

When Abby woke up, she could tell by the colour of the light in her room that it was late afternoon. Her head felt thick and heavy, as if someone had stuffed it with cladding. Snowy was yelling for food—that's what had woken her—and Abby realised it had been hours since she'd been fed.

Slowly, her body tender, she sat up and rubbed her face. She felt heavy and light all at once, the sort of confusion she'd felt all those years back when she'd first met Dan. When she'd wake up next to a boy and be longing for a girl. Except now, she was waking up next to a kitten and longing for something she told herself she must avoid wanting ever again. And the universe must have agreed, because Chris could never be hers to have.

Abby padded to the kitchen, pulling a wedgie out of her butt as she scrolled through her phone. A couple of missed calls from Evan—she wondered what he wanted. Marli would still be around until the morning. Abby would call him back later. Right now, she needed water, Coke, and a toothbrush, in that order.

The house was empty. There wasn't even coffee in the pot. Abby sighed. She'd have to get used to this. Chris was leaving tomorrow, and soon, this would all just feel like a dream—a bizarre and beautiful dream.

As Abby slowly filled a large tumbler with water, she made a mental note to give the coffee plunger to Chris as a parting gift. She wouldn't have any use for it anyway.

CHAPTER SEVEN

It was four a.m., the only morning since Chris had arrived that Abby could hear her moving around the house. She'd tried to insist that Abby not get up to see her off, but Abby had downright refused.

Instead, she had set her alarm, chosen what she'd wear, thought about what she'd say by way of goodbye. But now, as she lay on her back in the dark with Snowy under her chin, she was frozen with apprehension. True, she was horribly sleep-deprived after yesterday's all-nighter. She was recovering from a hangover and she hadn't eaten a vegetable since… who knew? So, none of that helped.

She hadn't expected a bitch slap from the universe in the shape of Chris-fucking-Addison.

She crept out of bed and into her darkened bathroom, where she brushed her teeth and tried to wrangle her hair back into something resembling waves. But it wouldn't be tamed, springing instead like a fountain from the top of her head. She wrestled into a messy bun and applied a little makeup, but not so much that it would look obvious.

Back in her room, she pulled on her clothes, and over them, for the last time, Chris's purple bomber jacket. She zipped it up, inhaling every atom of scent, and then she climbed back into bed, wrapped her arms around herself, and closed her eyes. She listened to suitcases being zipped and rolled down the hallway. She smelled coffee, and that familiar rich fragrance, and allowed herself a final few moments of enjoying Chris's jacket wrapped around her before she'd cull it from her memory—something she fully intended to do.

"Hey," she called hoarsely as she emerged from her room. Chris was in the kitchen, pouring a cup of thick black coffee. Abby felt the need to whisper even though it was just the two of them in the house. Perhaps it was the fact that it felt like they were the only two people awake on Earth. It always seemed to feel like that when you woke up for an early flight.

"Hey, morning." Chris spun around, surprised. "You shouldn't have got up. Sorry if I woke you."

Abby shrugged. "Obviously I was going to get up to say goodbye to you." The "goodbye" caught in her throat, and she cursed silently. *Not cool, Abby.*

Over the rim of her mug, Chris watched Abby. She looked immaculate, the hallway light turning her hair merlot-red. Her makeup was flawless, just as it had been when she first strutted into Abby's house almost a week ago.

"Do you get up this early to say goodbye to all your FortyLinks guests?" Chris asked. "Or only the ones whose clothes you need to return?"

It took Abby half a second to register. When she did, she could feel her cheeks turning the same colour as Chris's hair.

"Oh, god, yes, sorry!" She'd forgotten to take it off, and now she yanked at the sleeves as if the jacket were on fire. "I'm half asleep…I only put it on so I'd remember…I mean, I didn't *sleep* in it—"

But Chris was smiling, walking around the counter to Abby, her arm outstretched. From her fingertips dangled Abby's leather jacket. "It's okay, I almost forgot to give yours back to you, too."

Jackets exchanged, coffee cup drained, there was nothing left to be said. All the words that Abby had planned had evaporated. It had been a fun week with a stranger, but now, regular programming would resume. For both of them.

The elder Mrs. Addison was fine—she'd confirmed it herself when Chris spent the afternoon with her yesterday while Abby slept off the night before. When Chris returned home in the evening, exhausted but visibly relieved, Abby didn't even have to ask. Chris told her all was well with her mother, and there was no reason for her to return to Bay View. She didn't say it quite so plainly, but anyway, as far as she was aware, there was no reason to sugarcoat the announcement to her remarkably hospitable accommodation host, was there? If they'd crossed any boundaries, it was barely by a hair, fuelled by too many mixed drinks and a fleeting sense of anonymous adventure.

The *toot* of the taxi outside. A stone in Abby's throat.

Chris turned to her and took a breath, but Abby sprang into action before she could say a word.

"I've got it," she said too brightly, grabbing a bag handle in each hand. They wobbled behind her as she hauled them to the front door, knocking into the furniture as she went.

Abby yanked open the door and dragged the bags behind her down the path, toward the taxi. The wheels scraped against the ground like sandpaper. Somehow, Abby wasn't doing it right. It was the same driver from the week before—probably the only dude doing airport taxi runs for the whole town—and he seemed less than enthused about loading up the car before the crack of dawn.

Abby spun around to go back to the house and found herself nose to nose with Chris—or nose to collarbone, really, since Chris was wearing dark boots with a high, square heel. Abby hadn't seen them before. She wondered what Chris's closet looked like at home.

The cab driver hadn't turned off the ignition while he waited, and the air was thick with exhaust fumes and a sense of impatience. Abby was irritated. Couldn't he just chill? He was mere meters behind them, and she tried her best to block it out.

"What a week." Chris sighed. She looked up and down the street as if she were searching for something, or perhaps something to say. Abby stared at Chris's collar and nodded. She didn't trust her voice.

Finally, Chris turned back to Abby, her eyes soft—softer, at least, than they'd been a week ago when she'd arrived. "Thank you for being my baggage handler," she said with a smile. "In more ways than you know." And with that, she softly brushed her lips against Abby's cheek and was gone—one, two, three steps into the cab, then down the street in a streak of red brake lights, and back to the city like a swallow escaping an icy winter. Abby watched until she could no longer see the car, but Chris didn't turn around.

Back inside the house, Abby stood still and silent for a long time. Eventually, she unglued herself from her spot beside the kitchen counter where the coffee plunger still sat, forgotten, with Chris's used mug beside it, a faint ring of red around the rim. She wrapped her fingers around the porcelain, but it was already cold.

PART TWO

CHAPTER EIGHT

When Abby was eight years old, her parents got it into their heads that she should learn to play the violin. She'd sucked at the piano and the recorder, so it wasn't clear why they thought her inner prodigy would be awakened by a Stradivarius knock-off. But off she trotted to weekly classes, where she'd saw away at the strings like a tree feller until the teacher couldn't hack it any longer and begged her parents to divert her attention elsewhere. She'd been terrible at playing chords, and the only note she'd been able to hit somewhat successfully was G. She liked to think it meant she was "Great" at violin, but she overheard her teacher telling her parents that the droning G note made the whole class feel "glum, glum, glum."

She thought about this as she sat, chin in hand, watching her class perform their regular Monday acting assignment. She felt glum, glum, glum.

A little trick she'd learnt to ease herself into her Monday morning drama classes was to get the kids to act out something interesting they'd done over the weekend. She'd separate them into groups, appoint one of them the director, and then let them perform for the rest of the class. If Evan had a free period, he'd come and watch, too, and they'd have entire silent exchanges through looks and winks alone.

Having spent four years tutoring young adults, she hadn't realised the folly in allowing ten-year-olds free rein in crafting their stories, and she quickly learned that little humans lacked the emotional intelligence to tell a good story from a very bad one. She started vetting their stories after one of her groups acted out a dog being run over in stomach-churning detail, and another had reenacted her dad's affair after eavesdropping on a conversation between her mother and her aunt. But now, as she watched Jordan's group dramatising a visit to the grocery store—possibly the only thing more boring than actually going to the grocery store—she was severely regretting the censorship. Oh, what she'd give for a bit of soap-opera-style drama right now.

It had been particularly hard to get going this morning. After Chris had left, Abby had drifted through the house searching for something she couldn't quite put her finger on. Only when she'd come full circle with a rubbery feeling of disappointment in her gut did she realise what she'd been doing: searching for any tiny bit of Chris left behind. A hairbrush. A drop of perfume. A note.

She'd barely left a trace, bar the tepid coffee in the pot and a tangle of sheets on her bed. Abby had stood in the doorway for a long, long time, fighting the urge to bury herself in the rumpled bedding. She knew what it would smell like.

Then finally, like a magnet drawn to its mate, she'd launched herself at the bed. But instead of taking a final hit, coiling the fabric around herself like a second skin, she ripped the sheets off as quickly as she could. Holding her breath, she tore the fabric from the pillows and mattress as if it were on fire, her fingers burning from the friction. Then she'd bundled it all into the washing machine with a short, powerful exhale and hit Start before she could change her mind. Water gurgled into the machine. Abby stared, stuck.

Then she'd panicked and raced to check on Snowy to be doubly sure she hadn't bundled the tiny cat into the machine with the sheets. (She hadn't.)

Finally, she'd returned to the haven of her bathroom (she checked for traces of Chris here, too, even though she'd never had any reason to use the room), and had run a deep, hot bath. It was here that she stayed until the very last minute she could—long past her regular wake-up time, long past 7:03 a.m., when she was usually checking FortyLinks bookings in bed with coffee, long past the time she should be pulling on her clothes and checking the contents of her backpack and running through her day's lessons in her head.

She'd skidded into school a minute or two late, avoiding the disapproving looks of her colleagues and the relieved expressions of straggler parents—*Hell, even the teacher is late* was written all over their faces. She heard her email ping on her phone as she legged it to class—a useful reminder to put her phone on silent—and ploughed straight into the dense brickwork of Evan's chest. Coffee went everywhere. The kids were hysterical. Evan looked dismayed—strange, Abby thought, since nothing really bothered him. Shit! She'd never called him back last night. Perhaps something had happened over the weekend. She'd figure it out when they connected at lunchtime. For now, she muttered a quick apology and thanks, and raced into her classroom to get started on her kids' riveting off-off-off-Broadway productions.

Jordan's family was at the checkout counter now, in "a very verrrrryyyyy long line," with Poppy behind the till. With her pained expression and distinct air of apathy, she fit the part perfectly. Abby wondered whether she should be finding these little plays charming. Wouldn't other prep-school teachers be enchanted by these silly, overacted dramas?

Abby had loved her tutoring job at the university. She adored teaching first-year students who were training to become researchers and teachers themselves. They were smart and opinionated, and they sparred with her daily. When she was new in the role, insecure and inexperienced, she responded to these challenges with a defiant "because I'm the teacher and I'm right" mentality. She held her chin high and hoped none of her students saw it quaver. But as she grew into the role and realised how little she knew, she began to welcome the debates. They were, after all, only a few years her junior, and it wasn't unheard of to have students her own age or much older. They were determined and eager and fun—often it was difficult to turn down their invitations to join them at parties or check out their music gigs or stand-up shows, but she knew it was important to maintain proper boundaries, especially because she was so young and so similar, in many ways, to the kids she taught. Boundaries were hard, because she cared for her students. But she had a goal, and if she were going to grow into a respected lecturer and perhaps even a professor one day, clear boundaries were essential.

Abby wasn't entirely sure what her future might look like, but she knew for sure that the two things she wanted in it were the university, and Dan. Those were the no-brainers. Everything else was negotiable.

Work fulfilled her in happy times and fuelled her when life had left her gutted. Carol, her students, her research—those were the constants in her life when it became suffocatingly clear that Dan wouldn't be.

Which was why leaving her job had felt like tearing the skin from her bones. It had left her vulnerable and bare, exposing the rawness of her feelings for the first time and forcing her to face the pain without distraction. So, when Abby arrived in Bay View, she leapt at the chance to fill the void with something, anything, that would divert her from it… and a bunch of ten-year-olds fuelled by snot and tater tots seemed the most perfectly imperfect fit. Besides, it wasn't like she could afford to be unemployed for long. Dan's freelance career had floundered when she got ill. Two years on, Abby was still feeling the strain of having carried their lives singlehandedly on her tutor's salary—even with the welcome addition of her FortyLinks side hustle.

Now, as she felt irritated, she wondered—not for the first time— whether she hadn't been a little hasty in taking up this position. True, the kids had been a wonderful distraction for the first few months, when she vacillated between agony, numbness, shock, and confusion. But while she wasn't cut out to teach kids, there was no university here, and barely a college to speak of. So where did that leave her?

"So, is it true, Miss Massey? Is it?"

Abby's eyes flew open. Her daydream had nearly surfed into slumber, and her chin hovered dangerously close to her desk. She sat bolt upright and cleared her throat, searching the twenty flushed little faces in front of her for a clue to the question. It was clearly something naughty, but beyond that, she had no clue.

"Oh, uh, I'm sorry, Jacob…is what true?"

Jacob rolled his eyes and sighed in that dramatic way that ten-year-olds do, as if Abby had proven that she was just as dense as he'd suspected.

"That if you eat cabbage you'll grow boobs!" He mimed having large breasts, and the rest of the kids fell to pieces laughing. Even Poppy hid a smirk behind her hand.

Jesus. Christ. Not even grocery store stories were a safe bet.

"For people who grow breasts, they grow regardless of how much or how little cabbage they eat," Abby said in a tone she hoped would put the line of questioning to rest, and when Jacob took a breath to answer back, she raised her eyebrows in warning. "Hey, let's get back to the grocery store checkout, okay?" Even to her own ears, she sounded exasperated— something she tried to avoid with her kids.

By lunchtime, Abby was hungry, scratchy, and drained. She'd done her best to push any other feelings aside, and she pulled out her phone to distract herself while she waited for Evan.

She squinted at the screen in the sun. Texts from Lulu and the virtual pub quiz group. A bunch of emails, most of them FortyLinks enquiries.

It was hardly surprising, now that her little cottage was one of the only accommodation options in the whole of Bay View. She'd check them properly when she got home. Apart from slowly repairing her debt hole, she now had a new reason to fill the room as quickly as possible: She wanted to put Chris behind her. The faster the better. There was also a missed call from Carol with a follow-up message: *Feel the need 2 check in with u. U OK? Love C x*

Carol seemed to have a sixth sense about things.

"Hey." It was a sigh as Evan slid down into the chair next to Abby. She'd barely heard him approaching. He tossed his lunch container onto the table but made no move to open it. She caught a hint of coffee stain on his white T-shirt before he folded his arms across his chest.

"Hey!" Abby said, overly cheerfully. "You okay? What's with the neg vibe?"

Evan sighed and dropped his head into his hands. When he looked up, Abby was stunned to see his eyes were misted over.

"Hey, hey," she said, gently this time. She stood and wrapped her arms around his thick shoulders. "What's happened, my friend?"

"Marli. She broke up with me. I didn't…I didn't see it coming."

So that's why he was calling last night. Abby felt awful.

"Oh, my god, Evan, I'm sorry, I had no idea."

"Yeah, well." Upset as he was, he was magnanimous enough not to remind her about the missed call.

"What happened? I mean you guys were just talking pets…and kids! I don't understand."

He was staring into the distance, shaking his head slowly as if he were still trying to figure it out himself. "She wants me to move to the city with her, and I don't want to leave Bay View. Do you know it's been nearly a year? Long-distance is fucking hard, man. It's not like we can have long-distance pets, or kids. I love her, but this is my home, and she can't stand the place. She says we're just wasting time with each other."

Abby, seated once again, reached across the table and squeezed his arm. There wasn't anything to say. He was right. They seemed to be at an impasse.

They sat in silence for a few moments while the playground erupted around them, kids playing tag and trading sandwiches. Two boys were roughhousing under a tree. Abby could tell that their game would descend into a scuffle at any moment. No sooner had she thought it than they began laying into each other with fists and feet, and she hurried over to break up the fight.

Evan was still staring into the distance when she returned, his jaw working overtime. Nearby, the two kids now sat sulking, one repeatedly stubbing the toe of his boot into the dirt, the other watching him warily.

"Is it so bad to want to stay in a small town your whole life?" he asked, focusing on Abby with pleading eyes. He looked so vulnerable, it broke Abby's heart.

Evan loved Bay View. He'd lived here his entire life, and he was deeply content with his lot. While many youngsters couldn't wait to leave, he had always been vocal about his affection for his hometown.

Evan was a good man, and Abby felt a flash of irritation toward Marli for making him question the things he held so dear. He was happy in his job, happy to help the townsfolk with odd jobs, happy here. But Abby knew she needed to see it from her perspective, too. Why was Evan's home more important than Marli's?

"No, Ev, I don't," she replied at last. "And I know you hate the idea of living in a big city. But you could fall in love with someone and your whole perspective could change."

"Are you're saying that if I loved Marli enough, I'd have been willing to move to the city for her?"

"No. Maybe. Or maybe she'd have been willing to move here for you."

"That would be a huge sacrifice for her," he said, lacing his fingers together. "Bay View bores her. And besides, where would she get a job in tech?"

Abby shrugged. "Aren't a lot of tech jobs remote? And how could she be bored with a stud like you?" She grinned, but his mood only seemed to decline further.

"I can't expect someone to give up their entire life for me."

"Do you feel like you'd be giving up your entire life for her, if you moved?"

"No. Well, yeah, actually. Bay View *is* my life. It's my…" He searched for the right words and then pressed the heel of his palms into his eyes. "It's my home, Abby. It's everything I know. I don't want to leave." Evan's voice faltered. "I feel like I'm being forced to choose between my two greatest loves—my home, and Marli."

"I'm sorry, Ev," Abby said softly, feeling overwhelming sadness for her friend. She seldom saw him this exposed and vulnerable. But she wished she could shake him by the shoulders and help him see reason. Sometimes, you had to do scary things for love. She'd always told Dan she'd move anywhere with her, and then Dan had picked the one place she couldn't go. What she would give to be in Evan's shoes right now.

The bell rang, signalling the end of break time, and Evan reluctantly unfolded himself into a standing position. Neither of them had eaten. Those chicken nuggets had been the last thing Abby had eaten, but she didn't have much of an appetite.

As if reading her mind, Evan asked, "Hey, how's your weird old house guest? She still there?"

"She's actually neither weird nor old," Abby said testily as they crossed the field to the main building. "And no, she left this morning."

Evan shot her a look. "Do I detect a little defensiveness?"

Abby felt her ears redden. "No, I just…She's cool, okay? She was great."

"Great? Do you have a thing for her?" This seemed to lift his mood slightly, and Abby relented. She really needed someone to talk to about it.

"Well, I'm sure I don't. But…maybe?"

"Really? I thought you were committed to spinsterhood."

"I am."

"Well, what gives, then? Did you guys bone?"

"What? Jesus, no. No! It was nothing like that."

"But you wanted to."

"She's basically married." Abby sighed. "Anyway, it's all irrelevant. She's gone, so there's nothing left to say about it."

"Wow, we really are quite a pair today, huh?" he said as they climbed the stairs to their first-floor classrooms.

"Sheesh, understatement of the day. What are you doing tonight?"

Evan rolled his eyes. "Running, showering, probably some crying. You?"

"Well, as appealing as every one of those things sounds, I think we should go for pizza instead."

"Ah, fuck yes," Evan replied a bit too loudly, and a few kids nearby overheard. They were little ones, probably around seven or eight, and their eyes flew wide open. Abby gave the kids a sheepish grin and elbowed Evan hard in the side.

"We have got to start being better role models to these kids," she hissed.

CHAPTER NINE

Something was gnawing at Abby as she sat outside in the late afternoon sun, trying to enjoy her porch as she always had, trying to let Snowy's purrs soothe her restless mind. Perhaps it was her broken routine of the past several days. But today, she'd come home from school, dumped her things, scooped up her cat, and painstakingly scrolled through all her FortyLinks enquiries. She'd all but ignored the requests throughout Chris's stay, suspended by the intoxicating energy in her house, but now she'd made headway. She'd accepted several bookings, including one starting tomorrow, which meant she'd need to get the room cleaned and ready. She'd replied to friends' texts and emails, and finally she'd returned Carol's call, saving the best for last, knowing that hearing the voice of her mentor would bring much-needed comfort.

"Hello, my dear," Carol had said in that low, soothing way she always did. "You've been on my mind. This semester is simply flying along. How are you?"

Abby pictured her grey curls bobbing as she spoke, her feathery earrings tangling in her hair as she chatted animatedly. Carol's hair reminded Abby of an old-fashioned telephone cord, the kind you'd wrap tightly around your finger as you talked your best friend's ear off for hours on end—or until someone needed to use the Internet. Your finger would turn a throbbing red, then purple, until you released the cord, and then you'd do it all over again.

"You should visit…" It was what Abby always said, and Carol always said she would, but she never did. Abby was fine with that. They cared about each other, but wouldn't it feel awkward to pursue a personal friendship? She knew Carol cared about her deeply and had been sad to see her leave the university. Abby couldn't help but feel she'd let her down—even though Carol understood better than anyone. Then, of course, there would always be that sliding door between them: the unspoken fact of Carol having stepped out of Dan's path and Abby into it, like a relay race in love. Carol's grief was different to Abby's, and sometimes that helped. But she didn't necessarily want to build a friendship on it.

Carol was chatting away about the university—the students, the curriculum, posts opening up. She was always careful not to make Abby feel any guilt or shame for leaving but smart enough to tend the seeds she always sowed. Painstakingly and with every conversation, she made sure Abby knew she would always have a home at the university, should she want it. That consistency and unwavering support over the years were some of the many gifts Carol had given Abby.

"Have you made any new friends lately?" Carol finally enquired, almost hesitantly, like she always did. It was so old-fashioned. Abby liked to answer in the most purposefully obtuse way she could.

"I got a kitten, if that counts?"

Carol was an animal person, so the news delighted her. But of course, it wasn't the answer she'd been looking for.

"How's Layla?" Abby deflected, knowing Carol wouldn't push it.

"Oh, she's fine, the usual. Bottling things, pickling things. She's starting another herb garden—she says the mint needs a whole garden to itself. Aggressive stuff. I can't stand it myself, but she puts it in everything. Next time you're in town, no doubt she'll feed you several of her special mojitos and tell you they're a cure-all. Well, who'm I to knock it? She's healthy as a horse."

Carol paused, and Abby knew what she'd say next. "We do worry about you, darling. Won't you visit sometime? You know how huge the house is. You can stay up—" She stopped. "Well, we'll set up one of the downstairs rooms for you. Plenty of room. Stay as long as you like."

Abby had absolutely no plan to return in the foreseeable future, so she demurred as gently as she could. She hated disappointing Carol.

Later, as Abby scanned the laminated pizza menu at Luigi's, she couldn't shake a strange feeling of longing—but what exactly she was longing for, she had no idea.

"Why do we even bother with these?" Evan said, dropping his menu onto the sticky placemat. He had a point. They never wavered from their regular order at Luigi's.

With its red checkered linen and faded photos of Italian landmarks hanging crooked against the walls, Luigi's was like every other pizza place as far removed from Italy as it was possible to be. The only authentic thing seemed to be the garlic, strings and strings of the stuff hanging all over the place as if Luigi knew something about nearby vampires that no one else did.

Unlike the trendy pizza places back in the city, Luigi's didn't do "light" or "fresh" or, heaven forfend, "healthy." Your options were doorstop with tons of cheese, doorstop with tons of cheese and pepperoni, or doorstop with all the above *and* pineapple which, Abby wasn't surprised to discover, was what the locals seemed to love. That Bay View was a pineapple pizza-loving town really didn't shock her at all.

But at times, like tonight, there was nothing like a cheesy, greasy round of stodge to distract you from any other kind of gnawing in your gut.

"Yeah, no idea," Abby agreed, covering an unidentifiable red blob on the tablecloth with a napkin.

They were sitting outside, staring across a parking lot. It felt chillier tonight than it had been for the past few days, and Abby hunched over the table.

"I never thought I'd say this, but I miss The Dolphin Inn," Evan said, lazily following her gaze.

"Yeah, me too. It was easy there. Comfy. How are you feeling?"

"Ugh, not great. You?"

"Same. Weird," Abby replied. "Trying not to think about it. I have a new booking starting tomorrow, so there's that. It'll be good to get back to normal."

"You sound so bummed out, dude," Evan said. He started shredding a paper napkin and rolling the scraps into tiny balls. The waiter arrived with their drinks—a tray of lukewarm beers—and then with his free hand, scooped the napkin scraps onto his tray. He took their pizza order and left, and Evan got started on a new napkin.

"Me? Nah, I'm okay. I'm not the one whose girlfriend just broke up with them. How are you managing?"

Evan pulled his mouth down at the sides. "Just gotta get through it, I guess."

Abby took a sip of beer, and her mind slipped back to Friday night, to the hours that she and Chris had spent pouring their hearts out to each other. A bolt shot through her. She forced her attention back to Evan.

"You know, I've been thinking about it a lot," she said, watching his steady progress through the napkin. "Maybe you and Marli just weren't right for each other."

"Yeah, you've mentioned that before." His jaw muscles clenched. "You never liked her."

"Hey," Abby protested. "*She* never liked *me*, and I still maintain that if she hadn't known about what happened between us—one time!—we could have been friends. You should never have told her."

"Telling her was the right thing to do." Evan's eyes hardened.

"Really?" Abby challenged. "You tell all your girlfriends who you've slept with in the past?"

"Stop it. You know this is different."

"It is different. Because our friendship is really important. If your partners know you and I once slept together, of course it could make them insecure."

"What made her insecure was how we are now, not what happened then," Evan snapped, flicking a piece of napkin across the table.

"Wait, are you serious, dude?" Abby asked, sitting up straighter. "Do you blame me for the break-up?"

"That's ridiculous. Obviously I don't blame you. You know very well what the issue was."

"Yeah, the issue was that you're both too fucking afraid!" Abby blurted out before she could stop herself. "Afraid to take a chance, afraid to leave your cosy little comfort zones. What are you sticking around here for? What's she sticking around there for? Jesus, you should put each other first."

"That's such an oversimplification, Abby," Evan growled, the cords in his neck sticking up. He rarely raised his voice. She must have really struck a nerve.

"Shit, Ev, I overstepped." Abby slumped back in her seat. "I'm sorry."

"Just drop it," he said, deflated now. "I don't think I should be taking relationship advice from you anyway."

"What does that mean?"

"Nothing. Never mind."

"No—I'm not 'never minding.' Tell me what you meant."

"I mean…" He seemed to search for the right words and then gave up. "You sit on your high horse, dishing out opinions on my relationship, but you're the one benching it out for the rest of your life. You've taken yourself out of the game. You're the one who's afraid."

Abby blinked. "I'm not afraid, just pragmatic."

"Oh, really? Fine, call it 'pragmatism' if it makes you feel better. You're fucking terrified, ever since Dan, and that's no way to live."

"Well, I have a pretty compelling reason to be afraid, don't you think? Don't you think I'm entitled to a little bit of fear? Anyway, if I'm terrified, so are you. If you love Marli so much, why won't you move to the city to be with her? How can you just throw love away? Don't you know how lucky you are?"

"I'm not you, Abby, and she's not Dan!"

"You think I don't know that?"

The waiter appeared with their pizzas. Evan shot Abby daggers as the server hastily set them down and retreated. The slices were bubbling with thick, yellow cheese, and shiny with grease.

Softer now, Evan muttered, "It's actually none of your business."

"Whoa," Abby replied, arching an eyebrow. "That is seriously not cool, bro. We're supposed to be best friends. We're supposed to be able to be honest with each other."

"This doesn't feel like honesty. It feels like an attack."

"An attack? I'm just trying to help you workshop this thing. Don't take out your bad mood on me."

Evan sighed and shook his head. "You're right. I'm sorry. That was uncalled for, Abs. I apologise."

Abby gave a rueful smile. "It's fine, I get it, and I'm sorry I high-horsed you. That was douchey."

For a few minutes, they ate in silence. Abby always begrudgingly enjoyed Luigi's pizzas, and for the umpteenth time, marvelled at how much her tastes and tolerances had changed since arriving in Bay View. This was such a far cry from her favourite fresh, gourmet pizzas that they may as well come from different planets. But for once, as she chewed through the thick, glutinous base, she didn't hear Dan's horrified voice in her head.

Eventually, their conversation returned to all their well-worn topics: work, town gossip, The Dolphin Inn. And, after they'd paid their bill and gathered their takeaway boxes, Abby found herself leading them home past the shell of the burnt-out hotel.

"You reckon old Roy will ever get this place running again?" Abby asked, looking up at Evan. He was standing with his hands on his hips, surveying the wreckage of the building. Abby couldn't be sure, but she suspected he was flexing, even in the dark. The monochromatic orange glow of the streetlamp ricocheted off his cheekbones, casting deep shadows on his face that looked like gashes.

"Who knows?" He shrugged. "But it would be a shame if he didn't. This place was legendary, even if it was kind of a mess."

Abby nodded as she surveyed the piles of rubble around her. It was hard to believe her tiny little cat had emerged from the soot-filled detritus.

"Hey, what's that?" Evan asked, breaking Abby's concentration. He was pointing to the far corner of the bar—or at least, what was once the bar—and Abby fully expected to see a tiny creature emerge. Instead, her eyes caught something shiny in the far corner. What *was* it?

"No idea," Abby murmured. "Let's go see."

They picked their way over the debris, Evan using the light from his phone to illuminate their path over shards of glass and broken brick, until they reached it: scratched but intact, half-buried under the muck, the stainless-steel ice scoop from the faulty machine.

"How eerie," Evan said as he picked it up, smudging the layer of soot.

"And ironic," Abby said, peering over his shoulder.

"Should we take it with us? Throw it away?" Evan asked, turning it over in his hands. "I'm not sure how old Roy would feel seeing it lying here…"

"Yeah, you're right. Let's take it."

They made their way back onto the road, in the direction of home.

"Tonight was great—well, mostly great," Evan said, nudging Abby with his elbow. "I needed it, so thanks."

"Yeah. Me too. You know we'll both be fine, right?" she said and really hoped she was right. The fleeting whirlwind of Chris had knocked her.

"Yeah, fuck it, definitely," Evan agreed as Abby's house came into view. He always walked her to her door, even though Bay View was safe as houses, and Abby always insisted he need not.

Later, after she'd climbed into bed and balled Snowy into the crook of her arm, Abby reached for her phone. It had been less than a week since she'd last spoken with her parents, but she was wide awake. A call to the mothership might help lull her to sleep.

"Hey, Mom. Where in the world are you?"

"Abigail! Can you believe that your father and I just did an art class on the Italian Riviera? Led by an actual famous *artista*! It was a still life, and—"

"There's *still life* in us yet!" her father boomed in the background, roaring with laughter. Her mother dissolved into giggles.

"Oh, your father is hilarious. Anyway, we painted oranges…"

"Tangerines!"

"Tangerines. Sounds easy, but oh, it was tricky! I'll send you a photo when we're back on Wi-Fi…"

Abby listened with half an ear as she played with Snowy's tiny paws. The conversation was light and distracting, but when it was over and Abby turned off her light to go to sleep, she blinked into the dark for a long time, thinking about her parents, about Evan and school and Dan, thinking about anything, absolutely anything at all, that wasn't Chris Addison.

CHAPTER TEN

The soles of her gladiator sandals slipped against the asphalt as Abby neared the old Dolphin Inn, and she stepped onto the grassy curb for better footing. Up ahead, the black shell of the building cut into the sky, today a hazy baby blue and completely cloudless.

At some point over intervening weeks since the fire, Abby's route had permanently changed to bring her past the structure, as if by some sort of subconscious pull. She always slowed as she passed, fascinated by the living, breathing deadness of it—a deadness that felt impermanent, as if it were only suspended in death and awaiting the right moment to reanimate itself.

A few remaining bits of fireman's tape clung to the burnt bricks as if by sheer stubbornness, and Abby looked down as the words "LICE LINE" flitted near her feet, the "PO" long since ripped away. For some time now, she'd had the sense that a new, small but unpluggable hole had opened somewhere deep in her soul.

A cough startled her from her thoughts, and she looked up to see Roy at the far corner of the property, hitching up his chinos at the thigh like old men did and peering at something on the ground. Abby yelled a greeting and waved.

"Morning, Roy," she said, making her way over. "How's it—"

"Awful. Awful, awful, Abby." Roy tutted as he straightened up, still staring at the ground. "Those insurance crooks…Apparently, I was negligent. Negligent! After all those years of paying their levies, every month, even when business was bad. Nonexistent sometimes! Crooks and thieves, I tell ya. Crooks and thieves!" Spittle caught the light, and Abby watched drops of it land on the coals at their feet. Roy seemed even greyer than before, as grey as ash really. Her heart sank for him.

"So, what now?" she asked hesitantly. She felt glad that she and Evan had removed the ice scoop from the scene last night.

"Ah, my dear, I don't know." He sighed, looking into the distance. "They'll pay me out some, but it won't be enough to rebuild the place. It'll barely cover the costs to repair the remains."

Abby glanced to her left, where parts of the building—and Roy's room—remained relatively unscathed. Even so, they'd need a good industrial strength scrubbing down and repaint. She also imagined that whatever furniture remained intact inside those rooms would need to be replaced.

Abby kicked the toe of her shoe into the dirt, then immediately rubbed her toes together to get the grit out. She'd spotted the sandals at the bottom of one of the boxes as she'd been packing Dan's clothes away. She and Chris had left rather a mess of things after their private fashion show, but the arrival of her next guest had forced her to get her ass into gear and clear up. In sorting and packing the clothes away once again, Abby had rediscovered items of her own that she hadn't worn since she'd left the city. Clothes that had reminded her of date nights and dinner parties and fun times in fairy-lit apartments. She remembered where she'd bought these bronze sandals, and the first time she'd worn them— the housewarming party of one of her former colleagues—and as she'd slipped them on, she'd smiled. And so, she'd dug around and unearthed tank tops and dresses and brightly coloured garments she hadn't worn in years. And, sure, some of them were a few seasons out of date by now, but who in Bay View would care? Her new-old clothes were now in steady rotation in her wardrobe and were slowly replacing the shapeless garb she'd draped herself in since arriving.

"But, Roy, surely you can appeal the decision?" Abby was indignant on his behalf. How dare this insurance company find some silly loophole to cheat him out of his payout? "This doesn't seem fair at all. And we need The Dolphin Inn. It was such a special part of this town."

Roy just shook his head sadly from side to side. "I've tried, Abby. I've tried everything. There's only so much headway I can make without going to court. Lucy Allrick—you know Lucy, the lawyer on Main Street? She's been helping me bona fide."

"Do you mean pro bono?"

"Whatever." Roy waved his hand dismissively, as if Latin verbiage was the least of his concerns right now. It probably was. "Pro bono. She says I'd have to go to court to fight it—and I'd probably win, too. She'd do it for me…pro bono. But I don't have that kinda fight in me—what do I wanna go to court for? Just too much angst for me, I'm afraid. Too much angst."

"I'm so sorry, Roy," Abby said sadly, and Roy nodded.

"Me too."

Abby sighed. The fire had been a shock, but everyone had assumed that once the insurance claim paid out, The Dolphin would be rebuilt, as good as new—or as "new" as The Dolphin Inn could ever be. A degree of dilapidation seemed to be baked into its bones. But no more Dolphin Inn? It was unfathomable.

"The very first day I arrived in town, I came to The Dolphin Inn for a drink."

"I remember. You were crying at the bar."

"I was." Abby grimaced. The sticky bar counter, the grimy glasses, the fact that the bartender—Roy, as it turned out—had never heard of her favourite drink had all been too much for her. *What have I done?* She'd panicked. *What was I thinking, picking a random town because of its pretty name? This place is ghastly!* Not wanting to be a hideous cliché, she'd done her best to swallow her tears through giant glugs of bottom-shelf vodka. And it had worked—until Evan had broken away from his group of friends, flexed, and introduced himself. The moment he'd asked Abby, with real concern, whether she was all right, she'd lost her fragile grip on her composure.

"You and Evan, been fast friends since that night."

"Yeah, we have," Abby agreed.

"Held my bar up many nights, and I appreciated that."

"The stories that bar must be able to tell!" Abby joked, then instantly regretted the words. The bar counter was just ash now, and given how much booze was soaked into it, it must've burned up pretty fast.

"Roy…" Abby began awkwardly. "We came past here the other night, Evan and I. And we found…well, we found an ice scoop. Don't suppose you want it, do you?"

Roy laughed wryly, the wryest laugh Abby had ever heard. "Throw it away. I have no more need for it."

"Okay," Abby replied, but she knew she wouldn't. Something told her to keep it, even though she didn't know why. And she'd probably never have figured it out if it weren't for Snowy's disappearance, and Chris, because everything these days seemed to come back, inexorably, to Chris Addison.

* * *

Malcolm was some sort of municipal worker, on his way to a conference on potable water. The conference was three towns over, and he'd stopped over in Bay View to visit a cousin for a few days. He was friendly enough, and Abby was polite and helpful, even though it chafed having someone else occupy the room she now reflexively—annoyingly—thought of as "Chris's room."

It had been over a month since a taxi had spirited Chris away and out Abby's life as enigmatically as she'd appeared, as if Abby had dreamt the whole thing up. How else to explain the visceral intensity of the week they shared, and the interminable silence that followed?

At last, Abby had stopped anticipating the *ping* of her phone.

Malcolm was fine, really—an easy guest with few demands. Tomorrow morning, he'd be driving for several hours to get to the conference on time, and he told Abby he'd probably be leaving before she woke up.

Through the fog of deep sleep, she became aware of Malcolm rustling around in the early hours—the sound of water running and zippers being closed. She turned and snuggled her nose deeper into Snowy's soft belly. The kitten liked to sleep pressed up against Abby's face.

Abby must have drifted off again because she awoke with a fright to the clanging sound of keys being dropped into the metal lockbox.

Oh, good—he's followed the instructions, Abby thought as her heart rate slowed. It was far too early to get up—Malcolm said he'd be leaving around three a.m.—and Abby burrowed deeply into her pillow.

Her cold, empty pillow.

Her eyes sprang open. First gingerly, then more urgently, she felt around the bed for the small, warm puff of fur she'd grown so accustomed to. "Snowy!" she called, knowing it would be futile—the cat never responded to her name, she was too little to know it. "Snowy!" she called again, sitting up, her feet landing on the floor. She leapt up and yanked open the bedroom door. She always left it open a tiny crack so

Snowy could use her litter box in the night, but Abby just *knew* that's not where she was. She knew she was gone.

She checked the house anyway, flipping on light switches as she lurched through the rooms. And then: an open window in Malcolm's room—the lowest window, the one she'd asked him to keep closed when she explained that her cat was curious but far too small to go outside alone. Last month, the vet estimated Snowy to be around six weeks old. She was too young to be alone outside, in the dark, in the road, amid the charred rubble of The Dolphin Inn.

Shit. Shit, shit, shit.

"Snowy!"

Abby jammed her feet into a pair of sliders she'd left in the sitting room and, armed with the torch light from her cell phone, tripped into the garden. She pss-pss'ed frantically as she searched bushes, trees, and the high branches reaching into the black sky. Then she stood still, her breath on pause, and listened…

Nothing.

Abby's heart pounded in her ears and under the hot, thin skin of her neck. Her next move would be to cover the streets close to her house, and she did, her sliders smacking against the tar as she scampered to cover ground. Snowy could move fast, so Abby had to, too. She called for the kitten, trying not to wake the neighbourhood but also hoping to rouse at least one or two somnambulant humans to help with the search.

She went almost as far as Main Street, her torch sweeping trees and gardens and the spaces underneath sleeping cars. Then back up, past Evan's house, around the corner and toward Mrs. Addison's place, nestled in its overgrown garden. Abby couldn't shake the feeling that if Chris had been here, she'd have known what to do. She'd have been able to solve this, decisively and without panic. And Dan? This simply wouldn't have happened to her. Snowy would never, ever have left her side, not for a moment. Abby just knew it.

Outside of old Mrs. Addison's house, as the night sky began to crank open and the first rays of light slipped through, Abby started crying. She felt very afraid, and very, very alone.

Her fingers working faster than her brain, she turned over her phone, the torch boring its light into the ground, and found herself scrolling through her contact list. Scrolling, scrolling, until—

"Abby?" Surprise. Confusion. Phlegm. She'd been woken from a deep sleep. Obviously—it was five a.m.

"I'm so sorry to call you so late. Or early," Abby said, doing her best to choke back her panic. "Your mom's fine," she quickly added, realising the shortsightedness of her early morning call.

"Good, okay. Though you don't sound so fine." Her tone was cool. Abby suddenly regretted calling. *What was I thinking?* In the background, she heard shuffling—presumably, Chris getting out of bed so the call wouldn't disturb Karys. She waited a beat for the rustling to stop.

"No, I…Snowy's gone and I…I'm sorry, I don't really know why I'm calling you…" Abby's mind whirled. What had she been hoping for? "I…I probably shouldn't have."

"Snowy's gone?"

"Yeah. My house guest, he left the window open in your room—*his* room—and Snowy got out."

"I see." It was clipped, and Abby wondered whether she was about to tell her to get lost, to ask Abby what she expected her to do about it, from hundreds of miles away, from a different life, a different planet.

But she didn't.

Instead, in a firm voice, she said, "Okay, here's what you need to do. Take notes."

Time, really, is the only thing that will bring a cat home, if it comes home. Time, and a litter box placed strategically in the breeze, surrounded by your worn clothes and tinned fish, ripe and rank from exposure. Abby repeated the tips back to Chris as she slowly made her way home, eyes sweeping the asphalt as the morning turned it from black to blue to grey.

"Let me know, okay? Cats have a way of finding their way home. Stay positive, Abby."

Abby nodded, then croaked her assent. "Yeah." There was nothing left to say, but she dreaded hanging up. Chris was silent too, but she didn't hang up.

Finally, "Thanks for all your help, Chris. I feel so silly for calling you so early…"

"Don't. I'm glad you did. Team Crabby, right? We've got this."

Abby smiled weakly into the phone, but her heart flipped all the same. And she didn't feel so alone—not at all, actually—anymore.

"Team Crabby," she repeated, her insides squeezing. "I…Thank you."

"Don't mention it. Bye, Abby."

"Bye, Chris." She ended the call before she could say any more.

Abby couldn't have foreseen that Snowy's disappearance would be the catalyst for a chain of events that would ultimately change the entire course of her life in Bay View. She certainly couldn't have predicted it during those dark days of despair.

Abby tried to stay positive, at least outwardly. At school, she forced herself to be even more upbeat than usual, pushing her worry to the back of her mind until she could properly focus on it. Chris said it would all be okay, and Abby believed her. She had to.

"Oh, honey, I'm sure she'll be home in no time," Moira Fresh said throatily at the staff table later that morning. "Cats can be real little so-and-sos, I tell you." She reached into her pocket for a packet of cigarettes and then hoisted herself up, one liver-spotted hand pressing against the tabletop. She was kind, Moira Fresh, but also tough—two essential traits of sixty-plus schoolteachers. "Once my Jackie was gone for three months. Three months! He turned up at a shelter an hour away. Chasing tail, no doubt, and got lost. The little shit."

Abby pressed her lips together and shrugged. "Thanks, Moira. I really hope so. I don't think I could go three months wondering."

Abby raced home the moment the school bell rang. She was sweating by the time she reached her house, her heart pounding. She took a cursory look around the front before flinging open the door and racing through the house.

She'd taken to leaving the window open in the second bedroom, in case Snowy tried to return. But there was no sign of the kitten.

"Whoa, Abby!" Evan appeared in Abby's living room, skidding to a stop as they almost collided. He grabbed her arms. "Abby, jeez. Are you okay? I've never seen you move so fast."

Abby shook her head. "No. Snowy's still not back, and I just don't know what to do." She felt her eyes filling with tears and bit the inside of her cheek.

"I'm sorry, Abs. I don't know either. But you heard what Moira said. She'll turn up—everyone's sure of it."

Abby pulled away, shaking her head again. "She's just so small," she whimpered, feeling miserable and helpless.

"Right. Get your laptop," Evan ordered. "We're going to design 'missing' posters and stick them up all over town." He pulled out his phone and tapped on the screen a few times. "And if we hurry, we can get to the printing shop before closing time."

"You're pretty smart for a dumb blonde," Abby said as she returned with her laptop.

"I know, right?" Evan waggled his eyebrows. "But there'll be plenty of time for compliments later. Right now, type, and find a good photo of Snowy."

An hour later, posters freshly printed and warm between Abby's fingers, she and Evan split up outside the print shop to cover the town before it got dark.

Abby tacked posters to windows and lamp-posts, her heart tugging each time her eyes fell on Snowy's little face, grainy on the poorly printed page.

"Hey, dude," Abby heard behind her as she stuck a poster to the front of the ice cream shop. During the day, it was one of Bay View's busiest hangouts. It was closed now, but the windows were strangely warm.

"Oh, hey, Cody," Abby said, glancing around to see the woman coming up behind her. She was scanning the poster over Abby's shoulder.

"Ah, shit, man, your kitty's missing? That's balls, dude. I'm sorry."

"Yeah, it really is." Abby sighed. "And thanks. Maybe these posters will help."

"Yeah, definitely they will," Cody replied enthusiastically, and Abby smiled. She was a good person, Cody. "Here," she added, holding out a hand. "Pass me some of those. I'll help you put them up."

Cody chatted as they tacked up the posters in prominent spots around town. They were back in front of the print shop just as darkness fell, Evan there already and sitting on a low wall as he typed on his phone.

"All done?" he asked, looking up. "Oh, hi, Cody," he added with a wave.

She responded with a salute. "Hey, dude."

"Yes," Abby replied, feeling slightly more upbeat since bumping into Cody. She realised that Cody's perennially positive outlook had buoyed her spirits. "Fingers crossed these posters will reach the right person."

"I'm sure they will," Evan said, hopping off the wall. "Let's stay positive. Wanna get some chow?"

"I dunno," Abby replied, scanning the vicinity—for what, she wasn't sure. "I'm not in the mood for Luigi's premium plastic pizza."

"Hey, why don't you guys come to ours?" Cody said, hands jammed into the back pockets of her jeans. "We're right around the corner. Jade's got a fire going, and we've got loads of beer. Would be cool," she added with a shrug.

"That actually sounds really great," Abby heard herself replying, then smiled. She was enjoying Cody's company and was fond of Jade, too. "You sure Jade won't mind?"

"Jade? Mind?" Cody scoffed. "She loves people. The more the merrier, as far as she's concerned."

"It sounds great, thanks, Codes," Evan replied, slipping his phone into his pocket. Abby knew he and Marli were still on speaking terms, and she wondered if he'd been texting her—and if so, what about.

They headed in the direction of Cody's house, chatting amicably as their eyes scanned their surroundings for the little white kitten. Abby did it automatically now, and she could see the others doing it, too.

Abby had, of course, been to Cody's house that one time, but she pushed the awkward encounter to the back of her mind as they arrived. The air smelled like jasmine and wood fire. Abby realised she couldn't remember the last time she'd sat around a fire. Group of friends, she mused. When last…?

"Babe!" Cody called as they entered the house through the back door. "I found company."

Jade was in the kitchen, squeezing fresh lemon juice over a salad as they walked in. She dropped the fruit and flung her arms wide.

"Heyyyy!" She embraced each of them in turn. She gave Cody a smooch, then grabbed a tray of meat off the counter and plopped it into her arms.

"Just in time." She grinned. "Fire's good to go."

"You sure it's okay that we're gate-crashing?" Abby asked, looking around. They didn't seem to be having a party, and she hoped Jade hadn't been planning something quiet or romantic just for the two of them.

"Oh god, yes." She laughed, squeezing Abby's arm. "We always have people popping in. We love it."

She spun around and opened the fridge. "Wine? Beer? Something else? We also have fruit juice, and I think some…" Her words were muffled as she moved bottles and containers around inside the fridge. It was filled to capacity. "Whatever this is," she said as she held a bottle of pink liquid aloft. "Someone must've left this here."

"Creamy Strawberry Kiss." Evan read the label aloud. "Er, I think I'll stick with beer, thanks. That stuff looks nasty."

"Yeah, gross," Jade agreed, reaching for the beers and popping a few open. She handed them around and they headed outside to where Cody was grilling steaks over the coals. The small backyard was lit up by fairy lights and filled with flowerpots of every colour and size. It looked like a nursery, every plant bright and healthy and spilling over the edges of its pot. The barbeque was set up at the far end of the yard, with a handful of plastic chairs scattered around it.

Once they settled, Cody explained how they'd bumped into each other. Jade's face fell. She reached out to squeeze Abby's hand.

"I'm so sorry, love," she said, shaking her head. Her eyeliner-ringed eyes were earnest as she spoke. "We need to send all our positive vibes into the universe to bring her home."

"Yeah, and we will," Cody added, flipping the meat over.

"Thanks, guys," Abby replied, taking a sip of her beer. The mild evening and the taste of the drink flung her mind back to her evenings with Chris—the hair-combing, the heart-to-hearts, the unshakable feeling that, no matter what happened next, her life would never be entirely the same.

"I, um," she started, taking a sip of her beer. "I actually spoke to Chris Addison about it. She gave me some pretty good advice." Abby wasn't sure why she mentioned it. Perhaps she just wanted to feel Chris's name on her tongue.

"You did?" Evan asked. He seemed taken aback. "You didn't tell me that."

"Why would I?"

"Well, I mean, I just didn't realise you guys were still chatting."

"You and Marli are still chatting," Abby shot back defensively and instantly regretted it.

There was an awkward pause around the fire. Abby saw Cody and Jade exchange looks.

"Well, I think Chris is awesome," Jade said, stretching out her legs and lacing her fingers behind her head. "People here still talk about her," she added, rolling her eyes but then winking to show she was teasing. "It doesn't take much to excite them."

"Yeah, she made quite an impression on some of our friends," Cody added with a grin.

"On some of mine, too," Evan added cheekily, and Abby shot him daggers.

"Well, it's not like there's much going on here in Bay View," Cody said. "Any new person coming in is bound to get people talking. Especially someone as glamorous and so obviously out-of-town as Chris Addison." She lifted the steaks off the heat and placed them into a clean bowl. "And Cookie Addison's daughter? That quiet, little old lady? I think people's minds were a little blown."

"Minds blown, mmm," Evan repeated, wiggling his eyebrows at Abby. Abby longed to throw something at his head.

"What are you on about?" Jade laughed, looking from Evan to Abby and back again. "Oh my god—Abby, you and Chris?" She leaned forward, eyes sparkling, ready for the juicy details. "Are you guys—"

"No! My god, no," Abby spluttered, shaking her head emphatically. "She's *in a relationship*, guys. How does that keep escaping you all?"

"That means nothing," Cody said drily.

"I should hope it means something, babe," Jade replied, sounding a little hurt. It was no secret that the two of them had virtually picked their wedding date. The fact that neither of them had actually popped the pivotal question yet seemed a minor detail. Perhaps, to them, it was.

"Of course, my love," Cody said quickly, coming over and squeezing Jade's shoulders. "I meant other people. I fuckin' adore you. But other people can be real dicks. I've dated real dicks. So have you. We probably all have."

The conversation was starting to feel horribly awkward. Abby was eager for a new topic.

"Codes, those steaks look great!" Abby said brightly. "Is there anything I can help with?"

"Nope. Just resting them a few minutes, and then we can eat."

"Actually, Abs, you can help me dish up the salad," Jade said, standing and beckoning Abby to follow her into the house.

Abby found herself enjoying the girls' company more and more as the evening wore on. As they tucked into their meals, a few other friends arrived and pulled up chairs.

"See what I mean?" Jade laughed as she introduced people called Jon, Alexia, and Chipper.

"Chipper?" Abby repeated, bemused.

She recognised the tall, hippie-looking guy as Roy's nephew. He grinned, showing off an impressive set of front teeth. They seemed larger and whiter than any front teeth she'd ever seen, except that one had a very obvious chunk missing. "Windsurfing accident," he explained. "I'll never live it down." Chip pulled a face like a bunny, emphasising the raggedy tooth, and Abby giggled.

It was late into the night before Abby and Evan left, making their way home through silent streets plastered with Snowy's picture.

"That was a really great evening," Abby said, realising that it had taken her mind off things for several hours. "I like them a lot."

"Yeah, they're cool people," Evan agreed. "Maybe now you'll start socialising more in real life and less on that damn laptop?"

"We'll see. That laptop doesn't give me nearly as much shit as you do."

"That's probably true." Evan laughed, then clapped his hand over his mouth to stifle the sound. For the most part, Bay View was not a late-night town.

When they arrived at Abby's house, she reached up and hugged him goodbye. It was something they seldom did—in fact, hardly ever since they'd slept together. At first, Evan seemed taken aback.

But Abby didn't let go. Instead, she squeezed harder, and finally, he pulled her closer and she felt his body relax into the embrace. It felt so good to be wrapped in someone's arms, to feel the warmth and connection of another person's body pressed against hers.

"I really miss Marli," Evan mumbled into Abby's hair.

"I really miss Snowy. And Dan. And…" She drifted off, not wanting to say Chris's name out loud, to turn it into fact. "I'm so tired of all the missing."

Evan didn't reply. He just held her.

"Thanks for being my friend," Abby whispered.

"It's not a bad gig, most of the time." He chuckled.

Finally, Abby let go and looked up at Evan. "We have to do something to get ourselves out of this grump dump."

"Yeah, I agree. What do you have in mind?"

"I don't know yet, but I'll think about it. And no—" She saw him taking a breath. "Before you say anything, it's not going to be a virtual pub quiz."

"Thank god for that," he said with a laugh. "I want my life to be *less* sad. And before you say anything…" He cut her off as she took a breath. "Drinking alone is still drinking alone."

"It's different with virtual pub quiz!"

"Yeah, sure, whatever helps you sleep better at night," he said, sauntering off down the path. "Now go to bed, Massey!"

"Love yooooou," Abby sang in reply.

"Obviously," Evan joked, flexing his biceps. "Night!"

CHAPTER ELEVEN

It was dusk when Abby returned from school a few days later to find a package on her doorstep. It had been a long day; the kids had been especially wearing and she was feeling harried and distracted. So much so that she'd missed the package entirely and stumbled over it as she went to put her key in the lock.

She looked down, startled, then bent to pick it up. She wasn't expecting a delivery and there were no sender details on the plain manilla box, and no return address.

Quickly, Abby opened the front door (she'd finally stopped doing it gingerly, expecting a darting kitten to try and escape), slammed it shut with her foot, and made her way to the kitchen counter. She used her key as a makeshift box cutter, ripping through the tape that tightly sealed the package.

Yanking open the lid, she discovered another box inside, this one a beautiful smooth matte black. It was embossed with a logo she could never forget—one from her old life.

Carefully, she lifted the black box and placed it onto the kitchen counter, feeling her eyes welling as past and present collided. How could it be?

With her fingertips she traced the logo, taking in its dips and edges, remembering all the times she'd done this before.

She took a breath and eased off the lid. There was a note folded on top of the white tissue paper. Gingerly, Abby picked it up and opened it, but she already knew who it was from.

I thought you could use some cheering up. I know how much you loved this piece. C x

Abby stared at the note as the words blurred before her eyes. She hadn't realised she'd been holding her breath until she exhaled in a rough, raggedy burst.

She knew even before she unwrapped it what she'd find swathed in the tissue paper: the purple silk bomber jacket, the same one that Chris had worn to The Planetarium.

Well, not the *same* one.

Abby lifted it up and brought it to her face. This one was new. It had that shop-floor smell and the swing tag still attached, price subtly removed.

Of course, Chris wasn't to know the real reason Abby had loved the jacket so much. It was because it had belonged to Chris. It had smelled like her and felt like her, and while Abby wore it, she'd been able to imagine…what, exactly?

It didn't matter, though, as Abby stared at the garment between her fingertips. Chris had thought about her. She'd sent her a gift. A gift that she'd carefully chosen, just for Abby. She held it against her chest and smiled.

"You're so fucked," Evan said into the phone moments later. "I mean, whether or not this means anything, you're so fucked."

But she grinned as he said it, already zipped into the jacket, the swing tag in the trash.

Now to thank Chris. A phone call? She didn't know if she had the courage to call her twice in a single week. A text seemed impersonal, an email even more so.

A selfie.

Abby never bothered with pictures of herself or worried about what she looked like in other people's photos. Lulu always told her it was because she had the luxury of being "every-angle beautiful."

"You couldn't take a bad photo if you tried, Abs," Lulu had once said, barely concealing her jealously. "Try—just try taking a bad front-camera photo. See? See! You can't even fake a double chin. Ugh! You're just perfect or something. I love you but I also kind of hate you."

But now, Abby took a dozen selfies to get one she was happy sending to Chris—one that looked natural and spontaneous after an hour of posing, preening, fiddling with the lighting, and changing locations. One that said "I've just opened the box and thrown this on," and not "I've agonised over this photo for an hour because I desperately want to impress you."

An hour of fretting was fifty-nine minutes too many for Abby. Eventually, frustrated and worried she'd lose her nerve, she picked the photo she disliked the least and hit Send.

Fuck. She hadn't meant to send it without a caption. So she fretted over that, too. By the time she'd decided what to say (a short thank-you had won out over several wordier versions peppered with exclamations marks and emojis), too many minutes had passed. She knew she'd appear to be "double messaging" if she sent it—something that memes had led her to believe was an absolute no-no. When had she become this out of touch?

It had been seventeen minutes. Chris hadn't read the message. Maybe she could still send the follow-up text? Didn't it seem rude to send just a selfie? She really needed to say thank you.

Gah! She tossed her phone onto the sofa. A scatter cushion fell on top of it.

This wasn't her. She wasn't this girl, and now that she was starting to rediscover the old Abby, the happy, pre-trauma Abby, she was determined to stay true to her.

She marched over to the sofa and snatched up her phone. It had been thirty-nine minutes.

Thank you… This was so thoughtful of you. I love it xx

Then she placed her phone face down on the table and walked over to a full-length mirror to admire her new Saint Jamie jacket. She'd be able to debut it in a few minutes when she dialled in to tonight's pub quiz.

"Wa-hey, look at you," Nathan exclaimed when Abby popped up on screen. "Killer jacket, dude."

"Right?" She popped a shoulder and winked at the screen. "Isn't it great?"

"I didn't know they sold couture in your neck of the woods," Lulu commented, taking a sip of wine. "I thought it was all polyester and hand-me-downs."

Abby scoffed. "You're such a snob, Lu," she said, zipping the jacket up to her neck. It didn't smell like Chris, but it did feel soft and lush.

"Actually, I noticed some pretty trendy fashion at The Planetarium. Maybe I've underestimated these folks."

"Would you still recognise 'trendy'?" Lulu teased.

"Ha!" Abby scowled playfully at the screen. "But you're right," she said. "It was a gift."

"Oh, yeah?" Lu asked. "From whom? Surely Evan doesn't have such good taste."

"From Chris, actually. The woman who stayed here a while ago. Not sure if you remember…" Her nonchalance sounded forced, and she knew Lulu could tell.

"Remember?" Lulu whooped. "How could I forget?"

"Whoa, okay, people, are we doing this quiz, or what?" JD cut in. He could always be relied upon to keep to the programme.

"I'm calling you after this," Lulu said conspiratorially, pointing her wineglass at Abby.

She did call, except that it was early the next morning as Abby was scrolling idly through her FortyLinks bookings and waiting for her coffee to cool to something slightly less than scalding. It had tasted burnt upon first sip. And, as it turned out, once it had cooled, too.

"Ugh," Abby said as she took a few bitter gulps. "Chris has ruined coffee for me. The cheap kind, anyway."

"Mmm," Lulu replied. Abby knew what was coming. Last night's quiz had run until late, as it often did. Once Abby had finally shut the lid of her laptop, she'd barely had time to brush her teeth before her eyelids decided. She'd hung the jacket over a chair, and it was the second-last thing she'd glanced before she fell asleep. The last was her phone, and the little blue ticks that indicated that Chris had read her messages.

"So, you managed to dodge me last night, but there's no getting away from it now, missy," Lulu said, and Abby's heart did a little flip as she glanced over at the chair. "What's the deal with you and this woman?"

Abby chuckled. "This woman? You sound like my mother. Well, not my mother. A mother."

"Nice deflection. How are your folks? Still sunning themselves on the Mediterranean?"

"Something like that. Except less sunning, more crafting. And I have no idea where they are."

"Nice work if you can get it."

"Tell me about it," Abby said. "But it's way easier this way."

"I know, now stop trying to change the subject. What's the deal?"

Abby shrugged and hoped it carried across the airwaves. "There's no deal. I think she just wanted to make me feel better, after Snowy and all."

"Oh, come on, Abs. I've known you since before your feet stopped growing. And you've been a size seven since forever. Talk to me."

Abby chuckled. "Honestly, Lu, there's—"

A beep on the line: a call waiting. She looked at the screen but didn't recognise the number.

"Sorry, Lu, gonna have to call you back. I have another call coming in."

"Oh, how very convenient."

"I'll call you back, promise. Just end the call, I don't know how to switch between."

"Okay-love-you-bye!" Lu trilled before cutting the call.

"Hello?" Abby said into the new silence.

Nothing for a beat, and then, "Hello. May I speak with Abigail, please?"

It was the voice of an elderly person. Abby didn't recognise it.

"Speaking. Can I help you?"

"This is Cookie Addison, from number four Marble Close."

Cookie Addison? Why on earth would she be calling me?

"I believe I have your cat. Well, I suppose it's a kitten, really. But all the same, it's here."

"What? Oh, oh my god, Mrs. Addison, thank you!"

"When will you collect it?"

"Right now. I'm, uh, just getting some shoes on."

"Good." Mrs. Addison sounded like she'd been dressed for hours already. "The doorbell doesn't work, so do knock hard, dear."

"Will do!" Abby said in a voice several octaves higher than usual, but the line was already dead.

* * *

Abby lived on Bay View Street, perfect for anonymity, she remembered thinking the day she moved in. How easy to disappear into a town unimaginatively named Bay View when you lived on a street with the same moniker.

It was an easy town to navigate on foot, and quick to do at speed. From the front path of her house, facing east, school and the town centre were down on Main Street, accessed by the imaginatively named Hill Street, now blighted by the gaping remains of The Dolphin Inn. The bay was far in the distance; the higher up the hill you were, the better your view of it—incrementally speaking, of course. Cody's place was to the left and up another hill (so she had an extra sliver of famous view), and Evan was down the hill to the right. Just around the corner from him was Mrs. Cookie Addison, at number four Marble Close.

As she zigzagged through the grid of neat suburban streets, Abby thought back to the moment she'd burst into tears in front of Mrs. Addison's house. How she'd called Chris sobbing from the sidewalk she was rapidly approaching now. Had she just missed Snowy by a hair?

The front lawn of Mrs. Addison's home was brown and crackly under Abby's feet. As she approached the front door, pretty little flowers that were actually weeds bobbed at knee height. The rest of the garden was bare.

Abby knocked on the door, loudly, as instructed. "Hello, Mrs. Addison! It's Abby, er, gail! Abigail!"

Shuffling inside. Doors being closed. Furniture scraping. Why did it always sound like elderly people needed to rearrange their furniture to get to their front doors?

Finally, after some protracted latch sounds, the door opened a few inches.

"Abigail?" Mrs. Addison eyed her through the crack. Her face was grey. A beaded spectacle chain swayed around her neck.

"Yes, hi, Mrs. Addison. Just here to collect Snowy."

"Okay," she agreed, as if it had been Abby's idea all along. "Come in."

Abby followed her down the dimly lit passage into an equally dim sitting room. It was a carpety place, the air thick and musty. Sheer white curtains were drawn against the morning sun, and the house had a dusty, coppery tinge to it. Abby squinted but couldn't discern anything kitten-shaped in the dimness. Just a lot of heavy, dark-wood furniture.

"I don't leave the house very often, you know," Mrs. Addison was saying as she walked to the far side of the sitting room. She was tall, like Chris, but stooped, her movements stiff and slow. Abby knew her hair was grey, but in this light, everything was a silhouette. "Which is why I only saw your poster this morning. You're very lucky. I seldom walk farther than the front gate, just to get my mail, you know. Your poster was all the way at the streetlamp, three houses away."

Abby couldn't quite work out the old woman's tone, but she was only listening with half an ear—like how you turn down the car radio when you're looking for a parking spot.

"...I don't abide animals in the house, but it was very small. Too small to be outside..."

Wish I'd brought a headlamp.

"...certainly not on the furniture..."

Mmm, not a huge surprise.

"…so I made this box for it, and it seems happy."

At last, Mrs. Addison gestured to a shoebox near her feet, pushed up against one of the sofas. Abby crept over. Inside, curled up in a cosy nest of newspaper and fast asleep, was Snowy.

She knelt, scooping up the small cat and pressing her into her neck. She looked a little grubby, and even more delicate than before, but otherwise fine. It had been a week, and Abby was amazed she looked this good, considering. Promptly, she burst into tears.

"Thank you so much for finding her, Mrs. Addison." She beamed up at the woman before kissing Snowy's head through her tears. The kitten was mewling, clearly hungry.

"I didn't. It found me," she said over the yowls. "I thought it would leave of its own accord, but it's been two days and I started to worry it was getting rather comfortable."

"Cats certainly are presumptuous little things," Abby agreed, sniffing.

"Yes, well, this isn't a home for cats," Mrs. Addison replied. "I have too many ornaments. Too many things that can break."

"Well, I appreciate it very much, that you took her in, especially under those circumstances," Abby replied, straightening up. The air in the house felt oppressive, not helped by Mrs. Addison's terseness. Or was it barely concealed irritation? Abby wasn't sure, but she understood why Chris wouldn't have wanted to stay here for a moment longer than she had to.

And yet…

"Mrs. Addison?"

"Yes?"

She wasn't quite ready to leave.

"Are you feeling better now? Your daughter, Chris—she stayed with me a little while back. She'd been…"

Even in the dim light, Abby could see the shadow that crossed the old woman's face. Quick, but unmistakable.

"Oh, that was you? She mentioned she was staying nearby."

"Yes, just up the hill."

"Right. Well, it was good of you to put her up. After the fire, I mean. Lucky that she had a friend so nearby."

"Oh, no, it wasn't like that," Abby replied quickly. "What I mean is, I rent out my second bedroom. Online, you know?" Now that Abby's eyes had adjusted, she could see just how pale and drawn the old woman was, as if someone had wrung the colour out of her. She was giving Abby a strange look as she babbled on. "I don't know Chris—I mean, I didn't know Chris, before this. Just a place to stay. We aren't…friends."

Abby was regretting bringing up Chris at all. She inched closer to the front door, and to her relief, Mrs. Addison took the hint. With jerky movements, she fiddled with the latches until freedom appeared on the other side.

"Well, either way, I suppose we're even now," Mrs. Addison said as Abby stepped gratefully into the bright light.

"Even?"

Mrs. Addison, an eyebrow twitching, looked pointedly at Snowy, who was now tucked into the crook of Abby's arm.

"Oh! Oh, yes, kind of, I guess." She didn't feel like explaining the economics of FortyLinks. She just wanted to leave before things got more awkward.

"Thank you, again, Mrs. Addison. Please, let me know if I owe you anything? Like for food, or anything…?"

"No. It was just a bit of milk."

Ah! That explains the yowling.

"Well, thanks. And I'm glad you're better."

"I am. Take care, Abigail."

Abby started to reply, but the door had already clicked shut.

If it wasn't cool to double text, then it certainly wasn't cool to triple or quadruple text. But it wasn't like Abby had ever been concerned with cool before, so why start now? Last night's brief text-based anguish certainly wasn't how she intended to while away her hours.

"Have you ever tried to be cool?" Lulu had once asked Abby as they tried on clothes. They'd been inside a stiflingly hot tent at a music festival, idly picking at items that may or may not have been previously worn. Abby was appraising her reflection in a long, cracked mirror, debating the white crocheted top she'd thrown on, and Lu was scowling at her reflection behind her. The Panama hat perched on her head simply wouldn't work with her face, no matter how she tipped it.

"No?" Abby had replied, surprised. It hadn't occurred to her, ever. "Should I be?"

"No, that's exactly my point!" Lu had been exasperated. She tossed the hat back onto its hook and folded her arms with a huff. "You just are. Your very essence is cool. Everything you wear, everything you do, it just works. And now you're a cool lesbian, too. And your girlfriend! Even I'm gay for her. Have I told you yet today that I hate you?"

Abby had laughed and hugged her and said that she was full of shit. Then she helped her to find a hat that suited her.

"Fedora, see? Same, same, but different. These suit everyone."

She wondered where that white crocheted top was. She'd bought it and worn it for two days straight with a hot pink bra underneath. She had a vague memory of turning it into a bed for Alice when they had first adopted her.

"Oh, if Lu could see me now," Abby said to Snowy as she debated the message she was about to send. Snowy, having gorged herself until her belly bulged (Abby had had to stop her), was now perched happily on a pile of blankets on Abby's bed, purring like a tractor.

"Before you go to sleep, we need to take a selfie," Abby told the cat, scooping her up with one hand, pressing their faces together, and quickly taking the shot. Snowy wasn't impressed, pushing her little paws against Abby's cheek until she released her back onto the bed.

Look who's come home! She captioned the photo, then deleted it.

My baby's back! Eew, no. Delete.

Hot off the press! Snowy's home! Ugh, corny. Delete.

Abby clenched her jaw and sighed. "Argh!" She tossed her phone onto the bed. "No. No, no, no," she said aloud. "I'm not this girl."

Grabbing up her phone, she fired off the photo—no caption, just like last night—then followed up with: *Best news! Snowy's home xx.*

She was proud of herself for not mentioning how, exactly, she'd found her.

* * *

It felt like it started slowly, little quips and check-ins, the odd meme. Chris had indeed wanted to know how Snowy had been found and couldn't believe the irony of it all.

"Of all the places to have got herself," she'd said into the phone. "My mother hates pets. She must be going soft in her old age, allowing a kitten to sleep in a box inside the house."

"That's your mom going soft?" Abby replied. "Sorry, that was rude."

"Oh, don't apologise. I grew up with it, remember? I get it."

The next day, Chris had resumed their conversation over text.

How's Snowy? Recovered from the trauma of my mother?

Barely! She's eating her feelings about it 🐱

Haha! How did my mom seem to you? Besides being an old sourpuss, I mean. You think she's OK? x

Hmm, I don't know her very well but she seemed OK? I wasn't there very long.

OK, thanks. xx

Then there'd been the cat photos—*This guy likes to hang out in the hotel lobby—he looks a bit like Snowy, don't you think?* (he didn't, really)— and Abby's requisite sarcasm to camouflage, just barely, her attempts at flirtation.

Do you actually do any work, or just travel from fancy place to fancy place shopping for clothes?

Ha! That IS my job. And anyway, sometimes I find myself in decidedly UNFANCY places, hint hint ;-)

Oh, I know you're not referring to Bay View!

After that, their conversations evolved. Before Abby knew it, she was glued to her phone in a way she'd never been before. Her attention was constantly divided, her phone screen smudged from endless tapping and scrolling. Phone-free outside time was long forgotten.

With Dan, things had escalated so fast that there'd barely been time to strike up a text-based romance. Also, Dan had detested cell phones. She'd never wanted to feel beholden to her device. They hadn't been a couple who'd called each other incessantly or took a million selfies. In fact, whenever Abby had tried to find photos of them in the past, she'd struggled. Her favourite was one that a friend had taken, catching them both unaware in their apartment as they hosted a dinner party, Dan in the background of the shot, slightly blurry, her head tossed back, her mouth open in laughter—a belly laugh Abby knew so well. In the foreground, Abby was leaning over the table and smiling coyly—it had been a dirty joke, she remembered, the kind Dan loved and Abby pretended not to. Just a little game they played. There were a couple of posed shots, too—the kind taken at weddings and work functions—and a handful of selfies. When Abby had realised how few photos of them existed, she'd panicked. In those last few months she took a whole lot— hundreds, maybe thousands—which felt forced and irritated Dan. The motive had been so obvious. "Grotesque," she'd spat.

Abby had never been able to bring herself to look at them, not even once. She always returned to the dinner party photo.

But with Chris, it was different. Suddenly, this little device bridged the miles between them with texts and calls and voice notes that Abby would play over and over again. She was falling for the sound of Chris's voice rendered digitally, the double entendre she imagined into her phrasing. It was a risky, inappropriate crutch, and Abby knew it. But it was also irresistible.

"Abby, hellooooo?" It was Cody, her hand coming into focus as she waved it in front of Abby's face. "Anyone there?"

Abby snapped into the moment. "Sorry, guys. I was a million miles away there for a second. What did I miss?"

They were at Luigi's for the two-for-one Wednesday special: she, Evan, Jade, Cody. They were falling into an easy friendship, the way queers (and honorary queers) in small towns often did. Abby was glad for it. In her previous life, she'd never had any difficulty making new friends and growing her social circle. Now, with each passing day, her life filled up a little more. The old Abby Massey was coming back.

They'd all gone to The Planetarium one night. Abby had worn her new purple bomber jacket and danced all night, mostly with her head thrown back in laughter. She'd ordered drinks named after planets and, toward the end of the night, made out with a girl as they waited in line to use the bathroom.

"In line to use the bathroom? But how? How does that even happen?"

"It just does! I can't explain it." Abby giggled as she relayed the story to Chris. She hoped she was jealous.

"The only clubs I find myself in these days are carpool clubs," Chris had said. She never spoke about Karys, but she talked about work, the kids, their exams, the mounting pressure as they approached the last weeks of their final school year.

Chris would call Abby while she shopped for groceries or drove home from the boutique. When she walked home from school without Evan, Abby would tap her phone twice—Recent Calls, then Chris A, always the first on the list—for another hit. She'd tell herself that their conversations were that of friends—good friends. But she knew she didn't feel about Chris the way she felt about Evan, or Cody and Jade, or Lulu, Cassie, or Carol. Her heart never pounded against her ribs when any of them called her.

Abby wondered what Karys must think of this constant communication, but she was too afraid to ask, and Chris never volunteered. It was as if there existed a silent understanding to never mention the one thing that would force them to evaluate their supposed "friendship." Perhaps that was the very reason why.

Late into the night, Abby would lie in bed reading and rereading Chris's messages until they pixelated before her eyes. She never texted Chris in the evenings, when she was home, and Chris was always quiet.

One afternoon, Evan loped into Abby's classroom, brushing the door with his knuckles as he did. The class was empty and Abby was marking assignments—or she would have been, if she hadn't been doodling her name with Chris's surname on her desk pad.

Abby Addison. Abigail Addison. Abby Addie. Chris Massey. Christmassy! She was laughing out loud as Evan walked in.

"Hey, what's so funny?"

"Huh?" She sat up with a start, quickly shoving a stack of books over her scribbles. "Um, oh, you know, kids say the darndest things. What's up?"

Evan was leaning on the chair in front of her desk. "I'm heading out soon but just wanted to check if you're cool with me swinging past at seven. Will you be ready?"

Abby stared at him. "Um, what's happening at seven?"

"Abby!" Evan was exasperated. He turned the chair around and sat down in it, backward. "We literally confirmed on the group chat this morning. I don't know how you could've missed it—you're always on your phone."

This morning…this morning. "Oh, yes, sorry. The games night at Cody and Jade's place. Yes, seven's good. What do we need to bring?"

Evan gave her a withering look. "Really? It's all on the group, if you took a moment to actually read it."

"Sorry. I'm sorry. I will."

"And you're leaving your phone at home."

"What? I don't know—"

"It's not a debate. You need a break from that thing, and we all need a break from watching you staring at it all googly eyed."

"I don't do that!"

"Oh, you do."

Abby felt her face reddening. "Fine. I'll leave it at home. It's just—"

"'Really good conversation.' I know," Evan said, mimicking Abby's voice. "And there'll be good conversation tonight." He stood and turned the chair the right way round with a flick of his wrist. "I'll fetch you at seven. Just you. No phono, homo."

"Yeah, yeah, I heard you the first time. Now, go. I have a lot of work to do before I go homo."

Evan laughed. "'Work,'" he said, putting the word in air quotes. "Sure, Little Miss Lovebird. See ya later."

Cody and Jade's place was already filled with familiar faces, and a few new ones, when Abby and Evan let themselves in through the back door.

"The world's best guacamole has arrived," Abby called by way of greeting.

"Yay!" Jade squealed, coming into the kitchen and giving them each a hug. "You can put it in the sitting room with all the other snacks." She lifted the plastic covering, stuck a finger in, and licked. "Oooh, yum! This is amazing, dude."

"Gross, babe," Cody said as she came into the kitchen, swatting Jade's hand away from the bowl. "Who knows where those fingers have been?"

"Well, you should," Jade teased, wiggling her fingers in Cody's face. "Babe!"

"TMI, guys," Evan said, pulling a face. "I think I'll pass on the guac."

"Aww, Evan, I'm just kidding." Jade grinned. "I've washed my hands, promise."

"Who's definitely lying about washing their hands?" said a voice like wind chimes, and Abby turned around. It belonged to a tiny, pixielike human, all delicate features and large brown eyes.

"Oh, you know, just us lesbians talking about our fingers, as usual," Cody said before turning to the others. "Guys, this is my cousin, Drew. She's staying with us for a bit while she figures out how to adult. Apparently, we're supposed to be the ones to teach her. Crazy, I know." She rolled her eyes and shook her head in wonderment. "Drew, this is Abby and Evan."

"Hi!" Drew stuck out her hand and shook theirs in turn. Her grip was unexpectedly strong for such a small creature. "It's really cool to meet you guys. These dorks have told me about you. Can I get you some drinks?"

"See? We've already trained her." Cody grinned. "In lieu of rent money, she's our beer bitch."

"Pretty much." Drew nodded. "Except you forgot to add that I'm also dinner bitch, barbeque bitch, cleaning bitch…the list goes on." She gave a dramatic sigh.

"Just getting you used to the real world, sweetie." Jade shrugged. "You gotta work, bitch. It's called 'adulting.'"

"Oh, yes—they force me to listen to Britney Spears, too."

"Drew!" Cody gasped, putting a hand over her heart in mock horror. "You were supposed to take our Britney secret to the grave!"

"Rookie error, dude. The help always sings like a bird." Drew grinned.

"Britney, really?" Abby said, stifling a laugh. "I wouldn't have pegged you guys as pop fans."

"Ah, well, everyone needs a guilty pleasure," Cody replied. "And we all know what yours is." She winked, and Abby felt herself flushing.

"Firstly, you are all full of shit, and secondly—yes, please, Drew. I'd love a drink. Is that punch? I'll have some of that."

"Certainly." Drew winked, then spun on her heel to get it.

"And won't you grab one for me, too, please? While you're there?" Jade asked.

"I'll have a beer!"

"Me too!"

"God, you guys, you better be tipping!"

"Yeah, yeah, let's start with a free room." Cody rolled her eyes and then grinned sheepishly at Abby. "I'm just teasing you, Abs. Come, let's join the others."

Abby greeted the group as she entered the sitting room—Jon, Alexia, and Chipper were all there, and a few others. She found an empty sofa and sat, trying to catch up with the conversation.

"…So, like, maybe fifty percent of the total cost, if he's lucky," Chipper was saying, shaking his head. The others looked glum.

"Hey, what's going on?" Cody asked, pulling up a dining chair. "When I left you, you were all raucously debating tequila shots. What happened?"

"Yeah, the tequila got us thinking about The Dolphin." Jon shrugged. "Fuckin' miss that place."

"Yeah, me too," Abby chimed in. "What's happening there, anyone know?"

"Probably not a helluva lot," Chipper replied, taking the last slug of his beer. "Roy's payout isn't enough to rebuild it completely, so he may just clear up the area, repair the section he's living in, and leave it at that."

"It's so awful," Alexia said. "Jon and I went there on our first date, like seven years ago."

"Ah, Lex, you can't tell people that! It makes me sound like a total cheapskate."

"You were a cheapskate back then. We all were. We were all broke."

"True." Jon shrugged. "I just feel so bad for the guy. Your poor uncle," he added, looking at Chipper.

"Oh, I didn't know that," Abby said, turning to him. His dark ponytail bobbed as he nodded. "I'm sorry."

Chipper shrugged and stretched his legs out in front of him. His feet, as usual, were bare. "Shit happens. At least he can still live there."

Abby felt a weight on the sofa next to her and turned. It was Drew.

"Here," she said, handing Abby a glass of punch. She smiled sweetly, her small teeth perfectly aligned behind her small, perfectly round lips. Nature's exercise in the beauty of symmetry.

"Oh, thanks," Abby replied, taking the drink. Drew didn't move.

"Is it okay if I sit here?" she asked, all big, innocent eyes.

"Yeah, sure."

"Thanks. I was just checking that you weren't saving it for your boyfriend."

"My boyfriend? Oh, Evan and I are just friends."

"Oh, I'm sorry!" Drew replied, sounding embarrassed. Impossibly, her eyes seemed to grow bigger. She placed a small, cool hand on Abby's arm, the nails short. "I just assumed…"

"It's totally fine." Abby smiled, shifting a little. Drew didn't move her hand. "Pretty much everyone assumes we're a couple. I'm used to it."

Drew's smile returned. "Yeah, I get it. People always think my best friend and I are together, but we're just super close. I mean, she's uh-mazing, but I don't want to date her. She's way too much drama."

"That's a bit of a turn-off in a relationship, I agree," Abby said, to make conversation. She took a sip of her drink. "Oh, wow, this punch is great. Did you make it?"

Drew nodded, her cheeks pink. "Yup. I learnt the recipe in college—basically just everything alcoholic you can get your hands on, plus some Sprite."

Abby laughed. "But nothing creamy, right?"

"Oh, god, no." Drew shook her head vigorously. "I made that mistake once. Curdled the entire bowl. I threw in a couple of cans of fruit to try and hide it, and we all drank it anyway. But the feeling of those curdled bits on your tongue…yuck!"

Abby grimaced. "Well, you nailed this one, so well done."

"Thanks. Here, give me your glass. I'll get us some refills. Keep my seat warm, I'll be right back."

There was a voice in Abby's ear as she watched Drew skip off.

"And that?" It was Jade, sidling in, waggling her eyebrows at Abby.

"Oh, you guys, give it a rest," Abby said with a sigh, swatting Jade away. Why was everyone so desperate to pair her up?

"C'mon, she's cute. Why not?"

"She's definitely not my type, but thank you for being so concerned about my love life. You're such a good lesbian."

"Well, you know I have to try. It's such a waste, you being single."

"That doesn't even make sense. A waste for whom?"

"Don't be like that. You know what I mean."

"I'm very satisfied with my life, thank you. Besides, Drew's a baby! What's she, like twenty?"

"Twenty-two. Not such a baby. And you're not much older."

"There's a big difference between twenty-two and twenty-eight. And I feel like eighty sometimes."

"Here you go!" Drew was back, thrusting out a hand and spilling some of the drink on Abby's arm. "Oh no, I'm so sorry," she babbled. "Let me get some paper towels."

"It's fine." Abby smiled. "Just a bit of a sticky wrist. I'll go rinse off in a bit."

"You sure?" Drew said, concerned. She was like an anime character come to life. "I don't want to mess up your jacket. It's stunning."

"Thanks," Abby replied as Drew fingered the silky purple fabric of the sleeve. She'd taken up position next to Abby once again.

"Yeah, it really is, Abs," Jade said, eyeing it appreciatively. "I actually thought it was Chris's. Wasn't she wearing it that night at The Planetarium?"

"No, she just has the same one."

"The same one?" Jade said, frowning. "How?"

"She sent me this a couple of weeks back, when Snowy was missing. She wanted to cheer me up. She knew I liked her jacket, because…Well, it doesn't matter. I just liked it."

"And you really expect us all to believe there's nothing going with you guys?" Jade rolled her eyes.

"There really isn't." Abby frowned and felt herself getting slightly annoyed. "It was a thoughtful gift, that's all. We're just friends."

"Ah, I'm just jealous of the jacket," Jade replied quickly, picking up on Abby's tone. "I wish we could get trendy clothes in Bay View. Or anywhere nearby that's not, like, a seven-hour drive away. When we get visitors from the city, I literally share my clothing wish list with them."

"Ohhh," Drew said, mouth downturned at the corners, her face thoughtful. "That explains those 501s. You still owe me for those, by the way."

"Oh, right. Take it off the rent this month," Jade said, then winked. "I'm just kidding. I've got the cash."

And just like that, the answer was obvious to Abby. So obvious, in fact, she couldn't believe it hadn't occurred to her sooner. Maybe she just hadn't been ready.

"Guys…" she started as the two bantered.

"You wanted a tip earlier?" Jade was joking with Drew. "Here it is. Get outta Bay View before next season, unless you want to be stuck wearing—"

"Guys!" A bit louder, stopping them both midsentence. They looked at her expectantly.

"I have boxes full of designer clothes at home," Abby said, hesitantly almost, as if she were running the idea past herself as much as the others. "They're…worn, but still in really great condition."

"Okay, and…?" Jade prompted.

"Do you think people—people here, in Bay View—would be interested in buying them? I mean, they're proper couture. A few years old, but they're classic pieces."

Now Abby had Jade's attention. "Really? Designer? Heck, I'll buy some—I mean, if I can afford to. Where did it all come from?"

"Some are mine, and other pieces belonged to my late girlfriend." Better out than in, Abby thought. Anyway, Cody knew the story and she assumed she'd have mentioned it, at least in passing, to Jade.

"Okay, so you *are* gay," Drew said breathily, and Abby frowned. "Sorry," she added quickly. "That's horrible about your girlfriend." She rearranged her baby face into something resembling solemnity.

"Thanks," Abby said and turned back to Jade.

"I'm sure you've heard about it from Cody"—Jade nodded—"And…I think it's time. I've hauled her stuff around with me for two years. It's long enough. And the timing is perfect."

"Perfect? What do you mean?"

"Well…" Abby glanced over to where Chipper and the others were setting up board games. She remembered how they used to gather at the corner booth at The Dolphin, playing Catan until all hours, and regretted avoiding the group for so long because of her ill-placed embarrassment over Cody.

"I'm thinking that the proceeds can go to Roy. To help rebuild The Dolphin."

"What? Really?" Now Jade's eyes were anime, too.

"Yeah." Abby was warming to the idea with each passing second. "Yeah! I mean, all these things, they're just gathering dust. What's the point in that? They're beautiful garments, so damn beautiful. They deserve to be enjoyed. And why not put all that toward a good cause? A great cause."

Jade's eyes were sparkling. Abby had a partner in this, and she could feel excitement welling inside her. As the others drifted off to join the game, Abby and Jade—with Drew barnacled on—huddled closer to discuss the finer details of the plan. It would be a pop-up sale, one day only, so they could take full advantage of the FOMO-factor. Prices would be fair—not too high, not ridiculously low—and customers would be encouraged to donate anything else they felt they'd like to. Jade, a talented graphic designer, would design the invitation, which they'd send out via email and text, and a poster, which they'd print and tack up over town. There'd be cupcakes on offer—a clever trick that Google had once employed to promote its new voice-activated speakers. Abby couldn't remember where she'd read about it, but she thought it was very smart indeed. Free food was irresistible, which is why she'd always promised cupcakes or cookies on the days she really needed her students to attend class.

"Let's pick a date," Abby said, pointing at Jade's phone on a table nearby. "Evan made me leave mine at home." She pretended not to notice Jade's smirk.

"Mmm…" Jade scrolled through her calendar. "It looks like I can do…any single day this year."

"And location?"

Jade pursed her lips. They'd agreed it would need to be somewhere central, but they didn't want to have to pay to rent a space. It would simply eat into their profits.

"I mean, we could just do it at one of our houses."

"We could…"

"Ooh, I have an idea," Drew piped up. "The Dolphin—that's the burnt-out lot you pointed out to me the other day, right?" She glanced at Jade.

"Yeah…?"

"So? Why not do it there? Just imagine this, like, burnt-out building and then these, like, gorgeous clothes hanging there," she said, all shining eyes and gesticulating hands.

"Oh, my god, you're right," Abby said, a mental picture emerging.

"And it would create a pretty powerful association between our sale and what we're wanting to achieve with the proceeds," Jade said.

"It's perfect. It's genius. You're a genius!" Abby beamed at Drew, cupping her face with her hands. Drew beamed back, and Abby quickly pulled her hands away. She didn't want to give the girl the wrong idea.

"I mean, we'd need to get permission from Roy, but I don't see that it would be a problem," Jade said. "And it looks like they're busy clearing all the rubble at the moment, so the space will be usable."

Abby could see it all in her mind's eye. This was necessary. This was good. And Dan would have loved it.

"Oh, my god, we're really doing this." Abby squealed, slightly dazed.

"We are." Jade smiled at her, squeezing her arm. "Let's say two weeks from Saturday?"

Abby nodded.

"This is so wonderful, Abs," Jade said, grabbing her hands. "You're so amazing for doing this. I know it's a huge step for you."

"It is," Abby agreed. "But I want to. It's time. So don't let me get cold feet."

"We won't." Jade squeezed harder. "We all want to see that shabby old shack back on its feet—or flippers, should I say. Come," she said, standing up and pulling Abby up with her. "Let's go tell the others. Chipper's going to be ecstatic. Everyone will."

Chipper was ecstatic. So much so, that he got his uncle Roy on the phone right away to share the news. Roy sounded astonished, but it was difficult to discern his tone over the phone—the speaker rendered it tinny, and the poor signal obliterated every second word—but Abby felt sure there was happiness beneath the disbelief. Evan came over from the other side of the room and squeezed Abby's shoulders. "I'm really proud of you," he whispered in her ear.

Jon and Alexia, both tall, lithe, and lovers of fine fashion, quizzed Abby on her collection.

"Gorgeous jackets and coats, mostly," Abby replied, smiling as she thought about Dan in silk and leather and pure, soft wool. Truly enviable items that she'd be proud to put on display. "And some amazing shoes, too, and jeans…You'll have to see for yourself."

Her friends' excitement was infectious. By the time she climbed into bed that night, having double-checked all the windows and tucking Snowy against her side, she felt something not too far from excitement herself. It would be a fresh start for her, a spring-cleaning that was oh-so necessary and so long coming, but which she was finally ready to undertake.

"No shrines," Dan had said as she'd packed clothes into boxes, her voice ludicrously upbeat under the circumstances. Abby clenched her jaw. She stared out of the window at the oak tree that stretched all the way up to their second-floor apartment and wished they could be leaves on its branches: light and free, dancing carelessly in the breeze. She and Dan would never dance carelessly again.

"They're just silly pieces of fabric," Dan was saying, but Abby knew she didn't really think that. "Donate them. Sell them. Turn them into yoga mats. I don't care, and you shouldn't either." Abby had stared wordlessly. Hot tears seeped from the sides of her eyes and ran down her neck.

"Abs." Dan had sighed, pulling her in close. Her smell was the greatest comfort Abby had ever known, and she inhaled it in great, gasping lungfuls. She wished she could inhale it all and store it forever. "You already have all of me, forever."

Abby smiled sadly at the memory and then rolled over to check her phone. For a brief moment, she almost expected a message from Dan. She'd barely thought about her phone all evening, but now, alone once more, she needed a hit.

Nothing from Dan, of course—or Chris. But there was a text from a number she didn't recognise.

Hey it's Drew :) So cool meetin u. Mayb we can hang sometime? I'll be in town awhile. TTYS :)

Abby tossed her phone back onto her nightstand and groaned. "Oh, Drew, noooo," she muttered, rolling over and rubbing Snowy's soft belly. "You're just a baby. Just a baby!" Snowy stretched, then curled into a tight ball, trapping Abby's hand with her paws and sinking her tiny shark teeth into Abby's flesh.

"Ow, ow, ow," Abby yelped, gingerly extracting her hand. "I get it, Snow! Women are a trap. So, don't make the same mistakes as me," she said as the kitten looked up at her, purring aggressively. "Avoid them at all costs, baby. I mean it. All costs."

CHAPTER TWELVE

The days whizzed by in a haze of preparation for the "Buy a Bargain, Save a Bar" sale. The name was a bit of a mouthful, but keeping things simple was key in Bay View. Sure, prices wouldn't really be bargain, but it was a clever psychological trick, so they went with it. Jade was hard at work designing the creative collateral, and almost every evening was spent sorting through Dan's boxes of clothes.

It wasn't as soul-crushing as Abby had thought it would be. Having sorted through everything with Chris had really taken the sting out of it.

Unexpectedly, Abby found that almost every evening after work, a friend would "spontaneously" show up on her doorstep, arms laden with wine or snacks, professing a random desire to hang out. After the third or fourth day in a row, she realised they must've set up a roster between them—a sort of "Keep Abby company while she sorts through all that dead-girlfriend detritus so she doesn't fall to pieces" rotation—and she felt loved, and immensely comforted.

"I know what you guys are doing, by the way," she said to Cody and Drew one night as she unfolded, appraised, sniffed, and ran her hands over the umpteenth item for that week. But she kept a smile in her voice.

"Whadaya mean?" Cody replied, her voice shrill, her eyebrows shooting up into her hairline. She was a terrible liar. Abby just shook her head, still smiling, and popped another homemade brownie bite into her mouth. "These are great, Drew. Yummy."

Drew grinned. "Glad to know I didn't go to chef's school for nothing."

"Deffahnty not," Abby mumbled around a mouthful of chocolate, already eyeing another.

"Well, there's plenty more where those came from," Drew said with a wink as she scratched Snowy's chin. The kitten, resettled at home, was eating—and growing—like a teenager these days. She chirped with pleasure at each rub and tickle.

"Oh, Drewsky, keep it in your pants," Cody said, rolling her eyes. She was lounging in an armchair and spinning her phone between her fingers. Every few minutes, Jade would text an updated design and Cody would gush over it before showing the rest.

"Look at this," she said now, as her phone pinged. With a sigh, she added, "She's so talented, my future wife."

Cody zoomed in with her thumb and forefinger. "I really think the design has nailed it." She leaned forward and thrust the phone first in front of Abby and then Drew, who was sitting on the floor and leaning back on her hands, legs stretched out in front of her as if she were on the beach. Neither she nor Cody were doing much to help with the clothes-sorting process. Abby was grateful for their company anyway.

"Oh, wow, yes," Abby agreed, glancing at the phone. She was holding up a tailored white shirt with gold-plated collar tips that Dan had worn exactly once, to a wedding. She'd loved this shirt, often running her fingers down its sleeves as it languished in her cupboard, waiting for another opportunity to be worn. "I think we're good to go. I told Jade that ten iterations ago, but something gives me the impression she's a perfectionist."

Cody nodded. "That she is. You don't get to be the creative design lead at an international digital publisher by not being a perfectionist."

"True," Abby said, distracted. This was a terribly tragic shirt.

"Wow, how long did it take you to rehearse that?" Drew said drily.

"Less time than it takes you to rehearse your god-awful pick-up lines."

The youngster guffawed. "Fuck you, old-timer!"

"Aww, I love you, too." Cody grinned back.

Later, after Abby's current guest had arrived home and the girls had shuffled off amid more teasing and jibes, she sat on her bed and picked up her phone. Chris was away on another business trip and Abby told herself that calling her now was okay, acceptable even, because she wouldn't be pulling her away from her family. But that conviction teetered on the edge of a steep precipice, ready to topple right over if Abby interrogated it too closely.

"My little fashion philanthropist," Chris cooed down the line after the second ring. As usual on these trips, she sounded tired, but happy.

Abby chuckled, abashed. The "my" warmed her cheeks.

"Less than a week to go," she replied, filing the "my" away for later. "It's actually happening."

"How are you feeling about it?"

"Good, actually. Strong," Abby said. "Thanks to you."

"Me?" Genuine surprise. "What have I done?"

Abby shrugged, then remembered Chris couldn't see her. "You've been there for me."

And she had been. Chris was not only supportive of the idea, but she'd given Abby helpful advice on cleaning and preparing the delicate fabrics for the sale, pricing them, and staying focused on the end goal.

"I know I had that wobble a few days ago," Abby continued. "But you were right—I just needed to go easy on myself. The next day, I felt surer than ever."

"I'm really glad to hear that, Abs," Chris said, and Abby thought she could hear a smile in her voice. "But this is all you. You're much stronger than you give yourself credit for. I think you're an absolute rock star for doing this."

Abby smiled again. It felt like she smiled a lot these days.

"I thought of you today when I was out shopping," Chris was saying now, and Abby wrapped up this treasure too, stowing it in her memory for later. "I saw a gorgeous shirt that would've complemented you beautifully."

She should have been flattered that she'd been on Chris's mind, but the "would've" brought Abby back to Earth. What were they doing here, she and Chris? This phoned-based folly, this friendship doomed before it ever left the starting blocks? *Friendship—spin another one, Abby.* It wasn't a friendship, and that was the very reason it could only end in pain.

Chris was still talking—she'd moved on to the topic of work, and the clothing sale, and now she was asking about Saturday and Abby had to ask her to repeat herself because she'd been so lost in thought.

"I was asking whether you're following through with that crazy idea to set up shop on that hideous disaster site," Chris repeated. "All that grime so close to those gorgeous clothes. Honestly, it sets my teeth on edge."

"Well, yeah, I am," Abby replied, slightly stung. She didn't like Chris thinking of her ideas as anything less than completely brilliant. "Obviously, we plan to be really careful with the stock. It wasn't my idea anyway, it was Drew's," she added defensively. "And I think it works."

Chris chuckled. "If you're into the whole heroin-chic idea, sure. Who's Drew?"

"New baby dyke in town," Abby said, then, feeling childish, added, "Super cute."

"Oh?"

"Mmm."

"Well?" Chris was impatient now, and Abby felt immensely gratified. "What's her story?"

Abby played dumb. "What story?"

"You're very annoying, do you know that?"

"And you're very impatient, do you know that?"

"As a matter of fact, I *Drew* know that."

Abby couldn't help it—she laughed, and gave in. She loved Chris's quick wit.

"Drew is Cody's cousin. She's in town for a while, trying to figure out life post-chef school."

"Good at making muffins, I take it?" Cheeky.

"I wouldn't know." Across the airwaves, a hundred or maybe a million miles away, she imagined Chris's knowing, slightly lopsided grin and wished she could see it. "But she's got great buns."

"Ahh, and here I was thinking you were a breast girl."

Abby instantly reddened. She squeezed her eyes shut and bit down on her lip, trying to think of a witty response.

"I'm just teasing you," Chris said into the silence.

"Yeah, hilarious," Abby replied feebly, suddenly out of her depth. "I have an early start tomorrow. But I'll talk to you soon, okay?"

"Sure." That easy shrug in her voice.

I...

Miss you.

Wish you knew.

"'Kay. Night."

"Night, doll."

Abby ended the call and pressed the phone to her chest, over the spot where her heart pounded so hard, she could see the phone rising and falling with each beat. By the time her breathing returned to normal, she was sure that Chris was already asleep, dreaming easily.

When Abby at last fell into slumber, her subconscious streamed a chaotic tangle of past and present: silly puns and ice cream cones, suntanned limbs and fairy lights and fingers pressed to lips. And hands— hands gripping until they ached, until they were bloodless and numb.

When she woke up, alone, it was to a life shaped around the absence of it all.

CHAPTER THIRTEEN

"Okay, let's see," Evan said, ticking items off on his long, tanned fingers. "Jon and Chip will bring the tables, Alexia's bringing the Bluetooth speakers—oh, and the playlist. I'm bringing the mannequins and rails, and Cody, you and Jade are—"

"Going to bring all the clothes. Plenty of room in my van. And we'll do the set-up."

It was the evening before the sale, and excitement was running high. The gang was huddling at their base of operations—Cody and Jade's place—to finalise the logistics. The invitations had all gone out, via email and text, and the posters had been stuck up all over town. Roy had even let Abby take over The Dolphin's Facebook page—an almost-forgotten little cavity of the Internet where a few souls still lurked, mostly posting conspiracy theories about Stonehenge. They probably weren't her target market, but Abby was casting her net wide.

But the achievement she was most proud of was getting flyers to most of the kids at school. The principal had been cool about it but he drew the line at Abby printing them with school equipment. Fair enough. So, she and Evan skipped out during a free period to have them done at the print shop.

"Wow, this looks super cool," said the young woman behind the counter. She snapped some gum as she read the flyer. "This is, like, such a sick idea. I'm gonna be there for sure. I dig vintage shit. Especially for charity." She stopped chewing and looked up, glancing from Evan to Abby and back again.

"You gonna be there?" she asked Evan.

"Yep." He grinned, instinctively uncurling his body into his signature stretch, bare skin flashing above his waistband. She looked away, but not before Abby's caught her eyes brushing over his V-muscles.

She blushed and handed the hot, thick stack of flyers to Abby. "No charge for these," she said, smiling coyly at Evan. "See you on Saturday."

"Dude!" Abby high-fived him once they were out of sight.

He shrugged, then flashed his guns. "What can I say? Just doing my bit for charity." And then, high on their victory, they'd popped into a bathing suit boutique, where Evan convinced the owner—a gloriously camp old queen—to lend them a couple of mannequins and a clothing rail for the sale.

"Oh, but oh! I just have to…" he'd breathed as he tried to circle Evan's bulging biceps with his thumb and forefinger. "Oh, but you are a treat!" The only condition was that Evan had to collect them, and return them, in person.

"Did I just…trade my body?"

"I think so," Abby confirmed. "But it's for charity."

Back at school, Abby handed the freshly printed flyers in bright rainbow colours to the kids. "Give these to your parents," she bellowed as they hurtled out of her classroom, waving a stack above her head. She hoped at least a few of the printouts would make it home—those that weren't turned into paper planes or crushed into the bottoms of kids' book bags.

Now, as Abby looked around the sitting room, filled with friends draped over sofas, she felt herself filling with gratitude from the tips of her baby-pink-painted toenails to the roots of her hair. Her friends, her boss, people she didn't even know had all come together over the past weeks to help bring her vision to life. Her life wasn't empty, or meaningless, or even sad. It was full—full of love and hope—and as she watched Evan firing up the gang, and Jade drawing up to-do lists with military precision, and Cody diligently stacking, packing, preparing for tomorrow, she wrapped the moment in silk and filed it under "new memories." *This* was what she needed to hold on to when the old ones rubbed her raw: her new unfurling, tender and green.

"Abs?"

The group was watching her as she snapped out her reverie. But instead of trying to cover it up, she spoke.

"Sorry, I was distracted. I was just thinking about how much I appreciate you all. And love you all." She looked around the room, making sure to look each person in the eye. "Thank you, all of you. I would never have been able to do this without you."

"Aw, Abs," Chip said, striding over and wrapping his arms around her. Her head rested against the soft part beneath his ribs, and she craned her neck up to look at him.

"You're saving our butts. My uncle's butt. The whole town's lazy, barfly butts. Like, dude, you're a legend."

"Total legend," Jade agreed, smiling at Abby. She was sitting with her arms wrapped around Cody, her head resting on her shoulder.

"Well, let's see if I actually pull it off. What if no one buys anything?"

"Never gonna happen," Alexia said firmly, and beside her, Jon nodded vigorously. "I've already picked my top three. And if I could afford more, I would."

"Guys, thanks," Abby said a final time, with all the feeling she could muster. She glanced at her phone to check the time. "I've gotta get home and bake. Those cupcakes I promised aren't going to make themselves."

As Abby gathered her things to leave, Drew sidled up. She smelled sweet and fresh, with something minty mixed in. Hair wax.

"Dude, I can help you bake if you like?" she said, more question than statement.

Abby turned to her, refusal already on her tongue, but something stopped her. The girl was all eyes and hopeful lips, and Abby really had no reason to reject her, except for the fact that she didn't want to fuel the flames of this crush. Her eyes flicked to the living room, where Evan was watching the exchange with a smirk. Abby would have to keep her boundaries very firm.

"You sure?" she asked, and Drew was nodding vehemently before the words were even out of her mouth.

"Totally, dude. There's sweet fuck-all going on around here anyway. And I'm a great baker."

I'm sure you are, Abby thought to herself as she hauled a heavy bag onto her shoulder, filled with clothes and equipment for tomorrow.

"And I'll take that, too," Drew said firmly, lifting the bag off Abby's shoulder as if it were filled with air. "I'm pretty strong." She shrugged even with the bag over her shoulder.

"Okay, Superwoman." Abby laughed. "If you're sure. We still need to walk back to my place."

"I prefer Wonder Woman. And it's, like, five minutes away. Let's go, lezzo."

They yelled their goodbyes and slipped out the back door, but not before Abby caught the knowing looks of Cody and Jade.

"It's not what you think," Abby called over her shoulder as they headed into the dusk. "We're just baking."

She turned to look at Drew for affirmation and was surprised to see the girl looking at her intently, slightly hunched under the weight of the backpack.

"You don't like me very much, do you?"

"Wh-aat?" Abby nearly stopped but then remembered the bag and decided not to ruin Drew's momentum.

"Of course I like you."

"Really?"

"Yeah…you're super cool, Drew. And sweet. Why do you think I don't like you?"

"You're always trying to avoid me, for one." She sounded a little winded, but Abby knew without asking that she wouldn't hand over the backpack. She'd slung it over both shoulders now to distribute the weight evenly, but she was walking at an odd angle to the ground. At least they were heading downhill.

"And you basically never reply to my texts." She sounded hurt.

"You're right. I don't, and I'm sorry. It's rude of me."

She didn't say anything, and Abby figured she hadn't been expecting the acknowledgment—or apology. They walked in silence until Abby's house came into view.

"Thanks for letting me help you out tonight," Drew said, huffing. "I was dying of boredom at Jody's."

"Jody's? Oh! Jade and Cody—I get it."

"Yeah, it's—oh, whoa. What's that?"

There was just enough light still for Abby to see what looked like a large pile of shrubbery on her doorstep, but as approached, she realised it was—

"No way! I've never seen such a massive thing of flowers."

"Me neither." Abby kneeled, bewildered, and touched a petal between her fingers. She'd never laid eyes on a bouquet so extravagant in her life—not in the city, and certainly not in Bay View. "Well, let's get it inside. Figure out what…who it's for."

"Lol, Abs," Drew said, dropping the bag to the ground with a metallic clang. "It's obviously for you. You think it's for Snowy?"

"Hmm," Abby muttered as she hoisted the arrangement into her arms, flowers dipping in every direction, almost completely obscuring the heavy glass vase that contained them.

"Can you get the door, please?" she said, trying to nudge keys out of her back pocket with a free hand. The vase wobbled dangerously.

"Here, let me…" Drew extracted the keys from Abby's pocket and let them in. She felt around in the dark as Abby set the flowers down on the kitchen counter and then, as she flipped on the lights, an explosion of colour: gerberas like burnished sunsets, tangerine roses tinged red at the tips, and lilies, yellow chrysanthemums, and a spray of tiny flowers the colour of oxblood. It was all held in place by a thick black silk ribbon and a card, which Drew gestured to silently, her face a mixture of curiosity and impatience.

Sensing what would be inside but anxious that her instincts were wrong, Abby teased the card off the ribbon. She ran her fingers over the embossed front—this was no cheap, plasticky-feel florist's card. It was fancier, even, than those from the artisanal florist back home, who wrapped his daily bouquets in organic hessian, labelled them "vegan" and "free range."

"Open it already!" Drew was exasperated now, shifting her weight from foot to foot. She sighed.

Abby scowled at her, but she did what she said. Inside, on a cream-coloured card, in pretty black handwriting belonging to a stranger, it said:

Abby, I'm so proud of you. I wish I could be there tomorrow, but I'm with you in spirit. You're one incredible woman! Love, C xx

A heart surge. Sure, "C" could be Carol… But no…no. No, this gesture smacked only of one "C" that Abby could think of, and it wasn't her mentor.

"It's your girlfriend, isn't it?" Drew shattered the silence. She was leaning against the doorframe, one eyebrow cocked.

"I don't have a girlfriend," Abby replied, placing the card back in the envelope. She'd have to park the glow for now and revel in it later, after Drew left. Annoying.

"No, I know, but I mean the chick that everyone teases you about. Kerry? Or something." Short, nervous laughter. She was smart enough to know she was treading on thin ice.

"Chris."

"Yeeees. Chris."

They blinked at each other. Abby didn't want to share this moment with Drew. Drew clearly wanted her to.

"Yeah, they're from her. But, like I keep saying, she's just a friend." Except this time when Abby said it, the words sounded empty and unconvincing, particularly in light of the evidence before them, red and vibrant as fire.

Abby smiled brightly and shoved the vase to the side of the counter. "More importantly right now, we have a lot of baking to do."

"Yeah, we do." Drew reanimated, standing up straight and trotting into the kitchen. She stopped, planted her hands on her hips, and surveyed the surroundings. "Okay so, in my kitchen, I'm in charge," she said with a stern voice, looking very much like she was in her kitchen, and very much like she was in charge.

"Oui, chef!" Abby saluted.

"Great. Now, here's what I need…"

Several hours and many, many pounds of sugar and flour later, Abby and Drew collapsed on the sofa, their clothes crusty with batter, cold beers in their hands. It was late, close to midnight, and the house was thick with heat and the sweet, slightly cloying smell of baked goods.

"Did we really just make a hundred cupcakes?" Abby said, slightly dazed. She looked over at the kitchen, where a wall obscured her view of the tower of pans stacked for cleaning. Future Abby's problem.

"Dude, one hundred and twenty," Drew corrected her. "Ten batches."

"Shit, people have to show up tomorrow. Otherwise, we'll be eating them all."

Drew blew out her cheeks, pretending to be nauseated. "I think I'm good for cupcakes for a while. You were a great sous chef, by the way."

"That's good to know." Abby grinned. "In case I ever need to find a new career path."

Drew winked, and Abby felt her cheeks flush. In the kitchen, the youngster had gone from doe-eyed pixie to master baker: skilled, focused, and decisive. She'd taken charge with the confidence and composure of someone infinitely well-versed in their trade.

"I think I was born a baker," she'd said, weighing flour on a scale Abby didn't even realise she owned. A frown of concentration briefly creased the flawless skin of her forehead, and Abby had felt a mix of envy and something else. Something less easy to place.

Drew took a sip of her beer, not taking her eyes off Abby.

"What?" Abby asked, lifting her fingers to her face. "Have I got batter on me?"

Drew looked pensive. "No. I was just wondering how you're planning to deal with…" She trailed off, eyes searching the walls and curtains as if the words might appear there. "I mean, have you thought about…the fact that everyone in this town will be wearing your dead girlfriend's clothes? Isn't that going to be weird for you?"

Abby pressed a thumb and forefinger into her eyes. For a moment the world turned black, and she could have been anyone, anywhere, with any story she liked.

"Yeah, I have thought about it. It might be weird. I guess I won't know until it's happened." Her voice sounded weary, even to her.

Drew shifted, leaned in closer to Abby. "We don't have to talk about it if you don't want to," she said, placing a hand on Abby's knee. Abby didn't move it, or shift away, and Drew left it there, small and warm.

"Thanks. I don't really want to."

Drew was close enough that Abby could smell the wax in her hair, notice the few tiny dark stubs of eyebrow hair that needed plucking. Now, she was moving her fingers gently, stroking Abby's knee, and Abby felt something surge inside her that she really wished wouldn't. She looked down, watching as Drew's hand stroked her and triggered feelings that started to spread all the way up and down.

"Look, Drew, I…"

"Yeah…?"

"I don't want you to have the wrong idea."

"And what would the wrong idea be?" Her eyes were playful as her fingers moved higher now, to Abby's thigh, and Abby shifted, but somehow the movement only brought them closer.

"That…well, I just need you to know that I'm not looking for… anything…serious."

Drew smiled, slowly moved her hand up higher—dangerously high now—and looked Abby in the eye.

"Oh, thank god," she whispered, and Abby thought she caught a glimpse of dimple, but it was just that cocky half-smile in the dim light. "You're hot, Abby, and I just really, really want to fuck you. That's it."

Abby opened her mouth and closed it again. What did she want? Her body, at least, seemed to know. No-strings sex? How long had it been? Months. Almost years. Would it really be so bad?

And then, somehow, the gap between them closed completely. Abby wasn't sure if she'd moved closer or whether Drew had pulled her in with her small, strong hands, now firmly gripping Abby's sides. Drew's lips were on hers, and Abby's hands were moving up and under Drew's T-shirt, feeling the soft curves beneath, familiar in shape, foreign in every other way. She'd always loved the feeling of pushing a hand under a bra, cotton or wire or elastic briefly pressing into the back of her fingers, and then the delicious silkiness of a breast, an erect nipple, the fullness of that soft, delicate flesh beneath the fingers.

Abby thought about how nice it felt to be touched like this, how good, how necessary. And Drew was a delight: expressive, enthusiastic, comfortable in her skin. It hadn't been like this with Cody, and she tried to push the thought out of her mind. They were cousins! But it was different with gays…

As batter-crusted clothes dropped to the floor, Abby noticed that Drew's pale body was covered in tattoos of every description: tiny ones behind her ears, large intricate etchings on her stomach and thighs, whimsical stick-and-poke jobs on her arms.

As she tongued Abby's nipple, Drew murmured, "This is cute," and Abby was taken aback until she realised she was talking about Abby's own tiny tattoo—half tattoo, really. Her one and only permanent inking, under her rib cage.

"What is it?"

"Oh, um, I'll tell you some other time," Abby said vaguely.

The truth was that it was an embarrassment. It was supposed to be a heartbeat gently drifting into a flatline and ending with their initials: *A.D.* Abby Dan. After Death.

It was supposed to exactly match the one Dan would be getting too. That's what they'd asked for when they skipped into that little tattoo place on the coast one sunny, salty day. It had been a spontaneous move, as was so often the case with Dan. But it had felt so right. Abby loved the idea of an inking that was meant to link them together forever, a daily reminder of the love of her life.

Dan had gone first. Abby had chickened out halfway through. Dan's design was complete. Abby's wasn't. A lot of things hadn't turned out the way they were supposed to.

"Yours are beautiful," Abby said, wanting to shift attention from the half-finished story under her ribs. She meant it, though she wasn't really here for the scenery.

Drew seemed to sense it, and soon she climbed on top and pressed herself into Abby, nothing but the thinnest wisps of fabric separating their flesh. Abby felt a bolt rush through her as Drew slowly ground, hot and wet, into Abby, her eyes fixed on Abby's, her body glistening with sweat. Roughly, Abby yanked down her own panties, then Drew's, and grabbed a small, taut buttock in each hand. She pulled Drew down harder, flesh on flesh, rising up to meet her, pressing, rubbing, thrusting. She needed more. Her hands had missed this, and they were eager to get to work as she slipped in a finger, then another, until Drew was riding her hard, her back arched, her own fingers finding their way deep inside Abby.

It had been *so* long. "Drew, I'm gonna—"

"Not yet!" she cried, pulling her fingers slowly out, letting her thumb linger, hard, for a few exquisite seconds.

"You bitch." Abby gasped, and Drew laughed, catching Abby's wrists as she reached up to grip Drew's hips. She pressed them above Abby's head, breathing hard, grinding slowly on top of Abby. Then she dipped low, bringing her breasts to Abby's mouth. And Abby—like the drought victim she was—sucked and licked and tongued like her life depended on it. Drew's skin was sticky and salty with exertion, her nipples hard and dark as her breasts pressed into Abby's face. Abby reached to gather them to her mouth, but Drew held her wrists firm above her head.

"Uh-uh." She teased Abby's lashes with her nipples, traced her ear with a tongue. "Not yet," she breathed.

Finally, Drew dipped her head down, moving lower and lower with tongue, lips, fingers until, at last, those plump, heart-shaped lips found their sweet spot. And there, they teased and played until Abby couldn't take it anymore, shoved her fingers deep into Drew's hair, and begged.

Afterward, as Abby lay against the pillows, Drew stood and began gathering her clothes.

"Wait, Drew. You don't have to…" Abby trailed off, barely able to sit up, her drenched body still trembling.

Drew paused, topless, a rumpled T-shirt dangling from her fingers. "Yeah?"

Strings or not, Abby just wasn't that girl. "It's so late. Why don't you just stay? In a totally non-U-Haul kind of way."

"Okay." She shrugged, and now they lay back to back in Abby's bed in their underwear, Drew breathing lightly, Abby awake thanks to the wail of a siren at, what? Five a.m.? She felt sticky, her eyes dry and sandy with exhaustion. Snowy lay between them, gnawing on a bit of Abby's hair.

Carefully, Abby edged out of bed, loath to wake Drew. Last night—well, a few hours ago, really—had been fun, but she had no intention of lazing in bed over coffee or breakfast with the girl. She took Snowy with her.

Chris's magnificent bouquet was the first thing she saw as she entered the kitchen, and with a jolt, she realised she hadn't thanked her yet. Quickly, she fed her mewling kitten and then crept back to her room, carefully disengaging her phone from its charger as Drew slept on.

With the card in one hand and her phone in the other, Abby returned to the sofa. She read the words again, ran her fingers over them, even though she knew Chris hadn't written them herself. It was just some anonymous florist with pretty handwriting. Still. It was the sentiment.

She unlocked her phone, typed up a message, deleted it, typed another. It was five thirty. Too early to message? But she was too tired—physically, mentally, emotionally—to play the game. If Chris was truly just a friend, she'd send the message without overthinking the phrasing, the timing, the perfect use of X's or emojis. So instead, she took a photo of the flowers and captioned it with a row of heart-eye emojis and a message of thanks. She hit send and tossed her phone behind the scatter cushions. She was too exhausted for post-send anxiety. So, there were some advantages to being worn out.

Into the shower. The steaming-hot water helped to revive her a bit. She dressed, put on some makeup, dried her hair. It was still so early, six-ish, and when she checked her phone, she could see that Chris had read her message, delivered at 5:31 a.m. No reply, though. Chris was a dawn riser, but this was early even for her. The idea of calling her floated vaguely through Abby's mind—she could do with Chris's encouragement before the big day—but she quickly dismissed it. Not appropriate, on any level, especially right now with Drew asleep in her room.

Instead, she returned to the sofa, coffee in hand, and settled in with Snowy on her lap. Outside, daylight was creeping in, smearing the sky navy blue. The bougainvillaea swayed slightly, and as Abby stared outside, she hoped it didn't mean wind for today. It was still *so* early. There was so much…time…to kill.

"Abs? Wake up, dude!"

What the…Who the fuck?

"We gotta get going. The girls are here!"

Oh, god.

Abby shot up, disorientated.

"Wha…? Oh, fuck," she mumbled as her brain caught up with her body. It felt like climbing up a waterslide the wrong way.

"What time is it?" she rasped, blinking in the daylight. She could tell by the brightness of the day that early morning was long past.

"It's time to guh-oh," Drew replied, elongating the word and kneeling down to hand Abby a mug of cement-coloured coffee. Some slopped onto the floor as Abby took it. Far too sweet.

"Ah, thanks. Shit, I was awake so early, and I must've—hey, are those my jeans?"

Drew grimaced.

"And my shirt?"

She wrinkled her nose. "Sorry, I didn't have time to go home and get fresh clothes. I hope it's okay." At least she had the good grace to look sheepish.

"Yeah, sure," Abby grumbled. She didn't know if she was more irritated by the fact that Drew had commandeered her wardrobe, or that she looked stupidly cute in Abby's clothes.

"I've done all the dishes, loaded the van..." Drew was saying, straightening. "We're pretty much good to go. We're just, basically, waiting for you."

"Shit, okay," Abby said, getting to her feet, smoothing her clothes. Her phone tumbled to the floor and she bent to pick it up, pressing the home screen to light it up. "Uh, thank you," she said distractedly to Drew, squinting at the notifications. Three missed calls from Evan. Nothing else. "I really appreciate everything you've done. You didn't have to do all the cleaning, too."

"Yeah, yeah, thank me later," Drew replied with a sniff and a shrug, her cheeks pink. "Now, go! It's your thing and you're gonna be late." She looked pointedly at the phone.

"Okay, I'm going," Abby said as Drew grabbed her shoulders and steered her down the hallway. "Two minutes. *Two* minutes!"

It was cool out, the sky pasty and grey like cold porridge. It reminded Abby of the day she drove to Carol's house in the rain, the day her life didn't change so much as it began—really began. But today, there were no torrential downpours, no gale-force winds, no thunderstorms to change the course of her life. Just a weak threat of drizzle as they drove the very short distance to the old Dolphin Inn. Silently, Abby worried that the poor weather might keep people away. What if no one showed at all? Bad coffee, lack of sleep, and mounting anxiety all collided in the pit of her stomach, and she clenched her jaw to keep the nausea at bay.

Dan would think of this as an adventure. I have to do the same.

Evan was setting up mannequins when they pulled up, and articulated limbs jutting out at impossible angles. Against the backdrop of a burnt-out hotel, it looked more like something out of an episode of *Dexter* than a clothing fair.

"Nice of you to show up," he said, looking pointedly from Abby to Drew as they hopped out of the van. "Here," he said, handing her an arm. "You're better with the ladies than I am."

Busying herself with the plastic limb as the others offloaded the van, Abby felt herself begin to relax. The crew was hard at work setting up:

Cody and Jade were lugging trestle tables to the flattest spots of ground they could find, and Jon and Alexia—tall, laughing, dressed almost identically as always—were ostensibly helping to arrange the clothes. Really, they were putting aside the items they wanted to buy. Against one of the remaining walls, Chipper was hanging the large canvas sign that Jade had been working on for several nights. *BUY A BARGAIN, SAVE A BAR!* was painted in luminous rainbow hues, adorned with ribbons and sparkling sequins and glitter. It fluttered in the light breeze, bold and brilliant against the dull tones of the burn site.

Abby smiled to herself as the arm finally popped into its socket. It did feel like it was all coming together. She just had to trust.

"Where should I set up the cupcakes, boss?" Drew asked, a large box wedged under her arm. She was chill, regular old Drew, as if she hadn't been eating Abby out just a few hours ago.

"Um, maybe that table, over there?" She pointed to where Cody and Jade were trying to align a dusty wooden top with the rickety trestles beneath. "People will see them as they arrive. Bribery, you know?"

"Gotcha," Drew said, saluting with her free hand, then she turned on her heel and nearly collided with Evan, who was walking in their direction with a hand behind his back.

"Sorry, dude!" she said, spinning away. "Things to do."

"Nice jeans," he called after her, and without turning around, she gave a thumbs-up. Evan grinned at Abby. "So, she finally wore you down, huh?"

"Oh, give it a rest," Abby said, suppressing a smile as she picked up another limb. "It's just some fun."

"Well, I came over here to say good for you."

"Thanks, dude."

"High five," he added, pulling the plastic hand out from behind his back and dissolving into fits of laughter.

"Oh my god, you are such a child."

"High five," he insisted, shaking the hand over Abby's head, his face creased with laughter. "Don't leave a dude hanging."

Abby rolled her eyes, half-heartedly slapping the hand because she didn't feel like indulging Evan's silly joke but knew he wouldn't relent until she did.

"Can't you let it—"

An ominous *crash* stopped Abby midsentence, and they both spun around to see a collapsed trestle table, several horror-struck faces, and a tragic pile of cupcakes, frost-side down, in the dirt.

"Sorry, Abs!" Drew called, waving her arm frantically above her head. "My bad. It wasn't the good batch, at least."

"Guess you can call it a 'snack-cident,'" Cody quipped, grinning sheepishly. "We'll sort it out, don't worry."

Abby turned to Evan and grimaced. He reached out with the plastic hand and patted her shoulder.

"Don't freak out, Abs. It's all going to be fine. I promise."

And Evan, it turned out, was right. The toppled cupcakes weren't a harbinger of disaster, and actually, the day turned out to be something of a roaring success.

By the time the first customers began dribbling in, Abby's friends had turned the dreary lot into a trendy vintage scene, bursting with colour and alive with music and laughter. Bountiful potted plants, procured from Cody and Jade's garden, brought vibrancy where there'd been lifelessness before. The mannequins were dressed in Dan's magnificent coats and decorated with jewellery from Jade's own collection of quirky costume pieces. Chipper had transformed the pile of unused limbs from eerie to cheery by draping them with scarves and placing brightly frosted cupcakes in the hands.

"I can't believe it," Abby marvelled to Jade as a banjo-heavy playlist floated through the air. "Thanks for bringing the speakers, by the way," she added, putting an arm around Jade's waist and squeezing her close.

"Oh, friend, this has been such fun," Jade replied, squeezing back, and suddenly, without warning, Abby burst into tears. "Oh, honey." Jade wrapped her in her arms, swaying gently from side to side. "I'm sorry. This must be so hard for you."

"No, no, it's not that," Abby said, embarrassed as she tried to compose herself. "It's you guys. All of you. And all of this." She gestured at the scene before them: Cody and Drew chatting animatedly to customers, Jon holding up a full-length mirror for shoppers to appraise their reflections, Evan chatting up the girl from the print shop, who'd shown up as promised. She was clutching several of Dan's signature white T-shirts in her hands, and nodding as Evan spoke, his muscles flexing as he ran his hands far too slowly through his hair.

Even Roy had shown up. He stood awkwardly on the outskirts, his hands jammed deep into the pockets of his faded brown chinos. In the distance, a broad, Lycra-clad shape was making its way over. Moira Fresh. She was waving animatedly and calling "Yoooo-hooo!" as she approached. A large shoulder bag was wedged under her arm.

Abby wiped her eyes with the heels of her hands, gave a deep sniff, then grinned at Jade.

"I love you guys," she said, and then, after giving Jade a final squeeze, she headed in Moira's direction.

"Wonderful, Abigail, just wonderful, all of it," Moira was saying as Abby approached her. A tuft of caramel-coloured fluff poked out from under her arm. The tuft growled as Abby got close, revealing a snaggle tooth and one small, rheumy eye hidden beneath a fringe.

"Oh, ignore Jonathan," Moira said, waving a bangled wrist. "He's a real grumper." She peered under her armpit. "A *real grumper!* Aren't you, Jonathan? Yes, you *are! A real grumper!*"

Jonathan glared at Abby from under his fringe. Abby backed away.

"Well, thank you for coming, Moira," she said. "It's so great to see the town supporting Roy."

"Of course!" Moira said emphatically, waving at Roy in the distance. He waved back less enthusiastically. "I truly want to see The Dolphin Inn restored to its former glory. Roy is such a *special* man."

"Mmm, he is."

"Sure, these items aren't really to *my* taste," Moira continued. Beside her, mustard-coloured cigarette pants clung snugly to a mannequin's waist, a leopard-print bandana slung loosely through the belt loops. "But what do you think of this scarf for Jonathan?"

"Oh, uh, for Jonathan? I think, perhaps…"

"You're right—it's perfect! I'll take it. How much is it?"

She handed over more than double the amount, and when Abby protested, Moira placed a warm, heavily jewelled hand over Abby's. "What's important is that we're here to *support Roy*. As much as we can."

"Well, please take a cupcake," Abby said, plucking one from the table next to her. "They're absolutely—"

"Oh, no, not with my diabetes, Abigail, but thanks all the same." Moira pressed the bandana into her handbag and then leaned in conspiratorially. "We'll put it on at home later, when Jonathan is feeling a little more relaxed," she said in a stage whisper. "Now, if you'll excuse me, I'm going to catch up with Roy. Ta-ta, Abigail!"

The initial trickle of visitors gave way to a steady stream of customers throughout the day, and by the time the late afternoon sun turned the sky pale orange, tabletops and mannequins were bare. Only a few items remained. Abby couldn't believe how far word had spread. There were locals, of course, and faces she recognised from The Planetarium, but there were also people she'd never laid eyes on before.

"How did you hear about our sale?" Abby asked a fedora-wearing skateboarder with pale pink hair who had chosen several denim items and a pair of sneakers.

"I saw it on Lara's Instagram story this morning," she replied as she counted out notes.

"Cool," Abby replied, having no idea who Lara was, or that anyone had taken to social media to share news of the sale.

"We never get things like in Bay View," the girl continued, bundling the items into her backpack. "Like, this stuff is amazing. Where did you get it all?"

Abby smiled and said she just had an eye for designer pieces. Only her close friends knew the backstory, and they'd agreed it didn't seem necessary to share it.

Even more surprising than the turnout, though, had been the donations. Almost no one had left without opening their wallets—even if the fashion hadn't appealed to them, even once the cupcakes had run out and the tinny sounds of banjo wore thin.

The oddly matched parents of studious little Poppy had rolled up midway through the day in a loud, backfiring heavy-duty truck with the branding *Woods' Construction and Design* along the side. Theirs was the most successful construction company in Bay View—which was a generous way of saying the only one—and together they built, designed, fitted, and decorated every major and minor construction in town. He was the muscle, but everyone knew she was the guts in the business.

"Oh, sweetheart, this is just gorgeous," Mrs. Woods gushed at her husband as she stroked a faux fur stole the colour of a fennec fox. With her slender legs, elongated torso, and tiny waist, she was the perfect match for many of the items, and she swept through the sale like a magnet, drawing item after item into her arms until she came to rest at the pay station at the end. Breathless, she dumped the pile of clothes on the rickety table. Mr. Woods traipsed up behind her. Short, stocky, and bald, he looked like he wouldn't be out of place in a Guy Ritchie movie, glowering down the barrel of a sawn-off shotgun. His hair seemed to have migrated south, curling dark and wiry above the neckline of his polo shirt and covering his arms in a thick, furry blanket.

"Sorry." Mrs. Woods beamed at Abby as she straightened up. "I'm not sure I've left anything for anyone else!"

Abby smiled politely as she began folding the clothes. As she lifted a moleskin blazer from the heap, a faint but familiar scent rose to her nostrils, hitting her in the chest, the back of her throat, behind her eyes. Suddenly, everything burned. Her chest clamped shut.

Just breathe. Breathe. Breathe, she told herself. She folded the clothes as quickly as she could.

"You know," Mrs. Woods was saying as she fished out her wallet, the movement causing a heady floral scent to engulf Abby. Her chest eased. "You just don't find such exquisite items here, so far from…civilisation!" With a dazzling smile and a flick of her bleached blond extensions, she handed over a wad of cash. It was far too much, and she refused change.

Mr. Woods leaned his carpety arms on the table. "Seeing as I couldn't find anything here to fit me, I'd like to donate some materials to Roy. Anything he can't cover himself. And my guys 'n' me, we can help with the rebuild on the weekends. We got some time." He straightened up and pulled a business card from his back pocket. He handed it to Abby with his short, stubby fingers.

"There's a lot going on here today, but ask him to call me next week, yeah? We can get started whenever he's ready. We miss the place. We wanna get it sorted."

"Oh, Mr. Woods, this is…Sheesh, this is incredibly generous of you," Abby stammered, taking the card. "But don't you want to tell Roy yourself? I'm sure he'd want to thank you in person. He's here… somewhere."

"Nah, no," Mr. Woods replied quickly, holding up his hands and shaking his head. "Let him call me. After all this is finished."

"My husband's a bit shy," Mrs. Woods explained, leaning in. "Not so good with great big displays of emotion, you know." He smiled awkwardly as he gathered his wife's purchases and made a beeline for the truck. Then, with a wink and a wave, she was off behind him, her blond waves bouncing as she trotted off.

Evan came up beside her as Abby stared after them. "What was that about?" he asked through a mouthful of cupcake. "These are great, by the way. You should keep Drew. She's a way better baker than you."

"Hey!" Abby jabbed him in the ribs. "How do you know I didn't bake those?"

"Because I've tasted your baking."

He skittered off as Abby scowled in his direction. But nothing could dull her mood now. It was midafternoon, and they'd sold most of their stock. But more to the point, Woods' Construction's generous offer meant that the reconstruction wasn't a possibility or even a probability, but a certainty.

"Guys!" Abby yelled across the lot, beckoning to the others to come over. "You won't believe what's just happened…"

* * *

Bath. Bed. Snowy cuddles. And at least twelve hours of sleep. That's what Abby was planning as they broke down the sale and packed up Cody's van. A long, hot bath with mustard salt to ease her muscles and a glass of wine to ease the rest of her.

"We should really celebrate," Drew said through a yawn as she dropped a trestle to the ground. It clattered loudly as it hit the gravel.

"I agree," Chipper said, also yawning. "Dammit, Drew, I caught your yawn!"

It was sunset, and the team was exhausted but high on the victory of the day. Going home seemed like an anticlimax, but Abby couldn't imagine summoning the energy for socialising. She'd had a handful of hours of sleep. Between that and the emotional stress of today, she felt like she could sleep for a week.

"I have an idea," Cody said, coming up and placing a hand on Abby's shoulder. "We dump all this shit at home, grab a few beers, and come back here to celebrate. Just a quick toast to The Dolphin."

Abby pursed her lips and looked around the group. They stared back hopefully.

"No pressure," Jade added. "But we've fucking earned it."

"I agree. And I dig that idea," Alexia said.

"All right, let's do it," Abby agreed, and the others whooped and high-fived. They were right: bed, bath, and half a day's worth of sleep could wait. Today's achievement deserved to be celebrated. "But I need to feed Snowy first."

Back at the house, Abby hopped out of the van and started offloading her things: hangers, pegs, the detritus of the day. To her surprise, Drew clamoured out of the van behind her. Abby saw Cody and Jade exchange glances in the front.

"Are you not, uh, going home?" she asked, hoping her voice sounded lighter than she felt.

"Yeah, I am. But some of my stuff is still here. And I thought I'd help you offload the van. I'll head home after drinks…if that's okay with you?"

"Yeah. I mean, yeah, sure. Thanks."

"Hey, if you can't get rid of her, just call the pound," Cody quipped from the van, grabbing a stray hanger and pretending to yoke Drew with it.

"Ha, ha, very funny, dickhead," Drew said, ducking out of the way and giving Cody the finger.

"Break it up, you two," Jade said, leaning over Cody to wave goodbye to the girls. "You're cutting into our drinking time. We'll see you there soon, right?"

"Yep," Abby replied with more enthusiasm than she felt. "Thanks guys, for ev—"

"Oh, god, shut up, already," Cody said as started pulling away. "You've thanked us, like, a billion times."

Snowy was waiting just behind the door as Abby opened it, and she gathered her up, planting kisses all over her as she walked through the house and flipped on the lights. Drew came in behind her, her arms full of Abby's things.

"Just drop it all," Abby called as she made her way to the kitchen. "Don't worry about where. I'll sort it all out."

"'Kay!" Drew called back as Abby opened some cat food, grabbed some beers out of the fridge, and scratched Snowy's head as she ate. She listened to Drew pottering around—bringing in bags, dropping bits and pieces in the entrance hall—and wondered about her motives.

They'd been on the same page last night, so why was she starting to feel a little…cuffed?

"Dude." Drew poked her head into the kitchen. "I left my phone in the van. Can you ask Codes to bring it?"

"Sure," Abby replied as she pulled her own phone out of her backpack. See? You're way overthinking this, she told herself as she typed a quick message to Cody. *She just called you "dude." Even friends with benefits are still friends.*

She fired off the message and held the device in her hands, staring wanly at the screen. She hadn't had a moment to check it all day, but even after all these hours, her last message to Chris still stared at her from the chat screen, pixelating before her tired eyes, still double-ticked, still unanswered.

A knock at the door startled her. How long had she stood here staring at the message?

"I'll get it," Drew called from the sitting room. "It's probably Cody."

"Cool," Abby replied, her eyes burning. She needed to keep moving or she'd fall asleep where she stood.

She heard the sounds of the door opening, low voices, and then Drew appeared in the doorway of the kitchen.

"It's, uh, for you," she said, jerking her thumb in the direction of the door.

Abby frowned. She wasn't expecting anyone, and her next booking was only in two days' time. A shot of panic through her body. Had she forgotten about a guest? Got her dates mixed up? She mentally ran through her calendar as she hurried to the front. Nothing she could think of.

At the door, it was indeed a guest.

But not a guest she'd forgotten about. Not a guest she could *ever* forget about.

She smelled her before she saw her. Florals, spice, leather.

Abby stood frozen in place, and with a wild pulse constricting her throat, she croaked, "Chris?"

The woman smiled wanly, her face pale in the early-evening light.

"Hey, Abby," she replied, her voice weary and thin. She was beautiful, and something else. Sad, perhaps. Lost.

Abby opened her mouth to speak, but nothing came out. She was trying—and failing—to bridge the gap between reality as she'd experienced it in her kitchen just moments before, and reality now, as the flesh-and-blood form of her imaginings stood before her, very real, and very much present. Questions tumbled through her head—What are you doing here? What's going on?—but she couldn't formulate the words.

She wished she could reach out and hug her. Or grab her hand or stroke her hair. Feel the realness of her against her fingertips. But it was all she could do to just keep breathing.

Abby's phone slipped from her sweaty fingertips, clattering to the ground and breaking her trance. As she stooped to pick it up, her head swam.

"My mother had a stroke," Chris said as Abby straightened up. "Sometime yesterday. Well, that's when we think it happened."

"Oh, god," Abby said, the sounds scraping up from her larynx. "I'm so sorry."

"She's at Newtown General Hospital. I had to come here to get some of her things, and I thought I'd see if you were home. I'm sorry, I didn't think to call ahead. You have a guest." Her eyes slid over Abby's shoulder, and Abby turned to see Drew hovering just behind her. She'd completely forgotten she was there—or even existed, at all.

"Oh!" Abby said quickly. "No, Drew's not a guest. What I mean is, she's just on her way out."

"*We're* on our way out," Drew corrected her, stepping forward and holding out her hand. "I'm Drew. Sorry about your mom."

Chris scarcely touched Drew's hand as she flicked her eyes up and down the girl. Then she glanced at Abby and raised her eyebrows, almost imperceptibly, just enough for Abby to read their meaning. So *this* is Drew.

The whole interaction took a matter of seconds, but it felt like hours to Abby. Why, oh why, had she tried to use Drew to make Chris feel jealous?

Finally, the sound of a car pulling up. Doors opening. Voices. Doors slamming.

"Hey, girls," Abby heard Jade call as they made their way up the path. "We wanted to make sure you weren't going to bail on us."

They stopped in their tracks as they reached the door, confusion plastered on their faces as they looked from Abby to Chris and back again. Cody was the first to recover.

"Chris, hey! I didn't know you were coming to town."

Abby watched with envy as the girls took turns to hug her. It was so easy for them to simply lean in and wrap their arms around Chris's shoulders, to press their torsos together, to brush their cheeks against hers. Something like acid rose in her throat and she swallowed hard to make it go away. Instead, it just felt thicker.

Chris smiled tightly as she pulled away. "Yeah, I didn't realise either, but here I am."

"Do you want to join us?" Cody asked, but her voice faltered. The girls didn't know what they'd walked in on, but they could sense that something wasn't right.

"We're celebrating the sale today," Jade added quickly, too enthusiastically. "But I'm sure Abby's told you all about it."

Chris turned to Abby, her face even paler. "I'm sorry, Abby, I haven't asked you—"

"No, it's all good! Really. You have your own stuff to deal with."

Her brain finally shaking off its inertia, Abby turned to Drew. The girl was still lingering at her shoulder. "Why don't you go ahead, and I'll meet you there? You can grab the beers from the kitchen counter."

Drew frowned. She looked hurt, and Abby felt bad, but she reminded herself that she owed her nothing. She'd been nothing but clear with her. And she desperately didn't want these worlds colliding.

"Yeah, dude, come with us," Cody added, and Drew grudgingly fetched the drinks from the kitchen.

Cody raised her eyebrows at Abby while they waited for Drew. "We'll see you there in a bit?" she asked, but what her eyes said was: *Dude! What the fuck?*

Abby smiled through a clenched jaw and nodded. "Yeah, sure. Wouldn't miss it."

And then, to Abby's unending relief, they all piled into the van and left, and it was silent after a few seconds, and she breathed for what felt like the first time in hours.

Then she turned to Chris and opened her arms and felt the warmth of the woman's body against her own. She felt Chris's own arms wrap around her back and pull her closer. Thought she could feel their hearts beating against each other's but knew that it was only her own heart pounding violently against her ribs, her own pulse straining against the walls of every artery and vessel and vein.

"I'm so sorry about your mom, Chris," Abby whispered over her shoulder, her eyes squeezed shut, her tongue tasting the cool night air.

But I'm so happy to see you.

Chris didn't say anything. After a moment, she disentangled herself, took a deep breath, and smiled—really smiled.

"Glass of wine before you go out?"

CHAPTER FOURTEEN

"The worst part is that I just feel so confused about what happened. And guilty. So guilty!"

Abby twirled spaghetti listlessly around her fork. It was Monday, and they were sitting at their usual spot along the edge of the school's soccer field. The pasta fell off the fork. Abby sighed.

"Sorry. I know I've been going on and on about this. I just need to know what to do."

Evan pushed aside his empty plate and leaned forward on his arms. "I don't think there's anything you can do. Or should do," he said, adjusting his baseball cap as he squinted at her in the bright sunlight. "I think you need to give her the space to deal with her mother."

Abby chewed on her lip. "You're probably right."

"I'm definitely right. Look." Evan sighed and leaned back in his chair, arms folded across his chest. "I know you don't want to hear this, but I'm gonna give you some tough love, okay?" He continued without waiting for Abby to reply, "You. Need. To Move. On. What happened doesn't really mean anything. Besides, the woman is married!"

"Not married."

Evan shot her a sideways glance. "Oh, right. 'Basically married' I think is how you put it? At best, you're wasting your time. At worst, you're setting yourself up for some major heartbreak."

Evan's words were a sucker punch—not because he was wrong, but because he was saying all the things Abby had feared herself. Saying them out loud made them real and impossible to ignore. Abby pulled in her lips and said nothing.

Evan continued, "I know we've been teasing you about Chris, but this is an unhealthy situation. And what you're hoping for is never going to happen."

"I know you're right."

"Look," he said, finally softening as he straightened up and put a hand on Abby's forearm. "I think you're being really hard on yourself. You feel guilty because you're happy she's here, and I think that's understandable. It's human. Don't beat yourself up about it, okay? But the other stuff… Abs, you gotta let that shit go."

"What about what she said?"

Evan shook his head as he slowly blew air out through puffed cheeks. "Yeah, I dunno. But I think you've gotta try to put it out of your mind and move on."

"I guess so," Abby said, but she didn't guess so. Not in the slightest.

That afternoon, she planned to grade assignments while her class completed their comprehension test. But, when the timer shrieked after thirty minutes to signal the cut-off time, Abby realised she'd done nothing more than stare out of the window and think about Saturday night, the night Chris had returned.

While no one could be certain, it seemed Cookie Addison had had a stroke on her way to the kitchen at some point during the evening. When her neighbour Colleen couldn't raise her on the phone, she thought she'd gone to bed early. But, unable to sleep for worry, she'd gone to investigate in the early hours of the morning. That's when she'd discovered the unconscious Mrs. Addison on the kitchen floor, a plate of food strewn all around. Blood was oozing from a crack on her forehead, and her mouth was ajar, but she seemed to be breathing. An ambulance was immediately called.

The siren I heard at five a.m., Abby had realised as Chris spoke. No wonder she had never replied to Abby's message. She probably didn't even remember reading it.

"I could tell, more from what the doctor didn't say on the phone than from what she did, that things don't look good for my mother. The least I could do was be here."

"I understand," Abby said, reaching for Chris's hand and wrapping it in her own.

In the silence that followed, Abby thought back to the hospitals of her past: the doctors, the drips, the painkillers, the metallic balloons.

Nothing had helped. Sometimes, it had felt like it all made it all worse.

"Let's just go to a beach and lie there until I die," Dan had said once through cracked lips as poison dripped, dripped, dripped into her veins. "It would be less cruel than this, surely?"

Chris was here to watch someone she loved die.

And Abby was so happy to see her, she felt physically ill with guilt.

"Where are you staying?" Abby asked, hating herself for even asking the question—for thinking of ways to cancel her guest reservation for two days' time. Then she felt stupid when she realised that Mrs. Addison's empty home would now be the obvious option. Chris would have no more need of Abby, and therefore, there was nothing more tying them together. It's what Abby had feared since she first picked up her phone to begin this pointless pursuit in the first place.

But Chris, of course, knew nothing of Abby's inner turmoil. She was pragmatic. "It makes the most sense to stay close to the hospital," she said, staring straight ahead, taking a slow sip of wine. "I booked a hotel room on the way to the airport. It'll probably be a shithole, but it's not like I'm here for a vacation."

The disappointment flowed icy cold in Abby's gut, immediately followed by guilt like burning coals.

"Yeah, that does make the most sense, for sure."

Abby pulled her hand away and hoped Chris didn't see it tremble as she wedged it between her thighs. She wanted to study Chris's face for hints of words unspoken, but instead, she swept her gaze to the wineglass in her hand, her eyes catching the thick metal rings on her fingers. She cleared her throat.

"And, uh, what about Karys?" she asked, already knowing the answer. "Is she not going to join you?"

Chris made a strange, bitter sound, something between a strangled laugh and a sigh.

"No." Chris drained her glass. "No. Karys is not going to join me." She set her face into a fake arrangement that Abby supposed was meant to portray excitement, or perhaps elation: toothy smile, eyebrows shot all the way into her hairline, eyes wide as caves. "She's preparing to move our lives to the other side of the world!" she said with forced cheerfulness. "So, I suppose you could say she's pretty busy."

Abby blinked quickly. She swallowed and willed her voice to work, because she knew she'd need it again soon. They'd never discussed this during all their conversations, and Abby had been able to push the nauseating possibility from her mind when Chris had said they wanted to take Saint Jamie international.

"I know, I know," Chris continued, mistaking Abby's silence for gainsay. "It's not a fair thing to say. Not when all she's ever experienced from my family has been rejection, and pain, and downright awful behaviour." She stared into the garden, its shapes almost indiscernible now in the dark. Her eyes, when she turned back to Abby, were misted over. "I still haven't told her that my mother asked after her. I haven't had the strength for that conversation. We haven't spoken much…about all this."

She shook her head as Abby offered her more wine, holding her hand over her glass to indicate she was done.

"No," she said firmly. "I'm keeping you from your friends and your celebration. Tell me how today went."

"It was amazing!" Abby grinned, a shot of genuine happiness diluting the unease saturating her body. "We still need to work out exactly how much we raised, but it was much more than we expected. So much more. And the donations!" She began tallying the items in her head as she spoke. "Chris, people donated money and building materials and their time. Even equipment. The owner of the liquor store store—dammit, I can never remember his name—he has old refrigerators he isn't using, just taking up space in his stockroom. I'm still trying to wrap my head around it all. We had no idea…just no idea what an all-out success it would be. Plus, there's hardly any clothing left. We sold pretty much everything."

Abby was breathless. She realised that despite the current situation, she felt happier and more fulfilled than she had in years. She was helping to make some sort of difference in this town, even if it was just a place for people to drink cheap beer and eat stale peanuts. She had purpose and drive and fulfilment and friends. Suddenly she *did* want to see them and hug them and toast to their incredible accomplishment today. Sure, there would still be holes to plug—with money and materials and insurance payouts and, yes, more donations—but Abby knew that what they'd achieved today was the difference between relegating The Dolphin to the annals of history and reviving it. She felt dizzy with joy.

Chris was beaming at her, and she held her hand up for a high five. When Abby reached forward to slap it, she savoured the brief brushing of their skin. "You're something else, doll," Chris said, whistling in appreciation. "An entrepreneur. Seriously."

"I'm not sure about that," Abby said, abashed. "My friends were all behind me. They worked so hard to pull this off. And you," she added quickly, with a shy smile. "All of your help and encouragement really powered me through this."

"Oh, shut up and own it." Chris stood, brushed her trousers with her hands, and looked pointedly at Abby. "You're a fucking force, Abby Massey. Got it?"

They made their way to the front door, and Abby could feel her jolly mood evaporating with each step. She dreaded saying goodbye. Newtown was two hours away. Mrs. Addison was in a coma. She had no idea when she'd see Chris again. She felt sick and guilt-ridden at the thought.

It only made it worse that as they faced each other on the porch, with the fresh night air curling around their necks, Chris touched Abby's arm and looked at her pensively for a long moment. "You know, it's funny. I…I missed you." She shook her head, looked away, chuckled softly. It was as if the realisation had caught her by complete surprise.

She squeezed Abby's arm a final time, then turned down the path to the rental car that would take her down a difficult road, and two hours out of town.

* * *

There was one person in whom Abby had yet to confide, someone who she knew would be honest, fair and trustworthy. And by Monday evening, she knew she needed to make the call.

"Abigail!" the voice exclaimed after just a couple of rings. "Lay and I were just talking about you. Were your ears burning?"

"Something like that." Abby chuckled, feeling immediately lighter upon hearing Carol's soothing and melodic voice. She lay back against her pillows and wedged her phone between her shoulder and ear. Snowy, her belly full of dinner, lay fast asleep and purring on Abby's chest.

"Let me put you on speaker, my dear, so Layla can hear, too."

Abby heard Carol's footsteps, the clattering of kitchenware, water running.

"Carol, I'm sorry—are you guys having dinner?"

"Dinner? What's that? All we do these days is drink kombucha. Though I feel like I shouldn't tell you that—you'll never want to visit us. Hang on, dear. Layla! Abby's on the phone." A muffled response, more footsteps, and then Layla's voice floating across the airwaves, smooth and deep.

"Abigail," she said in her husky voice. "We miss you. How are you?"

For the sake of politeness, Abby had planned to get the small talk out of the way first. But at the sound of kind voices on the other end of the line, it all tumbled out in a messy, convoluted word-vomit: Chris, Mrs. Addison, Karys, the saga of Snowy, and how it had all led to the strange…what exactly was the relationship between her and Chris?

"Emotional affair." Carol slapped a tabletop.

"Well, no, because I don't think she feels the same way—"

"I agree," Layla spoke over Abby. "Emotional affair."

Abby could tell she wasn't going to win this one so she carried on, the story culminating in Chris's unexpected arrival on Saturday night, and her own current state of confusion.

"Fucking lesbians," Layla muttered when Abby finished. "Always complicating things. And overthinking things! I tell my friends I miss them all the time."

Abby remained sceptical. "So, you think it was just a friend thing?"

"Yeah, I do."

"Well, I don't buy it," Carol declared. "I think there's more to it. Much more. I think it *is* complicated, and I don't think Abby's imagining things."

"Exactly. I mean, when she said—"

"But the romantic aspect is out of the question," Carol continued. "Completely." Another slap.

All three of them were silent for a moment.

"I mean, I can see the appeal," Layla said at last. "It's exciting, she's gorgeous, she's in your house, brewing you coffee and being all city-slicking-businesswomanlike—your very own Bette Porter. Us lesbians, we could fall in love five times a day if we tried."

"Ten, probably," Carol cut in. "Without even trying."

"Easily."

"This isn't like that. It's different."

"Fine, it's different. But she's taken, sweetie. So, no matter how different it may feel, it's the same old story."

"And if something does happen," Carol said, dropping her voice into her low, solemn lecturer tone, "what will you be left with? A big, stinking mess. A whole lot of regret and guilt. Heartache. Horrible, terrible heartache."

Abby said nothing.

"Oh, Abby, darling," she said into the heavy silence that fell, her voice gentler now. "Darling."

One word, two syllables, and Abby came undone. Guilt, confusion, anger, pain—her feelings were drowning her, and Abby gasped for air. She was supposed to love Dan forever. How could she possibly have feelings—whatever they were—for someone else? Someone else *taken*? How dare Dan leave? How dare Chris just…arrive in her life like this, being kind and vulnerable and…and…taken? How could she have let this happen at all—losing sight of Dan, focusing on something so unattainable? What was wrong with her?

This was the reason she'd hesitated to tell Carol, Abby realised. Carol had an all-access pass to the raw, gaping void that was now, and would forever be, a part of her. Most people wouldn't know it was there, or if they did, they'd have no idea how to get it to it. Carol had the map. And with a single word, she'd landed right on the X.

"I know you're terrified of being vulnerable again," Carol was saying now, her voice soothing and soft. "I know you're terrified of experiencing anything close to the pain you've survived. I understand. I was there. I witnessed it. I felt it."

"Now you're fixated on someone you cannot be with, and that makes perfect sense, really," Layla added gently. "But there is real risk of pain here, Abby. You don't have to be in pain all the time, no matter how familiar it may feel."

"Oh, my god, how are you guys so wise?" Abby choked out through her sobs.

"We're your fairy gay-mothers. It's our job," Carol replied, and Abby could hear the hug in her voice.

"So, what do I do? Say, 'Goodbye, Chris, see you never'?"

Both women were silent. They'd helped her understand the riddle, but she would have to solve it herself.

"God, why can't I have nice things?" Abby whined. It broke the tension and everyone laughed.

"Darling, do you like her?" Carol asked. "I mean, genuinely care for this woman?"

Abby took a breath to answer, then stopped. If she took away the attraction, desire, the frisson of excitement, did she genuinely care for Chris? The woman, the human being behind the designer clothes and polished appearance? The woman behind the steadily crumbling walls?

"I do, actually. I really do."

"Then be there for her. She needs friends now, possibly more than ever. So be there for her. Be her support, with no ulterior motives.

You've been where she is. You understand what she's going through, and it sounds like she could use all the support she can get."

"That's crazy," Layla interjected. "Far too risky. It could never work."

"Risky? Oh, come on. Look at us, Lay."

"It was different with us."

"Different how? You were in love with me for years before the notion of a romantic involvement even occurred to me. Give the girl some credit."

"It's not about credit, it's about risk. It's too much of a gamble after everything Abby's been through. It was hard for me to be around you, and I hadn't been through all Abby has," Layla insisted.

"But imagine if there's a real friendship under all this?" Carol countered. "It happens all the time with queer women. Our initial feelings confuse us. Do we want to be her, or be with her?"

"Or both," Layla cut in.

"Correct. That early chemistry is powerful and overwhelming and… bewildering. And when we don't take the time to interrogate the feelings from an emotionally mature place, we destroy something that could've been a great friendship. Or," Carol continued in a low, warning tone, "we don't even give it a chance to begin with."

But her partner remained sceptical. "I hear you, my darling, but I still think the risk is too great. Hell, the chemistry is too great. If nothing else, Abby needs a ton of time and space away from Chris if a genuine friendship can develop."

"Look, Abby cannot be with Chris, I agree. But that doesn't mean they have to lose each other altogether. Not if they really care about each other. Look at her friendship with Cody."

"That was a completely different situation," Abby finally cut in, adding her voice to the debate about her love life. "I was never in love with her."

"That's exactly my point," Carol said emphatically. "Cody was in the position you're in now—in love with you. But now that she's over it, you guys have a great friendship which would otherwise have been lost."

And it was all thanks to Chris, Abby thought.

"I suppose that's a good point."

"No one's saying it's going to be easy. And if it's too hard, that's okay. It's o-*kay* to walk away," Layla emphasised the word. "And to take care of your own emotional well-being first. In fact, it's essential, Abby. It's part of growing up. But you don't have to feel trapped by this situation. You get to make decisions. You get to take back your power. You're freer than you realise. And so much stronger than you're giving yourself credit for."

"Abby, you've already been through the very worst a person can go through. You survived it. You've got this, do you know that?"

Abby pushed her lips to the side. "Mm-hmm," she replied, because a realisation was occurring to her, if only she could grasp it, bring it into focus, like one of those 3D images. She knew the answer was in front of her.

She had it.

"Guys. Guys!" she cut in as the women continued talking. "I gotta go. I think…I know what I need to do."

She said her goodbyes and promised to call them again soon, and then double-promised to not to do anything silly. Yet before she even quite realised it was happening, she was crossing her fingers and squeezing her eyes shut and remembering how Lulu had once told her, "Just enjoy the good moments, and we'll get through the bad ones together."

She was probably going to do something silly.

CHAPTER FIFTEEN

Abby peeled a limp slice of pickle off the soggy bun and licked the remnants of mayonnaise off her fingers. She disliked how intensely sour it was—the kind of sour that makes your jaw seize up and your glands shoot saliva into your mouth. Usually, she asked them to leave the garnish off, but it had been so long, she'd completely forgotten. Three years? Four? Longer, probably.

Dan had detested fast food.

Obviously.

Abby had always had a soft spot for it.

She rubbed her greasy fingertips on a napkin and squashed the bun back onto the meat with her palm. Dan would've loved Bay View: no fast-food joints for miles and plenty of space to grow your own vegetables.

"A thousand dinner options to choose from, and this is the one you pick?" said a wry voice behind her, tired but unmistakable. Abby's heart leapt at the sound.

"How about a 'thanks for driving two hours to see me'?" Abby scoffed without meaning it, watching as Chris collapsed into the plastic chair opposite her.

There were, of course, not a thousand dining options to choose from in Newtown. Due to proximity and sheer lack of viable competition,

Newtown was "the city" in comparison to Bay View, but really, it didn't take much: a couple of fast-food places, a hospital with more than one X-ray machine, and a shop that sold Steve Maddens.

Chris dropped her head into her hands and rubbed her face. When she looked up again, her hair stood out at all angles, and Abby realised it was the first time she'd seen her without makeup. She looked younger, more vulnerable somehow.

"God, I'm finished," she said, her eyes sunken. "I can't believe you came out all this way. It's…It's really kind of you."

Abby shifted in her seat. "Yeah, just to drag you to this place," she replied, suddenly feeling exposed. She forced her mouth into a half-smile.

"I was just kidding about that," Chris said, a faint, familiar grin creeping onto her face. "I mean, it's a good break from the hospital, even if the walls are the same colour."

Abby scanned the interior of the restaurant. She knew that sickly, pale yellow shade all too well. Fifty shades of pain.

"Hospitals are just so shit, and you're here alone," Abby said with a shrug, finding it hard to meet Chris's eyes. "I figured you could do with a friend."

Chris shook her head as she took a deep breath, her eyes wide. "You have no idea," she said, leaning back in her chair. "Thank you, doll. I really appreciate that. And even this." She smiled, gesturing with her chin at the tray on the table. "Whatever it is."

"Oh, god, I forget what a snob you are, Miss McNopes."

Her mind snapped back to the moment in her kitchen all those months ago, and she flushed. Chris's expression hadn't changed, and Abby wondered if she'd forgotten all about it.

"How did you get here, anyway?" Chris asked as she unwrapped her burger with two claw fingers as if she were defusing a bomb.

"I borrowed Cody's van. She's super chilled," Abby said, watching Chris's progress on the burger. "That's a regular cheeseburger, by the way. Felt like the safest choice since I didn't know what you'd want."

With trepidation, like a child biting into broccoli, Chris nibbled the burger.

"Oh, this isn't the worst," she said with surprise around a small mouthful of food.

Abby laughed, relaxing a little. "That's the whole point of fast food. It's fucking amazing. You have some sort of mental block. You should really get over it because you're missing out on a whole world of deliciousness."

"Nope," she said, munching. "Designer clothing and fast food cannot coexist."

"You've gotta get over that, too," Abby teased, and then she watched Chris eat because she'd lost her appetite. She was going to give this "friendship" thing a solid go, but it wasn't going to be easy.

Behind them, meat sizzled aggressively in the industrial-sized kitchen—another batch of patties destined for flame-grilled mediocrity. A woman barked out an order number for the third, or maybe fourth time. Someone dropped a bucket of cutlery. A child wailed.

"Look, if you're done, let's get out of here," Chris said, her top lip curling as she glanced around the restaurant. Chaos. Noise. Strip lighting. It was a lot, even for Abby.

"Yeah, let's," Abby agreed, standing and scraping her chair back. You couldn't hear the sound above the racket. They dropped their rubbish into the bins, dumped their trays on the stack, and slipped out into the cool night. Gay efficiency, Abby thought to herself and smiled.

It was just after eight, almost dark but still pleasant out as they ambled across the street to the large park. Looming over it, square and squat, was Newtown General Hospital.

In silent agreement, they walked over to an empty bench and sat. They watched as a final few stragglers walked their dogs and finished their runs as dusk ebbed into darkness.

After a while, Chris leaned back and stretched her legs out in front of her. This evening, she wore brogues and a black sweater, and trousers that could safely skip an ironing. In other words, a more casual outfit than Abby had ever seen her wearing before. In the moonlight, the bare skin of her ankles looked almost translucent.

"My mom has come out of her unconscious state somewhat," she said at last, as if commenting on the weather.

"That's good, isn't it?"

"It can be. But they aren't sure yet of the extent of the damage, or what it means long term."

A jogger ran past, breathing heavily, a heart rate monitor strapped to his chest. Abby could see his puffs of breath against the darkness.

"So, what now?" Abby asked, watching the jogger and his steamy breath getting farther and farther away.

Chris sighed. She leaned her head back on the bench and looked to the sky, as if the answer may appear in the constellations. A celestial guidebook to adulting.

If only.

"More monitoring. More waiting. But fortunately, there's no real need for her to be all the way out here. They'll probably transfer her back home, to Bay View Clinic."

A wave of relief crashed over Abby, swiftly followed by a tsunami of guilt. How could she feel happy at the expense of a sick old woman? Even someone who'd behaved as despicably as Cookie Addison.

"I'll come and get her settled in," Chris was saying. "But more than that…I don't know. It could be days, weeks, months…I have no idea what to do. Am I supposed to give up my whole life? Or tuck her in and say goodbye? Take her home with me?" She laughed—a bitter, mirthless sound, the same she'd made a few nights before when she spoke about Karys.

"It's all just so fucked up." Her voice was softer now, thick with emotion, and Abby could hear that tears weren't far from the surface. But when she leaned forward to offer an empathetic touch, Chris shot straight up and shook her head, wiping her nose roughly with the back of her hand. She turned her back to Abby. "No, I'm fine. I'm just frustrated, you know? Being here, inexplicably bound to this woman who really, I mean, didn't even love me, let's be honest." She spat the words into the night. "And yet, for reasons beyond my comprehension, I feel duty-bound to her, like a dog who keeps being kicked but keeps coming back."

Abby, standing too, reached out once again, more gingerly now. This time, Chris didn't resist when Abby's hand landed just below her shoulder. She could feel Chris's body trembling with emotion. The touch felt awkward, but it was all Abby had. After all, what could she say?

"I hate her, and I hate myself for being here. It's pathetic."

"No," Abby said firmly, her hand tightening around Chris's arm. With effort, she swivelled Chris toward her, urging her to face her. Reluctantly, the woman turned her stormy face to Abby.

"Listen to me, Chris. You're entitled to all the uncomfortable, angry, confusing emotions you're feeling right now. And yes, even hateful feelings."

"Gee, thanks, Dr. Massey," Chris said with a sniff, and Abby jerked back in surprise.

"Hey, c'mon. All I'm saying is you're not pathetic for being a decent human—a better human than your mother ever was to you."

Chris stared at her, her eyes hard and unblinking.

"That's something to be proud of," Abby said gently. "Not to shame yourself for."

"Well, that's not what Karys—"

"Forget Karys."

Chris stiffened under her touch. "Forget my partner of twenty-five years?"

"N-no." Abby felt the air between them growing thick, and her pulse began to quicken. "W-what I mean is, she's your wife, and she's not being very supportive while you're—"

"*Not. My wife.*" Chris's face grew even darker, and Abby flinched. "Have you even listened to anything I've said?"

"Of course I have, but I just think—"

"Karys is *not* my wife. I've told you that. And she's not—You know what? Forget it."

"Forget what?" The conversation was going off the rails, and Abby was desperate to claw it back. She gripped Chris's arm tighter, but the woman jerked away.

"Never mind. You're not my therapist, Abby."

"I'm not trying to be, but I care—"

"You don't know anything!"

Abby froze midsentence, feeling fire in her cheeks. If anyone understood that grief didn't give a shit about innocent bystanders, it was Abby. Logically, she knew this wasn't personal. Chris was grieving and raw, and Abby was simply the closest target. The problem was, logic had left the chat. She didn't have enough emotional distance from Chris to take the hit.

Tonight had been a terrible idea.

"Look, I really appreciate you coming all the way out here." Chris's voice was cool. "You didn't have to."

"Well, as you can see"—Abby lifted her arms from her side and let them fall again—"I am here for you. I know that probably doesn't mean very much. I know I'm probably just some FortyLinks host to you."

For a moment, the women locked eyes. Abby's cheeks burned as silence pulsed between them. At last, Chris took a breath as if to speak, then shook her head, dropped her gaze, and turned away.

Abby swallowed hard. "I should be on my way…"

"Yeah…" Chris agreed, her gaze firmly on the perimeter of the park and the brightly lit hospital behind it.

Later, as Abby drove home, disappointed and shaken, she thought back to her own days, hours, months spent in hospitals under fluorescent lights, imprisoned by yellow walls and dotted ceiling boards. On some level, she knew what Chris was going through, but if she were truly honest with herself, she really had no idea. Their situations were entirely different. Tonight, she had shot off her mouth when she should have just listened. Friends listened. Abby had pushed too hard when Layla and Carol had only hours before cautioned her to take space.

But also, Abby reasoned as her cottage came into view, her dejection giving way to indignation, friends didn't lash out at friends who were just trying to help. And she really had been trying to help.

Friendship? Ha. She cut the engine, then climbed out and slammed the door in irritation. She was exhausted, annoyed, and more than a little stung. Maybe being Chris's friend wasn't such a great gig after all.

CHAPTER SIXTEEN

"Oh, my god. Is that…Drew?"

Abby frowned as she and Evan made their way across the parking lot to the exit of the school. As always after the final bell, the kids were shrieking and running around like wind-up toys. They whizzed past in little packs and huddled in clumps around the gates. But still, now that Evan had pointed her out, it was impossible to miss Drew, not towering above the kids but sticking out like a different species altogether. A species that wore acid-wash jeans and faded Metallica T-shirts.

"Yeah, I think it is. I wonder what she's doing here."

"Really?" Evan stopped and gave Abby a withering stare. "You wonder what she's doing here?"

"Yeah, yeah, okay, okay," Abby replied, embarrassed. "What should I do?"

"I dunno, go and talk to her, I guess. It's not like you can pretend you didn't see her. Her hand's about to fly off, she's waving so hard."

That was a bit of an exaggeration—Drew was waving at a pretty normal strength—but Abby took in the whole picture and accepted his point.

"Heyyyyyy, Drew," Abby said as they approached, aiming to sound friendly but not overly bright so as not to encourage this type of behaviour.

"Hey, guys!" Drew, however, did not try to hide her brightness. She leaned against a wall with forced casualness.

"Um, what are you doing here?"

"I was just, like, walking past as school let out," she said, tipping her head to one side, "and I thought I'd see what you—you guys—were up to now. Wanna hang out?" But her big eyes were fixed only on Abby. "Everyone works during the day. It's so boring in this town."

"It's called being an adult. You'll get there one day," Evan teased, and Drew scowled at him.

"Ignore him," Abby said conspiratorially. "Everyone else does."

"Oh, really?" Evan shot back, his muscles flexing as he yanked the straps of his backpack. "Not Michaela, for one."

Drew frowned. "Who's Michaela?"

"The girl from the print shop," Abby said helpfully. "Mr. Baywatch here has a date tonight."

"Yep! So, sorry, but I can't hang out. I'm not sure how you'll get over it."

"Cry myself to sleep, probably," Drew said, punctuating it with a stuck-out tongue. Abby laughed.

"I can't either, I'm afraid," said Abby. "I have a quiz tonight with my friends from back home."

"Back home? They're visiting?"

"No, we play online. On Skype."

Drew's eyes lit up, and inwardly, Abby panicked. "It's pretty lame, actually," she hurried to add. "You know, boring, old-timey quiz questions. We're obviously getting old."

"It doesn't sound lame at all. It sounds, like, kind of fun."

Shit.

"I would literally kill for a change of scenery, even something like, you know, a quiz or whatever."

Abby slid a look at Evan, so subtle that, to anyone who didn't know them, the subtext would be imperceptible. Evan shrugged with his eyes and Abby sighed on the inside.

"I mean, I guess you could join if you really wanted to, but it's not that—"

"Yeah, I'd love to!" Drew pushed off the wall with one sneakered foot, and with a little hop, landed next to Abby.

They headed toward home, Evan loping off with a "have fun, you guys" as they reached his street. "You, too" they unisoned with meaning.

"Hey, how about I cook us dinner, since you're hosting?" Drew said with a studied casualness that made it clear she'd been thinking about it for some time. Abby couldn't help but feel a vague twang of tenderness for the girl.

"Nah, it's okay. We'll order in." Abby turned to look at her, squinting as the midafternoon sun hit her eyes. "You don't always have to be doing something for me, you know."

"Yeah, I know," Drew replied quickly. "But…ordering in? In Bay View?"

"Basically, it's just Luigi bringing you a pizza."

"Is his name really Luigi?"

"No idea." Abby laughed. "Actually, I think it's Rob. But wouldn't it be so great if it were? I like to think it is."

They were both laughing as they arrived at Abby's place. After the roller coaster of the past few days, she found herself enjoying the girl's easy presence. Drew set about fixing them drinks, cuddling Snowy, opening up the patio doors to let in the mild afternoon breeze. When Abby plopped onto the sofa, Drew handed her a beer.

Some hours later, after Abby had disentangled her limbs from Drew's and set up her laptop for the quiz, she grabbed her phone and punched in the number for Luigi's. Her tummy rumbled as her finger hovered above the call button.

"I'm ordering," Abby called to Drew, who was shoulders-deep in the fridge looking for more beer. "Whatcha want?"

"Pineapple and pepperoni, please," she yelled back.

"Wait, what?" Abby dropped her arm to her side as she ambled into the kitchen. "You're a pineapple on pizza person? I thought you had good taste."

Drew laughed as she handed Abby a drink. "I could say the same about you. You're a cider person?"

"And to think, I've made out with that mouth."

"Jeez, you make it sound like I'm contagious."

"Hello? Hell-oh?" a tinny voice interrupted their banter. Abby slammed the phone to her ear.

"Oh, uh, hi, sorry. Can I order a pizza for delivery? Yeah, pepperoni please, with pineapple on one half only. No-no, the *pineapple* on one half only. Pepperoni everywhere."

Drew rolled her eyes at Abby and ambled into the sitting room. She poked Snowy in the belly until the kitten retaliated, grabbing her wrist with her tiny razor claws. Drew squealed.

"Okay, break it up you two, it's quiz time," Abby said, blowing fur off the keypad of her laptop. She logged into the call as Drew settled onto the sofa next to her, her thigh touching Abby's. Abby shifted. She hadn't told the group about Drew—not that there was anything to tell—and she was disinclined to do so now.

After the initial chit-chat among the group, and mercifully few looks askance, the game began. Drew's general knowledge was lacklustre at best, but she was a good sport, and the group seemed charmed by her spunkiness.

Was she charmed by her? Abby found herself wondering. She wasn't sure, and that comforted her. Could she be? Also not sure. Good. That was the safest place to be.

A rap on the door, short and loud, and Abby jumped up. She'd zoned out for a moment and the sound had startled her. "Pizza's here."

Drew looked up at her from the sofa. Her legs were crossed, a bottle of beer wedged between her folded legs. Snowy was curled up in her lap.

"Want me to go?"

"Don't be silly." Abby scoffed, eyeing the scene on the sofa. "Try not to get us kicked right out of the game, okay?"

"Can't promise anything," Drew called after her.

Just as they predicted, Luigi himself—or Rob, actually—was hunched on the doorstep, holding a large pizza box with oily fingerprints all along one side. His grubby apron was stretched across his paunch, and Abby wondered whether he'd left pizzas baking in the oven while he did a quick delivery run.

"Mmm, this smells amazing," Abby said as he thrust the warm box into her hands and garlicky steam wafted out of it.

He grunted the price, then felt around in the front pocket of the apron for change. He was out of breath from walking up the hill, and Abby saw a sweaty sheen on his forehead.

"No, it's cool, you can keep the change," she said, and then quickly added, "I mean, for your staff or the tip box, or whatever." Did one tip the proprietor?

He mumbled his thanks and turned to leave, using one hand to propel himself off the doorframe.

It was only then that Abby noticed that behind him in the dark, the entire time, had been Chris.

"Hi," she said as she stepped forward into the yellow pool of light spilling from the house. Her voice was soft. One might mistake it for shyness if one didn't know Chris Addison very well.

Abby blinked and said nothing. She couldn't get used to Chris randomly showing up in her life.

"Abby?"

"Yeah?"

"Please, can we talk?"

Chris was close now, just a foot in front of her, and Abby was rooted to the spot.

"I…um…" Her body felt frozen, but she managed to take a few jerky steps backward. "I'm busy, and we're about to eat dinner. As you see." She thrust the box in Chris's direction. Chris ignored it.

"Just two minutes. That's all I ask," she said, and Abby was surprised to see that her eyes were pleading.

She clenched her jaw. Unclenched it. "Two minutes," she agreed stiffly. Were these words really coming out of her mouth? Certainly, she had been unsettled by their last encounter, but until now, she hadn't realised how much Chris's outburst had hurt her. Or perhaps she hadn't wanted to admit it. Either way, she allowed herself to be guided by this newly emboldened version of herself. "Just give me a minute."

Inside, Drew was trying—and failing—to answer an eighties-themed music question when Abby slid the box onto the table. As wafts of pepperoni filled the air, Snowy opened her eyes, yawned, and sniffed the air.

"Dig in," Abby said, pointing at the pizza. "I'll be back in a minute. And the answer's Bon Jovi."

Drew frowned. "Where are you going?"

"Just—I'll be back in moment," she replied quickly and slipped out of the house before Drew could ask any more questions. As she shut the door behind her, she could see the girl's confused face staring out after her, framed by the living room windows.

Chris was sitting on the steps, her arms resting on her knees. She turned as she heard Abby approaching, and she looked so beautiful and so vulnerable, Abby felt her earlier resolve crumbling.

Dammit.

Abby stood in front of her, arms folded stiffly across her chest.

"You aren't going to sit?"

Abby shook her head. "Nope."

"Are you in a rush to get back to your girlfriend?"

Abby gritted her teeth. Part of her wished she'd never told Chris about Drew. Another part of her was glad she had.

"She's not my girlfriend."

"It's quiz night, tonight," Chris said, motioning to the house with a jerk of her head. How had she remembered that?

"Yeah," Abby said, frowning. "Good memory."

"So, let's see…" Chris pursed her lips, pretending to think hard. "You and Drew, you're Team…Drab." She looked up at Abby and smiled, proud of her quick joke, but Abby refused to give her the satisfaction.

"Sometimes drab isn't all that bad," Abby quipped back, dropping her hands into the back pockets of her jeans. "Sometimes," she added pointedly. "A little drab is better than a whole lot of Crabby." She knew she was being mean, and that Chris didn't deserve it, but it was definitely safer this way.

Chris's smile faded, and after a moment, she looked away. When she looked back at Abby, her face was serious.

"Abby, look. I'm really sorry about the other night. That's what I came here to say. Please," Chris said, patting the step next to her. "Sit?"

"I've gotta get back…" Abby said without much conviction.

She already knew she'd sit before Chris murmured, "Please…" once more.

Just before she lowered herself onto the step, she glanced back into the house and caught a glimpse of Drew in profile, chewing listlessly, her demeanour dulled. As her focus shifted, she saw her own reflection staring back at her, her jaw clenched, her lips tight.

She sat, refusing to look at Chris. Instead, she clamped her arms around her knees.

"Abby," Chris said, and Abby could tell she was looking at her. "I'm so sorry for the way I treated you the other night. I know you were only trying to be supportive, and the way I behaved wasn't very nice."

Abby took a deep breath, inhaling Chris's familiar scent. She knew she owed her an apology, too, but Chris continued.

"The things you said…well, everything was a bit overwhelming for me in that moment."

Abby winced. "I'm sorry, too. I overstepped, and—"

"No," Chris cut in firmly, and now she took Abby's hand—the one closest to her—and Abby's insides tightened. "You have nothing to be sorry for," Chris insisted, her face earnest. "You didn't the other night, and you don't now. I was an asshole."

She turned away and shook her head, running her free hand through her hair. Abby was acutely aware of the sweatiness of own palm still encased in Chris's.

"It's actually been keeping me up at night, the way I spoke to you. I'm embarrassed by it."

Abby started in surprise. Chris, embarrassed? It didn't seem possible.

"And it scared me," she went on softly, "that you may not forgive me."

"What?" Abby's jaw dropped. "Of course I forgive you, Chris."

Chris turned back to her, her face tinged with relief.

"I've really come to care about you and our…our…friendship. I was afraid I'd lost you. It."

Abby stared at Chris, dazed and clammy, her steely resolve long gone. Now, what she wanted more than anything was to drop her head onto Chris's shoulder, inhale her warmth, feel the soft skin of her neck against her cheek. But instead, she nodded silently, tried to speak, cleared her throat, and tried again before realising she had no idea what to say.

"Are you *ever* coming inside?" Drew, her voice sharp and irritable, was suddenly behind them. Abby dropped Chris's hand like it was on fire. She felt her cheeks flame as she turned to Drew, her irritation renewed but now redirected at this small, impish intruder in her home.

"Just *chill*, Drew, okay?" she hissed, surprising herself with the degree of annoyance that coloured her words. The girl's eyes were as wide as Abby had ever seen them, her eyebrows forming a deep V above them. "Please," she said, more softly now, as if talking to a child. "I'll be back in a minute. Go inside."

Drew looked furious, but she said nothing. She glared at Abby for another moment and then stomped inside, slamming the door behind her.

"You just got Uranus kicked," Chris said, giggling, and Abby, through a pressure-cooker release of laughter, threw her arms around Chris's shoulders. This time, Chris held her back, held her properly, tightly, slightly awkwardly, with a knee out to one side, but with the same gusto as Abby.

"Listen, you better get back to your girlfriend," Chris said, finally pulling away. "I'm worried she's going to come at me with the pizza cutter."

"*Not. My girlfriend*," Abby said, mimicking Chris's retort from the other night, and Chris grimaced.

"Not my finest moment."

Abby winked. "It's a joke, silly." Then she stood, turned, and offered a hand to Chris to help her up.

"I'm not that old," Chris protested, but she took the hand anyway.

"It's a friendship thing, asshole."

"Oh, god, I have a lot to learn, clearly."

Chris started making her way down the path. "I'm staying at my mother's house while she's in Bay View Clinic," she said, turning back around to face Abby. "So…I'll see you soon?"

"Yes!" Abby almost squealed as Chris strode away. It felt like every atom in her body was floating.

And just an hour later, a text pinged on her phone.

How about dinner tmrw, friend? My place. Xx

CHAPTER SEVENTEEN

Chris tossed the smashed garlic clove into a pan and picked up another.

"I learnt it years ago, when my go-to recipe for dinner parties was a garlic and parmesan pasta." *Chop, chop, THWAK!* "I think I thought it was exceptionally sophisticated, but really it was just a vulgar amount of garlic and half a bottle of cheap olive oil. I'm not even sure I used real parmesan."

She dumped a handful of garlic peels into the trash and rifled through the spice rack with a frown. "I assure you, my dishes are far more evolved these days." She pulled out a small, still-sealed glass bottle and wrinkled her nose. It looked about a hundred years old.

"Do you think onion powder could work as a substitute for garlic salt?"

"No!" Abby laughed and took a sip of her wine, better wine than she'd ever had in Bay View. To be fair, she'd only ever ordered the "house wine" at The Dolphin, and it either came out of a box or a bag.

"I think you have more than enough garlic already. And that onion powder does not look edible."

"Eh, you're probably right." Chris tossed the bottle into the bin. "Let's see what else we have here..."

Abby glanced around the dim, dark-wood kitchen. The home still had that heavy, oppressive air to it, even though Chris had flung open all the curtains and windows, flooding the place with fresh air and cool, early-evening light. She tried not to imagine where Cookie Addison had been found, unconscious from a stroke, on the kitchen floor.

"You okay?" Chris asked, looking up from the pan, to which she was adding generous shakes of…something.

"Yeah, I just thought of your mom, you know…here."

"Yeah," Chris replied distractedly. Abby couldn't read her expression. "Any more news?"

"Nope. There hasn't been much more progress. The doctors will monitor for a little while longer, but…" She trailed off, and Abby looked down at her wineglass. She became aware of the sound of the ticking clock—a yellowing melamine circle on the wall, covered in a layer of dust—and wondered if Mrs. Addison had heard that same ticking as she inched out of consciousness, or whether it had happened too fast for that.

"More wine?" Chris broke into Abby's thoughts, pouring already. "A little top-up to go with dinner."

She dished up two bowls of steaming, aromatic pasta. With a little flourish, she scattered over some basil she'd managed to find in an overgrown corner of the garden.

"Voilà!" she said with satisfaction. "Let's eat."

She led them out of the kitchen, through the dining room with its dark, heavy table, and into the lounge.

"I hate that dreary old dining room. Makes me feel like I'm in a convent or something."

Abby sat on a brown wool sofa, waving away the thick cloud of dust that puffed up around her as she did.

"This smells amazing," she said, cupping her hands around the bowl of penne in her lap. She speared a couple of pieces and shoved them into her mouth. She felt sauce smear all over her lips.

"Mmm, my god," she said, blotting her mouth with a napkin. "This is superb." Nutty flavours of mushroom and sharp cheese melted on her tongue.

"It's a crowd-pleaser, this one. All my kids eat it, which tells you a lot. Ditch the cheese, and it's vegan, too."

"Your kids are vegan?"

Chris rolled her eyes. "Some of them. Some of the time."

"Ah," Abby mumbled, taking another bite. "Do you do most of the cooking at home?"

"Not anymore. I used to, when they were little and Karys was away all the time. But now that they're basically grown-ups, we all take turns."

"You never really talk about your kids," Abby said, pushing a piece of pasta around her bowl to mop up some sauce.

"Not to you, no."

Abby paused, the piece of pasta halfway to her mouth. "Ouch! What does that mean?"

"Oh, it's not an insult," Chris said with a toss of her head. "It's nice not to have to talk about them for a change. They've been my whole life for seventeen years. And why would I want to bore you with stories of domestic mundanity? It's all just raging hormones and biology exams."

"I don't find it boring," Abby said, lowering her fork to her bowl. "It's your life. And I'm interested in you. So, tell me."

"Okay." Chris looked at her thoughtfully. "What do you want to know?"

"Umm…how about, what it was like to be a mom at twenty-six? No, not just a mom. A mom of a whole litter of kids."

Chris burst out laughing, the low light catching the curves of her chin and neck as her head tipped back.

"God, Abby, you're funny. A litter…Jesus, you're not wrong." She popped a piece of pasta into her mouth, chewing slowly as she stared at the bowl. "It was incredible, and terrible, and the hardest thing I've ever done, all at once."

"I can't even imagine."

"You know, I loved them so much, from the second I became aware of their existence. But in a lot of ways, it felt like my life was over at twenty-six, when it had just been getting started. I still remember cancelling the weekend plans I'd had when Karys showed up on my doorstep. Looking back, it's the moment I cancelled my life for her and the kids. You know what I mean? It's a horrible thing to say. It's crossed my mind from time to time, but I don't think I've ever said it out loud."

"Sometimes the truth is horrible. Doesn't make it less true."

"But it's not palatable. It's not what mothers are supposed to feel."

Abby nodded. "I'm not a mom, but even I know that many moms feel that way. Why are you so hard on yourself about it?"

"Really?" Chris said, arching an eyebrow. "I could give you a few reasons." She glanced pointedly around the lounge.

"You're nothing like your mother, and I don't even need to know her to know that."

Chris pulled in her lips. She didn't seem convinced.

"Do you want kids?" she asked, turning the attention to Abby, who hadn't been expecting the question.

"God, no!" spluttered from her lips before she could stop it. A squidge of chewed-up pasta landed on the coffee table. Quickly, she pressed it with her index finger and wiped it on her jeans. "I mean, no. I've never wanted kids. Sorry, no offence."

"None taken," Chris said with a shrug. "I think it's a smart decision—but then again, you're smart." She was watching Abby now, her brows slightly furrowed. "I'm going to tell you something."

"Yeah?" Abby said, leaning to push her empty bowl onto the coffee table in front of her. She'd ploughed through her pasta. Chris had barely touched hers.

"I never wanted kids, either. Karys knew that."

"Oh," Abby replied, surprised. And then, "Oh…Ohhhh."

"Yeah," Chris said, planting her bowl on the table next to Abby's. She drew her legs up under her and propped her head against a balled-up fist. "I'd never wanted kids. Not even when I was a kid and most other little girls were dreaming of it—you know, marrying some Prince Charming and popping out all these Baby Charmings. I had this idea that me and Karys…we'd magically get onto the same page…but as we got older, we just never did.

"I always thought it was because I loved Karys so much that I rolled with it and we made it work. And to a large degree, that's true. But Karys…"

She stopped. The sudden silence of the room compressed Abby's eardrums. Beyond the sitting room, the steady ticking of the melamine kitchen clock marched them forward: *tick, tock, tick, tock*. Specks of dust slowly settled onto the wooden coffee table.

Chris shook her head as if clearing a thought and picked up her wineglass. "I don't know why I'm telling you all this." She took a sip. "As usual."

"Because that's what friends do," Abby replied as lightly as she could. It was true, even if it felt a bit disingenuous. She took a gulp of her own wine and felt her salivary glands tighten.

"Karys," Chris eventually continued. "Was my whole world. Her family was my family. She was everything I had. And I was so grateful to her, and to them, and sometimes I wonder—"

She stopped again, squeezed her eyes shut, breathed out heavily through her nose.

"Sometimes I wonder," she said softly. "Whether I stayed with her out of a sense of gratitude. Because after everything she and her family had done for me, I couldn't ever possibly abandon her. She was there for me when no one else was. How could I desert her when *she* needed *me*? The guilt would've destroyed me. The guilt of just thinking about it came close to destroying me."

"So…you did think about it?"

"Yeah, once or twice. It came up after many years in therapy. I thought about unpacking it, but what for? So what if I had stayed out of a sense of obligation, or guilt? What good would it do knowing that, when Karys and the kids were everything to me? *Are* everything to me? I'd do anything for Karys, because she did everything for me, for so long."

"But what about what you want? What you need?" Abby asked gently.

Chris smile wistfully. "Well, my dear, therein lies the rub, as they say."

She reached for the wine, topping up Abby's glass, then her own. She placed the almost empty bottle back on the table, changed her mind, and spilled the last dregs into her glass. The bottle clanged as she set it on the glass top.

"I need this," Chris said emphatically, motioning to the brown lounge. "What I want is for my partner to realise that this isn't about my mother—that I need to do this for me." She let out an exasperated grunt. "Abby, I did it all! All of it! I raised those kids while she jetted around the world like a rock star with her dark sunglasses and Louis Vuitton luggage. I know you think my life is glamorous—and hell, it has been at times—but in the early, tough years, I was home taking care of the kids and running our shop—our shops, because one became two and then three—and yes, I get it. She's the people-person, the business-minded one, the one with the vision, yadda yadda. But when they were tiny—the hardest years, Abby, but also the most rewarding—she was never around. It's been almost two decades. When is it my turn to have my needs met? Why is it so selfish of me to be here?"

"It's not—"

"It's not! Thank you!" She threw her hands in the air. "Karys thinks that because the kids are about to leave, it's selfish that I'm here. But she forgets that I've always been there. I've always given up everything for her, for them. And for the first time, I need to do something for myself. I need her to do something for me. Is that so terrible? Am I seeing it all wrong?"

Abby shook her head. "I get that because it's about your mother, it complicates the situation and her feelings about it all. But maybe she's not used to you doing something for yourself?"

"Yeah," Chris agreed. "That's what I realised when I first came to Bay View. Almost thirty years we've been together, and all I've ever done is go along with what Karys has wanted. Did I even want this life, or did I just go along with it because I felt indebted to Karys? I don't even know if that would have occurred to me if she hadn't been so unsupportive of this trip."

Chris drew in a shaky breath. "You might be able to tell that I don't have a lot of friends to confide in back home. All our friends are couple friends, you know? I could never talk to them about this stuff. Most of it, I've never even said out loud."

"That's really tough," Abby said, feeling very grateful for her close circle.

"Please, let's change the subject," Chris said, standing and swiping their bowls off the table. "I don't know how we always manage to get so heavy."

"Leave those," Abby said, standing too. "I'll do the dishes. You cooked."

"Thanks for reminding me. There's no dishwasher here."

"I'll get you some of those yellow washing-up gloves," Abby teased, taking the bowls from Chris's hands.

"Don't you dare." Chris snorted, following her into the kitchen and leaning on the counter as Abby filled a sink with water. "I do not do dishes."

"Or beds, apparently," Abby said, and she heard Chris scoff behind her. "I mean, how are you surviving in this house?"

"With great difficulty." Chris sniffed, adding a dramatic sigh for good measure. "To be honest, I hate this place. I mean, look around."

Abby complied, peering over her shoulder to see Chris waving a hand expansively, indicating the general area.

"Not a single photo of any family member. Not me—which, okay, is entirely to be expected. But none of my sister. My father. It's as if once we're dead—or dead to her—she wipes us out of her existence entirely."

Abby thought about the absence of Dan photos in her own home. Searingly painful reminders belonged in shoeboxes and at the bottom of drawers. She wondered where Cookie Addison stored hers, and whether there were any of Chris among them.

"I'm so sorry, Chris," Abby said, slipping a plate onto the drying rack. "It must be very painful for you being here among all this loss."

"Ugh." Chris flicked a hand. "Let's not get heavy again. Distract me with something uplifting."

"Well," Abby said as the dirty water sucked out of the sink. "I have a great distraction for you. If you're up to it, that is."

"Oh, yeah?" Chris's head jerked up, and Abby realised she'd been looking at her phone. It was the first time she'd bothered with it all evening, unlike her last visit, when she'd been glued to it.

"Remember I told you about Mr. and Mrs. Woods from Woods' Construction? How they donated time and materials for the reconstruction?"

"Yeah?"

"Well, Roy got in touch with them, and things have moved incredibly fast. Mr. Woods got his guys round there earlier this week, and they've already prepped the new foundation. Chip's helping—that's Roy's nephew—and a bunch of his friends. It seems like they're working every night."

"That's great news, doll. But…wait, why do I feel there's more to the story?" Her eyes narrowed slightly and she ran a hand through her hair.

"Chip called me today and said that anyone from town can get involved. The more the merrier. The more the better, in fact. He says there are tons of tasks on-site that don't require too much technical expertise—just a hard hat and a willingness to help."

"Uh-*huhhh*." Chris's hand was frozen in her hair, her expression dubious.

Abby laughed. She'd come around to the other side of the kitchen counter, which now seemed to be holding Chris up.

"Well, I'm going to volunteer this weekend. Why don't you join me? I can't think of a better distraction than that."

"You must be joking." Chris's hand dropped to her side. "Have you met me?"

"Oh, come on. Don't be such a stuck-up snob."

"That's tautology. Either 'stuck up' or 'snob' would've sufficed."

Abby rolled her eyes. "See? That's exactly what I mean! Will you at least think about it?"

"God, no. Me, on a building site? Hilarious. I couldn't picture it, not in a million years."

"Could you ever have pictured yourself here, in this situation, in a million years?"

"That's totally different…"

"There's no room in this tiny town for high horses. So, get off yours and get involved."

"Abigail, look at these hands. Do these hands look like they have any business on a construction site?" She thrust her fingers under Abby's nose. Her skin was flawless. Her nails, as usual, immaculately manicured and painted in her signature deep red. Abby wanted so badly to hold her hands.

"Fine," Abby said, a cool sheen of sweat breaking out on her forehead. "I just thought it would be a nice distraction, but you're right." She spun away from Chris and stuck out her bottom lip, trying to blow cool air up to her forehead. Friends, Abby, her inner voice cautioned her.

Chris seemed not to notice. "I think it's fantastic you're doing it, though," she said. When Abby turned back to her, she was examining her nails with a frown. "Dammit, look. There's a chip there." She stuck a burgundy-coloured nail in Abby's direction.

"Well, then? They're already ruined, totally ruined," Abby concluded, her face cooling. "You may as well put your fingers to good use."

Chris smirked at her, and she felt her face flare up again.

"Oh, Abby, I'm just teasing you. You make it so easy!"

CHAPTER EIGHTEEN

"Where the fuck am I going with this?" Chris huffed, coming up next to Abby in a bright-yellow safety helmet. In her arms she held a large plastic crate loaded with rubble and building debris. She'd barely broken a sweat; she'd huffed out of irritation, not exertion.

"Right over there." Abby pointed to the far-left corner of the site. "But you're supposed to be in the human chain—like this one, see? You don't have to lug it the entire way."

"Oh." Chris shrugged despite the weight in her arms. "Fine. Well, I'll dump it and join them. See you later."

Evan whistled under his breath as she strode off. "That is one tough cookie," he said as he took a brick from Abby's hand. "So to speak."

"Right? And she would've done it in designer jeans if I hadn't insisted she borrow some sweats."

Abby grabbed the brick that Alexia handed her and tossed it to Evan. He passed it to Michaela on his other side.

Another brick. Another toss.

Chip had divided the volunteers into two human chains: one clearing the detritus, and the other offloading materials from the delivery truck. This allowed the actual construction workers, including Mr. Woods and overseen by Mrs. Woods, to work as quickly as possible. Chip was a natural at site management, and progress was efficient.

"How did you convince her to do it in the end?" Evan asked as they worked. "I thought she was vehemently opposed."

"She was," Abby confirmed. "But I don't think it had anything to do with my coercing. I think she just realised she needed a change of scenery, and this is pretty much the only thing going by way of 'new scenery' in Bay View."

This was an understatement. What had actually happened is that Chris had called early that morning and groaned, in a thin voice, "Okay, you win! I feel like I am eating, sleeping, breathing hospitals right now. The smell is stuck in my nostrils. The sounds are the sounds of my nightmares. I'll take your fucking construction site. Where and when?"

Abby had instructed her to come over—she knew Chris wouldn't have the appropriate attire—and after strong coffee and wardrobe changes, they'd made their way here.

It wasn't that Chris wasn't strong, or capable. She was both of those things in abundance. Abby watched her lift, lug, hoist, and haul not just with ease, but grace. Grace? On a construction site? It blew Abby's mind. Her brow, under the safety hat, was probably still cool and dry. At least, she showed no outward signs of strain. Except socially, that is.

"Dude, both your girlfriends on the same crew? Is that safe?" Jade teased as she came over, her helmet clamped under her arm.

"Well, at least they're both wearing their safety hats," Abby retorted. "So I'd say it's safer than you are right now."

Jade laughed and secured her headgear in place. "Fair point, dude. Listen, we're all gonna hang out at ours after this. We'll crack some beers, make some food. Bring Chris. And of course," she added, turning to Evan and Michaela. "You assholes are invited, too. Abby doesn't have a choice. She has to be there."

"I'll have to check my diary," Abby joked.

"Don't bother. It says, 'Jade's in charge of my social life.' There, saved ya the click." She grinned and planted her hands on her hips, surveying the scene before her. "Wow, we're making some progress, huh? Can you believe how we helped to make all this happen? It's pretty awesome."

"Yeah, it is," Abby replied, smiling to herself as she tossed another brick to Evan. Dan would have been proud of her, she just knew it.

"Oi, Earth to Abby. Bricks are pilin' up!"

"Sorry," she said, snapping back. Dan disappeared in a puff of rubble as a brick tumbled to the ground next to her. "Okay, chill! I'm on it."

For the next several hours, the teams put their heads down and sweated. Every now and then, Mrs. Woods would whistle, startling everyone except her husband, and insist that they all take a break. Bottles of water would be sucked down, cheese sandwiches inhaled. Then, they'd return to their stations and progress would continue.

"You were absolutely right, Ms. Massey," Chris said during one of their breaks. "This is exactly what I needed to get my mind off everything. All I can think about is the atrocious state of my nails."

Abby loved it when Chris called her that, making the "S" of "Ms." sound like a lazy "Z." Before she could feign temporary loss of hearing and ask Chris to repeat herself, Mrs. Woods barked over to them.

"We have about an hour of daylight left, so let's get back to it."

"We should do something relaxing after this, like join a chain gang," Chris grumbled as they headed back to their stations.

Later, as the sun set, they all headed out together, peeling off as each reached their respective street.

"I'll see you all soon," Chris called as she began to veer off at the corner of Main and Marble, but Jade wasn't going to let her off that easily.

"Oh no, you don't," Jade said, skipping over and linking her arm through Chris's. "We're all heading to our place for beers. You're coming, too."

Chris tried to protest, Jade was having none of it, and Cody looked on indulgently. They all knew who'd win, and no one could understand why Chris even bothered to argue. Jade, with her warmth and charm and irresistible niceness, always got her way.

"At least let me get some wine from home…" Chris tried valiantly, but Jade wouldn't hear of it.

"We have plenty. You can bring some next time," she said breezily as she hauled Chris along.

They always did have plenty of wine. And beer. And hot dogs just waiting to be fired up. It was a feature of the fact that Cody and Jade's home was the warm centre they all gravitated to—like how, when you were a kid, there was always one friend's house with the best snacks and the nicest mom. These days, when anyone shopped for groceries, they always grabbed a few packs of burgers for "Jody's" place, or an extra six-pack or bottle of red.

And that's what Abby had been thinking about when Drew walked in and startled her in the kitchen, causing her to slosh red wine all over her sleeve and the floor. It was a bottle she'd brought a while back—a not-half-bad bottle—and she was relieved to have something semidecent to be able to serve Chris.

"This reminds me of the night we met," Drew said, handing Abby a damp cloth. "When I spilled all over your new jacket. Here."

"Don't worry, it's fine," Abby replied, blotting her sleeve mostly so that she didn't have to meet Drew's eye. "These are old clothes, anyway—you know, for today."

Drew shrugged and walked over to the fridge. The tension was excruciating. Abby knew she had to say something to break it.

Drew beat her to it.

"You want a beer?" she asked, hidden by the fridge door. "Or are you on wine tonight?"

"Oh, uh, I've got one already, thanks. I was just grabbing this for Chris."

"Of course you were," Drew said with a sigh, closing the door with more force than necessary. "God forbid she pour her own wine."

"Look, Drew…"

"Don't 'Look, Drew' me," she snapped, wrenching the cap off her beer. It fell to the counter and bounced onto the floor, coming to a rest in a splash of wine near her foot. She jabbed at it with the toe of her boot, sending it spinning into a corner. "You were just using me, Abby. You don't need me now that your girlfriend is back."

That stung. Mostly because it was sort of true.

"Drew, I thought we were just having a bit of fun?" Abby said as gently as she could. "Remember? That's what you said, right at the beginning. We both agreed."

Drew glowered at her but said nothing.

"I'm…I'm so sorry. I never, ever meant to hurt you," Abby said, stepping closer. And she meant it, but what was there to say, really? If she were completely honest with herself, she *had* used Drew.

Abby should have seen it coming. At any other time in her life, she would have.

She was about to reach for Drew when Jade walked in and Drew jumped back. She snatched her beer from the counter and scuttled away, knocking past Abby as she did.

"Looks like that went well," Jade remarked, rolling up her flannel sleeves as she walked over to where Abby stood. "You okay?"

"Me? I'm fine. It's Drew who deserves your sympathy, not me."

Jade waved a hand. "She's a baby, she'll get over it. If this town weren't so small, she'd have fallen for someone else already. You, on the other hand…"

Abby frowned. "Me?"

"Yes. You." The arches of Jade's eyebrows reached for the ceiling and her mouth pressed to the side.

"Oh, no! I didn't feel that way about Drew. I—"

"Not *Drew*."

She let her eyes move pointedly to the gathering outside, where their friends were installed around the fire with cold drinks and hot-dog-lined bellies. Chris was leaning forward in her chair, listening intently to something Chip was saying. Looking at her, it was hard not to let her breath catch in her throat.

"See? Like that. You've been staring at her like a weirdo all night."

Abby groaned and slouched against the kitchen counter, dropping her head into her hand. "Shit, dude, I didn't even realise. Is it that obvious?"

"No, I don't think so. Only to me. And Drew, of course. But she's been watching you like a hawk all evening. It's like an episode of *The Real L Word* here."

Abby scoffed and took a gulp of the wine she'd just poured for Chris. It was hard to meet Jade's eye.

"We've all been there," Jade said, putting an arm around Abby. "I remember when I used to look at Cody that way."

"Yeah, but that's different."

"Not really. She used to look at you that way. And now look. My Cody-Bear." At that last sentence, she raised her voice just enough to get Cody's attention. Cody froze for a split second, like a puppy hearing its name being called, then spun around in her plastic chair and winked at Jade. Jade blew her a kiss, then shrugged at Abby.

"See? You get over it. Either way. You get with the girl and the longing goes away. Or, you don't get with the girl, and eventually, the longing goes away. You're going to be okay."

"Yep!" Abby agreed, with forced cheeriness. "Look, you don't need to worry about me. Before we know it, Chris is going to disappear from our lives as quickly as she appeared, and it'll be like she was never here. And then, like you say, the longing will go away."

Jade narrowed her eyes. "Are you just trying to shut me up?"

"No…"

Jade frowned and poked Abby in the ribs. "Abby. Don't lie to me."

"Ouch, stop!" Abby squealed, skittering away. "Okay, okay, maybe a bit. Jeez, Louise."

Then they were back outside, dipping in and out of conversations, forgetting for a moment about longing and loss as laughter floated up to the sky.

CHAPTER NINETEEN

It was a chilly Monday morning, and as usual Abby was running late.

A guest had arrived early that morning, plus Abby had over-brewed her coffee and had had to ditch it and start again. She just couldn't bring herself to drink the cheap crap anymore.

Despite these setbacks, she came to a stop as she detoured past The Dolphin. It was hard not to stare.

What had been a charred wasteland just a week before was now the site of regeneration, a new foundation slowly emerging from the bruised ground. She wondered how long it would be before they were sipping drinks at the bar again, the counter sticky beneath their forearms, Roy calling for last rounds over the din of board games and sports debates.

With great effort, she tore herself away and continued her fast shuffle to work. She fully expected to get the stink eye from the principal when she careened into school a full three minutes late, but to her surprise, he gave her a meaty clap on the shoulder and a broad, tobacco-stained grin.

"Abigail! I couldn't believe my eyes when I drove past the ol' Dolphin this morning. Moira reminded that me it's thanks to your generosity that they've got the rebuild off the ground?"

"Oh! No, well, what happen—"

"I didn't realise we paid you that much!" He chortled as he hiked up his navy chinos. As usual, the waistband hung low, like a hammock for his belly.

"Yep. I always wondered about that extra zero at the end of my paycheque."

It wasn't that funny, but Principal Jones roared with laughter and thumped Abby's shoulder again.

"Ah, you kids. Such joy you bring to my days," he said, glancing at his watch. "Oof! Better not make you any later for class than you already are, Miss Massey." He widened his eyes and play-waggled a finger at her. "I'm giving you a little leniency today, only because we're all so excited to have our pub back!"

Then he turned on his heel and chuckled his way down the corridor, leaving Abby to scurry to her classroom with a wide grin on her face.

* * *

The week flew in a succession of lovely and unexpected events. On Tuesday, Abby got a call from Paint Shop Paul, the guy who—predictably—ran the paint shop in town.

"I heard about the donation drive for The Dolphin Inn," he said after introducing himself. "I have a ton of paint you guys can have—if it's not too late?"

It wasn't too late, so Paint Shop Paul came around in his van and offloaded barrel upon barrel in a spectrum of shades.

"We could do the flag," Jade whispered, eyes glazing over as she watched the tins being offloaded. "Look at that!" She gripped Abby's arm, her fingers squeezing the flesh. "Red, blue, green…yellow! We *have* to do the flag."

"I love the idea, but we'd probably need Roy's buy-in," Abby said, watching as the paint piled up where Dan's boxes once were. Just as well she'd made some space.

"That'll be easy," Jade said, eyebrows wiggling playfully. "His name *lit-er-ally* stands for 'Red, Orange, Yellow.' We'll be able to convince him."

"Ha, you're right." Abby giggled, bending to grab the glossy black Saint Jamie box that was about to be crushed by a twenty-litre can of paint. "Do you think he even realises?"

"No idea, but we're about to find out."

On Wednesday, snug in the silky embrace of her purple bomber jacket, Abby found herself wedged between Evan and Chris at Luigi's two-for-one special. Cody and Jade were there too, of course, and Chip, Jon, and Alexia, and they all squeezed in and ate greasy pizza with their elbows touching and oil dripping down their wrists. Every time Chris shifted, deep floral scents wafted into Abby's nostrils, mingling with her tiny nibbles of pizza. Sparks shot through her when their thighs brushed.

At quiz night the next evening, no one even batted an eyelid when Chris appeared next to Abby on-screen, nailing the questions on history and science, and bombing completely on 2000s pop. No one except Lulu, of course.

What's going on there? she texted Abby, followed by a row of eyeball emojis. It pinged as Chris debated an answer with Nathan, leaning forward toward the screen, a hand absently placed on Abby's thigh to anchor herself.

Same old, Abby had typed back, adding a smiley face and then slipping her phone between the sofa cushions. She only retrieved it the following morning when her alarm, smothered by upholstery, squawked through the early morning silence.

"Yeah, yeah, I know," she muttered as she lumbered into the lounge, Snowy winding around her legs, flirting for breakfast.

Abby's eyes felt puffy as she padded to the kitchen. Chris had left at midnight, neither of them having watched the clock. They'd chatted for ages after the quiz had ended, Abby with her legs drawn up under her, Chris with Snowy curled up in her lap, both of them twirling the stems of their wineglasses, sipping occasionally.

That's really *the most embarrassing thing that's ever happened to you? I can totally top that...*

Oh, I've always *wanted to go there! Is it really as amazing as everyone says?*

Wait—did you ever watch that film—shit, what was it called? Yeah, that one!

Oh, come on! Everyone *has a hall pass! Who's yours?*

Shit, it's nearly midnight! Those kids are going to destroy me tomorrow. At least you can sleep in.

I never do.

I noticed that.

And I especially can't, tomorrow. My mother's doctor has requested a meeting with me.

Oh...

Yeah. I never thought I'd be the one to...

I'm so sorry.

Is there any more wine in that bottle?

Back in bed with her strong coffee, she felt guilty for her self-pity. Sure, she was exhausted, but how must Chris be feeling this morning, under the weight of the heart-stopping decision she'd probably have to make today?

She fired off a text to Chris—*Thinking of you today… see you later? xx*—then scrolled idly through the FortyLinks app, her brain taking in nothing. She forced herself to focus. A booking request for Sunday—a couple, for a few days. She forced herself to feel excited about it. She forced herself to stay awake. The kids really were going to run rings around her today, and her subpar cup of coffee wasn't helping.

She took a sip anyway, wrinkling her nose, and then she was moving, showering, brushing her teeth, throwing on a happy yellow shirt to trick her brain into feeling bright and sunny, kissing Snowy, and stumbling out of the front door.

"TGIF," she called as she saw Evan up ahead, jogging to fall into step with him.

"Hell, yeah," he agreed, squinting his eyes against the sun as he grinned at her. "I'm already counting the hours 'til final bell."

"I really don't feel like doing this," Abby said with a groan as school came into view. Today would feel like trudging through mud.

"You never feel like doing this." Evan stepped aside to let Abby pass through the pedestrian gate as the bell pierced the air. It sent the kids into a frenzy, and Abby sighed as a small red-headed one careered into her thighs, bounced off, and joined its clan.

"Okay, that's not true. You never feel like doing this *lately*," Evan corrected himself as kids shrieked his name and waved with small, stubby fingers. Evan really was an across-the-board hit.

"Hmm, I think you're right," Abby agreed, though she'd never really considered it before. Was she…over this job? She'd loved it in the beginning…or needed it. Perhaps that need had felt like love, back when she was stuck in a joyless void. Now that she was emerging from it, maybe she no longer needed the frantic distraction of this Mad Hatter's sugar-free, peanut-butter-banned, soy-milk tea party.

She mulled over it a lot, that day. Several times, the kids had to draw her attention back to the classroom, where they whined and cried and threw sharpened pencils at each other's heads. *Perhaps I'm dead*, she'd mused as she watched a kid pick his nose and grind his findings under his nail. *And this is hell.*

Her mind was in so many different places today, none of them Bay View Junior.

She and Evan were both buried in their phones as they walked home later. Earlier, Abby had texted Chris to find out about the meeting with the doctor. Still no reply.

"Come for a beer," Abby said, swapping thoughts of blue ticks for blue skies. "It's a nice day to sit out in the garden."

"Mmm," Evan mumbled, tapping away.

"Is that's a yes?"

"Yeahhh…Oh, uh, hmm?" He finally stopped tapping and looked up, sheepish. "Was distracted."

"I noticed. Beer?"

"I can't, sorry. But I'll see you tomorrow at The Dolphin, right?"

"No, you won't," Abby replied, wondering why he was being cagey. It wasn't like him.

"Oh. Oh, yeah. Shit, Abby, forgot for a moment." He focused fully on her at last, his face filling with concern. "You sure you don't want company?"

"Yeah, I'm sure," Abby said with more confidence than she felt.

"You know I'm here, right? Just say the word."

"I know, thank you. But it won't be like last year. I promise."

"Okay," Evan replied, but he didn't sound convinced. "It doesn't feel right, you being alone tomorrow. And, you know, doing…that."

"I'll be fine," Abby said, with much more confidence than she felt. "Go, go. I'll call you after."

Reluctantly, Evan left her side to head home, and Abby pushed thoughts of tomorrow out of her mind.

This was actually perfect, she thought as she neared her house. Some downtime would give her a chance to get Chris's room—ugh, the guest room—ready for Sunday's arrivals. Tomorrow would be—would have been—Dan's forty-first birthday, and she had more important things to do than house admin. On Sunday, if she felt up to it, she planned to join The Dolphin crew.

Now that the rubble had been removed and the new foundations laid, excitement was mounting. The revived Dolphin was almost a reality, and they worked faster and harder to make it happen.

As the days passed, more locals turned up to lend a hand, or to drop off snacks and energy drinks (and beer, if you were lucky). Ironically, The Dolphin Inn was already, once again, the place to be whenever you had a little free time on your hands—or *with* your hands—and it wasn't yet serving a single drink.

When a knock at the door interrupted her battle with a fitted sheet, she knew, from the rhythm and weight of the rap, that it was Chris.

"I should just give you a key," Abby teased as she opened the door. *Imagine.*

She took in Chris's drawn form and instantly changed her tone. "So…How did it go?"

Chris sighed. Her face was pale, her lips were pale, even her clothes seemed somehow paler. The only thing that remained vivid as ever was her hair, and as she lifted a hand to rake through it, Abby flicked her eyes away. It felt almost too intimate: Abby could predict the move by now, and seeing it ached in a strange way.

"Tomorrow's the day."

"Oh, Chris. I'm so sorry."

She shrugged, turned her mouth down at the corners.

"I have to turn the lights out on my mother," she said, making a motion like she was flipping a switch. "Just like that."

"Come," Abby said, guiding her inside and shutting the door.

Chris sagged into the house and wordlessly accepted the glass of wine Abby offered. But she didn't sip it. Instead, she leaned against the kitchen counter, her eyes glazed, her bottom lip caught between her teeth.

"Do you want to talk about it?" Abby asked softly.

Chris shook her head.

"Are you hungry? Do you want a hug?"

Chris continued staring at nothing. "No."

Abby moved closer to her, then hesitated.

"Okay. I'm just going to leave you be."

Chris finally tore her eyes away from nothing and stared at Abby with a wounded gaze. "No," she said, hoarsely. "Please, don't."

Abby nodded. "Okay," she whispered.

The sun had set but it was still warm out, so they went into the garden and sipped their wine. The sounds of birdsong eventually gave way to far-off music and laughter, and closer, the occasional *prrrt* of a chubby kitten chasing crickets and bugs.

It was Chris's phone that ultimately fractured the silence, and Abby jumped when it did. She saw her name before Chris set the phone against her ear with a gruff "Hey" and slipped into the house.

Abby tried not to eavesdrop. Not that it was easy anyway, with the thick glass door shut between them. But she caught glimpses of Chris pacing up and down the sitting room, free hand gesticulating, jaw clenching. It reminded her of the early days of Chris, when she'd first arrived and had spent all that time pacing up and down the patio, phone glued to her ear, hand working endlessly through her hair.

Chris was planted with her back to the garden, her shoulders slumped, one hand on her hip. Abby watched her, wanting more than anything to go in and hold her. But instead, she drew her legs up under her and wrapped her arms around them, waiting patiently for Chris to return.

"Sorry about that," came the sound of Chris's voice sometime later, a hand briefly touching her shoulder. With a sigh, she slid back into her chair.

"Does Karys know it's happening tomorrow?" Abby blurted. Whatever conversation had happened inside, it hadn't looked good, and Abby felt angry that Karys would want to put Chris through more stress—now, of all times.

It was hard to read her expression in the dark, but Abby heard Chris breathe in deeply through her nose and then exhale. "Yes. She does. But it doesn't matter."

Abby frowned, waiting for Chris to continue.

"Karys and I are separated."

"What?" Abby's feet fell to the ground, the tip of her sneaker hitting the table leg as they went. Her wineglass wobbled dangerously and then fell, smashing against the wrought iron and sending glass chips flying in all directions.

"Ah, fuck," she cursed, jumping up as Chris reached across the table to help.

"Careful, doll. Don't cut yourself," Chris said as she picked up shards of glass with her silver-ringed fingers—except on *that* finger. How had Abby missed it?

Abby felt frozen. She watched Chris's fingers move but all she could hear was *Karys and I are separated, Karys and I are separated, Karys and I are separated.*

"Get me some newspaper."

"Huh?"

Chris paused, gingerly cupping a handful of glass shards. "Paper. To wrap up the glass before I throw it in the bin."

"Oh! God, yes…yes, I have some. I'll be right back."

Abby stumbled through the house, blinking as she snapped on the kitchen lights. *Newspaper, newspaper…they're separated. Separated! Why didn't she tell me? Fuck, what was I doing in here again? Newspaper! Paper… got it.*

Back outside, Abby handed the newspaper to Chris and watched as she carefully wrapped up the shards. Then she folded it neatly and disappeared inside, reemerging moments later with another wineglass filled almost to the brim.

"Seems you need this as much as I do," she said as she handed it to Abby, giving her a look Abby couldn't quite read.

"I'm just surprised, is all," she said quickly, her hands sticky from the now-evaporated wine.

"I'm not," Chris scoffed, taking a gulp of wine. "Surprised, that is."

"When did it happen?"

"A while ago. After I got home. From here," she added, motioning in the general direction of Bay View with her wineglass.

Abby nodded weakly. Why hadn't Chris told her sooner? She felt utterly blindsided, even though she technically had no right to. What else was she feeling? Relief? Happiness? Guilt? That was it. Guilt at feeling relieved, and happy.

"Abby, I'm sorry I didn't tell you. I—"

But now it was Abby's turn to wave a hand, and she did it wildly, nearly upending her glass again. "Oh, it was none of my business." She winced at her overly shrill voice.

"I'm sure it didn't escape you that things were…tense around that time, to say the least."

"I didn't really pay that much attention…"

"Oh, please. I was staying here. I think it was pretty obvious."

Abby looked away. It had been obvious—and when Chris had been on the phone to Karys a few minutes ago, it had reminded her very much of those anguished days.

"Sure, but…I wanted to respect your privacy. As a FortyLinks host, I do my best not to get involved in my guests' lives."

"Oh, come on!" Chris spluttered. "A 'host', Abby? You are much more than a host. To me, anyway."

Abby felt warmth in her cheeks. "You mean, like, a super host?" She tried to deflect, but Chris didn't laugh.

"You know what I mean."

"Well," Abby said, clearing her throat. "I'm just really sorry that you've had to go through all this alone."

"Alone?" Chris leaned forward and touched Abby's arm. "Abby, I didn't go through this alone. I had my kids. My friends. *You.* I was never alone."

Abby didn't trust herself to reply. She dipped her head and lifted Snowy into her lap, cooing to the kitten, fighting to keep any awkward silence at bay.

"Karys isn't a monster, you know," Chris said softly.

Abby looked up. "Oh, I…I didn't think she was. You two obviously just have your stuff to work through."

"We do," Chris said. "She's just…she's tired. She's so, so tired of my family drama. She's cried my tears, burned with my rage, fought my battles, mourned my losses, held me through endless tears. She can't understand why I would choose to come back for the woman who threw me away like garbage. I can't understand it myself, but all I know is that something inside me compels me to do it, and I *have* to answer. I have to do the right thing. And it's the right thing for me, you know?" Chris's eyes searched Abby's, desperate for understanding.

Abby nodded earnestly. She understood that for Chris, there was no other choice. You couldn't look into her anguished eyes and not see that. But Abby hadn't spent the last twenty years looking into them.

"As angry as I am with Karys—as much as I wish she could come around to my point of view—I do understand hers. She's worked so hard to support our family. To make sure we felt her love and devotion, even if she wasn't around much."

Chris sipped from her almost empty glass. "Karys regrets not spending more time with the kids when they were little. Now, she's clinging to every last moment with them. That's her journey right now, and this…This is mine."

Their glasses empty, their heads swimming with exhaustion, they called it a night.

"I was thinking," Abby said, just before she slipped into her bedroom. "Would you like me to be there tomorrow? With you? So you don't have to do it alone? *Be* alone?"

Chris shook her head. "No," she said quietly. "No, I don't. I'm afraid you'll force me to eat fast food again."

And then they were both howling, laughing until tears streamed down their faces and their lips tasted like salt.

* * *

Abby felt a heaviness in her chest the moment she woke up.

Today. The third birthday she'd celebrate for her. Without her.

Happy birthday, my beautiful free spirit. Oh, how I miss you.

A lump, hard and heavy, in her throat. Soon the number of birthdays she celebrated alone would outweigh the number they had celebrated together.

You shithead. How could you have left so soon?

At least this morning, unlike last year, she wasn't crying so hard she vomited and burst all the blood vessels in her eyes.

As Abby lay still in the dim room, she wondered what forty-one-year-old Dan would have been like.

Would her forties have changed her? Illness had changed her, but would ageing have? Abby doubted it. Dan would have been a forty-, fifty-, eighty-, ninety-year-old free spirit. Adventurous, passionate, spontaneous…still refusing to microwave plastic. It was getting harder and harder to remember the cancer-embittered Dan. With every passing year, it was the old Dan—healthy, sparkling, alive, free—who endured in her memories.

After her bath, she stood in front of her full-length bedroom mirror, naked from the waist up, and stared at the inking below her breast. By this time tonight, it'll look the way it was always supposed to, she told herself as she pulled on a baggy sweatshirt. An exhilarating prospect after all this time.

Then she took a deep, steadying breath, and headed out into the sunshine.

There was a single tattoo shop in Bay View, one more than Abby had expected there to be. It was dingy and outdated, like the sort of place you went to get weed or tongue piercings when you were underage in the noughties.

Abby took her seat on a weathered black leather sofa, as instructed, and waited. The shop smelled sterile, but not in the same way a hospital did. Hospitals smelled like death and disinfectant. This place smelled like adrenaline, anticipation, and surgical spirits. And very much alive.

Abby's hands were sweaty, and she wiped them on her jeans as she waited. It hadn't taken more than thirty minutes, start to finish, to complete the permanent inking on Dan. So this wouldn't take long—surely no more than ten. She just needed to grow up and deal with the pain.

"Abby?"

Her head jerked up.

"Yes!" she said, with a lot more enthusiasm than she felt.

"You can come this way. I'm Seth. I'll be tattooing you today."

He led her to a cushioned table, hidden behind a privacy screen, and motioned for her to hop on. This time, she wasn't fooled by the massage-table appearance of the contraption. This would be far from a relaxing experience.

He sat down in the chair opposite her and smiled encouragingly. "So," he asked, his hands clasped loosely in his lap. "What are we doing today?"

Abby swung her legs over the side of the table, feeling like a kid at the doctor. It calmed her as she thought about divulging her ailment, hoping he'd be able to fix it quickly and…relatively painlessly.

"Well," she started, lifting her hoodie to expose the ink, interrupted. "I would really like to finish this."

"May I see?" Seth asked.

"Yes, of course," she replied, and he came closer.

"I chickened out a few years ago because I couldn't stand the pain. Like, *really* could. Not. Stand. It." She focused on a drawing of a sugar skull on the wall as he inspected the tiny design. "But it's incredibly important to me that I finish it."

"Cool, we can do that," Seth said, straightening up. "But what is it supposed to be? Like a mountain range or something?"

"No…here you go," Abby said, rolling onto one butt cheek and easing her phone out of her back pocket. She tapped until she reached an image she hadn't looked at since this day last year: Dan, high on endorphins, beaming into the camera with her perfect teeth and shining marble-grey eyes. One hand held up her sweatshirt, and with the other, she pointed to the fresh, slightly inflamed tattoo.

"This. It needs to be identical to this."

Seth took the phone and zoomed in like it was nothing. Abby looked away, squeezing her eyes shut.

"Okay, got it," Seth said as he handed the phone back. "It won't take long to finish it. Do you think you'll be okay? You've had some breakfast?"

Abby took a deep breath. "Yes. I refuse to be a baby this time."

"Aww, nah, you're not being a baby," Seth replied kindly as he assembled his equipment. "Tattoos are painful, man. Especially over your ribs." He sterilized Abby's skin with an icy-cold swab and ever so gently drew a razor across the skin to remove any fine hairs.

"Okay, here we go. The first two minutes are the worst, then it's all plain sailing."

The pain was about as bad as Abby remembered it, and it didn't get any better, not one bit. But somehow, today, she was better able to tolerate it.

Seth was gentle and patient. He spoke in soothing tones. When he succeeded in drawing Abby into conversation, it almost distracted her from the relentless cut-burn feeling of the needles puncturing her flesh over and over again.

"You're a champ, Abby. You're doing great," he murmured, his head low and close to her ribs.

"I don't feel like a champ." She gasped in pain, focusing on the peeling paint of the ceiling as if her life depended on it.

"This is one of the most painful parts of the body to get tattooed, and you're handling it like a total pro."

Abby laughed weakly. "I don't feel like I am."

"I'm gonna be done here in, like, five minutes."

"*Seriously?* Oh! Ohhhh, it's getting real now."

"Yeah, that happens," he chuckled.

"It does feel a bit more tolerable than last time. I just…I feel like I had no excuse for not pushing through the first time. My, um"—some days it was just too much effort—"the other person who got the matching one…she was going through so much at the time. She was really ill. And she breezed through like it was nothing."

"That's really impressive," Seth said, "but you shouldn't be hard on yourself. Everyone's different."

"Yeah, I guess so," Abby replied.

"And maybe there was, like, stuff you were going through and you just couldn't carry it at the time, you know? You've gotta be in the right headspace."

"What do you mean?"

"Well," Seth started, turning to top up the ink. "I have some clients who come in when they're mad, or sad, and it really helps—like a pressure release. But others, they can only commit when they're in a good space. Some are in, like, a bad way emotionally. They don't have the capacity to take on any more discomfort. They're at their pain peak, and they have to wait for it to come down before they can add more. I know it sounds kind of woo-woo, but it's just what I've picked up from my clients. And even myself."

"That…that actually makes sense."

"Yeah."

"No, really. That makes me feel a lot better."

And then, just as Abby felt the endorphins kicking in, like hitting the second mile of a run, it was all over.

"You're a legend," Seth declared, motioning toward the mirror. "Go have a look."

"No, *you're* a legend!" Abby gasped in awe. It was finally done, and it exactly matched Dan's. Abby didn't even need to look at the photo to know it.

"I really don't know how to thank you," Abby said as she paid. "This has…bothered me for a long time. And you got me through it. Today of all days." Of course, Seth wouldn't know what that meant, but he grinned broadly at the sentiment.

"Just doin' my job," he said. "Let me know if you ever want another."

"Now that's pushing it!" Abby laughed as she stepped back into the street, nearly colliding with Michaela.

"Sorry, Abby," she mumbled as she slid into the shop, not stopping to say hi.

"No worries," Abby called back.

Outside, the sky had unexpectedly clouded over, and Abby felt a drop of rain. It seemed somewhat appropriate.

Her phone rang and she yanked it out of her pocket.

"So?" Evan's voice was a mix of excitement and apprehension. He'd been the one left with tear-saturated T-shirts for the two birthdays past, so Abby understood his anxiety.

"Dude! Let me switch you to video call."

She tapped onto selfie mode and with the other hand pulled up her hoodie just far enough to reveal the now completed design.

"Bro! You did it!"

"Yep!" Abby beamed. "Were you worried I'd be a crumpled heap on the floor?"

"We-ellll…Let's just say the thought hadn't *not* crossed my mind."

Abby chuckled. "I get it. But I'm okay. More than okay, really. Now I know why Cody has so many tattoos. It really does give you a kick."

"You know, you could always just run with me in the mornings and you'd get the same kind of rush. Ever heard of 'runner's high'?"

"Yuck. I'd rather get a tattoo every morning, thanks."

"Spoilsport."

"That still implies some sort of sport. So no, I'm definitely not that."

Evan laughed. "Smart ass."

Abby turned off the camera and wedged the phone between her shoulder dend ear as she readjusted her top.

"Seriously, though. You sure you're okay? Because I'm here, if you want company."

"I thought you had some mysterious thing to do today?"

Evan ignored the unsubtle hint. "I'm always here for you, Abs, no matter what."

"I know, Ev. You're the best. But no, no tears for me this year. Well, no sobbing. It's progress."

"Yeah it is!"

As Abby approached her house, she spotted a familiar shape coming down the front steps, holding an overnight bag. She was wearing a hooded jacket, her hair covered, but Abby would know her shape anywhere. She felt her heart beating faster and a wave of concern rush over her. What had Chris had to endure today? What life-altering decisions? Life-*ending* decisions?

"Dude, I gotta go."

"Cool. Call if you need anything."

"I will," Abby replied, already slipping her phone back into her pocket.

"Chris!" she called out as she picked up her pace. "Wait, I'm here," she yelled as she jogged closer, catching up with Chris as she was about to get into her car.

"Oh, hey," Chris greeted her as Abby pulled up, huffing. "Don't hurt yourself," she teased.

Abby pulled a face and planted her hands on her hips. "Funny."

She scrutinised Chris's face, trying to gather clues about how things may have gone. She was unreadable, but then she sagged against the car.

"It's over. It's all over," she said, folding her arms across her chest. That's when Abby realised that her face wasn't unreadable; it was drained by shock and exhaustion.

"Oh, Chris. Oh, my god. I'm so sorry."

"Yeah." She pressed a thumb and forefinger into her eyes. "At least she went on her own, this morning. I didn't have to…"

Abby reached out and gently touched Chris's arm. "What can I do? What do you need?"

"Do you mind if I stay here tonight? I don't really want to talk or anything. I just can't face going to her house right now. I'll pay the normal rate—"

"Chris, of course! Don't even worry about that," Abby said as they made their way into the house. Snowy immediately wound herself around Chris's legs, and Chris bent down to pick her up, speaking to her in a sweet baby voice.

"Can I make you some tea? Something to eat?"

"No," Chris said quietly, not taking her eyes off Snowy, who purred against her chest. Cats just knew. Amazing little creatures.

"Okay…" Abby was hovering, but Chris had made it clear. She didn't want to talk, and Abby needed to respect that. "Well, if there's anything you need, I'll be here, okay? You just shout."

"Mm-hmm," Chris murmured into Snowy's velvety belly, and eventually, Abby retreated. As she reached her room, she heard Chris call out, "Thank you, Abby. Really."

"Yeah, of course," she called back, suddenly exhausted herself from the knot of emotions tied up in her chest.

A light knock on Abby's door, much later.

She threw her laptop aside and scrambled to get under the covers. She was wearing only a tank top and panties, not expecting company. The house had been silent for hours.

"Come in," she said shyly, trying to act natural.

"Hi," Chris said, equally shyly, leaning around the door. "I, uh, changed my mind. I could use some company. Do you mind?"

"No!" Too bright. She cleared her throat. "No, not at all. Come in." Chris entered in a cloud of her familiar scent.

"What are you up to?" she asked, perching gingerly on the edge of the bed. She, too, wore a tank top, but she'd had the luxury of planning, so she'd paired hers with sweatpants. Designer, naturally.

Abby turned her laptop screen in Chris's direction. "Just watching some lesbian porn and drinking hot chocolate."

"Huh?" Chris nearly snapped her neck doing a double take. "Wait, that's not lesbian porn!"

Abby chuckled. "What do you mean it's not? It's *Ocean's 8*!"

"Hmmm…" Chris narrowed her eyes. "Cate Blanchett."

"Sandra Bullock."

"I'm starting to see your point."

Abby chuckled as she spun the laptop back around, snapping the lid shut. "So, um, silly question but…how are you feeling?"

Chris took a deep breath. "Honestly?"

Abby nodded.

"Relieved. Disappointed. Exhausted. Sad. Guilty. The order constantly changes."

Abby nodded again, saying nothing, allowing Chris to continue, just as she'd done for Abby that night at The Planetarium. It felt like a lifetime ago.

"I think you understand that. Even though our circumstances are so very different." She leaned forward, elbows on her knees, frowning at the floor. Snowy pirouetted against her bare ankles. "You know I did my mourning a long, long time ago. I'm relieved that it's all over, because it's been a mind-fuck to be thrust back into something that's been dead and buried for so long—to me, anyway. I feel like I can finally get closure… there'll be no more 'Maybe one days' or 'I wonder ifs.' I'm relieved for so many reasons! Relieved that I did the right thing—the right thing for *me*. Relieved that I didn't have to be the one to flip that switch. I didn't want to have to kill my mother. Even though it felt like she buried me a long time ago." She turned around and looked at Abby. "Is this making any sense?"

Abby nodded sadly. "Yeah, it is."

Chris nodded too, then returned to her position staring at the floor. Snowy jumped up and began rubbing her face on Chris's side.

"I'm disappointed that things had to end this way, with these lingering questions. Did my mother finally accept me? Accept that I'm gay? Is that why she called me up here in the first place? Or was she just confused and drugged-up when she asked me about Karys? I'll never know. I'm exhausted from trying to figure it all out. Argh!" She lifted her hands to the sides of her skull and shook her head, her fingers disappearing into her hair. "I wish I could just stop my brain whirring all the time! I need a break from it all."

"I get it," Abby said, leaning forward to place a hand on Chris's back. "Trying to find peace, or acceptance, or whatever…it's the most exhausting part of all. But you know, you don't have to figure it out right now. Or ever. I know it happened years and years ago…but it also happened right now. Today. It took…what? Nearly thirty years for your lived experience and reality to line up? You're going to need to give yourself a lot of grace, and a lot of kindness, as you work through all this."

"I might need you to remind me of that."

"I gladly will."

Chris cleared her throat and shifted so she was facing Abby. "There's something else I wanted to ask you," she said, her brows furrowing.

"Mmm?"

"Would you come to the funeral? I just don't think I can face it on my own. Obviously, I'll understand if funerals are not your thing. Some people can't…and perhaps you, especially, after…you know—"

Abby placed her hand on Chris's, gently silencing her. "Chris. Of course I'll be there."

She sighed, visibly relieved. "Why are you so good to me? All I ever do is dump my shit on you."

Abby took in the drawn yet exquisite face of the woman beside of her, the woman who had turned her life on its head. The woman who, she was realising, had given her her life back.

"I owe you."

"You owe me? Whatever for?"

Abby frowned. "You don't know? You…you opened up my world again. I had such a tiny life before you arrived. And you forced me back out there. Not forced. Gently encouraged." She chuckled.

Chris pretended to look shocked before conceding with a smile.

"You allowed me to say things I'd never felt comfortable telling anyone. You helped me to face the things I didn't want to. Silly things, like seeing Cody again. And really big things, like sorting through Dan's clothes. And all of those things have come together and entirely transformed my life. This Dolphin project…I'm not sure it would ever have happened if it hadn't been for you and I getting tipsy together and going through those boxes I hadn't been able to touch in years, except to push them further out of sight. You helped me to find joy in the things that had been too difficult and painful to face, and…it's changed my life, Chris." *You've changed my life.*

"Oh, Abby!" Chris flushed in a way that Abby had never seen before, and Abby couldn't help but laugh.

"It's true! Even if it embarrasses you. You've had a massive impact on my life. On me."

Chris rolled her eyes to the ceiling and shook her head. "Well, thank you," she said, finally looking Abby in the eye. "Now can we stop being so fucking cheesy?"

"God, yes. Please."

"Good." Chris leaned back on her arms, and her eyes drifted to the laptop resting on Abby's thighs.

"I want to watch with you," she said. "Shift up."

"Oh, er…" Now it was Abby's turn to blush. "I, uh…" She shifted awkwardly like a seal on dry land, trying to keep the covers over her waist while holding the laptop steady.

Chris laughed as she slid in next to her. "Don't pop a hip out, doll," she said, then stopped and looked at Abby, who could still feel her cheeks flaming. "Is this okay?"

"Yeah, of course. I just…I don't have pants on," Abby blurted. "And it's Dan's birthday today."

"*What?*" Chris shot Abby a look, her back suddenly ramrod straight. "Did I forget? Did you tell me and I forgot?"

"No. I didn't tell you."

Chris was aghast. "Abby, why? Why wouldn't you tell me?"

"Chris, come on. You've had a lot going on. A lot."

Chris rubbed a hand over her face. "And here I was asking you to come to a funeral! Well, are you okay? Stupid fucking question."

"No, it's not." Abby finally looked Chris in the eye. "A stupid question, I mean. I appreciate you asking, and yes, I'm okay. I'm much, much better than I was before."

"Before?"

"Yeah. The first birthday…I'd just moved to Bay View. I don't really remember much of it, I was so traumatised. And last year…Well, last year would've been Dan's fortieth birthday, and she'd been planning this crazy island celebration even before I met her. So Evan and I, we created this ridiculous island scene in the living room…" Abby chuckled at the memory. "Inflatable palm trees and leis and this really, really terrible punch. It was great until I ended up sobbing all over him and massacring his white T-shirt with my mascara."

Abby trailed off, pulling her lips into her mouth. She leaned back against the headboard and closed her eyes, becoming aware of Chris's body so close to hers. She took a deep breath to steady the trembling of her limbs.

She felt Chris lean back too. "Did you do something special today?" she asked softly, and Abby could sense her eyes on her.

Slowly, she opened her eyes and rolled her head to face Chris.

"Mmm, I guess you could say that," she replied, fiddling with the hem of her tank top. "I drank hot chocolate in the bath, and I got loads of messages from my friends back home." She paused, took another breath. "And…I did this." With clammy fingers, she slowly rolled her top up.

Bemused, Chris cocked her head as Abby moved.

"Dan has—had—the same one," Abby was explaining as Chris's eyes travelled to the pale, slightly inflamed skin below her breast. "We got them together, but I couldn't handle the pain, so I chickened out halfway through. Today, I finally finished it."

"Oh, my…" Chris murmured, leaning in closer to see the design. "Does it hurt now?"

"Now? No, not really."

Chris nodded. Then, she reached out and brushed the tattoo with her fingertips.

Abby's breath caught in her throat. Chris looked up with concern.

"Did I hurt you?"

Abby shook her head vigorously. "No," she choked out. "You can touch it."

So Chris bent her head—so low, Abby could feel her breath against her skin—and rested her fingers on the curve of Abby's ribs. And then, with exquisite tenderness, she brushed her thumb over the tender tattooed flesh, the tip of her finger grazing the soft underside of Abby's breast.

Abby squeezed her eyes shut as a thousand tiny fires erupted under her flesh, burning through the last of her resolve and ruining any chance she may have had of escaping this friendship unscathed.

Oh, shit.

"It's beautiful, Abby," Chris murmured, straightening up and pulling her hand away. Almost instinctively, Abby reached out and took it. Her skin throbbed where Chris's fingers had been, and she didn't want the feeling to end.

"Please stay," Abby said softly, locking eyes with Chris as she held her warm hand between her own.

Chris didn't answer. Instead, she reached her free arm around Abby's waist and pulled her in close.

"Just tonight," Abby said. "I just don't feel like being alone."

"Me, neither, Abs. Are you feeling sad?"

"Yeah. But not…not because of today."

"I'm feeling sad, too…but also not because of today. Not *only* today."

Abby nodded. "I don't want you to leave," she whispered, but it was too soft for Chris to hear, so they held each other as the movie played and the credits rolled and nine o'clock became ten o'clock and eleven. When neither of them could keep their eyes open any longer, they slid down under the covers without saying a word and closed their eyes.

In the middle of the night, when Abby woke from something like sleep, cocooned in warm and fragrant embrace, she realised that their fingers were laced together.

She could have been asleep for one minute or forever when she was wrenched from it by alternating banging and grating sounds. Then, all at once, she was aware of Chris scrambling for something next to the bed.

She cursed as she fumbled in the dark.

A phone. Vibrating over and over on the bedside table.

She pressed a button and switched it off. "Fuck!"

More banging.

"Is that…the front door?" Abby croaked, clawing her way out of sleep.

"Yeah." Chris panted, now up and frantically running her hands through her hair. "Karys is here."

"Jesus!" Abby was bolt upright, her heart in her throat. "What?"

But Chris was already gone, barrelling down the hallway and calling, "Yeah, I'm *coming*!"

The sound of the front door opening, and then a woman's voice she didn't recognise.

Abby sat dead still in her bed, her legs pulled up to her chin, her roaring pulse making it almost impossible to hear what the voices were saying.

Panic, like wet cement, poured into her chest.

Karys, here? But how? Why?

She shook her head, trying to unscramble her thoughts.

Nothing happened last night.

And, anyway, they're not even together.

But the thoughts crumbled as quickly as they formed and Abby shook her head again, hard.

What happened last night wasn't nothing.

And Chris and Karys were together, right now, in Abby's living room.

The heartbeat in her throat turned to a lump of stone.

What is going on?

Abby forced her breathing into a more normal rhythm so she could try to hear what they were saying. She caught only snatches.

"…was a mistake, and I'm sorry…"

"…about you, not her…"

"…deal with it alone, and it was wrong…"

And then silence. She held her breath, but nothing more was said.

The slam of her front door broke the spell, and Abby leapt up. She yanked on a pair of shorts and crept to the door, listening for any signs of life.

The distinctive sounds of luggage and zippers were coming from Chris's room. Gingerly, Abby tiptoed over and peered around the door.

"Hey," she said softly to Chris's frantic form.

"Hey," she replied without turning around.

Abby felt panic rising into her throat. "Chris, what's going on?" But Chris either didn't hear her or chose not to.

"Chris!" Abby repeated, straining to keep the dread from her voice. "Chris, *speak* to me!"

Chris reeled around, breathless and pale. "Karys is here. With the kids. They flew in this morning and they're waiting for me outside."

"Your whole family? But…why?"

Chris returned to her frenzied packing. "She says she didn't want me to go through this alone."

Abby scoffed. "Wait, you're serious? And you're *going*?"

"Yeah," Chris replied, hoisting her bag onto her shoulder. "Abby." She finally looked her in the eye. "I'll talk to you later, okay?"

"Sure," Abby mumbled, following Chris as she hurried down the hallway. "I just don't understand…How did she even know you were here?"

Chris waggled her phone in the air without stopping. "It's easy to trace me, doll."

Outside in the street, a car idled. The sun was just starting to rise, slashing red and yellow claw marks into the sky.

Chris strode down the pathway and in two fluid movements threw her bag into the car and climbed in after it.

The car revved a few times before tearing off. Even though it was too dark to see, Abby knew that Chris hadn't turned around as she disappeared into the red light of dawn.

CHAPTER TWENTY

The progress the team had made on The Dolphin in just a few short weeks was nothing short of remarkable. At the rate they were going, Mrs. Woods was telling Roy, he'd be back behind the bar as soon as next month.

Abby listened with half an ear as she helped Michaela slap plaster onto a wall.

"Just imagine, Roy," Mrs. Woods enthused, ponytail bobbing. "This time next month, it'll be like the fire never happened. Actually, scratch that. The place will be even better than before."

Roy was dubious. "Well, that's not the story I hear from your other half. Not even close."

Abby glanced over at him. With his stooped shoulders and slightly loose jaw, it looked like someone had let all the air out of him. The last few months had really aged him, and Abby made a mental note to check in on him.

"Well, I'm a lot more positive than he is," Mrs. Woods said, her tone only slightly dulled. "Roy, I know we'll find the money. We've come this far. We just have to keep going, okay? You'll see. It's all going to work out."

Roy grunted and shoved his hands into his pockets, rounding his back even more. "Well, we'll see," he said, sloping off. "See ya later, Penny."

Abby dropped her trowel and grabbed an old rag.

"Roy," she called, wiping her hands as she hustled after him. "Roy!"

"Oh, Abby." He finally stopped and turned around. "Sorry, my hearing is pretty shot these days," he said, pointing at his ears. His medic-alert bracelet tinkled on his wrist. "I guess that's what ya can expect when you're seventy-eight. Everything just falls apart."

"Seventy-eight? I wouldn't have put you at a day over sixty."

"Yeah, well, I feel every minute of it," he grunted, ignoring the compliment.

"At least The Dolphin is the opposite of falling apart. Just look! In a few weeks, it'll be good as new. Even better, perhaps."

"That's what they tell me," he grumbled.

Abby was starting to get annoyed. They were all working so hard. "Aren't you happy you'll have your bar back? And your hotel?"

"No!" he barked, and Abby jumped.

"No?" She shook her head in confusion. "What do you mean?"

Roy squeezed his eyes shut. Then he let out a long, defeated sigh. "I'm sorry if I sound ungrateful, Abby. I'll never have enough words to thank you. I'm just tired. So, so tired."

He was quiet for a moment as the sounds of drilling and hammering punctuated the air. Abby watched as Mrs. Woods yelled orders at the team, sending men scattering in every direction.

Roy followed Abby's gaze. "When this place burnt down, I was gutted—if you'll forgive the pun. But then, as the months passed, I realised that I was…relieved. I don't miss the late nights, or the drunken customers. Sure, we had good times, didn't we?"

Abby nodded, even though Roy didn't seem to be expecting an answer.

"But I don't know if I have the energy to do it all over again. And I certainly don't have the money."

Abby frowned. "The money? What do you mean? I thought everything was covered."

"Nope. I guess these things always end up costing more than one expects."

He mentioned a figure and Abby gasped. "We're that much short? What are we going to do?"

Roy shrugged, his hands still in his pockets. "Penny seems optimistic. I'll leave it to her. Until then, I'm going home to nap. And then I gotta figure out how I'm gonna run a bar I don't wanna run."

Abby watched Roy retreating, feeling deflated. She'd come to The Dolphin today to distract her from her thoughts and the ache behind her ribs. But now, with Chris gone and the project broke, the ache was worse.

Abby's new FortyLinks guests were ensconced on the sofa and watching TV when she got in. Usually, she would have kept Dan's birthday weekend guest-free in case she needed to melt down at midnight in the living room. But the couple—in town for a long-planned family event—had originally booked at The Dolphin, and she hadn't the heart to turn them down. Given how she was feeling today, she was quite pleased for the distraction.

Abby greeted them and slipped straight into the shower before sequestering herself in her bedroom. It suited her just fine, actually. Even Snowy had given her a wide berth—she was perched, purring fatly, nose in the air, on the woman's lap.

Abby glanced at her phone, feeling a jolt at the sight of a missed call. It was just Evan.

"I just got back from The Dolphin," she said as he picked up. "Thought I'd see you, actually. Michaela was there."

"Yeah, I had some other stuff going on," he replied, still as uncharacteristically vague as he'd been last week.

"What other stuff? Why are you being weird?"

"I'm not being weird! I just...I had to sort some things out with Marli."

"Marli?" Abby sat up straight. "*Marli* Marli?"

"See, this is exactly why I didn't want to tell you."

A beep came down the line and Abby glanced at the phone screen.

"Listen, I want to hear everything, okay?" she said, her palms suddenly clammy. "But I have to take another call."

"Now who's being weird?" Evan retorted, but he hung up and Abby took a breath before answering.

"Chris?"

"Hey." Abby could hear voices in the background, and then the sound of a door closing. "I wanted to call to find out how much I owe you. For the room last night."

"For the...what?"

"The room. I stayed last night. I would like to settle for it." Her tone was icy: brusque and businesslike.

Abby gasped like she'd been punched in the stomach. Was this some kind of joke? She waited for a laugh or a "Just kidding!" but none was forthcoming.

"Is this why you're calling me?" she choked out at last. "You didn't even sleep in that room last night."

"Abby."

"No, Chris! Why are you calling me?"

"To find out how much I owe you."

"Jesus…fine!" Anger and humiliation began to unfurl inside her. What the *hell* was going on? "You really want to know? Eight grand. That's the current daily rate for unused FortyLinks bedrooms in Bay View. Payable directly to Roy at The Dolphin Inn."

Chris paused. "What?"

"What do you mean, what? You asked."

"Abby, please."

She swallowed hard, suppressing a laugh or a sob, she wasn't sure. "Never mind, Chris. Just forget it."

Another long pause.

"There is something else I wanted to say," Chris began, but at that moment, the sounds once again: a door being opened, voices, a rustle over the line.

"I'll call you back, okay?" she said and abruptly cut the line.

But she didn't, and late into the night, Abby finally fell asleep.

On Monday, she dredged every last bit of enthusiasm she could muster, but she felt emptied-out and hollow.

"Dude, it was always a ball-of-shit situation," Evan had said around a mouthful of pastrami sandwich, and while the observation had deeply irritated Abby, she'd had to admit he was right. If she were honest with herself, she'd known it, too.

She worked hard to distract herself for the rest of the school day. It had worked until she got home and saw Chris's rental car parked outside. Her insides lurched. The memory of Chris's fingers laced through her own flashed through her mind, and she reached out to steady herself against a tree.

The car was empty, so Abby walked slowly up to her front door, casting an eye around but seeing no one.

She certainly wasn't expecting to open her front door and find a stranger inside her home.

"Whoa!" she exclaimed at the sight of Karys, who spun around and glared at her, a tight smile cracked into her face.

Abby had never seen her picture, but somehow, she knew exactly who she was.

"Hello, Abby. Or do you prefer Abigail? I'm Karys."

"Abby is good," she answered warily as she took a step back. "And, uh, hi." What the *hell* was Karys doing here, inside her home? "I wasn't expecting visitors. How did you get into my house?"

"Oh, your guests let me in," Karys said breezily, jerking her chin in the direction of the bedrooms. "I thought I'd take a look around, in case we'd like to stay here."

Abby felt her jaw tighten. "Stay here?"

"Mmm," Karys said, slowly casting her eyes around the room. "That other house is so…suffocating." She settled her cool gaze on Abby once more. "But I'm sure you know that."

Abby sidestepped the trap. "I imagine it must feel like that, especially now. I'm very sorry for your loss."

Karys waved a hand dismissively. "Are you? I can't say I am, really. Anyway, your place won't be big enough for our whole family."

"No, sadly not," Abby replied, not feeling sad about it at all. "I'm sorry I can't help you."

"That's okay. You've helped a lot already, I hear." Her smile was like a crocodile's.

"Well!" Abby replied brightly, alarm bells screaming. "Thank you for stopping by. Usually, people would just look and book online."

Karys ignored the hint. "It is a pity, though. Your bedroom is cute. Tiny, of course. But cute."

"My bedroom?"

"Oh!" A short little laugh. "Silly me. *Guest* room, I mean."

Still the woman made no move to leave, and Abby felt the room closing in around her. It felt like all the air had been sucked out of the house, and Abby was desperate for Karys to go. But she was also intrigued by the woman who had been something of a spectre in her life for months.

Karys wasn't much different to what Abby had expected. It struck her that here in front of her was an adult. A real adult. If you looked around a room in a crisis, Karys was the person you'd ask for help, like if your appendix burst, or your plane crashed and you had to flag down a rescue chopper using just the life jacket you were wearing and some tin foil. Karys would pull it off.

Her look, too, was impeccable, and her scent a musky mix of high-end clothing and expensive cosmetics. In a different time, she might have worn leather gloves, which she'd pinch off at the fingertips and drop onto a table with mild contempt. But when Abby looked down at her hands, there were no gloves, just unclad fingers with a visible white rind of nail protruding above each one. Abby saw that Karys had been watching her the whole time.

"Well," she said crisply, stepping toward the front door. "We won't be in town much longer, anyway. Just a day or two, until the funeral. We have a lot to do at home before Chris and I emigrate next month."

Next month?

Abby felt instantly winded, but she fought to keep her expression neutral. She knew Karys was scrutinising her every expression. She would not give her the satisfaction of knowing the statement had jolted her.

"Thanks for stopping by," Abby repeated, reaching across Karys for the door handle, hoping their physical closeness would encourage her to move along.

But instead, the woman leaned in closer, her face so near to Abby's, she could smell spearmint gum on her breath.

"Oh, one more thing," Karys said in a low voice, and Abby pulled back, her hand dropping from the door.

"How long have you been in love with Chris?"

Abby was too stunned to speak.

"Ah, you see, a woman always knows," Karys said with a wink, tapping the side of her nose. Abby shrank back.

"I know you think you have a special connection with her because you happened to witness this…this personal crisis of hers."

Karys's gaze bore right into Abby's soul. Her smile was ice-cold.

"Because you—what?—went to a party together? Because she gave you a nice little jacket?"

Abby felt like the tips of her ears had been set on fire.

"But relationships, Abigail—real relationships—are about much more than an old jacket pulled out of the garbage pile. Oh? She didn't tell you that part, did she? It wasn't even last season. It was two seasons ago." Every word dripped with contempt. "It made no difference to her whether she threw it away or gave it to you."

Karys's words were roaring in Abby's ears, the way voices did when you were about to faint. She dug her short nails into the palms of her hands as sweat broke out above her lip, fighting to stay in the moment.

"What I'm saying is, don't construct some sort of love story out of a few acts of convenience. Because that's all this was to her."

Abby stared at her mutely.

"You're young, Abigail. So young. And beautiful." She reached out with a cool hand and touched Abby's cheek. Abby flinched. "And free! I have real responsibilities, you understand? Our business. Our children. I can't just…flit off on a journey of self-discovery on a whim. Someone has to keep the home fires burning. One day you'll understand that, Abby. One day, you'll discover what love really is. And sacrifice."

And at that, at last, Abby found her voice.

"That's. *Enough*."

Karys drew back her hand.

"You know nothing about me," Abby hissed, feeling a level of rage almost foreign to her, rage born of frustration and pain and the unfairness of it all. "And I might be young, but I'm old enough to know that all of this is a *you* problem, not a *me* problem."

Karys glared at her.

"All I have done is provide accommodation. Anything else, you need to take up with Chris." Abby was furious now, almost panting. "Because talking to me about your relationship is about as helpful as putting it in rice."

With a shaking hand, she yanked open the door.

"Now, please," she said, the words cracking in her throat. "Get out of my house."

"Gladly." Karys sneered, stepping out into the bright daylight. "Thank you for your hospitality, but your services are no longer needed. Chris has enough going on, what with her mother dying and us leaving so soon." Karys delivered each word with relish. "She doesn't want to hear from you. So please, stop calling, stop messaging, and for the love of god, don't bother coming to the funeral. Goodbye, Abigail."

Then she stomped to her car, slammed herself inside it, and sped away, almost colliding with Cody's van trundling down the road.

"Hey!" Jade called out of the passenger window, waving at Abby. "Hey, Abs!"

The van screeched to a halt and Jade leaned out. "Dude, you okay? You look like you've seen a ghost."

Abby nodded dumbly. "I feel like it, too."

Her head was buzzing from the confrontation as well as the bomb Karys had dropped. Chris? Emigrating in a *month*? Abby felt a headache setting in.

"Well, are you gonna get in?" Cody's voice penetrated her daze.

Abby frowned, shaking her head. "Uh, sorry—what?"

"I texted you earlier, silly. Didn't you check your phone? We're going to Luigi's. Get in."

"Oh, umm…yeah…Okay…"

Abby's legs felt like rubber as she lumbered to the van, her head beginning to throb.

"Abby." Jade twisted around in her seat. "What's going on?"

"Karys was just here," she replied in a voice that sounded very far away. "Chris's…partner, I guess."

She saw Cody and Jade exchange a look, and a twinge of irritation snapped her back into the present.

"And that look?"

"What look?" Cody was the picture of innocence. "There was no look."

Abby grunted but dropped it. They were already at the restaurant, and they piled out and into their regular outside booth. Soon, Evan joined them, stepping over a mess of rubble and a discarded neon *Luigi's* sign at the entrance.

Abby's head was still spinning—and it was pounding now, too. All she wanted was to bury herself under her covers.

"Hey, what's going on here?" Cody asked as the waitress came over. "You guys renovating?"

"Oh, you didn't hear?" she said, snapping on some gum. "Rob's sold the place to his brother. Turning it into a grocery store. What can I get ya to drink?"

"Wait, what? Why?" Jade looked crestfallen.

"Oh, he had a heart attack last week—not a bad one! But, yeah. His wife told him he's gotta stop working and stop eating so much cheese."

"Well, that's the end of an era," Jade said sadly as the waitresses sauntered off.

"Or the end of an error," Evan quipped, dropping his voice to a whisper. "I mean, it's really terrible pizza. Maybe we'll all be saved from heart attacks."

Everyone laughed except Abby, and Evan frowned in her direction.

"She just had a visit from Chris's wife," Cody explained, and Evan's eyebrows shot up.

"What? For real?"

"She's not her wife, and anyway, they're…Ugh, it doesn't matter."

"Abby, you have to tell us what happened!"

Abby shrugged her shoulders and sighed. "I got home from school and she was inside my house and told me never to contact Chris again."

The table erupted.

"Inside your house?"

"She warned you to stay away from Chris?"

"How did she get in?"

Abby answered all their questions but found herself growing more and more agitated. The word *emigrating* slammed around inside her head over and over again, and Abby felt desperate for answers. She pulled her phone out of her pocket.

"What are you doing?" Jade asked.

"Texting Chris," Abby replied, not looking up. "I need to—"

"I don't think that's a good idea," Jade cut in, putting her hand over the phone. "Abby, I think you should just—"

Abby wrenched away from Jade, her rage reignited. "Jade, you have no idea what things are like with me and Chris. We're friends, okay? I can message her if I like."

"I know that, Abby," Jade replied gently. "But from Karys's perspective…" She shifted uncomfortably, her shoulders hunching. "I have to say I do kind of understand where she's coming from."

"What's that supposed to mean?"

"Well, you and Chris…at times it almost seemed like you were…a couple."

"That is ridiculous." Abby scoffed, the sound harsher than she'd intended. "It's nothing like that."

"I'm not saying it is, I'm just saying—"

"What? What are you saying, Jade?"

"I'm just saying I understand Karys's insecurity around things."

"You're *serious*?" Abby exploded, shooting to her feet. "Why am I not surprised that you would side with her? You've always been insecure about me."

"Abby, whoa," Evan said, grabbing her arm, but she shook him off.

"No, Evan. You guys have no idea! You're supposed to be my friends and you're taking her side?"

She clambered over Evan to escape the booth, feeling hot and angry and embarrassed, knowing her words were wildly out of line but entirely powerless to stop them.

"Just forget it." She huffed as she lurched out of the restaurant, tripping over the stupid sign. "I'm going home."

And she did text Chris on her walk home, through a haze of tears and frustration, even as everything rational in her yelled not to.

Why did it feel like everyone was always leaving? As she tried to figure out where everything had gone wrong—where she'd fallen into the trap she'd been so determined to avoid—she felt angry with herself, and wildly out of control.

* * *

"I really hate these things," Evan muttered as they filed into the echoey town hall. The soles of their shoes squeaked against the linoleum floor as they shuffled toward one of the back rows, Abby's arm hooked through Evan's, his muscles straining against the unforgiving fabric of his jacket.

"Yeah," she agreed, wrinkling her nose. "It always smells like mothballs in here."

It had felt good to have his support, particularly as Abby had defied Karys's orders and the woman scared her.

Standing at the entrance to the hall had been Chris, of course. Abby had allowed her heart to surge at the sight of her. She was too tired, too confused, to lie to herself any longer. Besides, it seemed Chris had done enough lying for both of them.

"I've got you," Evan had whispered to her as they'd walked up, offering her his arm, which she gratefully accepted. He'd said the same thing when he'd arrived at her house an hour earlier.

"I know that no matter what any of us say, you're going to go today," he'd said as he'd pressed a coffee into her hand. "So, I've got you, okay? You're not going to do this alone."

Abby had sniffed. Nodded. She had appreciated Evan so much in that moment that she'd suddenly regretted giving him a hard time about Marli. He was sensible, and kind. He hadn't interrogated her intentions or tried to change her mind. And here he was beside her—dependable, consistent, forgiving—as she took in the hair, the form, the face that threatened to undo her.

"Hello," said the hair, the form, the face without emotion, encased in a tailored black pants suit, and Abby felt her stomach turn.

"Hi," she said back, taking in the three towering young adults flanking her and the glowering figure lurking behind them. Karys stared at her icily.

"I'm so sorry for your loss," Evan said in a low voice. Chris thanked him before turning to greet someone else.

Abby didn't realise until they were inside that she'd been holding her breath the whole time.

"Thank you for being here for me," she murmured now as they watched people dribble into the hall. "I'm sorry about the way I acted last night. I was such a brat. And I'm sorry for being hard on you about Marli."

"I know you didn't mean it," he said, nudging her arm with his.

"What's the deal with you and her anyway? You never got a chance to tell me."

He looked at her sheepishly. "Can we talk about it later?"

"Talk about what, exactly?"

"Abs, this thing's about to start…"

She shot him a look. "Well, it hasn't started yet. What's the deal?"

"We, um, got back together."

"What!" Abby yelped. An elderly man sitting in front of her turned around to glower.

"I told you, we'll talk later, okay? It's about to start."

A handful of people stood up to speak. Chris wasn't one of them. Instead, she sat with stiff shoulders in the front row, between Karys and one of her sons. Occasionally, she glanced around, and in those moments, Abby would avert her gaze, worried that Chris could sense her eyes boring into her.

Afterward, in the stark midday sun, people milled about, ostensibly paying their respects. Most were patently curious; they hadn't realised Cookie, a closed book to almost everyone in town, had a daughter. They gawked at her and Karys, and Abby could see them doing the mental gymnastics and coming up short—one man short, to be precise.

"Ready to go?" Evan asked, yanking at the top button of his shirt. "I'm fucking dying in this suit."

"No." Abby was staring at Chris in the distance. "I need to speak to her."

"Really, Abby?" He planted his hands squarely on her shoulders and wheeled her around to face him. "Listen to me. This is not the time. Or the place."

Abby shrugged, easing out of his grip and turning back to focus on Chris, who was deep in conversation with Roy and the Woodses.

"Abby, I'm serious. You have to drop it. You're going to embarrass yourself."

Abby spun back around. "Evan, I am going to speak to her. I don't care what you say. So you can go, or you can stay, but I'm doing it."

"Fine." He threw his hands up in the air. "The woman clearly doesn't want to speak to you, and her girlfriend told you to leave them alone. You are going to humiliate yourself, and I'm not sticking around to watch it."

"Fine!" Abby snapped. "Go. I don't care."

Evan stalked off and Abby, afraid she'd lose her nerve, made her way over to Chris. This might well be the last opportunity she'd have to talk to her in the flesh, but as the gap between them closed, her mind was clear and blank as the sky.

"Chris," she blurted as she came close. "Can I speak to you for a moment?" Her heart was racing so fast, she worried she might pass out.

"I'm a bit busy right now," Chris replied with a tight mouth.

"Oh, please," Mrs. Woods said, flapping a hand. "Go ahead. Ask my husband—I can talk for *hours*."

Abby looked hopefully at Chris, who clenched her jaw and shot a look at Karys. Abby could feel a forcefield of disapproval emanating from the woman, but Chris stepped aside anyway.

"Abby, this *really* isn't a good time."

"Don't you think I know that? But what else was I supposed to do? You've completely shut me out. You don't even reply to my texts."

Chris clenched her jaw again, studying Abby as she breathed out heavily through her nose. "Things are different. My family is here."

"Jesus, Chris, what does that even mean?"

"What do you want from me, Abby?"

"I want you to speak to me! I want to talk about what happened. I want to talk about us…whatever this weird thing is between us."

"Well, this is not the time. I told you that."

"So, you admit there's something?"

Chris pulled her lips into her mouth.

"When is the time, Chris? Will it be before you emigrate? Because I hear that's just around the corner."

Chris's eyes flashed angrily as she folded her arms across her chest. "That has nothing to do with you."

"Of all things, *that* has nothing to do with me?" Abby shot back, feeling her own anger rising. Frantically, she clawed around for the right words to de-escalate the argument, but her brain refused to budge.

"Abby, this is my mother's funeral. My entire family is here. I think it would be best if you left and didn't contact me again."

Abby shook her head, stunned. "I'm sorry—what did you say?"

"You heard her," said a voice from behind as Karys sauntered over. "Go away, Abigail. You're not wanted here." Abby could hear the sneer without even looking at Karys's face. "And Chris doesn't want to hear from you again."

Abby felt tears welling up as she looked from Karys to Chris and back again. "Is that really what you want, Chris? To never hear from me again?"

But Chris's expression didn't change. She stood there, rigid and silent, her dark eyes shining as she clenched and unclenched her jaw.

"*Abby*," she said at last. A plea.

Abby's whole body was trembling now. She wanted to scream at Karys to leave, beg Chris to stay, but as fat tears began to fall onto her cheeks, she realised she'd been utterly defeated.

"Abby, you're embarrassing yourself," Karys hissed, grabbing her arm and yanking her around. "Look! Everyone is staring at you."

It was true. As Abby glanced around the garden, she realised that all the conversations had stopped and everyone's attention was firmly on her.

"Just. Go."

Suddenly unable to see through her tears, Abby turned and stumbled straight into a wall of solid, warm, human.

"It's fine, we're going," Evan said gruffly, folding Abby into his arms. "We're really sorry to have caused a scene. And I'm terribly sorry for your loss, Ms. Addison."

A sweating bottle of beer hovered above Abby's head, gripped between short, purple-polished nails peeling at the edges.

"I heard you could do with another one of these," said the voice from above, and Abby twisted around to see Drew peering down at her.

"Yep." Abby hiccupped, taking the bottle and downing a big swig. "You can keep these coming."

Drew walked around to the back of the sofa and slid down beside Abby. "You're already double parked," she said, gesturing to the glass of red wine on the floor beside Abby.

"Am I?" She turned to look at where Drew pointed, but her neck wouldn't cooperate, and her head lolled against the back of the sofa. "Whatever."

"What are you doing, hiding out in here? Everyone's outside, eating ribs 'n' shit. Cody says it's the best she's ever grilled 'em."

Abby attempted to shrug, but she just slipped farther down against the back of the sofa. It was quiet here—in contrast to the mayhem in her head.

"Erryone'sh giving me a hard time," she said, stumbling over each word as she struggled to focus on Drew's face. "An' erryone'sh leaving. An' I wanna go home bu' Cody won' lemme go on my own."

"What do you mean, everyone's leaving? Who's going where?"

Abby groaned and dropped her head onto her knees. It was so obvious! But so hard to explain right now. It was clear in her head, but her tongue just wasn't cooperating.

"You mean Chris?"

"Yeahhh, and Evan."

"Evan's leaving?"

Abby grunted into her knees. "I jus' wanna go home."

"Okay, you want me to take you?"

Abby looked up, feeling hopeful for the first time since Evan dragged her to Cody's house for a barbeque, and on the way, dropped the bombshell that he'd decided to leave Bay View and live with Marli in the city.

He couldn't have picked worse timing if his life had depended on it. Yesterday, Chris. Today, Evan. Tomorrow… Well, everyone who mattered was already gone, so.

"Take me home? Really?"

"Yeah, sure. Come, get up. You'll have to have a glass of water first or something 'cos we're gonna walk."

Drew stood, then held her hand out to Abby, who lumbered to her feet and kicked the glass of wine over as she did.

"Shit," she mumbled as the drink spread through the carpet like blood. She crouched down and tried to blot it with the hem of her bomber jacket.

"Abby, no!" Drew yanked her back to her feet like a toddler. "Leave it. I'll sort it out tomorrow. You'll ruin your jacket."

"I don' care."

"Yeah, you do," Drew muttered. "At least, you will tomorrow."

"I don' care 'bout tomorrow, either."

"Jesus, you're such a drama queen," Drew said, watching as Abby poured half a glass of water down her throat and the other half down her front. "You gonna be able to make the walk?"

"Yeahhh." Abby groaned as cool night air hit her wet face and sobered her a little. "Jus' go shlow."

The rest of the evening Abby remembered in a tsunami of humiliating snapshots the next day: getting home and pulling all her clothes off, clumsily trying to seduce Drew, Drew firmly rebuffing her: *Abby, you're drunk. No. You're drunk.* Crying on her bed. Crying in the shower. Crying while puking, all the while naked and aching, not just in her soul but physically, every fibre of her, as if she'd been thrown down a flight of stairs. Drew drying her. Dressing her. Putting her to bed. The weight of a body next to hers, a body that held her gingerly and let her weep until sleep came, fast but fitful, and now, hideous-bright morning, the briefest of blank minds, and then—

"Oh god, oh god, oh god, oh god."

"Ah. You're awake."

Drew breezed into the room with a cup of her signature awful coffee and ripped open the curtains. "Your alarm's been going off for ages. Don't you have to get to school?"

Abby groaned into her pillow, wrapping it around her head, and felt every atom of her body lurch into violent warfare. "Oh *godddd*. I think I'm going to die."

Waves of nausea rocked her body, and when she tried to move her limbs, her head swam.

"I think this is the worst hangover I've ever had."

"Well." Drew's voice sounded muffled through the pillow clamped around Abby's head. "You have a shower and I'll make you some breakfast. I make the best hangover food ever."

"Please stop talking about food."

"Okay, at least have some coff—"

"Drew, shut it!"

Abby vaulted out of bed and made it to the bathroom just in time to slam the door and wrap her arms around the toilet bowl.

"Fuck my life," she groaned as stood under a cold shower minutes later, resting her pounding head against the cool tiles. The throbbing was in her ears, under her skin, in the tips of her fingers. Maybe she'd have a stroke. Maybe she'd explode like a volcano, right here where she stood.

She wasn't sure how long she rested like that. Perhaps she drifted off. At some point, she was roused by banging, like someone at her door. And words through the hiss of the falling water.

Can't be…can it?

Slowly she stood, pushing off the wall with weak arms, her neck aching as she did. With shaking hands, she closed the taps and listened.

Nothing.

That's weird. Maybe I really am going crazy.

Out of the shower, dressed, a towel wrapped around her head, she limped into the kitchen.

"Did someone come to the door while I was in the shower? I could've sworn I heard knocking."

Drew was at the stove, overseeing some yellow gloop bubbling in a skillet. "Nope," she said, not looking up. "You probably heard me banging these pans around. You know, you really need to sort out your cupboards."

"Yeah, I know." Abby frowned, then wrinkled her nose. "Eggs? Really?"

"Yes, Ms. Hangover." Drew stuck a spatula into the mush. "Trust me. I'm a chef."

"Trust me, I'm going to puke them back up."

Abby watched for a moment as Drew pushed the slop around the pan, feeling her stomach turn. Something was bugging her, and it was more than just the sight and smell of the eggs.

"Drew, are you sure there was no one...?"

Drew looked up, spatula poised above the pan, her expression vacant.

"Never mind." Abby shook her head. "I'm imagining things."

But back in her room, Abby knew there was one thing she wasn't imagining: Chris leaving. Chris emigrating.

Chris gone.

"Go, then," she said under her breath as she reached for her phone and began erasing texts, numbers, emails, every last shred of evidence that Chris Addison had ever existed, digitally or otherwise. Then she deactivated her FortyLinks account, blocked Chris's number, and tossed her phone into the back of her drawer.

"*There*. You're gone. For good."

Moments later she was stomping out of the house, hair piled on top of her head, forcing bits of rubbery egg down her throat. She felt Drew watching her as she left.

CHAPTER TWENTY-ONE

"Okay, so… that's a no to the books but a yes to the CD collection?"

"Mm-hmm." Abby nodded from her spot on Evan's bed, where she lay on her stomach surrounded by old books, clothes, and sports gear. "I haven't seen you read a book in the entire time I've known you."

"Well, have you seen anyone playing a CD in the last ten years?"

"True. But, c'mon, half of these will be collector's items one day. Goo Goo Dolls? Matchbox Twenty? Offspring? Gold, dude. You have to keep them."

"I agree with Abby," Marli chimed in from the laptop screen. Her teeth flashed in a wide grin. "And besides, I already have more books than I could get through in an entire lifetime."

"Okayyyy," Evan said, dropping a stack into a crate labelled *DONATE*. "Once again, you girls win."

"You know, if you'd been a bit more in touch with your feelings and made up your mind sooner, you could've added all your stuff to Abby's sale," Marli pointed out, her voice slightly tinny through the computer speakers. "Men, huh?" She winked in Abby's direction.

"Yup," Abby chimed in. "And Roy might've been able to reach his target."

Evan dropped another pile of books into the crate with a huff. "What is this, National Gang Up On Evan Day?"

The girls chuckled.

"Anyway, didn't you hear?"

Thwack. Another armful of textbooks into the crate.

"Roy got it. The money he needed. Apparently, some Good Samaritan donated the whole lot."

"Really?" This was news to Abby.

It had been impossible not to notice how, over the past few weeks, work on-site had slowed and slowed until it had almost ground to a halt. It was inevitable, really, as the pile of building material grew smaller while the gaping holes in the building remained worryingly large. If what Evan was saying was true, it changed everything.

"Yeah. And Luigi—Rob, whatever his name is—he's donating his pizza oven. Moira told me."

Abby sat up straighter as her mind started to whirr. "Seriously? That's phenomenal news. This could be the future of The Dolphin!"

"I know, right? I hear Roy's finally got a spring in his step again."

There'd been a lot of anxiety among locals recently, mostly related to the availability of cheese-laden carbs. It was safe to say that while Luigi's wasn't anyone favourite pizza in town, its imminent closure had left everyone rather bereft. It was, after all, the *only* pizza in town.

The one bright spot on the pizzaless horizon was that the shop would be replaced by a convenience store, and not just any convenience store: the largest and best-stocked one in Bay View's history. It would mean fewer two-hour trips to Newtown to get essentials, like the really good ice cream you craved on your period or when you were melting down over a personal crisis.

Abby and Evan had scooted into a sticky booth at Luigi's a few weeks back, once Abby had pulled herself together and was finally ready to hear him out.

"I know the timing sucked, Abs," Evan had said, fiddling with the menu in front of him. "I really am sorry. I don't know how many more times I can apologise."

Abby pushed her lips to the side. She watched him thumb the bent laminated corner of the menu he'd never look at because they always ordered the same thing, and felt overwhelmingly sad and tender all at once.

"I know. It's fine. I was kind of an asshole, too."

Evan pressed his lips together in an awkward smile. "Yeah, I guess you were."

In the weeks after Chris's departure and the revelation of Evan's imminent one, Abby had felt like something recently healed inside her had ripped wide open. The pain made her brain hurt and her behaviour irrational. Barely eating or sleeping, she'd dragged herself through each school day on autopilot.

She'd refused to communicate with Evan, with her friends, with anyone from Bay View, really, except her students and, on occasion, Drew.

She didn't spend her weekends helping out at The Dolphin.

She was humiliated and furious and hurting.

She left her phone in her drawer for five days straight.

Cody said later that if it hadn't been for Drew's reports from time to time, they'd have done a welfare check.

Abby didn't cry until weeks after it had all happened, when she found her crumpled bomber jacket in a ball at the back of her wardrobe. It had smelled terrible and had an ugly stain that looked suspiciously like wine. She examined it with almost scientific curiosity, like an archaeologist examining an old relic, then carefully washed it by hand. She hung it out to dry, and when she discovered, hours later, that the stain was gone and the jacket looked like new, she sat down, folded it into her belly, and sobbed.

After that, things got a bit better.

She still felt raw, but she was ready to hear Evan's side of the story.

And now he was telling her that it was all her fault he was leaving.

Well, kind of.

"It's actually you who inspired me to make the decision to move," Evan said as their pizzas arrived, and Abby remembered the horrible fight they'd had months ago, at this same table, when each of them accused the other of being afraid of love.

So much water had flowed under the bridge since then.

"Me? I inspired you to take a leap of faith for love?" Abby guffawed. "Or did you see how my life was falling apart and decide to run like hell from Bay View?"

Evan tutted as he lifted a slice to his mouth. "Your life wasn't falling apart. Do you remember…" He paused to chew. "Do you remember the night of Dan's birthday party last year, I mean, after the tears… much later, when we were lying on the grass, trying to make out the constellations, and I asked you if you had any regrets?"

Abby nodded, knowing where he was going.

"You said, 'None that I have any control over.'"

"I remember."

"That's been going around and around in my head. I realised I needed to take control of the parts of my life I could, otherwise I'd always have regrets."

"Regrets about?"

"Marli, obviously. I really love her, Abby. I was so terrified at the thought of leaving here that I let my fear sabotage our relationship. So yeah, I guess you were right all along."

He gave a small shrug, concentrating unusually hard on his food. "And yeah, I did think about you and Dan…None of us knows how much time we have. I don't want to waste any of it being afraid. Or any more of it. I'll never regret trying things out with Marli. But I'll definitely regret not trying and never knowing. And I have you to thank for that."

Finally, he looked up, and Abby noticed to her surprise that his eyes had misted over.

"I'm just really sorry that I've hurt you, Abby. I care about you so much, and I'd never, ever want to hurt you." His voice cracked and he took a gulp of his drink. "I thought you were never going to speak to me again."

Abby felt her eyes filling too, and she reached across the table to take his hand. "I am happy for you, my friend. *So* happy. I'm going to miss the shit out of you, but you are doing the right thing. And whatever happens, you'll always have my sofa to crash on. An entire room, in fact. But you're not going to need it."

"Yeah, Drew told me about that." Evan gave Abby's hand a squeeze and returned to his food. "Are you really done with FortyLinks? For good?"

"Yeah, I think so. After everything that happened with…Well, I just don't ever want to risk it again. What did you call it…benching it out?"

"Yeah." Evan grimaced. "Something like that. Sorry."

"No, you're right. I am benching it out, but I'm okay with that. This whole situation…what was I thinking? It nearly destroyed me. And right as I was finally starting to feel good again."

"Okay, *but*," Evan started carefully, "don't you think Chris actually had something to do with you feeling good again?"

Abby shook her head defiantly. "I'm done with FortyLinks," she said, ignoring his question. "I want my life to be simple and predictable. No more fucking surprises. Some might call it boring, but right now, I'll take all the boring I can get."

She wadded up a paper napkin and dumped it in her glass. It bloomed in the shallow pool of water at the bottom. "Anyway, how did we end up talking about me? This is about you and Marli."

"It's about all of us, really. And speaking of which, I really wish you and Marli would put all the weirdness behind you. You are both so important to me and all I want is for you to get along. Really, Abs—no, don't look away. It would mean the world to me. Besides, you're going to have to crash on *our* sofa when you visit."

Abby narrowed her eyes at her friend. "You really love her, don't you?"

Evan's cheeks glowed. If he were a cartoon character, his eyes would have turned into throbbing pink hearts. "Yep," he said with a sigh, unable to stop the grin spreading across his face. "I really do."

"Then you have my word that I will put the weirdness behind me."

Evan leapt up and squeezed into the booth next to her, wrapping his thick arms around her. "Thank you, my Abs. You have no idea what a weight that is off my shoulders. You're the best, you know that?"

"Life's too short for weirdness, dude."

He'd laughed into her ear and she'd hugged him back, hard, and now here they were, condensing his entire life into a handful of moving boxes.

"All right, let's see, we're done with books, CDs, sports stuff…" Evan surveyed the piles around him, hands on his hips. "I guess all that's left is my clothes."

"Well, that shouldn't take up too much space," Abby said, plucking a black tank top from the bed. "Since you always squeeze yourself into clothing three sizes too small."

She heard Marli giggle. "You know, Abby, while I agree with you, I don't exactly have a problem with that."

Evan waggled his eyebrows at the screen and pretended to lift his shirt, much to Marli's glee.

"Ugh, you guys, get a room!"

"Oh, we will," Evan replied saucily, he and Marli still locked on each other through the screen.

"Jesus." Abby leapt off the bed and grabbed her jacket. "I'm out. Bye, lovebirds."

CHAPTER TWENTY-TWO

Work on The Dolphin resumed with renewed vigour. The funds from the mystery donor combined with the delivery of Luigi's pizza oven seemed to spur on just about everyone in town. Suddenly, their goal was within spitting distance.

It was Abby's first time back in weeks, too. Since before her tattoo.

That was how she measured time now: before her tattoo, and after it. Before Chris had touched her body in a way that friends don't touch each other, and after it.

Before her carefully carved-out life had spectacularly imploded in front of the entire town, and after it.

"It's good to have you back, Abs," Chip said, coming up behind her as she sanded the new surfboard-shaped bar counter. She, Evan, and Drew had chosen indoor jobs today, mostly as a way to escape the heat.

Chip's denim overalls were covered in paint splodges, and a crackly blue streak ran the length of his face. She wondered how much he knew, then quickly pushed the thought away. Everyone knew everything in this town. It was best not to dwell on it.

"I'm glad to *be* back," she said, moving her dust buff from her mouth. "And I hear this design is your handiwork?" She ran a hand over the countertop. "It's so clever, Chip. What a great idea."

He beamed, his non-blue cheek turning slightly pink. "Aw, shucks, Abs, thanks. I'm glad you like it."

Abby motioned to his face. "I'm guessing from the paint all over you...you guys really are painting a rainbow?"

"Yep, the entire back wall. Come check it out."

"I will, soon as we've finished up here."

"Gotcha. See you later." And with a tongue click and some finger guns, he was gone.

Abby pulled the buff back on and returned to the task at hand, carefully working out the little imperfections in the wood with the sandpaper. She was concentrating so intently she didn't realise Evan was trying to get her attention until she heard Drew giggling.

"Earth to Abby...?"

"Hmmm?" She looked up, her eyes taking a second to focus. "Sorry, I was totally in the zone." She wiped her forehead with the back of her wrist. "What's up?"

Evan bit his lip for a second, and suddenly Abby felt nervous. "Have I done it wrong?"

"What? Oh, I have no idea. I just...I've been debating telling you this, but you're bound to find out and I'd rather be the one to tell you..."

"Evan...? What?"

"I bumped into Chris yesterday." He looked apologetic and worried. "She's here. In town."

Abby felt herself go cold. She leaned against the counter as the blood roared in her ears. It was easy to deal with something when you thought you'd never have to think about it again as long as you lived.

"I mean, I guess we always kind of knew it would happen after she put Mrs. Addison's house up for sale? She says it's just sold and she's here packing up..."

Abby stared at a spot on the floor as her head spun. "Yeah..."

"She, uh...she asked about you. She seemed genuinely worried, like...like it was really important to her that you were okay. And she..."

"She what?"

"She asked if you'd reconsider hearing her out. She says she's tried texting, emailing, calling...She says she even came to your house and you refused to come out."

Abby blinked. "What? What do you mean she came to my house? The last time I saw her, you were with me. And she all but told me to get fucked. Publicly!" Abby felt heat rising back into her face. "What the hell? None of that makes sense."

Evan shrugged helplessly. "I'm sorry, Abs, I don't have any answers for you."

"Well…What did you say?"

"Dude, obviously I said you were doing great."

"Okay. Good." She turned back to the bar counter, sandpaper poised above the wood, then immediately swivelled back.

"She wants me to 'reconsider' hearing her out?" Abby dropped the paper as she made the air quotes with her fingers. She realised she was trembling. "When did she even ask me to consider it in the first place? She can forget about it. I'm not speaking to her."

"Okay."

"Or maybe I should speak to her! How dare she try to pull this kind of stunt—using my best friend to do it?"

With force, Abby kicked a sanding block against the counter, taking a chunk out of the wood.

A small voice behind her interrupted her ragged breathing.

"Abby?"

"Yeah?" She twisted around to look at Drew, having forgotten she was there at all. The girl's face was pale. Abby frowned as she inched toward her, her arms held out in a gesture of surrender.

"Abby, I…I fucked up and I know you're probably going to hate me. I, I…" The girl looked stricken.

"Drew, what? *What?*"

Words started spilling out so quickly, it took Abby a moment to process them. "Chris came to your house the day after the funeral when you were in the shower and I told her to go away and that you didn't want to speak to her ever again."

Oh. My. God.

"But I *asked* you, Drew! I knew it!" Abby wailed, grabbing her by the shoulders. "You lied to me? Does *everybody* lie to me?"

Drew looked woeful. She started to reply, but Abby didn't care. She pulled her hands away roughly and Drew stumbled backward, still grasping at words that wouldn't come. She reached for Abby's arm, but Abby flicked her away.

"No!" she said gruffly. "I gotta go."

CHAPTER TWENTY-THREE

There'd been a moment in the bruising weeks after Chris's departure when Abby had briefly forgotten the feelings of betrayal, shame, hurt, and confusion. She'd remembered how her old-new life in Bay View had felt, after the worst of Dan had passed and before the worst of Chris had hit. When the old, happy Abby had merged with the new, hopeful one and at last everything had seemed okay. Good, even.

She held on to it for as long as she could, and then every day after that, she called it to mind instead of thinking about Chris's smell or the feeling of her fingers on her skin.

She realised that grieving a living person was excruciating in its own way, but that closure came easier when you pretended they no longer existed.

Chris was dead to her.

So was FortyLinks.

She bought new linens and curtains and plants for her spare bedroom. She rearranged all the furniture, filled the room with scent diffusers, and then stuck Snowy on the bed and said, "Look, a whole bedroom, just for you."

When she finally emerged from her fog, she didn't speak of Chris and no one mentioned her name.

It was like she had never existed at all.

Until today.

Now her legs were carrying her to Marble Close faster than her brain could keep up. Over the past month, everything that had brought her to this point of acceptance had been based on a simple premise: Chris had lied to her and left without ever giving her any answers. And so, it was easy to be angry and to write her off as dead.

But what if she actually had tried to give those answers? And what if those answers made everything else make sense?

She rushed closer and closer to the road she had been strenuously avoiding for weeks.

She didn't realise she was running until her lungs started burning and she had to stop and catch her breath as she rounded the corner to Marble Close. As she doubled over and panted, hands on her thighs, she saw the *SOLD* sign hanging outside Mrs. Addison's house and a large moving truck outside. All over the lawn were boxes and furniture, with more spilling out of the house, and men loading them into the van.

And there, standing in the middle of it all with one hand in her hair and the other pointing to boxes, was Chris. She wore a loose flannel shirt rolled to the elbows, and her hair was the same cherry-rich shade seared into Abby's memory. Was it longer now, or just messier?

It didn't matter. Abby was here for answers, she reminded herself, as the feelings of hurt and betrayal flooded through her again. She watched as Chris directed the movers, swooping to grab an antique hat stand they held at a precarious angle. How dare she be more concerned about a piece of furniture than about the terrible hurt she'd caused her?

Abby swallowed hard and stomped toward the house. She was propelled by indignation and renewed anger hot in her veins.

"I heard you wanted to speak to me," she bellowed as she approached, the words shooting out before she could stop them. Chris jerked around in surprise.

"Abby," she said, but almost no sound came out. She fumbled with the hat stand and it fell to the lawn. "I…yes. I did. I do. Hi."

Abby ignored the greeting. "Well?" She watched as Chris awkwardly righted the stand, further fumbling to make sure it wouldn't topple over again. When she straightened up and looked Abby in the eye, her face was as beautiful as Abby remembered it, just paler somehow, and wearier.

Chris smiled weakly. "I wanted to say thank you. And goodbye. Properly."

"'Thank you and goodbye'?" Abby repeated, gobsmacked. "Are you serious? That's why you've been so desperate to talk to me? To tell me 'Thank you and goodbye'?"

Chris opened her mouth to reply, then closed it again. Her hand autopiloted a path through her hair. Abby scowled. The sun was baking down on them, and she could feel a tickle of wood dust on her face. It occurred to her how she must look, clad in ripped clothes and covered in dirt and sawdust from the building site. She didn't care.

"Yeah, well, I realise that when I left last time, things were a bit nuts, and—"

"'A bit nuts'?" Abby spluttered. "Jesus, Chris, are you hearing yourself? A bit nuts? Things were not 'a bit nuts' when you left last time. Things were absolutely, unequivocally horrific. You lied to me, Chris! You treated me like total garbage, and then you convinced my best friend that you actually cared about me as a ploy to get me here to say… THANK YOU AND GOODBYE?" Abby was so furious she could feel her pulse in her eyeballs. Behind Chris, the men had paused in various states of box removal and stood rooted to the spot. Abby shot her gaze to them and in another fit of fury, yelled, "What? Have you never seen a pissed-off lesbian before? There's nothing to see here!"

"Okay, okay, Abby, come," Chris urged, her fingers closing around Abby's arm. Her skin burned where Chris touched it, and she knew she had to get away before she lost all power to the feeling. She'd flown too close to the sun once, and she wasn't going to let it happen again.

"No!" She wrenched her arm away. "It was a mistake, coming here." She turned away as tears burned in her eyes, her voice wobbling as she spoke. "You're lying to me, Chris. You're lying to me now, like you lied to me before. You know, I'd managed to convince myself that you were dead. And now I realise it was better that way."

"Abby, no," Chris pleaded. "Don't say that."

"Why not? Because it makes you uncomfortable when people speak the truth?"

"No. Because I can't bear the thought of you thinking something like that."

"Oh, spare me." Abby scoffed, but she refused to look Chris in the eye because when she did, she saw sorrow, and regret. "Look, I'm gonna go." Abby sighed, raising her arms and dropping them to her sides. "We're not getting anywhere here, and I'd like to get back to believing you don't exist."

"Abby, please. I'm flying out in a few hours and I just need you to wait so I can explain in private, after the movers—"

"Wait? *Wait?* You mean like how I've waited for you to figure out what's going on in your head all this time? In case you hadn't noticed, waiting around for bad endings has kind of been the theme of my life for the last few years and I'm about done with it, Chris."

She spun to leave, but Chris lurched forward and grabbed her arm, and this time when Abby tried to pull away, Chris caught her other arm and spun her in so that their bodies were pressed together and Abby was trapped like a wild animal, writhing but neutralised, feeling Chris's heart pounding against her own. She tried to fight but Chris held her, held her until she slowly stopped quivering with rage and fear.

"Abby," she said at last in a low voice, her lips against Abby's ear, her breath mingling with Abby's hot, ragged gasps. "I'm so sorry I hurt you. And I'm sorry it's taken me this long to say it. But I need you to know that I never lied to you."

Abby didn't reply. Her head was spinning as her face pressed into Chris's shoulder. She was no longer trying to get away, but Chris held her anyway.

"Karys and I *were* separated. For reasons that had nothing to do with me being here. But I was here, and for the first time in my life I started to feel like myself, like I was able to live for me. I'd never experienced anything like that before. And then my mother died and Karys arrived and I was so afraid, Abby. I realised I had no one. No one. And that I was trapped."

She gently released her grip on Abby's arms and stepped back. Her voice was shaky, and when Abby finally looked into her eyes, she saw that they were shining and raw.

"I'm not brave like you, Abby. I'm weak, and afraid. I don't want to be left behind when my whole family moves away." Her voice cracked and she looked away, clenching and unclenching her jaw. "That's it. Now you know," she said with a sniff and a shrug as she stared into the distance.

"Chris, look at me," Abby said, softened, feeling drained. Gingerly, she took Chris's hands. "Please."

Chris turned to her, tears spilling onto her cheeks, and the sight of it stole the air from Abby's lungs.

"What else?" Abby urged, squeezing her hands. "I know there's more."

But Chris just shook her head. "No…"

"I don't believe you." Abby searched the woman's face for answers, for the one answer she desperately wanted, but Chris tightened her jaw again, her face hardening.

"All I want to hear is that I'm not going crazy," Abby begged, her own voice cracking, her eyes refusing to look down and acknowledge the scuffed silver band pressing uncomfortably into her finger. "I know I'm not crazy, Chris. I know I'm not imagining things."

"I…I'm so sorry. I can't tell you…what you want to hear."

Abby dropped her hands.

"Abs, I never meant to—"

But Abby had stopped listening.

"Thank you for your honesty," Abby said, backing away, her feet like lumps of granite. "And thank you for your apology. I…I need to go."

And this time, when she turned to leave, Chris didn't try to stop her.

* * *

They'd been walking around The Bed Collective, fingering scatter cushions and cotton throws, when Dan had sprung the question on her.

"Do you think you'd still be with Matt now, if you hadn't met me?"

Abby paused, a rose-scented candle halfway to her nose. "But I did meet you."

"Yeah, I know. But imagine," she said with a shrug, leaning in to smell the candle. "Would you?"

"Why? Do you still think I'm a flight risk?"

"No, of course not, silly." Dan flashed Abby a dimpled grin. She tossed a cactus-shaped novelty pillow into their basket. "I was just wondering. Oh, here—aren't these the pillowcases you wanted?"

Abby inspected the package and nodded. "Yeah, exactly, but in grey."

She watched Dan rifling around until she found the right shade. She was so gorgeous and graceful and cool that Abby had to pinch herself. How had this perfect, ethereal creature chosen her? The thought of them never meeting made her feel panicky, but she'd be lying if she said it had never crossed her mind.

"Well, if I'm honest," Abby admitted as they wandered into the mattress department. "I have thought about it. And I hope I wouldn't still be with him."

"Really?" Dan raised her eyebrows. "You seemed to be pretty happy with him when we met."

"Well, that's because I had no idea what else was out there. Given what I know now, I shudder to think that I could've spent my whole life in that sort of relationship, believing that that's the best it would get." Absent-mindedly, she ran her fingers over a plastic-covered mattress. "So I have to believe that if you and I hadn't met, I'd have met someone else who would have shown me that I was living this muted life…that love and passion is so much more than I could ever have imagined."

Abby stopped and smiled up at Dan, whose face looked soft and filled with love.

"Wow, babe, you really have put some thought into this," she said, coming closer to take Abby's hand.

"I have," Abby agreed, feeling emotional because perhaps she'd thought about it too much. "Sometimes…" She stopped and stared down at her sneakers—or were they Dan's? She'd lost track.

"Sometimes?" Dan nudged gently.

"Ugh, it's embarrassing, but sometimes I have this horrible thought that you and I never met—like, what if I'd never gone to sit on those stairs and you'd never come out of your room at that exact moment? You'd be out there living your life without me, and I want to cry at the thought of having lost you forever."

"Oh, my baby, we were always going to meet. It was written. I know that in my soul. You were never going to lose me." Dan flung her arms around Abby, and they toppled onto the mattress, Dan giggling and Abby fighting back tears.

"It's not funny!" Abby huffed, feeling embarrassed but thrilled to be wrapped up in Dan's arms. She didn't care that people were staring as they rolled around on the plastic in the middle of the store.

"No, it's not funny," Dan replied, dropping her voice, her arms still tight around Abby. "And I'm not laughing at you, my love. I'm laughing because the idea of us never meeting is just so…so…preposterous to me, I can't even imagine it. I'm sorry I asked such a silly question." She brushed some hair out of Abby's eyes. "I love you so much, do you know that? Do you have any idea how much?"

"Not really," Abby grumbled, playing along. "You'll have to show me."

"Fine!" Dan declared, planting kisses all over Abby's face and neck and forehead until the manager came over and shooed them up and out of the mattress section and toward the tills to pay.

Later, at home, as they unpacked their purchases, Dan handed Abby a package roughly wrapped in newsprint.

"What's this?" she asked, her curiosity piqued as she began to peel the layers away.

Dan put her arms around Abby, resting her chin on her shoulder. "It's definitely not *that*," she joked, alluding to their previous conversations about marriage and Dan's steadfast opposition to it. "But it's close."

Abby removed the last piece of paper to reveal a white porcelain mug with the words *WORLD'S BEST WIFE* emblazoned in black. The dot of the "I" was a gaudy red heart. It was by far the stupidest and best mug she had ever seen.

"Hilarious," Abby said with a pretend pout as Dan twirled her around to face her.

"Abs…I know it's just a silly mug, and I know there are some things we don't entirely agree on. But I want you to know that you are the very best thing that has ever happened to me. I love you so damn much. With or without a piece of paper, you are my forever. Do you know that?"

"I do," Abby said, setting the mug on the counter and putting her arms around Dan's neck. She stared into her shining grey eyes and knew that the mug said the one thing Dan couldn't but wished she could.

"You're stuck with me, Dan Kelly. Paper or no paper. And besides…" She grinned up at her. "You love me so much, I just know that one day you're going to change your mind."

Dan laughed and shook her head.

Forever, Abby knew, was a state of mind.

CHAPTER TWENTY-FOUR

The mug slipped from her fingers and smashed into a million pieces. Tiny shards shot in every direction, covering the kitchen floor with a layer of razor-sharp glitter that cut into the soles of Abby's feet and the pads of her fingers.

Of course this would happen.

Up until this point, she'd been remarkably contained. She'd stumbled home from Marble Close nearly delirious with disappointment and humiliation. In a daze, she'd fed the cat, washed the sweat and sawdust off her body, put on fresh clothes, padded into the kitchen to fix a hot drink. The tears hadn't come until now, as she sat on the kitchen floor surrounded by the remnants of that stupid, precious cup, blood oozing from her wounds. She'd been so worried about Snowy cutting her paws that she'd rushed, barefoot, to clean up the mess, but it had been futile. There were just so many shards.

Snowy had taken one look at the pitiful situation and leapt out of the window with a flick of her tail, abandoning Abby for greener pastures. Asshole.

That's when the tears came, violent and thick, and lasted a long, long time. So long, in fact, that she fell asleep with her head pressed painfully against a cabinet, waking abruptly, minutes or hours later, to banging on her front door.

Dry-mouthed and disorientated, she pressed her hands into the floor to push herself up and felt a fresh wave of pinprick pain through her palm.

"Fuck!" she gasped as bright-red blood fanned out across her hand.

The banging was still happening as Abby hobbled out of the kitchen, stepping on only a few shards this time, and lumbered to the door. On the way, she caught sight of herself in the hallway mirror: she looked wild. Her hair was sticking up where it had smooshed against the cabinet and there was a smear of blood on her cheek just below her black-rimmed eyes. She hadn't looked this bad since… Well, it had been a while.

She supposed, later, that it was pretty obvious who'd be at the door at midnight. But at the time, she was shocked into speechlessness when Chris spilled over the threshold, looking pretty wild herself, wheeling that stupid suitcase behind her, still wearing her blue flannel shirt.

"Abby, you're not crazy," she panted, pink-cheeked and breathless, and Abby wondered whether she was still dreaming.

"Wh-what?"

"You asked me earlier. You said you needed me to tell you you're not crazy. And I tried to leave but I couldn't. I couldn't go without telling you that. That you're not crazy. Or, if you are, then I am too."

Abby closed her eyes and inhaled deeply. She was awake, and this was real life.

"Really?" she said at last. "Because I thought I was in love with you, but being in love with you feels a lot like being crazy. And I feel pretty crazy right now."

"Oh my god, you're bleeding!" Chris grabbed her wrists and turned them over in a panic. "Jesus, what's happened?"

Abby pulled her hands away and wiped them on her sweatpants. "Broke a mug. Didn't think through the clean-up process very well."

"Jeez, I can see that," Chris muttered. "Let me help you get cleaned up."

They shuffled inside, Abby on tender soles, Chris yanking her bag behind her, both of them ignoring the confession Abby had just made.

I thought I was in love with you.

Side by side on Abby's sofa, Chris gently cleaned the wounds.

"You know, you're actually a big baby," she said with a little smile as she mopped up Abby's hands. "See? You can barely even see any cuts."

"Well, thank god for that," Abby said, gingerly flexing her fingers. "I kind of need these."

They both started to speak at the same time, both stopped, both started again.

"I thought your flight was this evening?"

"It is. It was. I missed it."

"Well, that sucks. I don't have a spare room anymore."

"I heard. Abby…did you say you're in love with me?"

Abby sighed, a long and low exhalation, and dropped her head into her freshly cleaned hands. "I did. I mean, I thought it was pretty fucking obvious this whole time."

"No…" Chris shook her head. "It wasn't. At least, not to me. Karys figured it out."

Abby snorted. "Yeah. She did."

"She, um…she also figured out that I was in love with you. Long before I did."

Abby's head shot up. "She…what?"

"Yeah…"

Abby held her breath. Whatever was happening right now, she was afraid to shatter it by moving or breathing or blinking.

"I never tried to deceive you, Abby. If anything, I've been deceiving myself for a long, long time. And I couldn't leave without seeing you face-to-face and telling you that I…well, that you weren't imagining things."

The words were flowing now, a steady stream of truths, and Abby braced because the *but* was etched into every word, every gesture, into the very set of Chris's body. Somehow, she knew she was gaining and losing her all at the same time.

"Abby." Chris took both her hands in her own, and when Abby looked into her eyes, she saw they were filled with tears. "You shifted something fundamental in me. It terrified me. It's why I didn't—couldn't—tell you about the separation. It felt…" She searched for the right words. "Too dangerous."

"Abby…" she repeated, more urgently now, and this time, it shattered Abby's heart. "I'm in love with you. I have been since…almost the beginning, if I'm honest. And I'm truly, utterly sorry, because there's nothing I can do about it."

She sat motionless as tears fell from Chris's eyes onto their hands. There's nothing you *want* to do about it, she thought bitterly.

"I need to stay with my family. If I don't, Karys will take everything. She'll make sure I lose my stake in the business—she's set it up that way and I had no idea until recently. I'm a coward, Abby, and that's the truth. My family is all I know. And I know it's not fair to put this all on you,

I know that, but the one thing I knew I owed you was honesty. I never wanted to tell you how I felt. I fought to not tell you. Because what would have been the point? But I saw how I hurt you today, and you deserved so much better than that. You deserved not to spend your life questioning your own intuition."

It was a strange feeling, the consecutive body-slams of elation and devastation. The "I was right all along" and the "but it doesn't make any difference."

"Chris," Abby murmured, reaching out, tentatively touching her cheek. "It was always going to be this way. I was stupid for allowing it to happen. And I tried, I really did. I tried so hard to stop myself falling for you. Just ask Drew."

They both chuckled at that, maybe a bit too hard, and Abby wished she could kiss the tiny, lovely creases next to Chris's eyes.

"It was always going to end painfully, at least for me," Abby said with a shrug. "I knew that. But it turns out, you can't talk yourself out of falling in love with someone. And that's why I've cancelled my FortyLinks account."

Chris smiled again, and this time, Abby took her face in her hands and leaned in and kissed the crinkles next to her eyes, just like she wanted to, and her eyelashes, and the wet, salty skin beneath her eyes.

"Abby…"

She pulled away, peered into Chris's eyes. "Do you want me to stop?"

"No…I just…I don't want to hurt you. And I know I can't—"

"Shh," Abby soothed, but she stopped anyway. "I'm a big girl. And look at me." She shrugged, spread her arms. "I think I'm way past hurt."

"We really fucked up, didn't we?" Chris said sadly, and Abby nodded and looked down into her lap.

"I wish things could be different."

"Me, too."

After a while, Chris cleared her throat. "I have to go," she said, standing up, and Abby felt a tsunami of grief rising in her.

"Really? Now? But surely you won't get a flight until morning?"

"Yeah, sometime around six a.m."

"Well, stay. Please. Stay until the morning. There's no point in going to the airport now. Please." She tugged Chris's hand, gently urging her back down onto the sofa.

"You're sure?"

"So sure," Abby whispered. "It'll just take me a minute to get the spare room ready for you."

Chris flopped back down next to Abby and gave her a tired smile. "I thought you said you didn't have one of those anymore."

Abby gave her a playful shove. "The room is still there. It's the usage that's up for debate. But for you, I'll make an exception." Oh, the irony.

Reluctantly, Abby left Chris in the lounge, working as quickly as she could to clear the rest of the mess in the kitchen and remove all of Snowy's toys from Chris's room. She threw on fresh sheets—sheets that weren't covered in a stubborn layer of cat fur—ran her hands over surfaces to clear any dust, and spritzed her perfume into the air. Then, she raced back to the sitting room to find Chris…fast asleep on the sofa.

"Chris?" she whispered, gently shaking her. "You're too old to sleep like this. You'll wake up with your neck stuck at ninety degrees."

But Chris just gave a sleepy moan and burrowed deeper into the sofa, so Abby covered her with a blanket and gently lifted her head to place a pillow underneath. For a moment, her hand hovered above Chris's head, aching to stroke her hair and the soft skin of her cheek.

Chris stirred, her eyes opening a crack, and Abby jerked her hand away.

"Please, don't go."

"What?"

"Stay with me. Here." She shifted on the sofa.

With her heart pounding in her chest, Abby eased onto the sofa and curled herself around the soft, warm shape of Chris.

It couldn't have been later than four a.m., maybe five. Chris was sound asleep, her head tucked under Abby's chin. But Abby hadn't slept a wink. It had been hours that she'd been in the same position, inhaling Chris's scent and watching the rhythmic rise and fall of her chest.

She knew she had to get up. Her body ached from immobility, plus she needed to stop weeping into Chris's hair, lest she wake up and wonder about the suspicious wet patch on her head.

Carefully, inch by inch, she extricated herself from Chris's embrace, feeling pins and needles shoot through her limbs.

She crept to the bathroom and closed the door. She needed to pull herself together before Chris woke up.

In the dark, she felt around until she found matches to light a few candles. Then she poured an obscene amount of foam bath into the bottom of the tub to muffle the sound of the water pouring in.

As the scalding water filled the tub, Abby removed her clothes, carefully folding each item and placing it out of the way. She knew she wouldn't be washing them any time soon—not while the atoms of

Chris's perfume clung to their fibres. Then she stepped into the hot, foamy water, sliding lower and lower until the bubbles enveloped her almost completely.

The knock was so light, Abby thought she'd imagined it. But then there was the unmistakable click of the door latch, and when she sat up and turned around, Chris was there, silhouetted against the blue-black morning, her hair ruffled from sleep and spiking up at strange angles.

Abby's heart stopped.

"Tell me to leave," Chris whispered, one hand on the doorknob, her eyes locked on Abby's. "And I will."

Abby shook her head, the rest of her body frozen as steam rose off her shoulders in thick tendrils.

"Tell me to go, Abby."

"No…" Her whole body was quivering now, her heart pounding in the base of her throat. "No," she said, louder now, her voice trembling. "I don't want you to go."

Without taking her eyes off Abby, Chris unbuttoned her shirt and let it fall to the floor. She unclasped her bra and slipped the straps off her shoulders, revealing breasts that Abby had fantasised about more times than she cared to count, that she ached to touch, to kiss, to feel pressed against her own.

The room was silent but for the sounds of Chris's clothes falling to the floor and thousands of tiny bubbles fizzing and popping on the water. As Abby watched Chris undress, she felt a tear roll down her cheek. She hadn't even realised she was crying.

"Are you sure?" Chris asked, fully nude now, just inches away. It was all Abby could do not to howl like an animal *"I'm sure!"*

But instead she nodded silently, feeling in a trance, as if she were watching an illusionist about to perform her pièce de résistance. Finally, Chris sank into the bath behind her.

Abby exhaled in a burst as Chris's bare skin touched her own and she wrapped her legs around Abby.

Gently, so tenderly, Chris leaned forward and kissed Abby's bare shoulders, her neck, her back. Every touch sent a bolt through her spine and all the way down, down, down.

She lifted Abby's hair and kissed her nape.

"I…" she whispered into Abby's neck, and then stopped, and Abby bent her head and replied, "I know."

Slowly, she ran her hands along Abby's thighs, her arms, her shoulders, her belly, and then up, up to her breasts, cupping and stroking them until Abby felt she might explode from the touch alone.

"I want to stay like this forever," Chris murmured, wrapping her arms around Abby, her mouth in the warm curve of her neck.

By now, Abby's tears were flowing freely—she couldn't help it. She wept silently with love and despair, with elation and loss, knowing that she'd stepped into the very trap she saw coming and swore she wouldn't. She'd already lost her, but this moment was the culmination of everything she'd wanted all this time. Chris was whispering into her ear, stroking her hair, kissing her shoulders. The world could have imploded and Abby wouldn't have noticed.

After a long while, she disentangled herself and turned to face Chris. She was surprised to see that Chris's eyes, too, shone with tears, but unlike Abby, she was smiling, her face radiant and flushed. Abby let her fingers take in all of Chris's body—her legs, arms, belly, breasts, shoulders. She ran them through her hair and slowly, delicately, kissed the base of her throat, where she felt her pulse through her lips.

I love you, she mouthed into the soft skin of Chris's neck, but she said it soundlessly, just to feel the shapes it made.

Tepid water spilled onto the floor as they pulled each other closer, Chris arching into Abby's kisses, twisting to get closer.

"You're the most beautiful person I have ever met in my life," she whispered, cupping Abby's face in her hands and smiling, laughing, as she kissed her chin and her collarbone and her breasts and her nipples and then finally—finally!—she brought her salty lips to Abby's and kissed her.

It was better than Abby could have ever imagined. She felt herself untether and float away to a place that felt new yet utterly familiar. It was the place she knew she'd return to when she lay awake at night, when she opened her eyes in the morning, when she wandered through town or grocery aisles or the hallways at school. It was the place she'd go to when someone said *I have a friend for you...* and she'd smile wistfully and say *I'm done with all that.*

They sat entwined for a very long time, until finally, as the day grew bright and the bath water icy cold, Abby wrapped them both in towels and led Chris to her bed.

"I want to climb inside you," Chris said breathlessly as they melded together: hands, thighs, breasts, mouths, lips. Abby couldn't get enough of Chris, breathing in every inch of her skin, kissing every curve, every crease, every fold. When Chris pulled her close, it felt closer than she had ever been to another human.

"It's racing," Chris murmured as she lay her hand over Abby's heart.

"It has been since you walked into my bathroom. Well, my *life*, actually," Abby replied, trying to laugh, but her breath caught in her throat. "I'm sorry I'm such a mess," she said, covering her eyes with her hands and feeling fresh tears trying to escape through the gaps between her fingers. She couldn't quite believe that Chris was beside her, naked under her sheets, making love to her—and she knew that as quickly as it happened, it would be over.

"Oh, baby girl, you're not a mess," Chris soothed, gently pulling her hands from her eyes and entwining them with her own. "You're perfect." She stroked Abby's face, her eyes full of concern. "Do you want to stop?"

"No," Abby said with a fierce shake of her head. "I never want to stop."

Then she slid down to Chris's stomach, and lower still to where it was warm and wet and sweet, and wished like she'd never wished before that space and time would fold in on themselves and this moment would go on forever in an endless, exquisite loop. She wanted Chris to feel her love through every pore of her body. She couldn't let her leave without telling her everything.

They slept. They woke. They made love. They cried.

"Abby, Abby, Abby…" Chris moaned, holding her in her gaze. "I want you inside me," and Abby responded by going deeper…deeper… deeper.

Much later, they lay together like spoons, Abby's chin resting in the curve of Chris's neck, her hand cupping a breast.

"I wish I'd met you—" Chris began.

"Please, don't," Abby cut her off, holding her tighter. "Let's just enjoy this moment, for however long we have it."

"Okay."

"I think you missed your flight again," Abby joked later, guessing that it was late afternoon, maybe early evening. She'd become aware of the light changing, of Snowy yowling for food, of her own belly growling for attention. When was the last time she'd eaten? Food, that was.

"Oh, I've definitely missed my flight again." Chris chuckled, pulling Abby to her, burying her face in her hair and kissing her neck.

It was Chris who eventually rose, pulled on Abby's bathrobe, and headed to the kitchen. But moments later, she was back.

"The strangest thing," she said, holding out her hand. "I just stepped on this in the kitchen."

In her hand she held a piece of the broken porcelain mug, and when she turned it over in her fingers, Abby saw that it was the tiny red heart from the word *WIFE*.

"Oh, Chris, I'm so sorry—I must have missed it. Are you hurt? Are you bleeding?"

"No," she said with a laugh. "That's the weird part. It didn't cut me. Look...the edges aren't even sharp."

She tipped it into Abby's hand and left again, busying herself in the kitchen. Abby could hear her fixing them snacks and feeding Snowy as she rolled the heart over in her fingers.

"You're going to fly, Abby. You'll see. You're going to be just fine."

"I won't, Dan. I can't fly without you. I can't even breathe without you."

"Yes, Abby, you can. You did before me, and you will after me."

"There wasn't supposed to be an 'after you.'"

"I know, my baby. But you're going to be okay. You have to promise me that you're going to live, Abby. For me. Promise me, baby?"

A light throat-clearing jerked Abby back to the present.

"Sugar?" Chris stood in the doorway holding two steaming mugs.

"Er, sorry...What?"

"I asked if you wanted sugar in your tea," she said with a smile. "Come, let's go sit outside. It's such a beautiful evening."

Does this count as living, Abby thought as she followed Chris outside, when this isn't real life?

It must have been a warm day, because even though the sun was setting, it was mild out. Abby wore Chris's flannel shirt and she smiled as she watched Chris nibbling sandwiches and sipping tea in her bathrobe. They sat at the little garden table, like they had so many times before, but this time, they were hand in hand: no secret yearning, no wishing or wondering.

But there had been a question on Abby's mind for hours now, and as they watched the sun slip behind the bougainvillaea, it grew louder and louder in the silence.

"Chris?"

"Mmm?"

She was the picture of happiness as she turned to smile at Abby, and Abby loathed allowing reality to steal this perfect moment.

She bit her lip. "Isn't there...anyone wondering where you are?"

Abby watched Chris's face cloud over, and she wished she could take back the words but she had to know.

"Karys and the kids, they've already left. They've probably just landed, actually," she said, drawing her legs up. "It's made it a little easier to..."

"Hide?"

Chris sighed. "To take the time I need to wrap up here."

Abby pursed her lips. "And you?" she asked softly. "When do you go?"

Chris cleared her throat. Shifted in her chair. "First flight out tomorrow morning. And then the last leg…early next week."

Abby looked away, blinking hard.

It didn't matter. Chris had always made her intentions clear.

"Come," she said, standing up and reaching for Abby's hand. "Tomorrow is a whole world away. Tonight is just for you and me."

They curled into each other but neither of them slept. There was a whole lifetime to sleep, but an ever-diminishing window of time for them to lie suspended in this moment, hidden from their lives in this secret space just for them.

"Why didn't you and Karys ever get married?"

They were lying face-to-face in the dark, hands lazing over each other's bodies. Abby could feel Chris's breath on her lips.

"She always wanted to, but…"

"But?"

"To be honest, I could never fully trust her again. Not after she left the first time."

"The *first* time?"

Chris breathed out heavily. "Yeah. It doesn't matter. After that, I just never could, or would."

"But you wear a ring."

"Mm. It's always made Karys feel more secure." Chris wrapped an arm around Abby's waist, finding a way to pull her even closer. Neither of them acknowledged the irony of her words. "What about you—do you want to get married one day?"

"I do," Abby whispered, her voice cracking in the dark. "I really do."

Even in their cocoon, with their backs turned to the rising sun of reality, all too soon it was dawn, and they each rose and moved in silence. Chris made the coffee while Abby double-checked the flight schedule (devastatingly, no cancellations or even delays) and made the bed, knowing that she'd climb right back into it the moment Chris left. Chris showered and got dressed into the clothes she'd been wearing on the night she arrived. It was surreal to see, as if time had gone back on itself and the intervening thirty-six hours had never happened at all. Except that Chris's shirt was wrinkled from sleeping in it and speckled with dried soap suds.

Abby wobbled Chris's bulging suitcase to the door, and when she peered outside, she saw that the taxi driver was there. This time, he lifted his hand to wave. She closed the door again.

This moment was just for them.

As they held each other, Abby did her best to memorise how Chris felt and smelled and how their bodies fitted together. And when they finally came apart, Abby was surprised to find her own neck wet and Chris's face streaked with tears.

"I don't know how the fuck this happened." She laughed through her tears. "And I'm so angry with the universe for letting it happen. Or, you know, not letting it happen twenty years ago."

"Hey, I'd have been eight!" Abby exclaimed with a loud sniff. At this point, her entire body was made up solely of snot, tears, and a single bite of a cheese sandwich.

Chris blushed. "You know what I mean."

"One last thing," Abby said, holding out her hand. "Give me your phone."

Chris frowned but did as she was told. Quickly, before she could change her mind, Abby tapped several buttons on Chris's screen, and then on her own, and then handed it back.

"I've deleted your number from my phone, and mine from yours. And just in case either of us happens to work around that, I've blocked them, too."

Chris looked horrified. "But, Abby, how will I—"

"You won't, and I won't. And that's the point." She looked away, shook her head, marvelled at the fact that her tears seemed to be endless. The entire planet was drying up, but not the two tiny tear glands above her eyeballs.

"Chris, I can't do this." Abby sighed, turning back. "I can't be waiting for you to call, or book a room, or surprise me in the middle of the night. I know what you need to do. And I need you to respect what I need to do."

Chris nodded, swallowing hard, reaching to take Abby's face in her hands. "I understand," she said hoarsely, pressing their foreheads together. "And I…"

"I know," Abby whispered back "Me, too."

CHAPTER TWENTY-FIVE

"Charge your glasses, everyone! It's nearly midnight!"

Chip's voice rang out above the laughter and chattering in the crowded bar as Abby felt arms squeeze her from behind.

"I'm so glad you're here," she said, grinning as she turned around at the familiar touch.

"Me too." Evan beamed at her. It seemed impossible, but he was even more tanned than before, his teeth even whiter and his eyes shinier.

"And you, Marli," Abby added with a smile, touching her arm. "Thank you for making the trip."

"Of course," Marli said, beaming back. "We wouldn't have missed it for the world. Not after all the hard work you all put in."

"I still can't believe it," Evan marvelled as he took Marli's hand. "It's like *Extreme Makeover: Bar Edition*."

"Yeah." She nodded, looking around. "When I was here less than a year ago, this place was just rubble. You guys have worked wonders."

Marli was right. Just after Evan left Bay View two months ago, those working on the site had made a pact to complete the project by New Year's Eve. Roy's enthusiasm was waning fast, and they knew they needed to pull off a miracle so he didn't completely give up. People worked longer and harder, and Abby, with more time on her hands these days, found herself at The Dolphin almost every day. She worked shoulder to shoulder with Chip and the Woodses and an ever-revolving crew of townspeople who painted and woodworked and cleaned and decorated. As the dream of a New Year's Eve roof-wetting became more and more plausible, the more people turned up to help, until excitement reached a fever pitch and they found themselves here, tonight, minutes from midnight inside the all-new, freshly completed Dolphin Inn, now with pizza oven and, for the first time, floors that you didn't stick to. It was entirely transformed.

"I just can't believe how much better it looks than it used to," Marli said before clapping her hand to her mouth. "Sorry. No offence."

Abby waved a hand. "I think even Roy would agree with you."

"Before, it was kind of crummy and gross." She pulled a face. "But now…" She swept her gaze across the room, taking in the exposed brick walls and screeded floors, the vintage-style light bulbs, and the newly installed booths and leather barstools. "It's a proper, trendy restaurant. Totally Instagrammable."

"My thoughts exactly," Abby agreed, following her gaze. "And not to mention, not nearly as sticky."

The girls giggled as Chip clambered back onto the bar counter and his voice boomed over the crowd, "Ten, nine, eight…"

"Quick, hurry, hurry! It's almost time."

"Six…five…four…"

Abby felt herself beaming as she waited for the ball to drop. It was the first time in years that she'd felt happy, whole, *home*. Not happy-sad, or happy-but. Really, actually, happy. Life, at last, felt good. Around her, her friends laughed and cheered under hundreds of fairy lights, strung from every corner and wooden ceiling beam, and the room vibrated with love. If she could bottle a feeling to carry into the new year, it would be this.

"Three…two…ONE!"

Corks popped and people were hugging. Someone was pouring more champagne into Abby's glass. She felt a huge, sloppy kiss on her cheek. Evan pulled her into a hug and yelled, "Happy New Year, my Abs!" into her ear, and as she hugged him, she shrieked, "Oh, my god, look over there!"

In the centre of the melee, Cody and Jade huddled close together, Jade holding what looked suspiciously like—

"A ring?" Marli gasped. "Oh, that is so romantic."

"I always thought Cody would be the one to propose," Evan said as lovestruck pair squealed and kissed.

"I know, right? Me, too," Abby replied.

"How does it work with lesbians, anyway? How do you know who proposes?"

"Dude, even we don't know. I think you just—Oh, oh! They're coming over here," Abby whispered, turning away. "Act natural."

"Happy New Year, guys!" Jade shrieked, barrelling over. She was holding up Cody's hand and pointing frantically to the ring finger. "Look, LOOK! She said yes!"

Cody grinned from ear to ear as she held up her hand to reveal a beautiful matte-black engagement band with their initials engraved onto it.

Suddenly they were all squealing as more champagne was being poured and the group hugged and gushed over the ring. Cody stood grinning awkwardly in the centre of it all, pink-cheeked from the attention.

"I'm really happy for them," Abby said a little while later as she watched them from a quiet corner of the bar. She'd escaped under the pretence of freshening her drink, but really, she just wanted a moment to take it all in.

"Yeah," Evan agreed, following Abby's gaze to where the couple sat, animatedly talking to friends. "They're one of those couples you just know were meant to be."

"Like you and Marli?"

"I hope so," he said, swirling the ice in his glass. "I wouldn't have moved halfway across the country if I didn't think so."

"Well, I miss you like crazy, but I think you did the right thing."

"Really? That means so much, Massey."

Abby smiled. "I've never seen you this happy. And you landed your dream job! Head of sports at a private junior school? Talk about 'King of the Castle' stuff. The kids must adore you."

"Oh, stop," he said bashfully, the slightest blush colouring his cheeks. "And hey," he added, lifting his glass. "Here's to us for making it through this crazy year and coming out of the other side even better."

"You can say that again." She grinned, knocking her glass into his. "Who could have guessed that this is how our year would've played out?"

"And," Evan said, raising his eyebrows and pausing until he had Abby's full attention. "Here's to you, Abby, for being the strongest, bravest person I know. And for not falling apart when you had every reason to."

Abby started to mutter her thanks, but Evan cut her off. His face had turned serious and Abby stopped, her brow furrowing as he spoke.

"I was worried when I left, Abs. I really was. I hope you don't mind me saying it, but we all were. I don't mean because I was leaving, I just mean because of every—"

"I know what you mean," she said softly, lowering her gaze.

"I almost didn't leave. You and Chris had just…well, she'd just left, and I thought about staying…"

"I would've hated if you'd stayed for me. You'd have turned into…a beard. *My* beard."

Evan laughed and shook his head. "Well, cheers to you, my friend. You're a fucking legend. Are you really as okay as you seem, or is this just all an act?"

"An act?" Abby arched an eyebrow. "I think you know me well enough to know that I cannot act 'okay' to save my life. And I *was* falling apart when you left. Actually, I'd been falling apart the entire time you knew me."

Evan grimaced. "I hate to admit it, but you're kind of right."

Abby laughed. "Don't feel bad. It's the truth. But yes, I really am a whole lot better now. I was so tired of being sad, you know? I was so damn tired of being in pain, sooo tired of the taste of my own tears. It felt like I spent a solid three years just crying."

She paused for a moment, glad Evan had asked the question because she hadn't yet put the shift into words herself—the change that had begun to unfold in her the morning Chris left for good, when she had the choice to fall to pieces, once again, or finally, to fly.

"After she left, and you left, I realised that people leave. Things change, and to be honest, Evan…I needed to grow the fuck up. It's life! Being sad about it is okay, but sad cannot be the defining feature of my personality. And I figured, if I could feel sad, surely I could feel happy, too. So I faked feeling happy for a while, just like I faked forgetting about Chris for a while, remember?"

Evan nodded.

"Well, it worked. When people say 'being happy is a choice,' I kind of want to puke. So I'm not going to say it. But I am going to say that choosing to be something other than sad is kind of a revelation. Of course, 'sad' is automatic after what I went through, but it doesn't have to be all that I am. I can actually choose to feel however I want to feel about my life. And choosing to be happy, while still making healthy space for the sad, has been totally liberating."

"Have you heard from her since she left?"

"Nope. I made it so I couldn't. It was the best decision I could've made."

Evan nodded slowly, absorbing it all.

"So," he said after a moment, considering his words carefully, "is 'choosing to be happy' why you quit your job?"

Now it was Abby's turn to nod. "Yes! Exactly. You know that job wasn't right for me, but having you there made it bearable. After you left it just…wasn't anymore. You can't dislike teaching and be a teacher. It's not fair to the kids."

"They'd never have known you'd disliked it. You were so good, and good at hiding it, too."

"Yeah, but I knew. And the final straw was when there was another lice outbreak."

They both burst out laughing, and Abby felt a wave of relief that she could smile at memories rather than feeling Signature Sad. "It was triggering, Ev! You have no idea."

"What's next, then?" he asked once they'd stopped giggling. "What are you going to do for money?"

"Ahh, you're such a buzzkill." She groaned. "On New Year's Eve?"

"Sorry, sorry!" He held up his hands. "I'm just curious. I mean, I guess you could go back home if you wanted to. You did say that there'd always be a job for you at the university."

"Well, that's true about the job," Abby replied. "But you forget one thing."

"Oh, yeah? What's that?"

Abby smiled and cast her eyes around the room, filled with all the people she loved. "I'm already home."

Eventually, Marli had come over to find Evan, and as Abby watched them move off into the crowd, she felt a swift tap on her shoulder. She spun around to see Roy, bright-eyed and flashing the widest grin she'd ever seen on him.

"Oh, Roy," she said, thrilled to see him in such high spirits. "This is such a great night. You really know how to throw a party."

"Oh, no, no," he said, waving away the compliment with his crinkly-skinned hand. "It's all you kids. You did it all. You and your fancy friend—Mrs. Addison's daughter. If it hadn't been for her large donation, and all your work, we'd never be here tonight."

"Chris?" Abby choked. She was annoyed that her heart leapt at this new information, that so much of her life now—her happiness now—was because of Chris Addison.

"Yeah, Chris! And as for this party, Chip simply rang me up and said, 'Uncle Roy, get dressed, and don't wear your brown trousers!'"

Abby pushed the old feelings aside and forced a laugh. "Well, either way, you look unbelievably spiffy, and the bar is just amazing."

"It is, rather, isn't it? It's much more than I could ever have imagined it would be." He cast a furtive look around and then leaned in close to Abby. "I didn't think we'd pull it off."

"I did," Abby whispered back, giving him a wink and a grin to match his own.

"Always so positive, you." He smiled, patting her shoulder. "And actually, that reminds me, I've been wanting to speak to you about something."

"Me?"

"Yes. I hear you've left your teaching position at Bay View Junior?"

"Oh, that…" Abby groaned, immediately on guard. More questions about work? Couldn't people give her a break—at least on New Year's Eve?

"Oh, I don't mean to intrude," Roy said hastily. "I just have an idea I'd like to run past you."

Abby was dubious. "Uh-huh?"

"Well, I'm sure you didn't dream of growing up to work behind a bar in a little bumsville town, but perhaps you wouldn't mind helping me out here while you look for a new job?"

"Oh!" Abby said in surprise. She'd fully expected Roy, like so many other well-meaning busybodies in Bay View, to dish out some unsolicited career advice. "You mean, like, here at The Dolphin Inn?"

"I do. I really am too old for all this, Abby. It's great fun, but I can't keep up anymore, not with the late nights, and now with the pizza oven. And of course, you've had experience running a guest house too, haven't you?"

Abby chuckled. "Hardly a guest house. It was one bedroom in my house and I rented it out on an app called FortyLinks. Used to rent it out. I don't anymore."

"Well, this is just a couple of rooms. Just like it was before. I know it's asking a lot of you, after you've already done so much to help…" Roy switched on some big-time puppy-dog eyes and ramped up his plea. "But perhaps you could consider it, just for a short while, to help an old man out? I'm very negotiable on pay."

Abby opened her mouth to reply, but Roy held up a hand and cut her off.

"Don't answer yet. Think about it, all right? We only officially open next week. And…you can eat all the free pizza you like."

"Did someone say 'free pizza'?" said a voice behind Abby, and she whirled around to see Drew, wide-eyed and pink-haired, sliding up beside her.

"Just think about." Roy gave Abby an exaggerated wink before tottering away with a giggle.

"Yeah, uh…Roy just offered me a job here at the bar," Abby said, staring after him. Why did his offer sound so…logical?

"Hey, maybe it's not the worst idea in the world," Drew said, hopping onto the barstool beside her. "I mean, didn't you all say you used to spend every day here anyway, before it burnt down?"

"Pretty much, yeah," Abby replied, finally turning her full attention to Drew. "Anyway…hi! I haven't seen you around in a while. I like your new hair."

"Really?" She peered up at Abby from under a pink lock. "I felt like something new. I'm glad you like it."

"Look, Drew," Abby said, shifting awkwardly on her stool. "I've been meaning to talk to you for a while now."

"Oh?" Drew's face grew serious as she leaned forward. "What's up?"

"I just wanted to say…I'm sorry for the way I treated you those months back. Actually, I'm sorry for the entire way I treated you, the whole time."

Drew pressed her mouth into a smile. "It's okay, Abby. I under—"

"No, please, let me finish." Abby screwed up her face as she tried to find the right words. "I was in a really, really terrible place. Which is absolutely no excuse. But you deserved a lot better than being…" She inhaled deeply, wincing at the words she was about to say. "…used by me." She exhaled slowly. "I'm sorry."

"You done now?" Drew asked with a little smile. Abby nodded.

"It's fine. It was never supposed to be anything serious. I knew that you were in love with Chris. Fuck, everyone did. But I caught feelings for you anyway." She shrugged and looked down at her shoes. "I fucked up too. I lied to you, and I'm sorry. I should never have done that. It was stupid to think it would even help."

"Help?"

"Help make you forget about Chris and pick me instead." She let out a small, self-conscious laugh. "Anyway, can we just put it all behind us? I hate things being all like…weird and stuff."

"Yeah, absolutely. Of course."

"Okay. Because, you know, I'm the perfect person to help you out here at the bar. I need a job, and I know how to knock together a pretty good pizza."

Abby laughed. "Does that mean you're staying in Bay View?"

Drew looked thoughtful. "Yeah, that's what I've been thinking lately. This place has grown on me. I mean, there have been ups and downs…" Here she grimaced at Abby. "But I actually kind of love it, I think."

Abby shook her head, giving a little laugh of disbelief. "After all of that, Bay View has still won you over? Who would've thought." Then she lifted her glass to Drew's. "Well, cheers to that, dude. Welcome home."

EPILOGUE

Two Months Later

"Call for you, Abs!"

"Another one?" Abby pushed a strand of hair off her forehead with the back of her wrist and grabbed her phone from Chip.

"Well, that's what happens on your birthday." Chip grinned as he shoved the ice scoop into the machine. The brand-new, *regularly cleaned* ice machine, and the old, freshly buffed ice scoop she and Evan had retrieved from the rubble all those months ago. Never could she have imagined that she—and the scoop—would be here now.

"Hello?" Abby said into the phone, streaking it with flour as she wedged it between her ear and shoulder. She was standing at the low pizza counter overlooking the crowded bar area, and it was difficult to hear above the din.

"Happy birthday to *you*, happy birthday to *youuuu*!"

"Guys!" Abby laughed at the terribly off-key rendition of the song as Evan's and Marli's voices rang down the line. "Jeez, Evan, even from a thousand miles away, you really know how to pick your moments."

"Well, that's because you chose to work on your birthday."

"True," Abby replied, dumping a round of dough onto the counter. "But I would've ended up here anyway. Besides, it's so hard to find good help these days." She raised her voice at that last part, and when she caught Drew's attention, she winked and stuck out her tongue to show she was kidding. Drew flung a tomato end at her.

"Ouch," she yelped as it hit her on the cheek.

Evan laughed. "Well, did Drew at least wake you up with a birthday cake and some candles to make a wish?"

"Hrmph, not quite," Abby grumbled, still eyeing her. "She overslept and tried to bake it before I woke up, but obviously that failed spectacularly." Abby was laughing as Drew put her hands on her hips and rolled her eyes dramatically. "What?" Abby said innocently. "It's true. Honestly, Evan, she's the worst housemate ever. Out until god knows what time with her new girlfriend, and too hungover to stick a candle in a cake for little old me. Probably knew I'd use it to wish for a better housemate."

She swirled a spoonful of tomato sauce over the pizza base.

"Okay, but seriously guys, I've gotta go. I've got orders piling up, and—shit!" She cursed as she knocked the pizza paddle to the ground with an ear-splitting *clang*. She pounced to pick it up, and when she stood back up, everything in the room stopped.

Chris Addison.

Real and in the flesh and standing in front of her in a purple bomber jacket.

Abby's phone dropped from her ear, bouncing off the counter and clattering to the floor.

"Abby? You okay?" Evan's voice called out tinnily from the phone. Abby snatched it up.

"Uh, yeah…no…I'm fine," she stammered, not breaking eye contact with the woman in front of her. "Evan, listen, I've gotta go."

With shaking hands, she cut the call.

"Happy birthday," Chris said, sliding a single chicken nugget onto the counter in front of Abby. In the middle of it was a candle.

Abby was too stunned to laugh or even breathe.

"Am I too late?" Chris asked, slightly breathless, and a million thoughts flew through Abby's mind before she thought she understood, and her eyes slid to the clock on the wall.

"No," she replied in a voice that sounded very far away. "It's, uh, it's only nine o'clock. It's still my birthday for another three hours."

"That's not what I meant," Chris replied, and Abby realised she wasn't out of breath. Her voice was trembling.

Abby frowned. "I'm sorry, I don't…"

"Am I too late for us?"

Abby stared wordlessly, rooted to the spot until she felt a tug at her hand. It was Drew, gently taking the pizza paddle from her. "I'll take over," she said firmly.

"W-wait…All the orders, they'll…the pizza, we have so many…"

"Go," Drew said, shooing Abby. "I can handle it. I'll see you at home."

In a daze, Abby motioned for Chris to follow her.

"She just means—she's my housemate," she mumbled as they wound their way through the back of The Dolphin Inn and out into the cool night air. She was burning up, hot from the pizza oven and the shock of what was happening.

"I'm sorry, I…I think it's raining but I really need air," Abby said as she stumbled outside, Chris trailing her. Her brain was swimming and she didn't know where to look, what to do, what to think. With shaking fingers, she untied her apron. Fat raindrops were falling on them, but she barely noticed.

This can't be happening! Not when my life has finally come together.

"It's okay," Chris said, gently taking the apron from her hands and dropping it to the ground. "Are you all right?"

Abby tried to reply but nothing came out. So Chris held her arms, gently, firmly, until her breathing steadied. Rain pelted down now, and in a vague, faraway part of her mind, Abby felt sort of bad about it, but in a much keener part of her brain, she thought it was the least Chris deserved after everything she'd put her through.

"Chris?"

"Yes?"

"I really hate you."

Chris sighed. "Well, that's unfortunate," she said with a watery smile, looking very vulnerable and very hopeful all at once. "Because I love you."

Rain splashed onto her nose, and Abby shook her head, gritted her teeth. She had no plans to fall apart in the foreseeable future, and she certainly wasn't going to do so now—not even when Chris had just said the three words she'd dreamed of hearing for so long.

"Don't say that, Chris. I know we can't—"

"We *can*, Abby! That's the point." She held up her hands, wet from the rain, and her ring finger was bare. "Look."

Abby looked, and as her brain finally caught up with reality, tears sprang into her eyes. Hope, anger, indignance, and terror all crashed through her, her heart forcing to her to face the feelings she'd tamped down since the morning Chris had left all those months ago.

"I mean," Chris said into the silence. "If you'll have me."

Abby blinked hard, forcing back the tears. She didn't trust herself to speak.

"The day I left Bay View, I went home and ended my relationship with Karys. I didn't leave her for you. I left her for me. Something I should have done a long time ago." Rain was dripping down her face and her voice grew more urgent now. "I've spent the past four months alone, for the first time in my entire life, figuring out who I am and what I really want. And what I really want, Abby, is you."

Abby's heart was beating so wildly, the rain pouring down so intensely, she had to concentrate hard to take in each word.

"I thought about you every, single, day. I dreamt about you. But I couldn't—wouldn't—come back until I could be certain. The truth is, I was certain from the moment I left, and I am just as certain now. You're all I can think about. You're…you're everything to me."

Chris's teeth were chattering now, so Abby steered them around the side of the building, underneath an awning to protect them from the downpour. When she turned back to Chris, she saw the plea etched into every inch of her face.

"I understand if it's too late and if I've already caused too much damage. But there's one more thing I have to say."

Abby shook her head. She didn't feel like her brain—her heart—had the capacity to take in anything else.

Chris took her hands, held them tight, and then tipped Abby's face up hers. Her eyes were filled with tears. "If you hear nothing else, even if you refuse to give me a chance, please hear this. I am so deeply sorry for how I hurt you—for how my own terror and confusion caused you pain. I have no excuse, and I wouldn't try to insult you with one, anyway. You deserved so much better from me. I want to spend the rest of my life making it up to you. And I will, if you give me the chance. You have my word."

With every word, Chris was cracking open everything Abby had so carefully packed away, and by the time she finished speaking, Abby was entirely undone.

"Oh, Abby! Abby, Abby," Chris crooned as she tried to wipe the tears streaming down Abby's face. But her hands were wet, and Abby's face was wet, and they both laughed at the futility of it.

Abby took a deep, shaky breath. She knew what she wanted. She had all along.

"Do you realise that I'm just a girl working at a bar now?" she said at last. "A bar that serves pizza? Pizza with *pineapple*?"

"Oh, my god, do you think I care?" Chris burst out laughing. Abby watched relief flood through her. "I don't even *have* a job anymore. Karys kicked me out of the business. All I have is a big pile of clothes and a whole lot of paperwork to wade through so I can get my share."

"And where…where would we live? You're a city girl. You hate this town."

"I don't care, doll. I have nowhere to be, except with you. And besides, this place has grown on me lately."

"Jesus!" Abby spluttered. "Why does everyone keep saying that?"

Chris chuckled again. How was she this *sure?*

"And another thing," Abby continued, getting into her stride. "I refuse to make the bed every day. We take turns."

"That sounds fair—"

"And you make the coffee. Every day. Because you do it better."

"I fully agree."

Abby's eyes swept Chris's face, searching for hints of doubt. All she saw was a small, hopeful smile, and the tiny, lovely creases beside her eyes—creases she so loved to kiss.

"Aren't you scared?" Abby whispered, her teeth chattering now, too.

"Not even a bit," Chris whispered back, her smile widening.

"Last thing," Abby said with a deep breath, laying out her final card. "I want to get married someday."

"Me, too," Chris replied, gathering Abby into her arms. And then she bent and kissed her, melting the last of her resolve. "To you."

"Dammit," Abby said huskily as she pulled away. "That's the best pick-up line I've ever heard."

"I've been practicing for tonight," Chris replied with a chuckle.

Abby shook her head, and at last she met Chris's gaze. "I love you, Chris Addison. I can't believe I finally get to say that out loud."

"And I love you, Abby Massey. I hope we'll be saying it out loud forever."

Abby's heart did a little dance at the word *forever* and, blushing, she buried her head in Chris's neck.

"Oh, just one more thing," Chris said, and Abby jerked her head up. "What?"

"I took a chance and brought some luggage with me." She looked sheepish as she jerked her thumb behind her. "Any chance you know of somewhere Drew can stay tonight? I'll pay. I'll pay *whatever* it costs."

"Ha!"

Abby threw her arms around Chris's neck, dizzy with happiness. As she looked up over Chris's shoulder and saw the window to a little room above the bar, newly rebuilt and ready for its first guest, she said, "Yes, actually, I do know of a place. She could stay right here. And something tells me Roy may even give you a freebie."

Chris turned and followed Abby's gaze, taking in the soft light of the upstairs room. Then she turned back to Abby, holding her tighter than Abby had ever been held, and declared, "I think that's a *phenomenally* good idea."

Bella Books
Happy Endings Live Here
P.O. Box 10543
Tallahassee, FL 32302
Phone: (800) 729-4992
BellaBooks.com

More Titles from Bella Books

Jones – Gerri Hill
978-1-64247-598-2 | 260 pages | Mystery
One weekend getaway, six friends, and a deadly secret that will wash away everything they thought they knew.

Merry Weihnachten – E. J. Noyes
978-1-64247-610-1 | 292 pages | Romance
Christmas traditions aren't the only things getting mixed up when these two hearts collide beneath the mistletoe.

Sweet Home Alabarden Park – TJ O'Shea
978-1-64247-570-8 | 362 pages | Romance
She came to restore a royal estate—she never expected to rebuild her heart.

Dr. Margaret Morgan – Christy Hadfield
978-1-64247-628-6 | 286 pages | Romance
Facing the professor on campus everyone hates is terrifying—but falling for her might be even worse.

Overtime – Tracey Richardson
978-1-64247-630-9 | 278 pages | Romance
A charming romance about second chances, found family, and scoring the goal that matters most.

The Big Guilt – Renée J. Lukas
978-1-64247-657-6 | 206 pages | Romance
What if the one who got away became the one you can't have?

9 781642 477191